Praise for Karin Rita Gastreich and Eolyn

"Gastreich allows her heroes to have flaws—including moments of cowardice—and some victories bring new sorrows. Vigorously told deceptions and battle scenes will satisfy fans of traditional epic fantasy, with a romantic thread."

—Publisher's Weekly

"Ms. Gastreich's uncanny talent for truly creating a world her readers can become part of is a rare gift, and one she shares abundantly."

—Terri-Lynne DeFino, author of *Finder*

"A book to savor first at great length, and then revisit over and over again."

—Lucy Crowe, author of *Sugarman's Daughter*

"Although rooted in traditional fantasy, Eolyn stretches and breaks the bounds in many ways, leading to a read that is fresh and unpredictable."

—Shauna Roberts, author of *Like Mayflies in a Stream*

"Gastreich's Eolyn focuses on the emotional, political, and physical conflicts between powerful and three-dimensional characters."

—Carlyle Clark, author of *The Black Song Inside*

"Humour leavens the story...but never becomes intrusive or undermines the strong threads of loss, duty, romance and revenge that permeate the book. And the action is often superb."

—David Hunter, author of *A Road of Blood and Slaughter*

"Masterfully written."

—The Kindle Book Review

D0912606

Eolyn

Book One of The Silver Web

Karin Rita Gastreich

ORB WEAVER PRESS

Eolyn
Book One of The Silver Web
Copyright © 2011 by Karin Rita Gastreich

Cover art © 2016 by Thomas Vandenberg
Cover design © 2016 by Thomas Vandenberg

Trade Paperback ISBN 978-0-9972320-0-4

First Edition 2011 by Hadley Rille Books

Second Edition 2016 by Orb Weaver Press
Kansas City, Missouri

For Suzanne and Rafael

CHAPTER ONE

Simple Magic

THE AUTUMN MORNING DAWNED COLD AND CRISP, lacing dark pines and old oaks with the sharp smell of winter. Eolyn ran toward the forest, cheeks flushed in excitement. Tales of man-eating trolls, elusive Guendes, and witches who devoured children played through her mind. Somewhere in the vast interior of the South Woods, the creatures of legend were lurking. Perhaps today, she would find one.

Eolyn's steps slowed as she reached the forest edge. Passing one hand over the bark of a gnarled beech, she directed her eyes toward the canopy, her natural enthusiasm tempered by the respect her mother, Kaie, had taught her. High overhead, a tangle of ebony branches spread, silhouetted against a bright sky.

Leaves rattled in the breeze.

A flash of ivory on the forest floor caught her eye.

Mushrooms!

Eolyn knelt and brushed aside the mottled leaf litter, exposing the plump, white fruits. As she gathered mushrooms, a spot of ruby betrayed the last berries on a thorny shrub. Bright green leaves of alomint peeked out from behind a fallen log. Eolyn ran from one simple treasure to the next, filling her tallow-wood basket with foods and medicines, imagining her mother's voice reflected in the flow of a nearby stream.

"Come look at this one," Kaie used to call, and Eolyn would run to see her mother pluck a delicate herb from the dark earth. "This will bring down a fever in winter time."

The plant had a star-shaped flower and tiny, pointed leaves. It pricked Eolyn's fingers as she crushed it to inhale the bitter essence.

"And these." Kaie gathered several fresh mushrooms bearing the sharp aroma of soft cheese. "Will help fill our bellies tonight. A balm made from the leaves of this black nettle will heal an infection. But only use the black nettle, Eolyn. The white will kill you faster than you can sneeze."

1

Every time they had visited the forest, Eolyn learned more from her mother, whose knowledge seemed without end.

"You must guard all of this in your heart," Kaie had instructed. "It is Simple Magic and it will serve you well."

"Magic?" Eolyn's eyes had opened wide. She liked plants, but magic was dangerous. Last fall, a woman had burned for witchcraft in Moehn. Eolyn's friend Dels had seen it. Dels said the first thing to catch fire on a witch was her hair, and the last thing to die was her heart. According to Dels, a burning witch smelled so bad even the rats ran away when the pyre was lit.

Her mother had sighed. "It's not real magic, Eolyn. Not the kind they would burn you for at any rate. Still, it's better you don't talk about what you've learned back in the village, not even in our own home."

"Why not?"

"Because the walls whisper," Kaie had replied. "They hear what is said and repeat it at inopportune moments."

Eolyn's mother paused and sat on a large smooth rock. She loosened the ribbons that bound her hair, letting it fall in copper rivers over her shoulders. Her eyes, the color of spring leaves, disconnected from her daughter. She rubbed her forehead as if to alleviate a tension that had settled on her brow. After a long silence, Kaie drew a deep breath and stood.

"It's late." She bound her hair and took Eolyn's hand. "We should start back to the farm."

"But Mama, you haven't explained anything about Simple Magic!"

"Nor will I. Not today."

"Why not?"

Eolyn's mother did not respond. Her gait had grown impatient, and Eolyn had to run to keep up. "Why are you angry, Mama? What have I done?"

Kaie stopped abruptly. She bent down and placed a tender hand upon Eolyn's cheek.

"I'm not angry with you, my daughter," she had said. "I'm angry at the silence imposed upon our lives."

That was the first and last time Eolyn's mother had mentioned Simple Magic. A few weeks later, Kaie had ventured alone into the South Woods. She returned with a sturdy walking stick almost twice Eolyn's height and a worn leather purse secured to a wide belt.

Eolyn's father had grown angry, and Kaie's last nights on the farm were marked by bitter disputes between husband and wife. Yet the morning Kaie left, Papa had held her close, covering her face with kisses.

"Where is she going, Papa?" Eolyn had asked as her mother

departed north.

Papa took Eolyn up in a solid embrace. Eolyn wrapped her arms around his neck.

"Your mother's allies are dead," he had said, "but her loyalties are not. We must pray to the Gods for her safe return."

Eolyn had prayed, but the Gods proved slow in their response. Spring slipped into summer and summer faded to fall. Still Kaie did not return.

Saddened by the memory, Eolyn paused in her work. A frigid northern wind shook the trees. Frost had spread over the forest floor. The sudden chill felt unnatural, and Eolyn shivered.

Come, Eolyn. Look at this one.

Startled, Eolyn dropped her basket, spilling berries and herbs. The voice had been real, Eolyn was certain. She looked around, but there was no one to be seen. "Mama?"

"I am here, Eolyn."

Eolyn jumped at the sight of Kaie next to her, tall and pale as a moonlit tree. Mama's eyes were opaque green and her hair fell unbound to her waist. Instinctively, Eolyn reached out to touch her. Kaie shimmered and vanished, only to appear a few paces away.

Eolyn stepped back in fear. "What's happening?"

"Hush, my daughter. Listen to me. Find your brother. Tell him you must run. Tell him you must hide."

Then Kaie vanished on a gust of wind.

Squirrels chattered in the distance. Eolyn heard feet pounding against the earth.

"Eolyn!" Ernan burst into the clearing where Eolyn stood. He stopped breathless and grasped Eolyn's shoulders. "Where have you been? Why didn't you answer when I called? I've been searching everywhere for you."

Eolyn looked from him to where her mother stood a moment ago.

"Eolyn." Ernan put his hand to his sister's chin and forced her gaze to him. "How often do I have to tell you not to run off on your own?"

"I'm not on my own," Eolyn said. "Not here."

Ernan shook his head in exasperation. Five years her senior, Eolyn's brother was a lanky boy with sharp features, red hair, and intense green eyes like their mother's. Ever since Eolyn could remember, Ernan had been watching over her.

"I saw Mama." Eolyn's voice sounded very small. She wondered if her brother would believe her.

Ernan clenched his jaw. "You what?"

"I saw Mama, right here. Just a moment ago. She said we should run.

She said we have to hide."

Ernan's hand closed tight around Eolyn's. He straightened and sent his gaze like a lance toward their village. "Gods help us. They've found her."

"Found who? Mama?"

Ernan flushed with anger. "Father was wrong to wait. We should have left a long time ago."

"Where is she? Is she coming back?"

Without warning, Ernan took off toward the forest interior, dragging Eolyn behind him. They dodged trees and jumped over logs and stones. Twice Eolyn tripped. Her hands and knees stung as they scraped the earth, but Ernan did not ease his pace. They came to a small stream that cut through a narrow trench. Ernan pushed Eolyn into a hole in the bank, concealed by bushes.

"What is this place?" Eolyn said, overwhelmed by the smell of damp earth. "Ernan, what's happening?"

Producing an oil lamp from the shadows, Ernan ignited a steady glow with some flint. "I'm going to get Papa. You stay here. Don't make any noise and don't come out—no matter what happens—until we return. Do you understand?"

"No! No I don't understand because you haven't told me anything."

Ernan slipped out of the hideaway and covered the entrance behind him.

"Ernan, don't leave me here!"

But Eolyn's brother was already gone.

Darkness shrouded her, broken only by the flickering lamp. The air felt stale and heavy. Earthen walls crowded Eolyn's shoulders, threatening to suffocate.

I'm not going to stay here. I'm going to follow Ernan and find Father.

Eolyn moved toward the entrance, but a tremor made her pause.

Listen, Eolyn, her mother whispered. *Listen well.*

Eolyn pressed her hands against the dirt and lowered her ear to the ground. A thin thunder ran through the earth, rising like an obsidian wave toward her village. When Eolyn closed her eyes, the tremor sucked her in. Bloody visions roared and receded like wild fire fed by wind. Mounted soldiers swirled through acrid smoke. Friends crumpled under flashing swords. Peasants lay scattered upon the burgundy dust, their homes collapsing into crisp flames. Eolyn screamed, but no one heard her. She ran through choking smoke and stumbled upon her father. His limbs were twisted at odd angles. Life flowed out of his body in a crimson river that drained into the earth.

Eolyn's eyes flew open. Nauseating emptiness ripped through her. She scurried backwards, knocking the lamp over and extinguishing its flame. Hugging her knees to her chest, Eolyn hid her face and wept. For the rest of that long day, and the torturous night that followed, she listened and saw no more.

When at last the morning light peered through the entrance to her hideaway, Eolyn's limbs were cramped and stiff. The damp chill had penetrated her bones. She crept forward and peeked outside.

Mist hovered over the stream. On the opposite bank, a mottled brown rabbit searched through leaves for the last of the fall forage. Behind it, a pair of flame-throated warblers chirped in a small bush. Assured by the presence of these animals that no humans were about, Eolyn crawled out of the small cave and stood on shaky legs.

The moment she appeared, the animals melted into the forest, leaving a silence so deafening Eolyn covered her ears to shut it out.

Ernan should have returned by now.

Their farm lay near the edge of the South Woods. It wouldn't have taken him long to run there and back.

He would be here if he had survived.

Eolyn bit her tongue against the urge to call her brother's name, fearful that any sound might bring mounted soldiers from behind the trees. She considered crawling back into the hole in hopes of capturing a vision that would reveal Ernan's fate, but the thought of that dank shaft made her stomach churn.

I don't need another vision. I saw what they did. Ernan would not have been spared.

Story tellers of Eolyn's village had shared numerous tales of such raids. They said entire villages were destroyed by the King's Riders for treachery and subversive magic. They said no one survived his wrath and nothing was ever left behind. But Eolyn had always thought such horrors happened in other provinces, in faraway places like Selkynsen or Selen, where rebellious subjects still clung to old ways. Her family lived in Moehn. Who among the peasant farmers of her home could have incurred the wrath of the King?

It is Simple Magic, Eolyn. Her mother's words returned like a serpent's hiss. *And it will serve you well.*

The ground lurched. Eolyn stumbled to her knees. Bile burned up through her throat and spilled onto the forest floor.

Was that it? Had Simple Magic condemned them all?

Sobs shook Eolyn's body in an unbearable surge of loss and guilt. This was her fault. She had indulged in the treacherous and forbidden. She had learned the secrets of the plants.

5

The pale sun burned the mist off the ground and settled in the high branches long before Eolyn ran out of tears. Not until her sobs faded into exhaustion did the voices of the forest return in the rustling of dry leaves, the subtle murmur of the autumn wind, and the silver gurgle of the tiny stream.

Come look at this one, Eolyn.

The girl started at the voice of her mother, close again and very real. Sniffling, Eolyn wiped the damp from her cheeks and drew herself to her feet.

"Mama?" She called as loud as she dared.

A fluid movement caught Eolyn's eye, a subtle shift of light beyond the trees. Eolyn recognized the sway of her mother's skirt, the sinuous confidence of Kaie's flowing stride. The girl took a hesitant step forward.

"Mama?"

The shadow responded by slipping toward the heart of the South Woods.

CHAPTER TWO

The House of Sweet Bread

KAIE'S GHOST CONTINUED AHEAD, never quite within reach, always beyond the next tree or around the bend. It led Eolyn deep into the forest before disappearing altogether.

Confused, Eolyn turned on her feet, trying to identify the path that had brought her here. Unfamiliar trees gawked at her. Thick bark twisted into expressions of loathing and disapproval. A strong gust rattled the high branches and sent a shower of auburn leaves fluttering to the ground. The birds did not sing. The squirrels did not chatter. The South Woods had never seemed so cold and heartless.

Fear pricked Eolyn's skin. What if the legends were true? What if werewolves and seven headed rats and child-eating witches waited beyond those dark trees?

"How will I find the path?" Eolyn whispered.

The voice of Kaie returned. *Wander, my daughter. A woman's path is made by wandering.*

This was Eolyn's only guidance now, words on the wind. Memories in her heart. Drawing a deep breath, she placed one uncertain foot in front of the other.

Days passed. Although Kaie had taught Eolyn how to find late season berries and distill water from moss, every morning the girl woke a little hungrier than the last. The further she traveled, the thinner the harvest. Emptiness began to gnaw at her belly.

One night, the restless cries of a blue-winged owl startled Eolyn out of her sleep. Barks and yelps pierced the shadows. A pack of wolves was bearing down upon her.

Panicked, Eolyn scrambled up a tree in the darkness. Branches stung hands and arms, raising jagged welts. Jaws snapped at her heels. Howls rose toward her. She clung to her perch while the pack snuffled below. Tears streamed down her cheeks.

She felt like a fool. Why had she strayed so far? Why did she not wait for Ernan? What if her brother had survived? What if he were looking for her even now? She would die here before he found her, if not of starvation, then under the fangs of these terrible beasts.

By morning, the wolves had left. Limbs stiff from exhaustion, Eolyn climbed down the tree. After that night, she took to finding strong high branches in which to sleep.

About a week into her journey, as the new moon drifted behind the forest canopy, Eolyn awoke to see two Guendes leaning over her. They froze like a pair of fawns caught by surprise. The Guendes wore colors of night and forest. Their large eyes twinkled, and their button noses twitched. One held a simple lantern glowing orange-warm. The other laid a blanket of woolly moss and spider silk over Eolyn.

They seemed little more than a dream, but the Guendes gave Eolyn a sense of warmth and companionship, as if the forest had at last stretched out a comforting hand. Together, the Guendes began to sing in whispery tones. Eolyn shifted her position, closed her eyes, and slept.

The next morning, at the foot of the tree, she found a leaf dish full of ripe golden berries and a wooden cup with fresh milk from a Berenben tree. The generous breakfast delighted her. In thanksgiving, Eolyn gathered bright leaves and shiny brown nuts and left them for the Guendes, just as her mother taught her to do. From that day forward, the Guendes kept Eolyn warm at night and fed in the morning. They followed her with the invisible rustle of dry leaves.

By the time Eolyn arrived at a large stony riverbed, she had lost track of the moon's passage. In a few months, spring would fill the river's banks to overflowing, but now with autumn drying up into winter she crossed the water without wetting her feet by jumping from one stone to another. She paused on the opposite bank and considered following the current downstream.

Then another Guende appeared.

The creature stood a few feet away, reflecting hues of autumn. It wore colored leaves in its cap and an evergreen vest embroidered with seeds and nuts. Smiling eyes peeked out from under bushy brows. It proffered its hand. Eolyn was surprised by the feathery lightness of its touch, as if the Guende were not real at all, but a mere impulse that took hold of her and pulled her forward.

They left the river and walked almost an hour until Eolyn felt a subtle shift in the forest. The woods did not look any different, with old trunks, crusty bark, and draped moss. Yet something had changed.

Caught between curiosity and apprehension, Eolyn stopped. The Guende tugged at her hand. An intense drone filled Eolyn's ears, as if she were passing through an invisible hive of bees. The buzzing ceased, and the Guende disappeared.

Eolyn stood in a small clearing. The thick expanse of trees that defined her world moments before had melted away. The ground sloped downward under a cover of soft grass and then rose again. Beyond a low hill hovered a faint wisp of chimney smoke.

Taken with a sudden enthusiasm founded on the hope of human company, Eolyn bounded forward. On the other side of the rise, she found a simple cottage surrounded by a thick garden.

"Good day!" she called out. "Is anyone home?"

The bushes rustled. A dark hood rose up and a voice crackled like fire. "Well, well. Who is this mouse that calls upon my humble house?"

Eolyn stepped backwards, regretting her boldness at once. How could she have been so foolish? She knew the stories about hags living in forests. They were witches, all of them. They turned children into bread and ate them for breakfast.

Rising to her full and somewhat crooked height, the hag shuffled toward Eolyn. "Don't run away, my child."

Eolyn had no intention of obeying, but her feet rooted into the ground like stubborn weeds.

Locating a stump next to the girl, the old woman eased herself down. Several minutes passed in silence.

"You are not much of a talker," the hag said. "All the better I suppose. I've grown accustomed to an existence without chatter in this place. How long have you been in the woods?"

"Nearly a moon," Eolyn whispered.

"A full moon?" the old one repeated with surprise and interest. "How did you survive so long on your own?"

"I know the late harvest berries and mushrooms and how to find springs and draw water from the moss. Then the Guendes found me."

And led me here. Treacherous beasts!

"I see," the hag said. "What drove you into the forest in the first place?"

Eolyn blinked and looked away. Her eyes burned and a hard lump settled in her throat.

"Come, child." The woman's voice was gentle. "You can tell me."

Eolyn was not going to tell her anything, but then the words spilled out anyway. "There were horses and soldiers and terrible fires, and they killed my father, and my brother never came back, and then I…I heard my mother. I saw her, I swear! She told me to follow her, but it wasn't her after all. And then I got lost."

The hag folded her arms and gave a slow nod. "You're a very brave girl. How old are you?"

Eolyn shifted nervously on her feet.

"Nine summers, perhaps?" The old woman asked.

The blood drained from Eolyn's face. Proof of witchcraft! How else could she have guessed her age?

"Speak, child. A guest in my house must say what she thinks."

"Are you the witch who eats children?" Eolyn covered her mouth with both hands, shocked by her careless tongue.

The old lady's eyes sparked in the shadow of her cloak. She reached up to remove her hood. Eolyn expected to see an ancient face twisted into a sharp warty nose, unkempt hair splayed like straw, and inflamed eyes that would hex her on the spot.

The truth proved oddly disappointing. The woman's features were soft, lined with the many years that had bent her body. Her thick gray hair lay braided in a neat coil at the nape of her neck. Her nose was an unremarkable peak over narrow lips.

"Well that is not a question I get every day," she said, watching Eolyn with keen gray eyes. "Tell me...What did you say your name was?"

"Eolyn."

"Nice to meet you, Eolyn. I am Ghemena. Tell me, why do you think I am a witch who eats children?"

"Because you are an old woman, and you live alone in the South Woods."

"That is rather damning evidence," she conceded. "What else do you know about this child-eating witch?"

"She lives in a house made of sweetbread and children come to eat it. That's how she fattens them up before she throws them into her great oven."

"I see." The woman nodded, her face a mask of careful reflection. "Well, young Eolyn, you can see my house. It does bear the shade of honey-sweetened bread. Why don't you take a bite? If the legend is true you'll be able to eat it. Even better, I'll be able to eat you. But I will let you run first. I'll give you a full half-a-day's head start just for being such an astute little girl."

The proposition horrified Eolyn, but she saw no other choice than to accept. Half a day was better than none. With half a day she might outrun the old hag, unless the hag could fly as witches were supposed to do.

Eolyn approached the house and ran her hands over the cinnamon-colored shingles. Her stomach growled, and hunger took over. Breaking off a splintery piece, she bit down hard. Pain shot through her teeth. Wood scraped her tongue. Disappointment and frustration set in.

She would have given anything to be able eat the old woman's cottage just then, even if it meant being turned into a loaf of bread.

10

A loud snort made Eolyn spin around. The witch fell off her perch, wheezing. Tears streamed from the old woman's eyes. "Don't try too hard, child. You'll break your teeth!"

It took several minutes for the hag to recover from her fit. Gasping for breath and clutching at her ribs, she rose on shaky legs. "A house of sweet bread! Who would invent such nonsense? Why don't you come inside, Eolyn, and have some proper food?"

Unable to resist the force of her appetite, Eolyn followed the hag with a wary heart.

Inside, the cottage was dim and sparsely furnished. As Eolyn watched the hag stoke the fire in her meager kitchen, she considered her options. With winter standing restless at the gates of the South Woods, they were stark. She could starve in the barren forest before the first snows turned her into ice, or she could eat on Ghemena's hearth until the witch turned her into breakfast.

"You can stay here, if you like, the whole winter through." The old woman laid out a meal of hot vegetable stew, fresh bread, and Berenben cheese. "Come spring, I could send you back to Moisehén."

Eolyn's face descended into the bottom of her bowl as she drank Ghemena's peppery brew. *Cruel witch, to talk of sending me back when she has no intention of doing so.*

"I know a forester who wanders these parts," Ghemena continued. "He could accompany you home."

"I don't have a home. It's all gone. I told you that already."

"You spoke of the deaths of your father and brother, but what of your mother? Where is she?"

"Mama went away last spring. She never came back."

Ghemena's gray brows furrowed. "Why did she leave?"

"I don't know." Eolyn's throat began to ache. "I think she went to look for her loyalties because her allies had died. That's what Papa said."

Eolyn reached for a thick slice of bread and spread it with pungent cheese. She felt Ghemena study her every move, though whether the witch reflected on her father's words or estimated the disappointing width of Eolyn's arm, the girl could not tell. She wondered where Ghemena's great oven was, and shuddered at the thought of charred remains of children's bones inside.

"Was your mother the one who taught you about the forest harvest?" the hag asked.

"Yes."

"What else did she teach you?"

Eolyn looked away from the table, her bread forgotten. Why did the witch keep asking bothersome questions? Now her stomach hurt too.

11

Maybe the food is poisoned!

"Did she teach you medicines?" Ghemena asked. "Did she tell you how to use plants to heal?"

The air shifted hot against the walls. Eolyn set her jaw. "I'm not supposed to talk about that."

"I see." Ghemena nodded. "What was her name?"

"Kaie."

The old woman sucked a sharp breath through yellow teeth.

"I knew your mother," she exclaimed softly, the pleasure of her discovery evident in her face. "A long time ago. Of course. I see the resemblance now. She was a maga warrior, one of the best of her generation."

Eolyn's gut lurched. It was not possible, not in the darkest of worlds, that this hag had known her mother. "What's that? What's a maga warrior?"

"A maga is a woman who knows magic. A maga warrior is also trained in the arts of war."

"Mama was not a witch!" Eolyn's anger evaporated the stones in her gut. "Mama was *beautiful.*"

Ghemena inhaled as if to respond and then held her breath behind pursed lips. A troubled sadness invaded her eyes. She pushed away from the table and shuffled to the front door. Unspoken thoughts trailed behind her in wispy clouds.

Eolyn's head sank into her hands. *What was I thinking? I've just insulted a witch.*

She would be dead before first snow fall for certain.

"It's a fine afternoon," Ghemena announced. "One of the last of the season, I imagine. Why don't you wash the dishes, Eolyn, and meet me in the garden. We'll have a cup of tea together."

Anxious to undo her transgression, Eolyn obeyed.

After cleaning the table, she went outside and found the old woman on a bench, cloak pulled tight around her shoulders. Aromas of dormant herbs floated in the air. Inviting the girl to take a seat, Ghemena gave her a cup of water with a neatly placed sprig of mint.

"I want to show you something," the hag said. "Watch me."

Folding her hands around the wooden vessel, Ghemena closed her eyes, lifted the liquid to her lips, and uttered a short verse in an odd language.

Ehekaht naeom tzefur. Ehukae.

Steam began rising off the water.

"How did you do that?" Eolyn's curiosity shoved her caution aside. "How did you heat up the water?"

12

"Did you not see? Give it a try. I believe you can do it just like me."

Folding her hands around the cup, Eolyn repeated the verse as best she could, but the water did not heat up.

"That was very good," Ghemena said, "but it is not just a matter of imitation. Stand up straight with your feet firmly on the ground."

Eolyn did as she was told, gripping the cup and keeping her eyes closed tight.

"Wait, child. Open your eyes. Give me that cup. Take off your shoes and stockings."

Eolyn pressed her bare feet against the damp earth. A vaguely familiar warmth coursed through her legs, opening her senses and bringing every subtle sound of the season into her awareness.

Ghemena returned the cup of tea to Eolyn's hands. "That's it. Now relax and close your eyes. And breathe."

Cold air filled Eolyn's lungs, pressing sharp against her ribs. Eolyn felt as if she no longer stood in the same spot, as if Ghemena's garden were replaced by another that looked the same but worked very differently.

"What do you feel at your feet?" Ghemena asked.

"The ground," Eolyn said.

"Yes, but tell me what it feels like."

"It is solid and still." Eolyn spread her toes over cool soil. "But also in motion. How can that be?" She opened her eyes.

"Keep your eyes closed."

Eolyn obeyed.

"Now take a deep breath and tell me: What do you feel in the air?"

Eolyn drew in the evening air, paying attention to its passage down her throat, its expansion inside her chest, its departure in a warm and humid cloud. "It carries life, like…like an invisible thread."

"Very good. Now tell me about the water."

"It is still. Yet it flows in the cup, and…beneath my skin."

A tremor invaded Ghemena's words. "And finally your heart, Eolyn. What do you feel in your heart?"

This was the easiest question of all. "Warmth. My heart is warm, like the hearth in your home."

"Excellent, my girl. Now here is what I want you to do. Pull together all the elements you just told me about, the earth at your feet, the air in your lungs, the water in your cup, and the fire in your heart. Imagine all of that coming together into a single brilliant point of light. When you see that light, repeat the verse just as I said it."

The night thickened with Eolyn's effort. The task was not easy. The air could be smothered by earth or the fire extinguished by water. Eolyn

13

recognized this and worked with care until a small white glow illuminated her interior. She opened her eyes and exhaled the verse.

Ehekaht naeom tzefur. Ehukae.

The cup responded with a soft rise of steam.

"Very good!" Ghemena exclaimed.

The sound of chirping insects and shifting herbs returned. Eolyn looked around as if seeing the garden for the first time. She felt different inside. Warmer. Complete. As if she had found something she had always sought, something that had always eluded her.

"Come and sit with me, Eolyn," Ghemena said. "Let's enjoy our tea together."

CHAPTER THREE

The Silver Web

EVERYTHING QUEEN BRIANA CRAFTED during her life was destroyed on the twelfth night after her death. The Mage King Kedehen forbade Akmael from observing the rite, but the prince disobeyed his father and found a narrow window to spy on the vigil.

At sunset, the High Mages assembled in a castle courtyard. Queen Briana's belongings were laid on a large stack of firewood: dark velvet dresses and fine linen undergarments, ribbons that had bound her thick black hair, jewels that had adorned her throat, embroidered slippers, curtains from her apartments, tapestries, even the bed sheets. On top of these were placed countless objects of magical intent: her medicine belt and potted herbs, a large box of crystals, a store of carefully separated spider silks, a shallow silver dish she might have used as a seeing tool, collections of furs and insects, glass vials filled with mysterious liquids, a few remaining books, and her ebony staff.

When the pyre was complete, the wizard Tzeremond stepped forward. Despite his many years, Tzeremond's carriage remained tall and his aspect striking. Close cropped, charcoal gray hair accentuated gaunt features. He struck his rowan staff three times against the ground.

Ehekahtu, he cried.

Naeom ehaen avignaes, reohoert...

The High Mages took up the chant. Kedehen joined the invocation over his dead wife's belongings, his expression as dispassionate as the stone foundation upon which the castle rested.

As the chanting reached its peak, Tzeremond raised a bony hand and sent a blinding shaft of light into the pyre. The wood ignited, converting Briana's possessions into floating wisps of ash.

Smoke reached Akmael's hiding place, stinging his eyes and throat. He felt as if he were witnessing the murder of his mother all over again. His chest constricted, and he fought to control the rise of bile from his stomach.

Only two items of Briana's making escaped the pyre that night, both

15

of them secure in Akmael's clenched fists. One was an amulet woven with threads of silver silk, the other an armband etched with images of Dragon. The Queen had instructed Akmael not to wear the armband until he began his study of High Magic, so the prince kept it well hidden in a place known only to him. The silver web, however, Akmael wore with the singular devotion of a loving son.

More than a year would pass after Briana's death before one afternoon, during Akmael's lessons, Master Tzeremond caught sight of the jewel at the boy's collar. The wizard grabbed the medallion and tried to yank it from Akmael's neck. The fine chain held strong. A struggle between teacher and student ensued. Desperate to loosen Tzeremond's hold, Akmael bit the wizard's hand. Tzeremond cried out and released the boy.

Akmael darted away through the castle corridors. His feet pounded against the stone floor. Rage coursed through his veins. He wove a crooked path through servant entrances and back halls, down ladders and up stairwells, hoping to lose Tzeremond or anyone else who might pursue him. He scowled at guards who saluted him and servants who bowed and scurried out of the way.

Curse them all!

They made it impossible for a prince to pass unnoticed.

Akmael burst into one of the back courtyards and paused, gulping fresh spring air. Bright afternoon light made him squint. As his anger cleared, he realized the Gods had granted him a singular opportunity. No one was present in this barren space. He glanced up at the high ramparts, but even those guards had their alert gazes turned elsewhere.

Akmael crept across the courtyard, keeping to the shadows as he approached a small wooden door on the northern wall. He slipped inside and shut the door securely behind him.

He had arrived at a long corridor of rough-hewn stone. Silence reigned here, broken only by the slow pulse of the mountain's heart.

Akmael knew this place well. The passage led to the Foundation of Vortingen, where Dragon had appeared to the very first of Akmael's fathers and crowned him King of all Moisehén. He crept through the dark passage until it opened onto a grassy knoll. The flat area ended in sharp cliffs lined by scattered and twisted trees. In the center, a circle of pale monoliths reached toward the sky.

Retreating to a copse of trees near the cliff's edge, Akmael found a hiding place among tall bushes. He leaned against the rough trunk of an old beech and allowed his pulse to steady, all the while clutching the silver web.

I won't let them take you from me. I'll die first.

"I know, my love."

His mother's voice felt so real and close, it broke Akmael's heart. Tears escaped his eyes. He slid down the trunk and sat hard on the ground.

I'm so sorry, Mother.

How could she be gone? One moment Briana had been alive, laughing and vibrant. The next, she was sprawled and motionless. Akmael would never forget how the light had faded from her eyes.

Master Tzeremond often said Queen Briana's murder was a vivid example of the treacherous hearts of the magas. *So incapable of loyalty are they that they kill their own sisters. This is one of the many reasons we no longer allow women to learn magic.*

Akmael disagreed with his tutor on many counts, but in this, Tzeremond was right. Although the red-haired witch had arrived dressed as a servant, Akmael's mother received her as a friend and equal. They had embraced, but their warmth soon turned to discord. Akmael remembered how his presence had ignited the red-haired maga's fury, how his resemblance to Kedehen made her turn upon Briana.

"You know the danger of pouring the blood of East Selen into the line of Vortingen!" the stranger had cried. "This boy's power will be unstoppable."

But the red-haired assassin had been wrong. An unstoppable power would have extinguished the death charge that flew from the maga's staff toward Akmael. An unstoppable power would have kept Briana from flinging her body into its path.

An unstoppable power would have brought my mother back from the dead.

With a heavy heart, Akmael lifted the silver web off his neck. Made of quartz crystals woven into the silk of a Dark Moon Orb Weaver, the jewel sparkled in the afternoon light. Akmael heard the faint echo of Briana's laughter and felt the comfort of her presence. A lullaby she used to sing when he was a little boy returned to him.

He flicked the web, and it spun on its axis. The words of his mother's song took shape on his lips. As the melody wove around the medallion, the copse of trees where he had taken refuge melted away.

Startled, Akmael ceased his song.

He sat in an unfamiliar and dense forest. Afternoon light filtered through the canopy. Water rushed past in a small river littered with large boulders. Somewhere close by squirrels chattered, accompanied by the sweet lilt of a summer thrush.

Pressing himself against the nearest tree, Akmael studied the amulet. Thrilled by the power of the object, he was nonetheless immediately preoccupied with the problem of returning home.

It must be a simple spell. Mother always favored simple spells.

Closing his eyes, Akmael grounded his spirit and imagined the soft grass and tall monoliths of the Foundation of Vortingen. He spun the amulet and began to sing, but his melody was cut short by laughter, high and free, like a song of the forest.

Akmael opened his eyes. He put the silver chain back on his neck and tucked the amulet beneath his shirt. Then he moved cautiously toward the source of the laughter.

Rounding a large tree, he saw a girl about his age on the riverbank. She wore a simple russet dress patched in many places. Her hair framed her face in wild curls, like spun copper. Mud sloshed underfoot, but that did not stop her from dancing after butterflies and rabbits and squirrels. Soon she threw herself down on the grass, where she took to watching white clouds race past the tree tops.

Akmael took a step closer. A twig snapped underfoot.

The girl sat up and pinned him with a sharp gaze.

Akmael returned her stare, uncertain what to do or say.

"Good afternoon." The girl stood and attempted to brush the dirt off her skirt, but the effort was wasted since her hands were covered in mud. "You must be lost."

"I am not lost," Akmael replied. Then he added, rather sheepishly, "I'm just not certain where I am."

"You're in the South Woods, on the banks of the Tarba River."

Akmael drew a sharp breath. The silver web had flung him clear across the kingdom!

"My name is Eolyn," she said. "Who are you?"

Akmael glanced away. "Achim. My name is Achim."

"Do you have a place to stay, Achim?"

"Of course." Akmael forced more confidence into his voice than he felt. "I will return home."

"Do you have to start back right away?"

That seemed a strange question.

"What I'm saying is, would you like to play?" she said.

Akmael shook his head. "I do not play. Certainly not with girls."

She threw up her hands in disbelief. "How can you not play?"

"I am too old to play."

"You can't be more than a couple summers older than me."

"Yes, but I am not a girl."

"I have an idea," Eolyn said. "We can look for the rainbow snail. The snail is supposed to migrate up river during the spring, but I've never seen it. Ghemena says it grows as big as one's hand and has a shell made of pearl that reflects all the colors of the world. Would you like to help me find it?"

I really should try to get home.

Yet even if the amulet took Akmael straight back to the castle, what did he have to look forward to? An argument with his father, the confiscation of Briana's precious gift, the infuriating satisfaction of old Tzeremond.

"It's only for a little while." Annoyance crept into the girl's tone. "If you don't like it you can just go home."

A grin spread across Akmael's face. He reached down to pull off his boots.

Eolyn jumped and clapped her hands. Unfettered by shoes, she took off at once toward the river. "The first one to find it wins!"

Akmael followed Eolyn along the riverbank, both of them taking care not to wander too deep into the swift and icy current. Spring blossomed throughout the forest. Heavy southern winds were forcing back the frosty breath of the north. Pale herbs pushed up from the musty earth, and delicate pink leaves budded from tall oaks.

The elusive rainbow snail never appeared, but many other creatures danced in the water for their entertainment. Large silver fish jumped over deep rapids, strong bodies flashing in the sun. Darting guppies nipped at their toes. Tiny water dragons clung to the underside of rocks. Whirligigs filled the still edge of the river with frenetic activity. Bright blue shrimp scuttled along the rocky bottom. Eolyn caught several to take back home because, as she enthusiastically informed Akmael, they made for an excellent stew.

Soaking wet before long, the two of them sought a large boulder where they sat while the sun warmed their bodies and dried their clothes.

"I'll have to go home soon," Eolyn announced. "It's about an hour's walk from here, and it's not good for a child to be out at dusk this time of year. Ghemena says the wolves and bears are terribly hungry right now."

"Who is Ghemena?" Akmael asked.

"The woman who takes care of me. She's like my grandmother but she's not really. She lives in a cottage nearby. People believe she eats children but it's not true at all. Neither is the part about the house made of sweet bread."

Akmael was not sure what to make of this.

"Who takes care of you, Achim?"

He cleared his throat. "My father and my tutors."

"Where do you live?"

"A long way from here."

"Well if it's going to take more than an hour for you to walk home, you should stay with us until tomorrow."

"That won't be necessary. I..." He searched for the appropriate phrase. "I travel very quickly."

Akmael looked away, uncertain why being guarded with her made him uncomfortable. It would hardly be prudent to reveal his true identity to a peasant girl from Moehn.

"Tell me about where you live." Eolyn pulled her knees up to her chest. Red curls danced about rosy cheeks. Brown eyes sparkled beneath thick lashes. "Is it a forest like this one?"

"Well..." He considered the scattered tree trunk pillars around them. "Yes. It is rather like a forest, except it is made of stone."

"A forest of stone." Eolyn lifted her face to a shaft of sunlight. "It sounds beautiful. At Summer Solstice, the trees must be filled with emerald leaves, leaves that fade into ruby and amber at Samhaen. At Midwinter's Eve, the branches must weigh heavy with diamond ice and snow, and at Eostar, I bet the flowers bloom with petals of opal!"

The girl turned to Akmael as if eager for him to confirm her vision, but he could only stare back in silence. He had never heard his home spoken of with such poetry. He could almost imagine it just as she described.

Sitting up straight, Akmael extended his arm in front of him and focused on the space above his palm. After a moment, particles of light collected over his hand and swirled together. They assembled into a twig of polished brown stone with emerald leaves and sapphire berries.

"From your forest?" Eolyn asked, breathless.

"For you." He plucked the object from the air and presented it to her.

The gift would disappear within the hour. Akmael had not yet learned how to make his visualizations last longer. Yet he could tell Eolyn would gather as much enjoyment out of the jewel in that short time as a nobleman's daughter might during the course of a year.

Indeed, any other child would have responded to this magic with fear and trepidation. Under Master Tzeremond's instruction, Akmael was learning how to use fear as a source of power. But Eolyn projected neither surprise nor apprehension. She offered only a strangely pleasant glow that Akmael identified with some difficulty as appreciation and burgeoning affection.

"I would like to give you something from my forest," Eolyn announced.

Then the girl did something that truly astounded Akmael. She sat up straight and cupped her hands. After a moment, a swirl of light appeared just above her fingers and assembled into a small plant with thick leaves and an exquisite flower of white and gold.

20

"This is an orchid." Eolyn plucked the plant from the air. "It grows in the highest branches of the oldest oaks, and it is for you."

Scarcely able to breathe, Akmael accepted the gift and examined it. What Eolyn had done was impossible. Forbidden.

"Where did you learn this?" he demanded. "Where did you learn magic?"

"It's not magic," she objected hotly. "You just did it yourself! It's..."

The girl paused and stood up, her expression caught between indignation and realization. "It's magic? Are you certain?"

"This," Akmael set the plant firmly between them, "is the work of a student well advanced in the ways of Middle Magic."

"*Middle* Magic?!" Eolyn clapped her hands and brought her fingers to her lips. She gazed at Akmael with great intensity. "What is Middle Magic?"

"How can you not know? You have to know what Middle Magic is in order to practice it."

"Is it like Simple Magic?"

"No not at all. Simple Magic is just foods and medicines. Middle Magic is the language of the world, of the animals and stones and plants. It's about integrating the elements. Middle Magic is everything you have to know before you can practice High Magic."

"*High* Magic?"

Her ignorance baffled him. How could she invoke a visualization if she knew nothing about the different classes of magic?

"Do you feel the same way I do when you bring earth out of the air?" she asked.

"What are you talking about?"

"When you made the branch of stone."

"You mean when I visualized it," Akmael said.

"Did you get a tingle in the soles of your feet?" Eolyn insisted. "Whenever I draw earth from the air there's a sensation that makes me feel all warm inside. Does that happen to you? Does it make you happy like when the sun shines on a spring day or when winter's first snow begins to fall?"

"I don't know." Akmael had to think for a moment. "It's not exactly happiness I feel, it is more like a sense of power over great movement, as if a river were flowing through my hands. It reminds me a little of what it's like to ride a spirited horse."

"A horse?"

Akmael rolled his eyes. "A horse is an animal that—"

"Oh, I know what a horse is!" She gave an impatient wave of her hand. "There used to be horses in my village. It's just that I've never ridden a horse. Ernan used to ride them, though. He rode them a lot and it always made him very happy."

Eolyn's gaze wavered and disconnected from Akmael. An unmistakable color flickered through her aura, the signature of some terrible memory. Before Akmael could determine the source, she buried her thoughts with a quick shake of her head.

"So it must be the same," she concluded. "If it works the same way and makes us feel the same way, it must all be magic—you making the branch and me making the flower. And of course, you riding a horse."

Akmael opened his mouth to correct her but stopped himself. If the girl was this confused about the matter she could not get much further with magic, and that would be better for everyone.

"I have to go." Eolyn sprang forward and startled him with a hug. "You'll come back, won't you? I'll be by the river again in a quarter moon."

Before he could reply she took off toward the forest interior.

"Just wait 'til I have a word with that old witch!" she called over her shoulder. "She's been playing tricks on me since the day I arrived!"

Once the girl was well away, Akmael took out his amulet. He drew a deep breath, spun the silver web, and sang his mother's song. Much to his relief, the silver web took him back to his hiding place in the Foundation of Vortingen.

Sunset painted the sky crimson and purple. In the east, stars would soon begin to shine over the distant lands of his mother's home.

"Akmael!" Kedehen's shout made the prince jump. The Mage King was nearby, and angry.

Akmael secured the amulet in its place over his heart. Cautiously, he peeked through the bushes.

Kedehen paced among long shadows cast by the monoliths. His hand rested on the hilt of his sword. His war-hardened face was framed by chestnut brown hair.

Next to him stood the wizard Tzeremond and Sir Drostan, Kedehen's most trusted knight.

"You're certain the men saw him enter this place?" Kedehen asked.

"He was not seen, my Lord King," Drostan replied, "but the path of his flight leads here."

"Gods know we've looked everywhere else. Akmael!"

Despite his trepidation, Akmael admired his father's imposing build and forceful presence. Someday he hoped to be like Kedehen, respected and feared by all the people of Moisehén. Until then, he was bound by duty to obey.

He straightened his shoulders and stepped into the clearing.

Drostan caught sight of the prince first.

"My Lord King." The knight nodded in the direction of where Akmael stood.

Kedehen's black gaze settled on his son. He took in Akmael's disheveled appearance and soiled clothes. "For the love of the Gods, son, what have you been doing? Wrestling with a bear?"

"I…I was…"

"Never mind," Kedehen said. "Show me the medallion."

Reluctantly, the prince approached and drew out the silver web. He did not remove it from his neck.

Kedehen took the delicate jewel in his strong fingers. The King's expression shifted, a subtle softening around the eyes that Akmael had not seen since before his mother had died. He had learned long ago that this was not a sign of affection, but rather an expression of Kedehen's unfulfilled desire to feel affection.

"What kind of magic did you say this is, Master Tzeremond?" Kedehen asked.

"I do not know, my Lord King. I recognize the Queen's handiwork, though. The object was crafted by her."

"Indeed." Kedehen turned the web over in his hand. "When did your mother give this to you, Akmael?"

"On my birthday, almost a year before she died."

"Did she tell you how to use it? Any spells or chants? Rites that came with the gift?"

"No, Father." Akmael held the King's gaze. He was telling the truth, after all. Briana had revealed nothing about the medallion. That Akmael had just discovered its use was a different matter altogether.

"Drostan," Kedehen called to the knight. "You knew the magas better than any of us. Have a look at this object and tell me what you think."

A warrior trained under the Old Orders, Sir Drostan had served the King faithfully when the magas rose up against him. Now Drostan tutored Akmael in the arts of war. Akmael was a tall boy, but Sir Drostan towered over him as he examined the web. The knight's jaw worked beneath a thick red beard, and the faint smell of sweat and leather rose from his body.

"I have not seen anything like it, my Lord King." Drostan straightened and stepped away. "Not among the magas I knew, not at any time during the last days of the Old Orders."

"Very well." Kedehen nodded. "You may keep the gift, Akmael."

Akmael's heart leapt. He could hardly believe his luck. Was it really going to be that easy?

"My Lord King," Tzeremond objected.

"It is but a jewel, Master Tzeremond," Kedehen said. "It will do the Prince no harm. Even if it did have magic, I cannot believe the Queen would sabotage her son's glory from the grave. You know what she sacrificed to bear him. You understand, better than most, the choice she made."

"I respect your faith in her, my Lord King, but I cannot share your confidence. Queen Briana was a witch after all. A true daughter of East Selen."

"Yes." Kedehen set a solid hand on Akmael's shoulder. "And thanks to her, the legacy of East Selen is now mine. If this medallion concerns you, Tzeremond, then continue searching your records. Should you find evidence the silver web contains subversive magic, advise me and we will take the necessary precautions. Come, Akmael. We've wasted enough time on this matter. The evening meal awaits."

Akmael thanked his father and tucked the medallion back into its hiding place, keeping tight rein on the surge of excitement in his heart.

It does have magic!

Magic of the most wonderful and mysterious sort.

Tomorrow, he would begin exploring the full potential of his mother's gift. He would find out what determined his destination, and whether he could control where he went. Maybe he could get back to the river in the forest and find that girl again. What was her name?

Eolyn.

Akmael caught his breath.

He would like to see her again, he realized.

He would like that very much.

Chapter Four

The Origin of Magic

EOLYN BURST INTO THE COTTAGE, BREATHLESS. "Why didn't you say you were teaching me magic?"

Caught in the middle of preparing their evening stew, Ghemena set down her knife and dried her hands on a worn apron. The cards had foretold of this moment. They had promised Eolyn would see the reflection of her power in the shadow of the forest.

"Because you feared magic, Eolyn. You were born into a world where women who practiced the craft met their end in brutal ways. You blamed your magic and your mother's magic for the death of your family and the destruction of your village. You wouldn't have learned anything from me had I told you what I was doing."

"I'm not afraid anymore."

"Are you certain?"

Eolyn opened her mouth and shut it again. Her gaze wavered and shifted to the floor.

"You have experienced magic running through your veins," Ghemena said. "You have glimpsed the doors it can open for you. Now that you recognize your own potential, you have a decision to make."

Eolyn looked up. "But if I'm already learning magic, the decision has been made."

"No, Eolyn. I have shown you a path. That is all. A path that may have no future. Right now the only place for a maga outside of this forest is on the pyre. If you continue in the ways of the Old Orders, it may lead to a painful death. The greater your power, the more terrible your condemnation."

Eolyn brought her hands together and studied them intently. "But I can't die here. There aren't any roads, so there won't ever be any soldiers, and no one can ever come here to hurt me or you. Can they?"

Eolyn lifted her dark eyes, tentative and uncertain, to Ghemena.

"Sweet child," the old maga murmured. "Death can find us no

matter where we hide."

The girl drew a shaky breath. She brought her fingers to her eyes as if to stop an impulse of tears. After a long moment, she uncovered her face, straightened her shoulders, and lifted her chin.

"Well then," she said. "I suppose if I must die, I would rather die with magic inside of me. I don't want to die like the people in my village died. They all died a terrible death. I think now it would have been better for them to die having learned magic than to die as they did, with no magic at all."

Ghemena's balance faltered. She sought a nearby stool and eased herself down.

The forester, Varyl, had rebuked her when she decided to keep Eolyn. Varyl had called her a fool, and perhaps she was. A crazy, lonely old fool, unwilling to let go of a dream with no future. But in the end, Ghemena had held her ground. She had not come across a child with such innate talent in many, many years.

And what of Eolyn's destiny? The girl should have been killed by the King's Riders, for only in legend did people survive those massacres. She should have perished in the forest of starvation or fallen prey to wolves and wild cats. The thieves—Gods forbid—could have found her, had their way with her and left her to die. The South Woods extended vast and impenetrable in every direction from the girl's village. Yet according to the Guendes, Eolyn had walked an almost direct route to Ghemena's refuge, where she had taken to magic as a fledgling takes to the air in late spring.

Does not all of this mean something?

"Come, Eolyn," Ghemena whispered.

The girl approached and stood before her. Eolyn had grown taller these past years. Her once rounded face had begun to take on the finer features of adolescence. Well-defined brows sat in smooth arcs over dark eyes. There was depth to her countenance, a determination Ghemena knew would serve Eolyn well.

"You will be the only one left to command this knowledge, Eolyn. You will be alone, feared and hated by many. Are you certain this is what you want?"

"Yes." This time Eolyn did not hesitate in her answer. The flare in her aura confirmed her resolve. Ghemena felt something she had not experienced in many years: hope. A fleeting sense that not everything was lost. Perhaps the old ways could be restored. Perhaps the glory of the magas would not be extinguished after all.

"Then I have something to show you." Ghemena pushed herself to her feet. "And a story to tell."

Unsealing a hidden door next to the hearth, Ghemena opened a small alcove filled with the few remaining annals of women's magic. These volumes had found refuge here from the pyres of Moisehén, spirited into hiding when the maga took flight into the South Woods.

Eolyn gasped when she saw them and moved to follow her guardian.

"Have a seat at the table," Ghemena said. "There's hardly room in here for all these books, much less the two of us."

Ghemena chose a heavy volume from the alcove and laid its richly illustrated pages in front of the girl.

"What are these?" Eolyn's fingers drifted over the complex symbols that covered the page. "What do they mean?"

"This is a special kind of Middle Magic. In the common tongue, it is called writing. It allows us to share wisdom across generations, and you will learn to interpret it as part of your training."

"Mother told me about books. And writing and parchments. I never thought I'd see any though. She said books only existed in hidden places and that girls weren't allowed to touch them."

"This place is hidden well enough, I think. As for the separation between books and women, that is a recent turn of events. Under the traditions of the Old Orders, I would have shown you the secrets of these pages long before I taught you any other magic. But there are many things we will have to do differently here in the South Woods. Today, you will start the next stage of your journey, Eolyn. Today, you will learn how magic came to our people."

Ghemena turned the page and began to read:

Long ago, in a land that existed before time had meaning, there lived a woman called Aithne. She grew up in a world of ordinary ways. The plants held their silence. The animals moved in secret. The wind stood still, and the rocks lay cold and lifeless against the earth. The sun shone pale through gray days and the moon barely illuminated the starless nights. The essence of Primitive Magic haunted the land, but people were unable to give form to its song. They suffered from hunger and disease, and Aithne longed to help them.

Aithne spent long hours pondering this problem, until one day she noticed the animals were always healthy. Their dark coats were thick in winter, and their young energetic in summer. So she began to watch them. In this way she discovered from Bear which berries are good to eat, from Boar where to look for tasty mushrooms, from Squirrel how to choose nuts, and from Songbird how to weave baskets. This was the beginning of Simple Magic.

At that time, a young man named Caradoc fell in love with Aithne.

Aithne, seeing Caradoc understood her, fell in love with him. They consecrated their love under a full spring moon, and the heat of their hearts sparked a fire in the center of their village. The villagers gathered in awe to observe the blaze. With branches of pine, they divided the flame so that each family took a piece back to their own home. This is how fire came to our people.

Together Aithne and Caradoc discovered the secrets of Middle Magic. The joy of their love illuminated the world, allowing them to see the stones are not cold, but rather vibrate with wisdom of the ages. The plants and animals are not silent, but whisper timeless secrets for the well-prepared ear. Aithne and Caradoc taught Middle Magic to all those willing to learn it.

At this time, the Gods from the deepest and highest places of the world took notice of Aithne and Caradoc, and a division grew among them. Some of the Gods saw great beauty in their initiative. They recognized how magic illuminated and improved the lives of the villagers. But other deities felt threatened.

"Are we to let them continue down this path?" they objected. "To become Gods like us?"

Spurred by this division, the Gods sent two messengers to Aithne and Caradoc, each representing a different side of their argument.

The first messenger, Thunder, pursued the lovers through the forest and filled their hearts with fear. Aithne and Caradoc found refuge in a small cave in the mountains. Thunder raged all over the hills looking for them, but eventually gave up and faded away.

In the silence that followed, Aithne and Caradoc realized they were not alone. A dragon-serpent sat in the cave observing them with sharp silver eyes. Like all serpents, Dragon spoke only through silence, but Aithne and Caradoc, long accustomed to listening to the animals, adapted to this dialect with ease.

Do not fear, said Dragon. *The Gods who sent me find pleasure in your magic. They offer you the gift of High Magic so you may use it for the prosperity of your people.*

"Thunder told us the Gods are displeased and we can no longer use magic," Caradoc objected.

The Gods of Thunder are jealous and fearful, responded Dragon. *They believe your power threatens their dominion. You have nothing to fear from them. If you choose this path, I will show you how to protect yourself from their wrath.*

Caradoc hesitated, but Aithne stepped forward and asked, "What must we do?"

Dragon instructed Aithne to bring three elements and Caradoc to bring four. She sent Aithne east in her search and Caradoc west. After three days, both returned having completed their quest. Dragon helped each of them forge their first staff from these elements. Then she gave them a single command.

Practice magic as you will, but do no harm with this gift.

"And that is how magic was given to us." Ghemena closed the book with quiet reverence.

Eolyn put out a hand to stop her. "But what happened next?"

"Oh." The old woman smiled and caught the girl's fingers in hers. "Only the rest of history. But that's too much for one sitting. We will continue another day."

CHAPTER FIVE

Shape Shifting

"I've been an otter, a hawk, an oak, a wildflower, a turtle, a wolf, a beetle, a northern goose, and a rabbit!" Eolyn caught the lowest branch of a river willow in a single jump. She swung up to sit, her feet dangling above Akmael. The girl had a lithe figure, subtle in its curves, like a length of fine ash suited for crafting a strong bow.

"What about you?" she asked.

"I've been a wolf too." Akmael scaled the trunk to sit beside Eolyn, but she continued up the tree. "Master Tzeremond has also turned me into a fox, a spider, a snake, a lynx, a bear and a badger."

Eolyn looked down at him with a puzzled expression. "How odd."

"Odd?" Akmael thought his list impressive, not odd.

"They're all predators," she said. "Haven't you ever been a walking stick or something like that?"

"I was a dragonfly once."

"That's a predator, too."

Akmael shrugged and took hold of large knot with both hands to hoist himself up further. "I asked to be turned into a deer once, but Master Tzeremond refused. He said docile animals are a waste of my time."

"That's ridiculous. Ghemena says practitioners of magic should integrate diverse spirits into their craft. Deer have such a completely different way of *being* than predators. How can it be a waste of time to learn from Deer?"

"Master Tzeremond says my destiny leaves no room for assuming the ways of subordinate creatures."

"*Subordinate?*" Anger rose hot in Eolyn's voice. "Deer are *not* subordinate. Deer can get along just fine without wolves and cats and bears, but find a predator that can live without its prey? Now *that* would be some impressive magic."

"It is unfortunate you were not there to argue the point with Master

Tzeremond."

"He wouldn't have listened to me anyway." Eolyn settled on a high branch and let go a breath of exasperation. "I don't know how you can stand Tzeremond. Everything you tell me about him is unpleasant, and he's giving you the most boring education. I can't imagine shape shifting only into predators."

"Tzeremond is a great wizard," Akmael countered. "And the only Master left in the Kingdom. Father says I am fortunate to be his pupil."

In truth, Akmael held little affection for his overbearing tutor, but Eolyn's attitude annoyed him. It was not her place to question Akmael's training. Maybe Tzeremond had a grim personality, but the Prince respected what the Master taught. Dominion over magic would make Akmael a powerful king someday, maybe the most powerful in the world.

"Still," Eolyn said. "When you become a High Mage and learn to invoke shape shifting on your own, you should turn yourself into something besides a predator. Something *interesting*."

Akmael knew Eolyn well enough by now to understand they would argue about Tzeremond all afternoon if he did not change the subject

This situation will have to be reported soon.

The thought pained Akmael, because he knew it would mean confiscation of the silver web and the end of his adventures in the South Woods. Still, duty was duty. The crone Ghemena had to be arrested and burned. As for Eolyn, perhaps she could be brought back to the King's City and placed with an honorable family.

Akmael would see to it that no harm came to the girl. It was hardly her fault the witch was teaching her magic, and she was still young enough to unlearn her powers.

Perhaps I could even convince Father to take her under his wing, just as he did with Mage Corey.

Akmael's cousin, Corey of East Selen, had been spared as a boy at Briana's intervention. So Kedehen could be merciful when the mood struck him, and who would not want to be merciful toward a girl like Eolyn?

Akmael shifted his position against a wide limb and watched the cobalt sky flicker through the green leaves of the canopy. The smooth bark felt cool against his back, and the fragrance of sun-warmed herbs drifted up from the forest floor. The Mage Prince liked the steady hum of the South Woods. A deep magic ran beneath the earth here.

"I wouldn't have thought of an oak." He shielded his eyes from the sunlight to look at Eolyn. "I wouldn't have thought of turning into a tree or any other plant for that matter. What is it like?"

"It's the most magnificent adventure." She swung to a lower branch to sit near him, auburn curls flashing in the sun. "You and I and the animals are accustomed to the weight of flesh upon our bones, but it is different for trees. A tree catches water in the fan of its roots, collects it drop by drop until it runs in a constant river up its trunk. The river divides into branches and then into leaves, until the water bursts forth in a thousand tiny droplets.

"When you shape shift into a tree, you have the sensation of floating between water in the earth and water in the sky. The breeze wraps around your branches, and you feel the soil turning in tiny currents through your roots. When the sun shines, you feel perpetually satiated, but never full in the heavy sense we have after a large meal. And at night..."

Her voice drifted off.

Akmael, who had closed his eyes at some point during her discourse, opened them to find Eolyn peering at him with a curious expression.

"What is it?" he asked.

"I thought you were going to do it."

"Do what?"

"Shape shift. You started to shimmer, you know."

"Really?" Akmael examined his hands. He had felt something, he realized. A tingle in the center of his gut, a light surge of magic through his feet. "Are you certain?"

"Yes. You were about to shape shift. I've seen Ghemena do it. You had exactly the same kind of shimmer she gets just before she changes shape."

"That must be how it's done!" Akmael declared. "You visualize the creature you desire to change into. But who invoked the magic? Was it you or was it me?"

"I think it was both of us. I think we did it together."

"Fantastic!" Akmael clapped his hands. "We must try it again!"

They abandoned the high branches. For the rest of the afternoon Akmael and Eolyn tried to turn each other into rocks, squirrels, birds, wolves, bushes, fish, frogs, turtles and whatever else they could think of. Once in a while they managed to reach that elusive shimmer between their own shape and the desired form, but they did not achieve a true shape shift.

"I wonder what's missing," Akmael asked, frustrated at the end of yet another failed attempt. "Is it a special chant or incantation? A certain herb or mushroom or tincture?"

"Maybe we need a staff. Only High Mages and Magas can shape shift, and they all have staffs."

"Perhaps." Akmael was not convinced.

"We'll learn in any case, once we become Initiates and start studying

High Magic."

Akmael became serious. "You cannot go through with that, you know. You cannot learn High Magic."

"Why not? I've had no trouble at all learning Middle Magic."

"You know very well why not. There won't be a safe place for you in the kingdom if you practice magic. Already what you know is enough to sentence you to the pyre."

"Ghemena will teach me how to protect myself, just as Dragon taught Aithne and Caradoc."

"You don't know what you will be up against! Tzeremond's Order, the Council, the warriors of my...of the King's army. Ghemena hasn't so much as shown you how to use a knife, much less teach you wartime magic."

"I'll have you," Eolyn said. "I don't know any other mages to compare you with, but it's obvious you have very powerful magic. And Ghemena says one friend can make all the difference in a hostile world."

This declaration threw Akmael into an uncomfortable silence. Having the girl Eolyn as a secret friend in the South Woods was easy. Coming to the defense of the woman Eolyn, High Maga and threat to the peace of his father's Kingdom...that would be a different matter altogether.

"All I'm saying is that if you continue down this path it will become very dangerous for you," he insisted. "It is not right for women to practice High Magic anymore. It is not acceptable."

Eolyn stared at him as if he had slapped her in the face. She stood up and stepped away, eyes smoldering with rage.

"Do you really believe that?" she demanded.

"No. I mean, I don't know." The intensity of her reaction caught him off guard. "It is just, everybody knows women's magic is wrong. The magas brought death upon this kingdom, upon their families, even upon their own sisters."

Eolyn's cheeks lost their color. She folded her arms and turned her back on him. For a very long time she did not speak.

A mysterious anxiety ignited in Akmael's heart.

"It's late," Eolyn said, her voice tired and stiff. "I should head home."

In an instant Akmael was on his feet and at her side. "Wait, Eolyn. What I meant was...What I mean is, if you must learn High Magic, then at least learn how to defend yourself. I could teach you, if you like."

What am I saying?

He was only going to make things more difficult in the end.

"Of course, I am still a student myself," he added awkwardly. "But I

33

could show you a few things, like how to throw a knife and how to hold a sword."

Eolyn looked up at him as if through some invisible barrier. Akmael detected apprehension in her aura. With any other person, he would have taken that fear and made it his own, just as Master Tzeremond had taught him. But he could not do this with Eolyn. Indeed, it hurt something deep inside to have her watch him like that.

"I will not betray you, Eolyn," he murmured. "That I will not do."

Did she believe him?

He could not tell.

Without a word, Eolyn walked away, becoming one with the shadows of the South Woods.

Chapter Six

Tzeremond

From the moment Kedehen took Briana as his bride to the day the maga warrior struck her down, Tzeremond had watched the situation with unceasing diligence.

Kedehen had always impressed the wizard with his clear and level-headed thinking, but when it came to the ebony haired sorceress of East Selen, the King tended to lose his bearings. The strain of keeping the Witch Queen's power at bay all those years had so permeated Tzeremond's life that he did not realize his exhaustion until the day the Gods released him from his duty.

How intriguing the irony of my deliverance, he often mused, *that a maga warrior should have put an end to the most troublesome witch of them all.*

With Briana out of the way, Tzeremond had turned his hopes toward the possibility of a new queen, and with her more suitable heirs. Although Akmael had inherited his mother's gift for magic, he did not have the qualities of a true king. His rebellious nature interfered with his advancement in sorcery, and witnessing the violent death of his mother had only made matters worse.

As long as Akmael remained Kedehen's only heir, the kingdom was at risk. Yet three summers had passed since Briana's murder, and still the King refused to seek another bride.

Now, as Tzeremond sat in conference with the rest of the Council, the future of his people weighed heavy in his heart.

The Council was gathered around a long polished oak table in the largest of the antechambers to the King's apartments. Twelve High Mages occupied seats on the Council, many of Tzeremond's finest students among them. Military and magical artifacts adorned the room. An elaborate tapestry depicting the appearance of Dragon to the ancient warrior chief Vortingen covered the eastern wall. Large windows along the southern face provided a strategic view of the rolling plains of Moisehén, verdant under the late summer sun.

"The Prince continues to progress rapidly, my Lord King," Sir Drostan was saying. "If he maintains the focus he has demonstrated these past weeks, he will make a fierce warrior and an able leader."

"His focus has returned," Tzeremond said, "but his obstinacy has not faded."

The attention of the Council turned to the wizard, as it always did in the moment he chose to speak.

"He fights his tutors every step of the way, challenges our wisdom at every turn," Tzeremond continued. "His skills in magic cannot be doubted, yet he has trouble understanding the deeper truths of what we teach. He is a difficult child, my Lord King, and it worries me the future of this kingdom rests solely on his shoulders."

"With all due respect, Master Tzeremond," Sir Drostan said, "I believe a gifted student should challenge his instructors. Indeed, it would be a greater worry if Prince Akmael's questions were too few rather than too many."

"He disappears, my Lord King." Tzeremond kept his gaze on Kedehen. "For long periods of time. Sometimes an entire day can pass in which no one knows where he is."

"These absences have not interfered with his lessons," the knight insisted. "It is natural for a boy of fourteen summers to explore the world. He is a prince, not a prisoner."

"Sir Drostan, I speak with Prince Akmael's best interests in mind." Tzeremond turned on the knight. "A young mage unsupervised can fall to many malevolent influences, even within these halls."

Drostan drew a breath as if to speak, then retreated into silence with a deferential nod. Before the war, this knight had trained under the masters of the Old Orders, weak wizards whose indulgence of women's magic had brought Moisehén to near ruin. Though his valiant service had secured the King's trust, Drostan was not fool enough to argue with Tzeremond in matters of subversive magic. At least, not in open Council.

"I suspect, Master Tzeremond, that the flame of women's magic has been extinguished both within these halls and without, thanks to your very thorough efforts," Kedehen said. "Trials and executions for witchcraft are now rare events in Moisehén."

Tzeremond acknowledged the King's complement with a gracious nod. "The diligence of our mages in seeking out and destroying women's magic has served us well, and the oversight of the magistrates in the provinces is exemplary. Still, the shadow of the magas clings to this land. Our divinatory tools send mixed messages regarding our success. On the one hand they indicate the Order of Magas is finished. On the other, they insist a new age of female sorcery is set to arrive."

"And what do you make of this contradiction?" the King asked.

"I believe, your Grace, that the coming threat will be so new to our experience we may not recognize it. We hunt magas with old techniques. We need new strategies for finding the witches prophesized by our seeing pools and sacred symbols."

"Indeed." The King stroked his beard. His dark gaze flicked across the table to Mage Tzetobar. "Do you have anything to add to Master Tzeremond's observations?"

"I share his concern, my Lord King."

Tzetobar's rounded cheeks seemed permanently flushed under that thick blond beard. Like Drostan, he had trained under the Old Orders, but Tzetobar often showed greater wisdom and prudence in matters that came before the Council.

"What organized resistance existed after the war has long since crumbled under the purges," Tzetobar said. "Where memory of the great conflict has not yet faded, it is repressed by fear. The people's attention has returned to farming, commerce, and craftsmanship, but it is an uneasy peace we have achieved. The possible resurgence of any subversive magic cannot be taken lightly."

A general murmur of agreement sounded across the table.

"If I may make a suggestion, my Lord King." High Mage Thelyn spoke now.

The youngest member of the Council, Thelyn boasted a striking countenance accentuated with a thin beard. One of the few to achieve the status of High Mage after the war, he was an excellent student with a keen intellect. Tzeremond had recommended him to the King, believing Thelyn would have much to contribute with his understanding of the complex mysteries of Primitive Magic.

"I believe it would be wise to initiate a comprehensive study of alternative forms of magic," Thelyn said. "Magic as it is practiced beyond the borders of this land, by the Syrnte or among the Mountain People, for example. It is an idea I have discussed at length with some of the other High Mages. Such an endeavor might give us better insight as to what to look for."

"An interesting recommendation," the King acknowledged. This was the kind of project that would appeal to Kedehen. Though he did not have a natural aptitude for magic, his thirst for knowledge had made him work harder than any student Tzeremond had ever taught, transforming the young prince into a formidable wizard. "What do you think, Master Tzeremond?"

"I support Mage Thelyn's suggestion, my Lord King. As he himself mentioned, we have discussed it at length."

"The work Thelyn proposes must be undertaken with great care." Tzetobar, always the cautious one, interjected. "We would be prudent to keep it hidden, to disguise our efforts under a guise of friendship, cooperation, and exchange of magical traditions."

"Very well," the King said. "See that it is done, Master Tzeremond. I expect periodic reports on your progress."

"Of course, my Lord King."

Kedehen moved to dismiss them, but High Mage Tzetobar gave a tentative lift of his ruddy hand. "If I may, my Lord King?"

Kedehen nodded and settled back into his chair. The diplomat's blue eyes connected briefly with Tzeremond's before returning to the regent.

"I thought we might use this opportunity to analyze the proposal made by the King of Roenfyn," Tzetobar said.

Kedehen's broad shoulders stiffened. "I have already made my decision, Mage Tzetobar, as you well know."

A tense silence spread across the table. Tzeremond shifted in his seat. If Tzetobar could not resolve this, then perhaps no one could.

"With all due respect, my Lord King," the red-faced mage persisted. "The Third Princess of Roenfyn is a very suitable match, a virtuous maiden of excellent lineage, and her father offers a generous dowry of goods and territories. There are many advantages to this opportunity and many risks in denying it. Among other considerations, you must know that it is not..." Tzetobar cleared his throat. "It is not prudent to let the future of the Crown to depend upon a single heir."

"The destiny of my son cannot be questioned," the King said. "With him the glory of Vortingen and the magic of East Selen have been poured into a single vessel. I require no other heirs."

"My Lord King," Tzeremond spoke with care, infusing his voice with genuine concern. "I agree this boy, if the Gods continue to favor him, could be the greatest Mage and King to have walked these lands, but we must take care with our own pride and arrogance. What would have happened, after all, if your father had set all his hopes upon his eldest son?"

Kedehen stood abruptly and moved away from the table. His jaw worked beneath the hard lines of his face. For several minutes the only sound was the heavy fall of his boots as he paced.

Tzeremond's question burned in the air between them. Three of Kedehen's brothers had gone to their deaths before the weight of the Crown fell to him. Experience had proven a single heir was not enough. What in the name of the Gods kept Kedehen from recognizing this? The very thought of accepting another queen seemed to fill him with distaste, inexplicable for a Prince of Vortingen.

Perhaps he did indeed love her.

As improbable as it seemed. Briana had lived out her last years as little more than Kedehen's prisoner, confined to the East Tower behind doors sealed by magic.

Still, if there was no love between them, what force kept the King from taking another princess to his bed? What other explanation could there be for this strange attachment that transcended death itself?

The King took a resolute stance before them, powerful hands gripping the back of his chair. "I desire no other queen, and I require no additional heirs. The Mage Prince Akmael will assume the Crown of Vortingen, and the line of my fathers will continue through him. You may give this message to the King of Roenfyn: his offer is refused. I will suffer no further discussion of the matter."

With that Kedehen departed, and the Council was adjourned.

Tempted to let his weary head sink into his hands, Tzeremond maintained his composure. He stood and retrieved his rowan staff. He acknowledged Tzetobar's efforts with a silent nod.

Once again they had failed, but Tzeremond would not give up hope. The Gods had led him this far in his effort to heal the country of women's magic and to ensure its future against any resurgence. It was only a matter of time and perseverance before Dragon showed him another way.

CHAPTER SEVEN

Three Rivers

"I want to be a warrior maga like my mother." Eolyn's voice cut sharp through cool morning air.

Ghemena gathered a handful of bean pods, set them in her basket, and observed her charge for several minutes. Vexation marked Eolyn's every move as she wrestled carrots out of the soft earth.

"But there is no war to fight," Ghemena replied. "Why learn the arts of war if no war exists in which to apply them?"

"It would serve to defend myself against those who would punish me for my magic and…" Eolyn forced another carrot out of the ground and threw it in her basket. "It would serve to avenge the destruction of my village and the murder of my family."

"There are many strategies for self-defense that do not require wartime magic. As for vengeance, who speaks to you of such things? The impulse for revenge has no place in this household, much less in your lessons."

Ghemena received the girl's cross silence with concern. An agitated glow tinged Eolyn's aura, accompanied by a surprising spark Ghemena had not noticed until this moment.

"You have a friend you haven't told me about," she realized in astonishment. "Who would have thought? A child in this corner of the woods. And a secret you've chosen to keep from me."

Still Eolyn did not speak. She wrapped her fist around another bunch of carrot greens and pulled hard. Tension creased the girl's brow and the sweat of her efforts dampened the fine roots of her hair.

"Why did you not tell me?" Ghemena insisted.

The earth released the carrot unexpectedly, throwing Eolyn back on her heels. She stared at the vegetable for a long moment and then tossed it in a basket. "He asked me not to."

"Oh for the love of the Gods!" Ghemena lifted her hands to the heavens. "What is it with men that they can smell a virgin across such distances? Who is he, Eolyn? The son of a forester? He cannot be a thief, or I would have lost you to some terrible fate long ago."

"He's not a thief or a forester. He's just a boy who comes to visit the forest, a student of magic like me."

The words hit Ghemena in the stomach. The ground lurched and her vision blurred. She caught herself on unsteady hands and tried to recuperate her breath. A harsh rattle invaded her lungs.

Eolyn rushed to place her hands upon the old woman's back, but the girl's healing powers had not matured enough to penetrate Ghemena's brittle ribs.

"A mage!" Ghemena gasped. "But how? Where did he come from?"

"I'm not sure." Eolyn sounded distraught. "He just appears. He told me he lives in a forest like this one, only everything is made of stone. Ghemena, what is wrong? Where has your breath gone?"

The old maga closed her eyes. Her head sank into shaking hands. Only one place could be described as a stone forest, the great city of Moisehén, the King's City. A student of Tzeremond had somehow crossed the kingdom, penetrated the South Woods, and found Eolyn.

I do not have the strength at this stage of life to confront a disaster of such magnitude.

Ghemena lifted her face and found it wet with tears. "You cannot see him again. And we, we must leave this place at once to seek a new refuge."

Even as she spoke Ghemena recognized the impossibility of this task. Varyl would not return before spring, and Ghemena was too old to move without his help. At least two moons would pass before winter rendered the South Woods impenetrable. If the mages wished to track them down, they could do it before Samhaen.

She drew a deep breath. "Perhaps we can find a new place for you, Eolyn. Somewhere to hide in the coming months. You could stock it with supplies from the cottage and wait for spring to show you another path. I am too old to ask for a longer life. If they find me, little will be lost. But you, you cannot die now. You must run and hide."

"No, Ghemena," Eolyn protested. "I will not leave you."

"You have no choice! A student of Tzeremond has found you. He will betray you, if he has not already."

"That's not true! He's promised never to betray me. He wants only to protect me. He's even offered to teach me how to protect myself!"

Ghemena pinned Eolyn with a sharp gaze.

"What do you mean?" she asked, each word crisp and ominous.

Eolyn averted her eyes. A flush invaded her cheeks. "He wants to teach me how to fight, a little. How to throw a knife. How to hold a sword."

"So you wish to die like the magas of the Old Orders," Ghemena concluded in bitter tones. "On the battle field watching the blood drain from your severed limbs."

"No, Ghemena! It's just…I'm frightened. What's going to happen if I ever leave this forest? How will I know whom to trust? Who will I look to for protection if I can't protect myself? And Achim has already taught me so much, not just about fighting, but about Tzeremond and the King and the world outside of these woods."

"It does not matter. Even if he can remain loyal to your friendship— which he cannot—there are others in his Order who, at the slightest hint of your existence, will do whatever it takes to destroy you. You must put an end to this 'friendship' at once."

"I can't," the girl pleaded. "Don't ask me to do this, Ghemena, please! He has been such a wonderful companion. He's the only friend I have besides you. We have known each other many moons now. All summer we have been together. Don't you think he would have betrayed me already if that had been his intention? Please, Ghemena, I can't bear the thought of losing another friend. Not now. Please."

Ghemena folded her fingers tight over her forehead. Her inner voice was faint against her own anxiety and the clamor of the girl's pleas.

"You yourself said," Eolyn continued, "that in the Great War there were mages who supported the magas, who fought with them against the King and Tzeremond. What if my friend is like those mages? What if he is destined to help me when the time comes?"

"Your friend is not a mage of the Old Orders!" Ghemena snapped. "The Old Orders are dead. Tzeremond saw to that."

Eolyn retreated into confused silence.

The garden plants shifted under the autumn sun. Insects buzzed amidst leaves and branches, indifferent to the crisis at hand.

Ghemena took Eolyn's hands into her gnarled grasp. Such long fingers the girl had, already rendered strong by work and magic.

"For the greater part of my life, Eolyn, I believed the truism of the Old Orders that there is no evil in this world except that which we create by our own choices. Tzeremond changed all that. His wizardry had no place in the traditions of Moisehén, and yet he came from us, trained by our own masters.

"He has only ever turned his magic to destructive ends, yet the Gods leave him unpunished. He violated the greatest prohibition of our people and taught the ways of magic to a man of royal lineage. When that prince assumed the crown and the magas rose up in protest, Tzeremond did not simply defeat them. He destroyed all his rivals, mages and magas alike. He tore down the old ways and created his own order. Now the only magic left to our people is controlled by him. Tzeremond does not have students, Eolyn. Tzeremond has only puppets, and your friend is one of them."

"Achim is not a puppet! He's not, Ghemena. He's my friend."

Ghemena sighed at the stubborn set of Eolyn's jaw. She knew that look of determination. She had honed it. "You've always been such an obedient child. Why do you choose to be difficult in this of all things?"

Eolyn's expression softened. She shrugged and lowered her gaze.

"I will consult the cards tonight, Eolyn. Tomorrow we will decide what to do. Until then you must not go to the forest. You are to remain here with me."

Alone in her tiny room that evening, Ghemena removed her worn deck from its resting place and spread it in an arc illuminated by a solitary white candle.

Decades ago, a traveling Syrnte witch had left these illustrated plates with the Doyenne as a gift. In time she had learned how to interpret them, and ever since her flight from Moisehén, they had been her constant companions.

After meditating, Ghemena chose three items to accompany the reading: a polished black stone, a songbird's feather, and a broken knife. Closing her eyes, she passed her aged fingers over the cards in search of an ephemeral vibration.

She drew first for Eolyn.

Companionship. Two witches play in an open meadow. The sun sets in the west and the moon rises in the east.

Ghemena's eyes grew damp. This was not the answer she sought. The risk seemed far too great. Still, the cards rarely misled her. Should she doubt them now?

Returning her fingers to the arc, she drew a second card for herself.

Transformation. A solitary witch crosses a river as if on air, her face upturned. Stars illuminate her path.

Ghemena's heart slowed. She rested her hands on the rough surface of the table.

So many years she had lived, so much experience she had gathered. Yet in this moment under the flickering candlelight, age and wisdom seemed insufficient to confront the true meaning of this image.

The Gods will soon call me home.

For herself, the news felt almost comforting, but what would become of young Eolyn once she was gone? And how could she teach the girl everything she needed to know before crossing over the Plains of the Dead?

"How much time do we have?" Ghemena whispered.

The deck responded with two cards.

For Eolyn, three rivers.

For Ghemena, seven trees.

CHAPTER EIGHT

Akmael's Secret

IN THE WEEKS BEFORE SAMHAEN, the magistrate of Selkynsen brought a girl accused of witchcraft to the city.

At the King's request, Prince Akmael oversaw her trial. She was young like Eolyn, no longer a girl but not quite a woman, with flaxen hair and frightened blue eyes. Her parents, merchants of some renown, wept and raged before the court while pleading her innocence, but in the end the girl confessed under torture.

When they dragged her back before court to receive her sentence, Akmael could only see Eolyn, her face swollen and discolored, her hair matted with blood, her limbs broken and twisted until they no longer served her.

The night before the girl burned, Akmael could not sleep for the thought of his Eolyn thrown to the guards like some scrap of meat, to be ravaged by them so she would not die a virgin.

The Prince had not seen such violence perpetrated against a witch since the trial of the woman who murdered his mother. That red haired assassin had committed an unpardonable crime. In Akmael's mind, she deserved every moment of suffering imposed upon her.

But this girl from Selkynsen, what offense had she committed that would undermine the peace of the kingdom? What threat did she truly pose?

The zealous fury of the mages that destroyed her sobered Akmael and made him reconsider his plan to bring Eolyn to the city. As a prince he had no real power of intervention in matters of magical law, and if he could not secure his father's sympathy, what would become of his friend?

So winter passed, followed by spring and then summer again, and still Eolyn remained his secret in the South Woods. How long he could sustain this situation, Akmael did not know. Years could pass, decades even, before the Gods saw fit to call his father home and give the Crown to him. Every day Eolyn spent in the South Woods was another day lost

45

to the corrupting influence of that crone. Yet if Eolyn left the forest, Tzeremond's mages could find her. When that happened, she might be lost to Akmael forever.

"It doesn't feel right." Frustrated, Eolyn drove the blade into the earth and paced around it. Sweat glistened on her sun-warmed skin and dampened the roots of her auburn hair. "I can't do this, Achim. I can't fight with a sword."

"You've only just started. It takes a lot of time and practice to handle a blade with skill."

"It's not about practicing. It's what happens when I feel the metal in my hands. Something inside me rejects everything I try to do with it."

Akmael could not deny the truth of her observation. The moment she had wrapped her hands around the hilt, Eolyn's natural speed and balance deserted her. All afternoon her movements had been awkward and forced. She appeared to be fighting against, rather than with, the weapon.

Eolyn pulled the sword back up, sheathed it, and offered it to him.

"No." Akmael shook his head. "This weapon is yours."

It was the first sword he had ever used, a small instrument meant more for practice than for battle. Akmael had long since discarded it in favor of longer blades, but it was well crafted. He had chosen the weapon for Eolyn, knowing its light weight would sit perfectly in her strong hands, and that it would never be missed from the castle armory.

"I can't accept your sword, Achim. How will you fight without it?"

He laughed. "I have many other swords. One day I will inherit my father's sword and then that will be the only one I use. You need to practice, Eolyn. Keep the sword."

"Can't we just visualize another one for me?"

"A sword cannot be visualized. Magic cannot be used to create weapons of war."

"Why not?"

Akmael shrugged. "Sir Drostan says it is because magic and warfare had separate origins, magic being given to Caradoc and warfare to the ancestors of Vortingen. But maybe they simply haven't discovered how to do it yet."

"Even if I do keep this sword, where would I put it? Ghemena will destroy it if she finds it at the cottage."

"You can hide it here in the forest."

"Then some thief or forester might come across it and take it."

"I know a simple spell that allows you to drive a sword into stone so that only you can remove it again. We can use one of the boulders at the foot of Lynx's ridge."

Eolyn unsheathed the blade and let it rest in her hand. The length of metal reflected the autumn leaves against a blue sky. She studied the instrument, listening carefully to its silver hum.

"It's such a strange sound, the language of swords," she said.

"You understand the knife well enough."

Eolyn had learned the dialect of knives with ease. She could send her small blade singing into almost any target.

"The knife has a simple song," she replied. "It's not at all like the voice of this sword, not nearly as complex."

"It is the same language." Odd she could not hear that for herself. Distinguishing the voice of a sword from the voice of a knife was as simple as discerning between the accents of Selkynsen and Selen. "They are both metals."

She looked up at him. For a moment, Akmael lost himself in the oval line of her face, the curve of her rose colored lips, the lovely smile that spread through her dark eyes.

"This is a generous gift, Achim. Thank you. I will keep your sword. Perhaps with time she and I will learn to understand each other."

Eolyn sheathed the weapon and together they set out for the high ridge. Autumn leaves crunched underfoot. Trees crowned in gold and crimson shaded their path. Empty sounds of fall had invaded the South Woods, chasing away songbirds and driving bears toward their caves. Soon the white blanket of winter's death would spread over barren trees.

This would be the second time Akmael left Eolyn behind in the South Woods for the winter. Once again, he wondered whether he was making a mistake. The forest could snatch her away in its grip of ice, leaving nothing but her memory to greet the spring. If she survived, that crone would continue to confuse Eolyn with her web of subversive magic.

Akmael wanted to take Eolyn back to the King's City, wrap her in a fine fur cloak, and watch her fall asleep in front of a roaring fire. He wanted to deliver her to the comforts of Moisehén, but the specter of the battered girl from Selkynsen loomed in his mind. The smell of her burning flesh returned to his memory.

"How do you survive here the winter through?" he asked. "What do you do for food and warmth?"

"We always greet the season with plenty of supplies. What we can't grow in the garden or harvest from the woods is brought to us by a forester named Varyl. He comes only twice a year, but he brings everything we need. The South Woods has always been kind to Ghemena and me. I do not fear winter. I love its crystal breath and the starkness of its colors." Eolyn paused in her gait to expose the blade of the sword. She held it to her ear. "I bet this sword will have a different song in winter. I bet she will ring like the ice."

Akmael smiled and took the weapon from her hands. He coaxed a hum from its blade with a few idle slices through the air.

"She will sing only for you if you keep flattering her like that," he said. "Why is your tutor so opposed to you learning the sword? All the magas of her time understood the arts of war."

"That's not true! Only a small number of magas have ever been warriors, even during the last great conflict in which they all perished."

Akmael let out a breath of disapproval. *So many lies the hag was telling her!*

"Ghemena was not part of the warrior class," Eolyn continued. "She never condoned war, not even when the magas rose up against Kedehen. She supported the magas because they were her sisters, but she has no tolerance for war. She believes anyone who learns to speak with the sword will die by it."

"Better to die on a blade than on the pyre." The King's men weighed the honor of one death against another without a second thought, but Akmael could tell by the look on Eolyn's face that she did not find his comment amusing.

"I don't understand how magic can be applied to warfare," she said. "Magic should be used to create not to destroy. And in war one always has to destroy. How is it possible for a mage to become warrior?"

"It is easy enough." Akmael balanced the sword in his grip. "You learn the arts of war and then you learn the arts of magic. Then a mage warrior like Sir Drostan teaches you how to integrate the two. For example…"

Advancing toward a nearby tree, Akmael evoked a soft hissing ring from the blade. He ran up the trunk vertically while deflecting the advances of an imaginary enemy and returned to the ground in a short flight.

"Tricks like that give you a great advantage over your opponent. You can also alter the path of flying objects."

He threw the sword toward the trunk of young pine, willing it to swerve before driving solidly into the target.

"A skilled warrior mage detects the fears of his enemy and turns them to his advantage." Akmael strode over to the pine to retrieve the weapon. "A warrior mage trained in High Magic can use his staff to invoke a death charge."

His words stopped short when he turned back to Eolyn.

She stood deathly still amidst the falling leaves, her feet pressed tight upon the earth, her eyes wide and frightened. All the color had drained from her face.

"What is it?" he asked. "What's wrong?"

"Are you going to be one of them?" she whispered.

"One of whom?"

"Are you going to be a Rider for the King?"

"No. No, Eolyn. The Riders are not mages. They're just knights."

"They destroyed my family, you know. And my village. I only escaped because I happened to be in the woods that day. That's how I came to be here with Ghemena."

A chill took hold of Akmael. The trees creaked in a passing breeze and then stood silent.

"There must have been traitors there," Akmael said. "The King only sends his Riders to villages that harbor traitors."

"There were no traitors where we lived, only farmers."

Frost spread over the forest floor, painting fallen leaves misty white.

"Children can't be traitors," Eolyn said, "and as for their parents, what treachery is there in tending chickens and harvesting grain?"

"I do not know, Eolyn. All I am saying is he must have had a reason. Sending the Riders upon a village is not a decision the King makes lightly. There must have been some justification."

"What *possible* justification could there have been?" Her voice broke like a clap of thunder.

When Akmael offered nothing in response, Eolyn sank to the ground and began to weep.

Akmael had known Eolyn in many moods, but he had never witnessed this core of pain and anger. Then again, he had never asked why she lived so deep inside the forest with only an old witch for company, or what had happened to her real family.

Now with the truth laid out on the carpet of her tears, he felt torn between the loyalty he sustained toward his father and the brutal consequences of the King's justice.

Sheathing the sword, Akmael approached Eolyn and knelt down beside her. "Eolyn."

"Don't you dare tell me it's my fault!"

"Your fault?"

"That's what you think!" Eolyn's sobs coursed through her body in harsh shudders. "It's what you said!"

"What *I* said?"

"You said women's magic invokes tears and bloodshed. You said magas bring death upon their families, even upon their own sisters. But it wasn't my fault! I only knew Simple Magic back then. And even if I had known what I know now, what's wrong with that? With who I am? How can something so beautiful be *wrong?*"

Her words lost their way in a renewed round of tears.

Akmael sat back, uncertain how to respond.

Yes, he had said that, though he could not quite remember when. But he had not meant to hurt Eolyn, only to warn her about the dangers of women's magic.

He placed a tentative hand on her shoulder. "Eolyn, the attack on your village was not your fault. I don't know why the Riders came, but it could not have been because of you."

That much was certainly true. No hamlet had ever been punished just because one girl knew a few medicinal plants.

Eolyn's weeping wavered, fell, and rose again.

Akmael was reminded of the lamentations of his own mother, which haunted the shadows of his early childhood.

"I lost my mother, you know." His voice sounded small. He'd never spoken about this to anyone, not even his father. "She died defending me and I saw her fall. I had not yet seen eleven summers, but I blamed myself for her murder. I thought I should have been able to protect her, but I couldn't. It still gives me bad dreams, sometimes."

The tremor in Eolyn's shoulders faded.

Encouraged by her response, Akmael continued, "I'm not saying it's comparable to your loss. I mean, how can one grief be weighed against another? But I think I understand something of what you experienced."

For a moment Eolyn's sobs intensified. Akmael drew her close and inhaled the honey-and-wood scent of her hair. Embracing her like this gave him a sense of warmth and completion.

"I'm sorry the Riders destroyed your village, Eolyn. I'm sorry they took away your family. If there were a magic in this world that would allow me to undo what was done, I would."

At last Eolyn stopped crying. She wiped the tears from her cheeks and tried to recapture her spirit with unsteady breaths. She lifted her earth brown eyes to his. Short sniffles interrupted her words.

"I'm sorry about your mother, Achim. I didn't know. I'm so sorry you lost her. I would bring her back, if I could. I would bring her back for you."

CHAPTER NINE

Winter Vigil

EOLYN FLATTENED A SCRAP OF PAPER crafted from plant fibers and bay leaves. Taking a piece of charcoal from the edge of the hearth, she wrote a wish in sacred symbols. Then, with the hot fire warming her face, she folded the paper three times and offered it to the flames.

"May the Gods see honor in my desire," she said. "May my hopes for the future guide the sun back to Moisehén."

The fire accepted the note, curling and tarnishing its edges until the wish burst into a small white flame that faded quickly to red.

Sitting back, Eolyn wrapped herself in a coarse blanket and huddled next to Ghemena. They would keep vigil in front of the hearth all night, drinking hot berry wine, sharing stories, and singing songs as the sun made its perilous journey back from the Underworld on Midwinter's Eve.

"Ghemena, why have you never told me about the war?"

The old maga stiffened. "I have spoken often of the war."

"You've told me bits and pieces, but mostly you talk about everything *except* the war. You've told me how Aithne and Caradoc discovered High Magic and how Caedmon became the first mage warrior. You've told me about the invasion of the Thunder People and the Foundation of Vortingen. I know how the Old Orders came to be, and I've learned the legends of the Clan of East Selen. I know about the banishment of the Naether Demons and the magic of Syrnte witches. You've even told me about the fire wizards of Galia, whom I'm sure I will never meet, but you've never really talked about the war that destroyed our sisters."

Ghemena closed her eyes. She had grown thin this past year, and the lines on her face had deepened. When she looked again at Eolyn, it was through a misty gaze. "Why do you ask this of me now?"

Eolyn shivered and drew the blanket tighter about her shoulders. "I fear that my own future may hold war. I had a dream of smoke and fire, and of bodies scattered across a blackened plain. Achim was there,

51

covered in soot and blood. A great ivory sword came down upon him, and then he was gone."

Ghemena clucked her tongue. "That was only a dream."

"What if it was a vision?"

"Divination is a reckless form of magic. You should not give yourself over to it."

"You use your cards," Eolyn countered.

"I resort to those Syrnte toys because I've no one else to consult when making decisions." Ghemena's voice was bitter and thick with emotion. "In the old days, the cards were nothing more than an entertaining relic. I spoke with real people when choosing my path, companions and mentors who did not allow my hopes and fears to cloud my judgement."

"Then talk to me, Ghemena," Eolyn said. "If you'd rather I listen to a person than to my dreams, tell me about the war. Maybe if you explain to me what happened and how, I will have the wisdom to choose another path when my time comes."

Ghemena narrowed her eyes and turned her gaze back to the fire. "We cannot stop war. We can only run from it. Run and hide."

Eolyn's throat tightened. "Surely you don't believe that, Ghemena? You've always told me that magas have a choice."

After a long moment, the old maga gave a weary shake of her head. "Pay me no mind, Eolyn. A long time ago, I saw my world go up in flames. Now sometimes I rant without reason. It is true what you say: A maga's life is never bound to a single path, not even in war. I will tell you the story you want to hear, but first you must refill my wine."

Ghemena had a gift for making hot berry and primrose wine. Eolyn loved the way its sweet aroma stung her senses whenever she poured a glass. She also served a thick slice of nut bread for each of them before snuggling back into the warmth of her blanket.

"The conflict that dragged us into war began around the time I was appointed Abbess of Berlingen," Ghemena said. "One of the *Aekelahrs* of the Old Orders—a place of learning led by Master Tzeremond—accepted a prince of the line of Vortingen as a student of magic. This decision violated an important prohibition. Mixing magical power with royal power was considered dangerous. It meant too much dominion in the hands of one family. The Old Orders understood this, and the prohibition against royalty practicing magic was respected by all generations of the House of Vortingen, until the arrival of the fourth son of Urien, Prince Kedehen."

"The one who is now King of Moisehén?"

"Yes. But he was not king back then. Indeed, he had little hope of ever becoming king, or anything else of importance for that matter. It is a terrible thing, Eolyn, to be the fourth son of a king. A fourth son is worth less than his sisters, for while a princess inherits nothing she can at least forge useful alliances with her marriage and children. But what can a fourth son bring to a royal family that it does not already have? And what does he gain from being the spawn of a king if he receives no inheritance? Princes not destined for the crown often seek to prove their worth by becoming great warriors, merchants, or explorers. But Kedehen would have none of that. Kedehen wanted to learn magic."

"And only Tzeremond would take him in?"

"No other *Aekelahr* would accept him under the prohibition. When Tzeremond opened his doors to Kedehen, everyone fell into an uproar. Mages and magas summoned special councils and attempted to dissuade Tzeremond from his folly. The wizard held firm though, and the prince advanced rapidly under his instruction as the debate wore on.

"In the end, everyone tired of the matter and desisted. We realized Tzeremond would not be turned from this path except by force, and we did not want to send mages into battle against each other. Kedehen was the fourth son, after all. With three healthy brothers between him and the throne, it would take a great coincidence of fate for the crown to fall to him."

Ghemena punctuated the words *coincidence of fate* in sour tones. The flames of the hearth flared in her gray eyes, and the skin around her pursed lips paled.

Eolyn felt the icy sick hand of the visions she had the day her village was destroyed.

"He killed them," she whispered. "He killed them all to be king, didn't he?"

"Perhaps," Ghemena said. "If he did, the truth has long since been buried in places too dark to be found. Within a few years of the death of King Urien, all three of Kedehen's brothers had followed their father into the Afterlife. The first fell victim to form of dysentery so rare even the court physician could find no cure. The second was assassinated by his best knight, and though more than a hundred people witnessed the murder, the man went to his execution swearing innocence. The third prince, who had traveled far beyond the mountains to the land of the Syrnte, fell prey to thieves on his way home to assume the crown. With that, the unthinkable became reality. Kedehen, Prince and High Mage, stood ready to assume the Crown of Vortingen.

"Mages and magas from both Orders met in special councils once again. We signed petitions urging the Prince to abdicate. We summoned Tzeremond with instructions on how to advise his student, this time under threat of expulsion. All our efforts failed. Kedehen assumed the throne, and within weeks of his coronation, the magas rose up in rebellion."

"So the magas did start the war."

Ghemena pinned Eolyn with a sharp gaze. "Is that what your friend told you?"

"No. I mean, yes, but you just said—"

"No one starts a war. War grows like a slitherwort vine, choking everything and feeding on conflicts so deeply mired in history that many cannot remember the original argument by the time they meet in battle. The magas did not start the war. Unfortunately, we did not finish it either. We had many excellent warriors, women and men alike. Countless mages joined our cause against the King. We fought valiantly, but in the end we lost, and we lost miserably. After that the purges began."

"As punishment?"

"Not just punishment. Tzeremond taught that female magic is an aberration, an insult to Dragon. He had instructed Kedehen in this doctrine, and after the war used his influence to persuade the King this land would not be safe until every last witch was destroyed."

"How is it possible to believe female magic an insult to Dragon? Aithne, a woman, was the first person to discover magic. It was she who accepted Dragon's offer without hesitation, while Caradoc doubted Dragon's message and faltered under Thunder's wrath."

"Tzeremond taught a different view of history and assigned truth to a different set of legends. His was a small group of mages, radical in bent and considered unimportant in the grander context of the Old Orders. Before all this began, no one would have thought Tzeremond's *Aekelahr* destined to become the seat of such power. Anyone who suggested such a thing would have been laughed out of the room."

"Did you know Tzeremond?"

Ghemena drew a breath between her teeth. "Oh yes. We knew each other from the time he was a student of Middle Magic."

"What was he like?"

"Handsome, if you can believe it." Ghemena's gaze drifted inward. "He had a unique color to his eyes, a piercing amber brown that could leave a young maga like me very unsettled. And he was a skilled mage. But even then he feared the power of the magas. It was this fear that led him into hate. He never understood…"

Ghemena brought the steaming cup to her lips. Her fingers were trembling.

"It is enough," she said. "I've told you enough for one sitting."

"But I want to hear more, Ghemena."

"It wears me down to speak of these things. I am an old woman. I must save my energy for greeting the renewed sun in the morning."

"At least tell me how you came to be here. How did you escape the purges?"

She sighed. "By the grace of the Gods, Berlingen was left untouched during the war. We had shortages of food and medicines, but we were not dragged into direct conflict with the King. When the magas surrendered, we expected peace to be restored and the Old Orders rebuilt.

"Then news came of the massacre at East Selen. The rumors were frantic and garbled. First it was said none had survived. Then we heard Briana of East Selen was captured and raped. Others claimed she had betrayed her kin and given herself freely to Kedehen. We didn't have time to sort out the truth before they came for us.

"Kedehen's men attacked in the middle of the night. I woke up with noise like thunder crashing through my head. I thought I was having a nightmare. There were screams, and awful sounds of metal slicing through flesh. Everything was in flames. I ran around like a mad woman. All I wanted to do was save something, anything...The library, the books. Suddenly, my nephew Varyl appeared and dragged me away. To this day I'm not certain how we escaped. If it wasn't for him, I would have died with all the rest."

"Varyl? You mean the forester who brings us supplies?" Eolyn had not known Varyl was Ghemena's nephew. He seemed a bitter man with his ragged beard and raspy voice. Though he faithfully brought supplies every spring and autumn, the stocky forester had never so much as directed a word at Eolyn.

"He was once a Knight of Vortingen. After the war ended, he came to Berlingen to rest and heal. I was his only family at the time. Everyone else had died in the war. When we were attacked, he helped me escape.

"It was my idea to flee to the South Woods. I thought I could hide here until the terror ended of its own accord. But as the years passed, I listened to the trees and to the Guendes. That's how I knew Tzeremond and Kedehen did not stop until they had killed everyone. So here I am. And here I will be, I suppose, until my death."

"But you won't die here, Ghemena," Eolyn said. "Someday when I am a High Maga, we will return to Moisehén together and rebuild everything as it once was."

Ghemena shook her head. "That day will not come, Eolyn. When you return to Moisehén, you will do so alone. You will not be part of any Order. You will be just one maga in a hostile land, struggling to preserve a dying craft."

Eolyn set down her wine. A sharp pain settled like a stone inside her belly. "Then how am I to survive?"

Ghemena stared into the fire, her expression solemn.

"Ghemena, answer me."

"As the sun returns after Midwinter's Eve," Ghemena murmured, "so you will return to Moisehén, alone and through a world of darkness, fear, and death. Your path will not be easy. I have warned you of this from the beginning. But if you succeed, your magic will bring a new dawn to the troubled lands of our people."

CHAPTER TEN

Farewell

DURING THE YEARS OF THEIR FRIENDSHIP, Eolyn had learned to anticipate the moment of Achim's arrival.

Today she waited for him by the river where they first met. Summer was already announcing its approach with warm southern winds. The trees had begun expanding their rose green buds, and flowers unfolded over small patches of lingering snow. The water roared high, and silver fish leapt in its rushing folds.

In the shifting light that filtered through the young canopy, Achim appeared. For the first time he wore the dark green robes of a High Mage Initiate. They blended well with the nascent colors of the spring forest.

Eolyn stood to greet him, only to stop short with a gasp. "What have they done to your hair?"

Achim's hand went to his head. His thick black locks had been shorn off at the roots. "It was part of the ceremony to become an Initiate."

Eolyn stared at him in perplexed silence.

"Does it look that bad?" he asked with a grimace.

"No, it doesn't look bad. It's just so...different. You had such beautiful hair, Achim. If I had known what they were going to do, I would have thought to touch it the last time you were here." She stepped toward him. "Will you let it grow back?"

"Yes, I suppose I will. But I am not supposed to until I complete my training."

Eolyn nodded. She lifted her hand to where his hair used to be, and let her fingers drift to his face. A strange ache ignited in her heart, compelling her to register every detail of his face through touch: his thick brow, his dark eyes, his straight nose and full lips.

Achim went very still, like a deer that had caught the scent of a predator, or a lynx prepared to strike. Tiny sparks seemed to fire between her hands and his skin as Eolyn ran her fingers down his neck and across his shoulders. She wondered what had happened to the boy she first met here on the riverbank. She and Achim had been about the same height back then. She remembered him as lanky in build. When had he grown a full head above her? When had his shoulders assumed this breadth, his arms this strength, his chest this subtle vigor?

Abruptly she stepped back. Heat flushed her cheeks. She looked away. "I...I just hope Ghemena doesn't do the same thing to me when my time comes."

Achim blinked. "Do what?"

"Shave my head." Eolyn fumbled through her pocket and retrieved a small box. "I have a present for you."

The polished rosewood box fit easily into the palm of his hand. Achim lifted the lid, revealing an interior lined with tiny colored crystals. When the light hit them, a small three-dimensional image of the forest projected into the air, a miniature replica of the grove where they stood, the place where they first met.

"Ghemena helped me," Eolyn said. They had started crafting the object three years before, when Ghemena told Eolyn she would have to let go of Achim. "I chose the crystals, and Ghemena showed me how to integrate their song. Do you like it?"

"It is breathtaking," he said.

Eolyn let go an inward sigh of relief. Enthusiasm colored her voice. "It will change according to the seasons. In winter, you will see this place glazed in snow and ice. In summer, it will turn fresh green under the bright sun. I made it so you will always remember this forest, even in the coming years when you cannot return."

Achim's expression hardened. He snapped the box closed.

"What do you mean, *not return?*"

Eolyn lowered her eyes.

"You are saying good bye?" he asked.

She nodded.

"Why?"

She looked up at him, confused. "I thought you would remember. Ghemena gave us three years from the time she learned about our friendship. Now I must say good bye to you and dedicate myself to the study of High Magic."

Achim closed his hand over the small gift and shook his head. "I remember now. But three years! Have they already passed? When you first told me, I thought we had plenty of time to fix things, to make arrangements..."

His voice trailed off at Eolyn's puzzled expression.

"What did you mean, fix things?" she asked.

He set his jaw and looked into the forest, as if the trees might hold

58

the answer.

"In truth it has been a little more than three years." Eolyn spoke to fill the silence. "The appropriate time to start my training is in the spring, so Ghemena granted us a few more months until today."

"Why did you not say anything before now?" he demanded.

"I don't know! It was just easier not to speak of it, somehow. I thought you would…" A lump in her throat choked off her words.

Achim opened his hand and let the rosewood box float in the air beside them. "So it is decided then. You intend to study High Magic?"

"I begin my fast tomorrow."

He nodded, his expression stern. Eolyn knew he did not agree with her decision, and for a moment she thought he would ruin their last meeting by starting another argument.

Instead he drew back his sleeve and said, "I would like to give you something to remember me by, as well."

The symbols embroidered into the fabric of his robe reflected the forest in multiple shades of green. Underneath the folds, Eolyn saw a silver band around his arm. Removing the jewel with care, Achim offered it to Eolyn.

Awed, Eolyn turned the bracelet over in her hands. On the etched surface she recognized multiple forms of Dragon: winged serpent, snake, lion, butterfly, river otter, fish and many others. Each figure blended into the next, creating a single creature as fantastic as imagination itself.

"It's beautiful," she breathed.

"It was a gift from my mother." Achim's voice broke with quiet emotion. "She gave it to me before she died."

"Oh, Achim. This is too much for me to accept. If this jewel belonged to your mother, it should stay with you."

Retrieving the armband gently from her grasp, Achim slipped it over Eolyn's wrist and moved it just past her elbow. The metal coiled into a perfect fit against her skin. "I would say it was made for you."

Achim's hand traveled back down her arm. He caught her fingers in his and studied her for a moment. "I will miss you, Eolyn."

Then he leaned forward and kissed her.

Caught by surprise, Eolyn hesitated before sinking into the pleasure of his touch. The taste of Achim's lips was familiar, as if she had always known what it would be like to hold him this close. She loved the scent of polished stone and soft earth that rose up around her. His caress, hesitant at first, gathered confidence. A sense of urgency grew between them, until the unexpected force of their passion ignited a knot of panic inside Eolyn.

Flushed and trembling, she pulled away. Her breath came in gasps, as if the air had been taken from her lungs.

Achim drew her back, wrapped his arms around her and buried his face in her hair. His voice was muffled against her thick curls. "Don't leave me, Eolyn."

"It wasn't supposed to be like this," she whispered. Tears stung her eyes. "I don't understand. What has happened?"

"Come back with me. My father is...of some influence at court. I could protect you, even with your knowledge of Middle Magic. I am certain I could. Don't go down this path. Don't learn High Magic. Come home with me."

She pulled away, torn by her own doubts. "Three years I have prepared for this day. It wasn't supposed to feel like this. I don't understand what's happening."

"Eolyn," he moved toward her, but she stepped back.

"No, Achim. I have to do this."

He stopped short, as if she had slapped him in the face.

"I want to learn High Magic more than anything," Eolyn said, "and Ghemena is the only one who can teach me. If I go back with you, I will never learn any magic again at all."

Achim stiffened. His hands clenched into fists at his sides, and his eyes turned a shade darker.

"I see," he said, though it appeared to Eolyn he did not.

"In four years I will finish my training, and then you can come back to visit." When he did not respond she added awkwardly, "Or I will go forth from these woods to find you."

"I will find you." The severity of his tone frightened Eolyn. She could not tell whether his words were meant as a promise or a threat. "I will not rest until I find you again."

Eolyn searched for something else to say, but if words existed that could cut through this tension between them, they escaped her.

"I suppose I should take my leave then," she murmured.

A terrible aura had enveloped Achim. Eolyn was reminded of Hawk, how his focus reached its highest intensity just before diving after Fat Dormouse.

"I will miss you, Achim." Her voice sounded impotent against the shadow of his fury and the pounding of her own heart. She could not bear to have him look at her like that. "I will miss you more than you can know."

Still Achim said nothing, and Eolyn had no more words for him. Unable to bear the silence any longer, she turned and fled into the forest.

By the time Eolyn arrived at the cottage, a spray of bright stars hung over the meadow. Though her heart was hollow after her parting with

Achim, Eolyn found her spirit renewed upon seeing the care her mentor had dedicated to preparing the Initiate's Feast.

Ghemena had put a table in the garden and spread it with bread, nuts, dried fruits, roasted spring vegetables, pungent Berenben cheese, and a steaming pitcher of hot berry and primrose wine. Floating candles provided pale illumination suited to the shy habits of the Guendes, who had joined them for this special evening.

Ghemena greeted Eolyn with a strong hug.

"Tonight you begin your journey as a woman in magic." Eyes filled with joy, the old maga held Eolyn's face in her hands. After some contemplation, she added, "Though I dare say, this is not the only transition you began today. You have had your first kiss."

The whispery giggles of Guendes floated out of the shadows.

Eolyn flushed. "Is it so obvious?"

"Only to a skilled maga who knows how to read her student's aura." Ghemena winked. "The first kiss generates a characteristic spark. If it is a good kiss, that spark grows to reflect the colors of a woman's aura as a diamond in the sunlight. If it is a poor kiss, the spark fades to make way for the next opportunity. If it is an unwanted kiss, the spark must be treated with magic, or it will collapse into shadows that eclipse the true colors of a woman's heart."

"I think it was a good kiss."

"My dear, it is quite evident you have had a very good kiss."

"But it was so unexpected. And then I got scared and Achim got angry and I...I don't know. I ran away like a rabbit from a fox. What if I never see him again? All he'll remember now is the coward I was in the moment we said good-bye."

Ghemena beckoned Eolyn to the table, where she served two cups of hot berry wine. "We have spoken often about desire and affection, but no words or illustrations, no stories or exercises, can truly prepare us for this most powerful expression of Primitive Magic. In the old days—in my *Aekelahr*—you would have experienced the awakening of *aen-lasati* this very summer during the High Ceremony of Bel-Aethne. Your lover would have been a mask to you, and you a mask to your lover. This would have freed you from identity, from past and future, from the fear of your own emotions. Your act of passion, your offering to the Gods, would have been bound to the present and therefore eternal."

Eolyn sipped at her wine. "So I wouldn't have acted the coward today had I known *aen-lasati* in the same way as the Magas of Old?"

"What I'm saying is that you have special challenges given the circumstances of your training. Learning to dance with passion and desire is one of them."

"Sometimes I feel my studies aren't preparing me for anything. Nothing is the way it was before. How can I ever be a maga if the Old Orders aren't with us? If I can't even have a proper coven?"

"You must not confuse the form of magic with its spirit. In the end all rites are but symbols of deeper processes. You helped me remember this by demanding creativity in my instruction. Your training will serve you well when you return to Moisehén, precisely because all the old rites have been washed away. As for the coven you so miss, look around, young maga. I dare say such a coven has not been assembled in all the history of magic."

In that moment, Eolyn became aware of the murmurings in the garden: the chatter of Red Squirrel and the whistle of Wood Thrush; the wet slap of River Otter's tail and the sharp snap of Turtle's jaws. Rabbit thumped his foot, Owl gave a throaty hoot, and Giant Moth hovered over the table in lilting flutters. The Guendes chimed in with feathery laughter, and Fat Dormouse darted out of the shadows to steal a bite of cheese.

Ghemena had summoned them all, the many companions of her childhood. All of them except one.

"Achim should be here," Eolyn said.

"We have already spoken about that, Eolyn."

"He's the only true friend I have, and he's a mage."

"These, too, are your friends. They have always been with you, teaching you and protecting you."

Eolyn blinked back tears. She knew Ghemena was right, but it did not lessen her heartache. "What if Messenger doesn't appear? What if all my training is for naught? What if I just sent away my only friend in the whole world for a dream that will never come true?"

The old maga leaned back in her chair. The lines around her gray eyes softened. "I have taught many students, Eolyn, so I can say that if the Gods refuse your petition, it is not because you are unworthy. If Dragon does not appear, it is because the tradition of the magas must come to an end, for reasons neither you nor I can hope understand. All that is left for us to do on this night is to prepare ourselves to accept their decision, whatever it may be, with faith and humility."

CHAPTER ELEVEN

The Initiate's Fast

EOLYN WOKE BEFORE DAWN. Wrapping herself in a worn red cloak, she accepted Ghemena's many blessings and wandered deep into the sun-flecked woods. The voices of trees danced on the wind. Animals scattered at her approach. Solitude followed her like a living presence.

At midday, Lynx melted out of the shadows not more than ten paces in front of her. The wild cat stretched broad furry paws against the ground and sat on her haunches. She studied Eolyn with steady amber eyes. Then she turned and retreated into the forest.

Understanding the wordless invitation, Eolyn followed.

Lynx's steps fell silent against the leaf litter. Her musk trailed behind her in a soothing cloud. When they reached the foot of Lynx's ridge, the cat rolled onto her back and stretched her limbs, exposing the downy white of her belly. She dedicated several minutes to meticulously cleaning her paws before rising and disappearing like a ghost in the underbrush, leaving Eolyn to climb alone.

Although Eolyn had explored the base of Lynx's ridge on countless occasions, she had never approached the lair itself. The ascent proved arduous. It took the rest of the day to find the cave nestled on the south side of the rocky outcrop. With aching limbs, Eolyn crawled into the small space, sat down, and wiped the sweat from her brow.

Lynx's cave was dry and well ventilated. On the smooth dirt floor, Lynx had left fragrant grass and soft ferns to prepare a bed. The aroma of stone and earth reminded Eolyn of Achim.

I wonder what his fast was like.

She had not thought to ask him during their meeting by the river, but then she had not thought about much of anything except the singular power of that kiss.

Did his coven give him a banquet of friendship and transition? Did Tzeremond, like Ghemena, send his student off with affection?

Even though Achim studied in the company of a full order, Eolyn

63

could not shake the suspicion that his initiation had been a solitary experience.

At sunset, Eolyn settled at the cave entrance to watch the stars ignite against a deep purple sky. The forest spread in an undulating carpet below. The fragrance of pine and oak rose from its canopy. Rhythmic sounds filled the night: the scratchy chirp of crickets, bell-like tones of dink frogs, and occasional hoots from a pygmy owl. The unbounded space brought on a deep sense of tranquility.

When sleep called, Eolyn crawled back into the lair. Strange and vivid dreams greeted her. She saw ancient people drift through the forest and observed fantastic animals that no longer existed. She witnessed the first sacred fire invoked by Aithne and Caradoc, and watched the path of their flight as Thunder pursued the lovers into the mountains.

She found herself transported to battlefields where Caedmon and his mage warriors defeated the People of Thunder. Then she followed their sacred tradition as it flowed generation past generation into the life of her own mother, Kaie.

Eolyn stood by the initiate Kaie as she accepted the staff of High Magic. She accompanied the knight Kaie into war against metal-clad opponents. She watched the mother Kaie share the arts of Simple Magic with her daughter in the South Woods, and she comforted the prisoner Kaie as she faded toward the Afterlife on a cold stone floor, her face bloodied and her limbs shattered.

In the wake of Kaie's death, an ebony haired witch appeared. With tapered fingers, she gathered a thousand broken threads of friendship left by the war and wove them into a shimmering web that stretched from one end of the kingdom to another.

You are not the one I sought, little Eolyn, she whispered, *but you are the one who was found. The Gods have spoken. Destiny has revealed its hand. If you choose the path of High Magic, you are bound to restore our tradition to Moisehén, to renew the heritage of your sisters. If you refuse this oath, then you cannot accept the gift of Dragon.*

Eolyn awoke with a start, muscles stiff and cheeks wet with tears. When she emerged from the cave, dawn was spreading its pale light along the misty horizon. A dense fog had settled, leaving the rocky ridge floating in a soft sea of white. Ribbons of salmon and pale blue heralded the arrival of the sun. As the bright orb peeked over the edge of the world, the tips of the fog bank ignited in misty gold.

Dragon, Ghemena had told Eolyn, *can assume the form of any creature that walks the earth. The Initiate must therefore open her mind to the greatness of all beings, lest she fail to hear Messenger's voice in the sinuous movement of a millipede or in the fearsome roar of an angry bear.*

Eolyn scanned the ridge, but detected no movement across its rocky face. She searched for tiny creatures among the rough crevices, but neither spider nor beetle nor lizard appeared.

The forest was strangely quiet. Even the birds refrained from their dawn chorus.

Time passed. The orange sun drifted upward through the fog bank. The jagged stones warmed, and the frost dissipated.

With a sinking heart, Eolyn wondered if she had misunderstood Lynx. Perhaps she was not meant to come here. Perhaps Dragon waited somewhere else.

Then a shadow passed over the rocks.

Eolyn straightened, uncertain whether the shifting light had played a trick on her eyes. The shadow passed again, sharper this time and unmistakable in form and meaning.

Incredulous, Eolyn turned toward the rising sun.

Dragon flew toward the ridge in her true form, a dark silhouette against the bright sky. Her flight was smooth and rhythmic. Her wings whipped the golden clouds beneath her. Sunlight reflected off her silver scales in brilliant and blinding colors. Three times she circled Eolyn. Then she lifted up over the rocks and prepared to land.

Eolyn stepped back, caught between wonder and fear. She breathed deep the crisp morning air in an effort to sooth her pounding heart.

Not a sound was heard nor a tremor felt as Dragon set her massive feet on the ground. Only the wind from her wings marked her arrival, blowing back the hood of Eolyn's cloak.

Dragon's translucent scales shone like fine cut crystal. The graceful movement of her long neck and undulating tail gave the impression of a sparkling river in constant motion. She folded her wings and set opaque silver eyes upon Eolyn.

Do not be afraid. Dragon spoke in her quiet tongue. *The Gods who sent me look with favor upon your petition. Not since the time of Caedmon have they instructed me to appear in my true form, and before that not since the time of Aithne and Caradoc.*

Eolyn stared at this wondrous creature, trying to grasp the magnitude of what was happening. On instinct, she went to her knees. Her words came in trembling starts. "I…I am not worthy of this honor."

Dragon tilted her head. Amusement sparked inside those silver orbs. *That is precisely why you are judged worthy. You have embraced your gift with joy and humility. Now your journey brings the promise of a new era of magic.*

"I don't understand."

Don't you, Eolyn? Your sisters spoke to you in your dreams last night. Have you already forgotten their message?

Eolyn bowed her head and closed her eyes. The full weight of the burden she was about to accept settled heavy upon her shoulders. She steadied her pulse and focused on her connection with the earth.

"My gratitude to the Gods is unending," she said quietly, repeating the invocation Ghemena had given her. "You gave me life while so many others met death. You gave me magic even as my sisters burned. I pray to you, break open my spirit, so that I may receive your instructions and see your will fulfilled."

Dragon nodded.

Go to the Oldest Oak. She has prepared the branch from which your staff will be forged. You will find the branch at her feet, along with a feather from Midnight Owl. Bring these to me, together with a water crystal from River, and the sword given to you by your mage friend.

With a reverent bow, Eolyn took her leave. She gathered all four elements, finding them just as Dragon had indicated. On her way back to Lynx's lair, she paused in the place where she kept Achim's sword. Wrapping both hands around the hilt, she sang the incantation he had taught her and pulled the weapon from its resting place.

The sun hung low in the west when Eolyn returned to the ridge. The fog had long since burned off, and the scales of Dragon shimmered with copper and scarlet hues of evening.

Dragon accepted the branch from Eolyn and stripped it of leaves and bark. She placed it on the ground, positioned the water crystal at its tip, and laid Owl's feather along the base.

The sword, Dragon commanded.

Eolyn offered the blade. With a single blow against the rocks, Dragon smashed it into a thousand pieces.

Eolyn cried out in horror. "Achim's sword!"

It is not his sword, Dragon reprimanded. *It is yours, as it has been since the day he gave it to you. And it will serve you much better like this.*

From the scattered shards, Dragon chose a single splinter and balanced it carefully along the midsection of the branch. Then she paused and raised her silver eyes to the setting sun.

You must pray to the Gods, for guidance and strength in this path you have chosen.

As Eolyn finished her incantations, Dragon ignited her fiery breath.

Eolyn watched in amazement, for the staff did not burn under the white flames but rather became pliable to Dragon's touch. The winged serpent worked well into the night. She imprinted the feather at the base of the staff, drove the shard of Achim's sword into its heart, and secured the crystallized quartz firmly to its head.

Although Eolyn intended to keep vigil with Dragon throughout the night, the rhythmic ebb and flow of the winged serpent's movement lulled the initiate to sleep. When at last the young maga awoke, Dragon was but a shadow receding into the rising sun.

The new staff stood upright on the rocky ground.

Eolyn approached with caution and closed her hands over the magically cured oak. The smooth surface responded to her touch with a hum unlike any she had ever heard, beautiful and complex. When the morning light hit the union of wood and quartz, the image of Dragon in flight was revealed, etched into the heart of the river crystal.

Filled with sudden and intense joy, Eolyn lifted the staff from its resting place and bounded down the ridge toward her home.

Ghemena rose well before sunrise to prepare the sacred fire. She stacked dry branches of Beech, the guardian of ancient knowledge, Birch to provide balance, and Walnut to give power in times of transition. For kindling, Ghemena used twigs of Linden, the protector of Children's Magic. Once she had laid the fuel, she settled down to wait. The sacred fire could not be ignited until Eolyn arrived.

Uncertainty plagued the old maga. Years ago, the Gods had granted Kedehen victory over the magas. Was it their will that the tradition of Aithne and Caradoc perish?

Today, she would know the answer. If the Gods rejected Eolyn's petition, there would be no others. The craft Ghemena honored every day of her life would die with her, here in the South Woods.

Unable to sit still any longer, Ghemena left the cabin and moved to the edge of the garden.

The rising sun illuminated the trees in hues of gold. A fresh breeze brought aromas of spring flowers, new leaves, and wet loam. Songs of birds dominated the forest.

Ghemena tilted her head and strained to listen.

Her heart leapt when she heard Eolyn's voice in the distance. The shouts rose in volume and excitement, until Eolyn burst from the forest and into the clearing.

"Ghemena!" she cried. "Look what Dragon has given me!"

Ghemena caught her breath. Eolyn held a staff fully formed her hands. The crystal head sparkled under the sun's bright rays. Stunned, the maga started toward Eolyn as fast as her stiff limbs would allow.

"Messenger appeared to me as Dragon!" Eolyn announced breathless when they reached each other. "Oh, Ghemena, she's beautiful! Her flight is swift and silent, and she shines as if she were made of river pearls and water crystals. She forged my staff for me and accepted my solemn oath to bring women's magic back to our people."

Trembling, Ghemena laid her hands on the polished oak.

"What is this wondrous gift?" she murmured. "No staff has been forged by Dragon since the time of Caedmon, and before that since the time of Aithne and Caradoc."

Eolyn laughed out loud. "The Gods have granted us their blessing, Ghemena. They have shown me the path, and given me leave to make it my own. They have promised they will be with me always."

Ghemena closed her eyes, absorbing the staff's complex and haunting melody. Dancing upon the surface of this song, Ghemena heard all the elements that had brought joy to Eolyn's young life. Yet beneath that beauty lurked a more ominous mood. When she recognized it, Ghemena's blood ran cold.

"I don't understand." Ghemena opened her eyes. Her voice shook. "I cannot teach you how to use this."

"Dragon said you would know what to do," Eolyn replied with a radiant smile. "She said the Gods would show you the way. When can we start? Can we start today?"

"No." Had the girl not heard? "Listen to me, Eolyn. I will not teach you how to use this staff."

Eolyn's smile faded. "But why? You are the only teacher I have. If you do not show me then—"

"This is a weapon of war. I will not make you a warrior. I will not teach you how to kill." Flushed with anger, the old maga snatched the staff from Eolyn. She raised it to the heavens and shouted at the Gods. "Do you hear me? I will not do it! I will not allow you to soil her magic with violence and bloodshed!"

"Ghemena!" Eolyn laid hand on the old maga's shoulder. "Please, don't say such things. Wasn't it you who taught me that the instruments of magic are just instruments? That it is the maga who commands her staff, not the other way around?"

Tears stung Ghemena's eyes. She sank to the ground. Her many burdens weighed heavy on frail shoulders. She felt weary and spent, worn to the bone by the endless trials of a cruel age.

"Dragon has linked this staff to the deepest places of the earth," she said, "where rivers of power run thick and virtually untapped. In the legends of old, dark wizards from distant lands used those rivers as a means for destruction. In the time of King Fahren, the magas and mages of Moisehén summoned this same magic to trap the Naether Demons and condemn them to the Underworld. I have great respect for this power, Eolyn, but I bear it no love. It is dangerous and unpredictable. I do not wish to see you bound to it."

Eolyn's shoulders deflated. She looked from Ghemena to the staff.

Sadness washed over the girl's features, causing Ghemena to regret her quick tongue.

I could have at least let Eolyn feel joy on this one day.

"I am sorry, my daughter," she said. "I have become an old and bitter woman. The future I want for you is not the future I see foretold in this staff. Dragon's gift brings a great burden, greater than even I imagined. I would give anything to spare you the sacrifices this instrument will demand."

Eolyn's eyes turned damp. She blinked and ran her hand slowly along the length of the staff, fingers coming to rest on its crystal head.

"Would you give up your magic, Ghemena?" she asked in subdued tones. "Should I then give up mine?"

Eolyn's quiet resolve softened the cold knot of fear that had taken hold of Ghemena. With shaking hands, Ghemena drew her last student into a firm embrace.

"So be it, beloved daughter," Ghemena murmured. "The Gods have spoken. Let us find a way."

CHAPTER TWELVE

Songs of Passage

IN THE FIFTH YEAR of Eolyn's training, Ghemena sent her into the forest to gather the elements needed for a maga's ward.

Eolyn harvested abundant silk from three different varieties of spiders: the ghostly sheet weaver, which wove its web at midnight; the dawn mist orb weaver, whose delicate orb could be seen only at the first light of dawn; and the giant harlequin jumper, a multicolored creature whose thick silk would lend strength and resilience to the fabric.

To complement the spider silks, Eolyn collected everything she could find that held the power of deception and hiding. She trapped walking sticks, thorn bugs, bark lizards, and pale rose crab mites. She found pebble homes of tiny water dragons on the river bottom and dusted scales from the wings of cryptic butterflies and moths. She took tufts of fox fur caught in thorny brambles and followed the path of a slipaway velvet snake until it shed its skin for her.

When the time arrived to prepare the ward, Ghemena put everything except for the silk into a large pot. The old maga added portions of rue, houseleek, juniper, rosemary and valerian. She completed the recipe with a healthy dose of wrinkled dusky night mushrooms, known and feared for their capacity to cause blindness.

For an entire day, Ghemena let the ingredients simmer over a low fire, occasionally sending Eolyn to add fresh spring water and stir the mixture while singing whispery incantations.

As night fell, Ghemena and Eolyn took the pot off the fire and separated the brew into three large bowls, one for each variety of silk. They then let the silk soak overnight under the last sliver of the waning moon. In the morning, they separated the threads, washed them in pure rainwater, and laid them out carefully to dry under the sun.

Ghemena set out a loom crafted for weaving wards. As the sun went into hiding behind the trees, she lit candles impregnated with cress and oregano. Only then did she and Eolyn begin the task that would occupy them until morning, for the fabric of a ward had to be woven in a single sitting under a dark moon.

"The magas devised the ward during the struggle against Tzeremond and his Mage King," Ghemena told Eolyn as they worked side by side. "Before the war, magas had no reason to hide their power. But during the war, the capacity to conceal one's abilities became synonymous with survival."

"Can mages break the ward?" Eolyn asked.

"Every ward, no matter how expertly crafted, has seams. A skilled mage can find these flaws, but he must know what he is looking for and where to search. Even then it is difficult, but Tzeremond's mages are very astute. They usually start by looking for other indications of magic. Knowledge of medicines and plants. A gift with animals. Exceptional beauty or an outspoken nature. Anything that sets a woman apart, in their minds, can be evidence of witchcraft. Once they have their eyes on a suspected maga, it is only a matter of time before they find her ward, or catch her in a moment of carelessness."

"Carelessness?"

"Perhaps that is not the right word. A well-trained maga is rarely careless. Yet magic is second nature to us, like instinct. You must find a way to control your impulse to use magic, Eolyn. Every time you express your magic, the ward will slip from its place, exposing the true colors of your aura."

Eolyn paused in her weaving and cast a glance to Ghemena. "I can't use any magic at all while wearing this?"

"Several forms of Middle Magic compatible with hiding and deception may be employed. You may also practice Simple Magic in its entirety, but you must take great care in doing so, as this is one of the signs mages look for when they hunt magas. If you use High Magic the ward will falter in the moment you invoke the spell. It will, however, resume its strength as soon as you finish your invocation."

"How long would it take for a mage to recognize my signature in such a situation?"

"He will likely recognize your magic first, which will be more than enough to send you to the pyre. But if your invocation is not detected, or if it cannot be readily traced to you, a mage could take several minutes to find the aura he seeks. Under such circumstances, this might be just enough time for you to slip away."

"All these years I've dedicated to becoming a High Maga, and now I must hide behind a ward and avoid using my skills at all costs."

"If you keep the vow you made as an Initiate and return magic to the women of Moisehén, your days of hiding will come to an end," Ghemena replied. "But when you leave these woods, you must be very cautious. Until you discover true friends and safe places, you must assume that any act of magic will send you to your death."

"Maybe I shouldn't go back," Eolyn said. "What is the point, if everything I've learned and most of who I am must be so thoroughly concealed? Better to stay here in the South Woods where I can practice magic freely with you."

"Loneliness will convince you otherwise," the old maga responded quietly. "You will soon be compelled to leave the South Woods in order to seek the company of your people."

"But you are my people, Ghemena! You raised me as your own daughter. You opened up a world of magic for me. All they did was destroy my village, murder my family, and drive me into exile. Why would I want to go back to that?"

Ghemena set her focus on the fabric that grew beneath her fingers. When she spoke, it was in low tones that matched the rhythm of her weave.

"Many terrible things have come to pass in Moisehén, but this does not change the fact that they are your people. You are bound by the craft to serve them, no matter what they have done to you in the past, and no matter what they might do to you in the future. On the day of their need you must respond, for you will be the only High Maga left to them."

A few days later, Ghemena did not appear for breakfast.

In the years since the old maga had adopted Eolyn, not once had she missed the first moments of the day, when the light of the sun lifted the pale mist off the forest.

Disconcerted, Eolyn knocked quietly at the entrance to Ghemena's bedroom.

"Come in, my daughter."

Relieved at the familiar cackle of Ghemena's voice, Eolyn pulled back the worn curtain and stepped into the cramped space. With the window shutters closed, Ghemena was but another shadow in the tiny alcove. She huddled beneath the covers, eyes peeking out from under the rough weave.

"Why are you still in bed, Ghemena?" Eolyn felt a tremor in her voice. She sought Ghemena's frail hand.

"My time has come, Eolyn." Ghemena's breath rattled through her lungs. "Prepare a place beneath the willow. I would spend my last day in this world under the spring sun."

Pain invaded Eolyn's throat. She tried to force a laugh. "Don't say such things, Ghemena. As if I would let you leave! As if the Gods would call you away before I finish my training."

"I anointed you High Maga at the last moon."

"But I've so much left to learn!"

"Not from me. Prepare a place, and do not argue the will of the Gods. I would spend my last day in peace."

Eolyn stood up. Her limbs had gone numb. Without another word, she left Ghemena and stalked out of the house.

In the garden, bushes and herbs lay in full bloom, pastel flowers interspersed with the pale flush of spring leaves. Vegetables pushed new growth up from the dark earth, and fruit trees rustled under the buzzing dance of wasps and bees.

A maga should not be sad on such a day, she told herself as she wiped the tears from her cheeks. *A maga celebrates spring and partakes in its joy.*

Or so Ghemena had told her on countless occasions. But all the things that ever made Eolyn sad returned to her now. How far did she have to run to escape death? What pleasure did the Gods derive from leaving her alone, again and again?

Eolyn closed her eyes and struggled to ground her spirit. She had to subdue her anger and recover her calm. If she did not bring her emotions into balance, she would endanger Ghemena's passage to the Afterlife.

Drawing a deep breath, the young maga returned to the cottage.

"The candles." Ghemena's voice rasped like dry leaves. "The ones we made last summer, of night berry, winter sage and iris root. Bring them now so we may put them to use."

Eolyn wrapped a blanket around the old maga's frail shoulders. She accompanied Ghemena to a willow tree that stood on the edge of the meadow. She brought the candles and placed them, nine in all, in a circle around the base of the trunk. When she finished, Eolyn settled next to Ghemena and took her hand.

The transformation of a maga was a delicate event. To reach the Afterlife, she had to pass through the treacherous landscape of the Underworld. There she risked falling victim to the lost souls, who confused the light of magic with the call of the Afterlife. Even worse were the Naether Demons, who hunted and feasted on the souls of practitioners.

"Mother didn't have any of this." Eolyn gestured to the circle of candles. "She did not have nightberry or winter sage; she did not even have a friend nearby when they destroyed her. Does that mean she was trapped in the Underworld?"

Ghemena lifted her face to Eolyn. How the old woman had changed! Her eyes sat in weary dark hollows. Her nose drooped over thin lips. Her cheeks had lost their color.

"Warrior magas prepared differently for death," Ghemena said. "They carried winter sage in their belts and recited incantations before each confrontation, sometimes every day. They bore the purple mark of nightberry on their bodies; some stained the soles of their feet, others painted elaborate designs over their arms or backs. Kaie observed all of these practices. From what I remember, she was a devout maga."

"But how can we be certain?"

"You said you saw Kaie the day the King's men attacked your village."

Eolyn nodded. "She appeared to me in the woods and urged us to hide."

"Then she survives in the Afterlife. It is impossible for a soul trapped in the Underworld to reach back into this realm."

"Why are you leaving, Ghemena?" The words jumped out, angry and unbidden.

"You speak as if I have a choice." Ghemena managed a quiet chuckle. "All of us die in the end. Your time will come, as well."

"But you are all I have. There must be some kind of magic that can keep you here for a little while longer."

"Perhaps you brought such magic with you when you arrived as a little girl. Maybe that is why I lived all these years until now."

"Ghemena!" Eolyn's voice filled with exasperation. She did not want trite answers. She wanted ancient spells and secret escape routes.

"You will not be alone for long," the old maga said gently.

"Is that what your cards told you?"

"The cards, and the dreams of an ancient woman."

"Divination is a reckless form of magic." Eolyn did not bother to hide her sarcasm.

"It is. But it brings comfort at times, and that, at least, can be of some use." The corners of Ghemena's lips turned up in a weak smile. Her eyes shone in quiet amusement.

Eolyn looked away. She was not in the mood for jests.

"I speak the truth, Eolyn. The Gods have given me a glimpse of your future. Your friends wait for you. You will recognize them..."

Ghemena's words ended in a ragged gasp. Her body contracted around her chest.

With a start, Eolyn took the old maga in her arms. Summoning the powers of the earth, she laid her hand over Ghemena's heart and murmured a lengthy spell.

Ghemena's breath settled into a slow and rasping rhythm.

"You have become a fine healer," she said. "Such heat in your hands. Your magic depends on this place, Eolyn. You must never forget that. You will always be drawn to the forest to restore your power and renew your magic."

"You were talking about my friends. Where are they? How will I know who they are?"

"They have unique magic. They hide in visible places."

Eolyn frowned. Did the dying always speak like this, in riddles and contradictions?

"And what of Achim? Have you seen Achim?"

Ghemena closed her eyes. "No. I have looked for your friend, Eolyn, but he is covered in shadows. You must be very careful. Do not let your affection for the boy cloud your judgment of the man. He has been through years of the most rigorous training. If Tzeremond anointed him High Mage, it is because he has accepted a way of magic that leaves no room for a woman of your power."

Clarity returned to Ghemena's gaze as she opened her eyes.

"He knows your name," she continued, "and by now others may have heard of you. So you must use a different name when you leave the South Woods. Do not invoke any magic unless necessary. Do not do anything that would allow them to find you before you are certain who your allies are."

Eolyn nodded, but in her heart she could not accept the idea that Achim would ever betray her.

Ghemena sighed as if speaking so many words had demanded extraordinary effort. Her eyes closed again. For a time she lay so still Eolyn would have thought her passage had begun, were it not for the continued warmth of her frail body.

The Doyenne slept the better part of the day, occasionally waking to shift her position or to watch the creatures of the meadow before dozing off again. It was not until the sun dipped low over the trees that Ghemena spoke once more.

"Eolyn," she said. "Light the candles."

Breaking into wretched sobs, Eolyn wrapped her arms tightly around her tutor. "I can't, Ghemena! Don't do this."

The old maga placed a trembling hand on her student's face. "Light the candles, Eolyn. Sing to me. Sing the songs of passage. They will help us both."

Eolyn choked back tears. She lifted one hand toward the candles. Her invocation came harsh and unsteady. The violet wicks flared like fireflies over the meadow. A soothing scent of winter sage and nightberry filled the air.

"You have brought me great joy, my daughter," Ghemena whispered. "I thank the Gods for sending you to me, for giving me hope in a time when all hope had fled. I am sorry...I am sorry I will not live to see you fulfill your destiny."

"Oh, Ghemena!"

"Sing to me, Eolyn. Sing the songs of passage."

Eolyn focused all her effort on opening her throat. When at last her voice found its way to the surface, it sounded weak against the gathering night, like a wisp of smoke undone by the evening breeze.

I sing for the passing of this witch
This wise and beautiful friend
Who brought joy to my days
And laughter to my nights
I call to her companions in the Afterlife
Those who recognize her with love
Reach out to me
So that we may be the bridge
Upon which she finds safe passage

Ghemena's body relaxed and her face lost all tension. A deep chill overtook the old maga. Then her hands went limp, and her body settled into the simple cold of the dead.

Eolyn's song faded. She laid her mentor down, extended the thin legs, and crossed Ghemena's hands gently over her small chest.

That is all, then.

The last maga of the Old Orders had joined her dead sisters.

Eolyn covered Ghemena's body with her own and wept. When her tears faded into exhaustion, she kissed Ghemena's forehead and sat back on her heels.

The evening birds were silent. The rhythmic chirp of crickets began to rise from the forest floor. An owl hooted nearby. Fir trees hissed in the wind.

On the ridge, Lynx would be emerging from her lair to hunt for rabbits now poking their noses out of their dens. Somewhere above, stars were spreading across a black sky.

The night forest was coming to life, yet for all its rich activity, Eolyn felt only absence and remorse. She lifted her face toward the sky and let forth a deep, aching moan.

Only the wolves responded, their sad chorus faint and unbearably far away.

CHAPTER THIRTEEN

A Den of Wolves

EOLYN BURNED GHEMENA'S BODY according to the tradition of the Old Orders, on a carefully laid pyre of Beech to preserve the old, Alder to protect the new, and Ash for wisdom during times of loss. Twelve days after the sacred fire consumed Ghemena's body, Eolyn scattered the ashes across the meadow.

Ghemena's absence excavated an aching hollow in Eolyn's heart. Food lost its taste, herbs their aroma. The voices of the trees became misty and muted. Animals disappeared. The arching blue sky turned flat and gray.

Even as she clung to the routines that had governed her life with Ghemena, Eolyn sank in a sea of remorse. As much as she wanted to remain in their home of so many years, she began to realize Ghemena was right. She could not continue without human companionship.

So a few weeks after Ghemena's transformation, Eolyn packed her satchel with flatbread, roasted nuts, and dried berries. She added a change of clothes and lined her medicine pouch with herbs, including an ample supply of winter sage. She secured her knife to her belt and filled the kitchen with rewards for the Guendes, who would expect many gifts in return for maintaining the refuge in her absence.

Though it was safer to fly under the cover of clouds, Eolyn decided to leave on a clear night. She wanted to see the forest beneath her and the stars above. As evening fell, she lit a fire of spruce, fir, and pine under the open sky. She mixed henbane, laurel and mugwort with precisely measured white magenta, the spring mushroom that conferred the power of flight. In a small pot of rainwater, she brought everything to a boil. Then she set a dense branch of fir over the rising steam. When all the needles shimmered with droplets of moisture, the fir began to pull toward the sky.

After fixing the branch to the base of her staff, Eolyn offered the spent brew to the fire, extinguishing its flames. She put her satchel over

77

her shoulder and balanced her weight on the floating staff.

Ehekaht

Naeom da-uwaen

Ehukae

With a strong push from Eolyn's foot, the ground descended, carrying with it the cottage, garden and meadow. Eolyn felt the memories of her childhood fall away as well, like a thousand tiny weights that would always anchor her to this place.

At the edge of the meadow, a subtle movement indicated the arrival of Lynx, come to bid farewell with the simple gesture of her presence. Above Lynx, restless shadows of Guendes moved through branches with whispery wishes for a safe journey.

At the level of the canopy, a strong buzz indicated the limit of the ward that surrounded the refuge. The landscape blurred and then melted into a mirage of continuous tree cover.

Directing the staff north, Eolyn gave impulse to her flight and retraced the path that had taken her to Ghemena so many years before. Aromas of pine and oak hung over the forest deep. The breeze refreshed her cheeks. The waxing moon illuminated scattered clouds with shades of slate blue and silver white.

Eolyn flew only at night, hiding beneath the cover of forest at dawn. Occasionally, Owl accompanied her under the starlit sky, the silent beat of its wings a soothing source of companionship. Bat also emerged once or twice, circling the staff in an impatient flutter and descending back to the forest with a high-pitched song.

When night began to fade into the fifth day, Eolyn descended once more to a place of haunting familiarity, the hideaway where Ernan had left her the day their village was attacked.

In all these years, very little had changed. The stream fell in crystalline waves over gray stones. The terror of little Eolyn had long since disappeared in its dancing bubbles.

The entrance to the hideaway was wider then Eolyn remembered. In the moment she noted this, the scent of Wolf filled the air. Eolyn turned to see a large gray male with shining black eyes only a few feet behind her. The creature tensed and bared its fangs.

I mean no harm, she assured the wolf in its own tongue. *This place protected me once. I only wish to see it again.*

With a twitch of his ears and a sharp nod, the male directed Eolyn's attention to the hideaway, where an ash gray she-wolf emerged. As a child, Eolyn had harbored a great fear of these creatures, but as a High Maga, she knew they would respect her as long as they did not detect malice.

Eolyn held her breath steady as they sniffed her feet, robe, hands, and staff. After a few moments they lost their stiffness and began to wag their tails. Eolyn reached down to let their wet tongues caress her palms. This was the first time since Ghemena's transformation, she realized, that she had enjoyed the touch of another living creature.

Whimpers gathered into short barks, and without warning a group of energetic pups tumbled out of the hideaway to attack Eolyn's feet and skirt.

"Oh," she smiled, kneeling to meet the family, "I see you have put this place to very good use."

Eolyn remained with the wolves that day, caring for the pups while the adults hunted. When darkness fell, she made her bed next to their lair. The male slept beside her, his mate taking refuge with their offspring in the den. Snuggling against the musky warmth of his bristled fur, Eolyn drifted into soothing dreams of the forest deep.

By the time she awoke, the male had departed. The female watched her from the edge of the stream, pups scampering at her feet and nipping her tail.

After bathing in the cold water, Eolyn made a breakfast of flat bread, dried fruits and herb tea. She then took her leave, thanking the wolf mother and pups for their hospitality and blessing their refuge with her magic.

Over a decade had passed since Eolyn ran through these woods in panic. The passage of time had left no mark, except perhaps in a slight thickening of tree trunks and the subtle rearrangement of herbs across the forest floor.

Eolyn found the grove where her mother had appeared and spoken for the last time. From there only a short walk remained to the place that used to mark the edge of the South Woods and the beginning of her village.

The forest had extended its reach into the fields once inhabited by her family and their neighbors. A loose stand of alder and birch stretched upwards over thorn bushes and hardwood saplings.

Carefully, Eolyn retraced the path to their former home. Her eyes searched the ground for any sign of her father's remains, but the forest had long since reclaimed him. Nor did anything persist of the stone and wood structure he and her mother had constructed with the loving intention of raising their family in peace.

Eolyn walked the faint boundaries of their old residence, recalling the location of the hearth, her parents' room, the room she had shared with Ernan. Standing in the center, she marveled at how everything had vanished beneath the encroaching forest.

The ground lurched and gave way with a sudden snap. Eolyn fell through a cloud of dust. Before she understood what was happening, her descent was cut short and pain shot up her legs.

She stood in a hole up to her chest.

The cellar. How could I have forgotten the cellar?

She flexed her ankles and tested the weight on her knees. Other than numerous stinging scrapes, she was unhurt. Pushing back the crumbling planks, she sought an edge where she could pull herself out. As she removed the rotting floor, sunlight spilled into the cellar and illuminated a formless heap in a forgotten corner, a broken pile of bones.

Eolyn's breath caught against her throat.

Kneeling down, she ran her fingers over the miniature skull.

Ernan.

He did make it back to the house! He must have hidden here while their father went to look for her in the woods, and suffocated when the Riders set fire to their home.

Eolyn had always remembered Ernan as bigger, older, stronger and wiser, but now with his fragile skull cradled in her hands, the loss of his life touched her with renewed and bitter sorrow. How young he had been when his world came to such a brutal end!

"I'm sorry I couldn't help you, Ernan," she said softly. "I'm sorry I was not yet strong enough."

Collecting every bone with reverence, Eolyn took her brother back into the sunlight. She used her staff to open a hole in the ground, choosing the place where they used to harvest pumpkins. She then covered his remains with rich brown earth.

Eolyn kept Ernan company as long as she could, telling him stories of everything she had done since their parting so many years before.

The sun turned over them, passed its zenith, and began to descend in the western sky. As evening approached, Eolyn stood up, reluctant to leave but aware she could not linger. Night would unveil doors to the Underworld, torn open by the violence of the King's Riders and never properly closed. The Lost Souls would recognize her light and send dreams of terror before dragging her down with them.

Eolyn called her staff. She removed the fir branch and converted it to ash in a flash of orange flame. From her satchel she retrieved the ward she had woven with Ghemena's help. Unlacing her bodice, Eolyn removed her dress.

The afternoon sun warmed her bare skin, and she felt her body drink up the freshness of that moment in preparation for hiding to come. Eolyn tossed the glittering fabric toward the sky and allowed it to drift back down upon her.

Ehekaht

Naeom enem
Enem semtue, faeom semtue
Ehekaht Ehukae

The fine silk disappeared on contact with her person, expanding and clinging invisibly to her skin, so light she felt only an occasional tingle when she moved.

She donned her dress and gathered her satchel. Using a small piece of cloth cut from the same fabric as her ward, Eolyn covered her staff, rendering it indistinguishable from a common walking stick.

Then she bent down to lay her hand upon Ernan's fresh grave.

"Sleep well, dear brother," she said, "for you are lovingly remembered."

CHAPTER FOURTEEN

Mage Echior

AS A CHILD, EOLYN HAD VISITED the Town of Moehn only once. She remembered little of that journey, except that they followed the road leading north from her village.

The first stretch of that route was now little more than an overgrown trail, but after a few days' walk it widened into a small dirt road. Fertile hills spread low in all directions, with fields of wheat and lentils, grazing cows and placid sheep, thick gardens, and scattered fruit trees.

People labored intensively upon the land, acknowledging her passing with little more than a sideways glance or an idle wave. Eolyn observed them with great discretion. Afraid to draw too much attention to herself, she spoke to no one.

One sunny afternoon, she passed through a village filled with shouts, laughter and song. She had never witnessed so many people in one place, and the sight at once frightened and fascinated her. Villagers turned around each other in waves of dancing. The revelry tugged at Eolyn's heart, igniting distant memories of laughter once shared around the fires of her village.

"It is a wedding."

Eolyn jumped at the voice of a man next to her. He was older and portly, with round cheeks and bushy white eyebrows. He wore the earth brown robes of a Middle Mage and studied her with keen blue eyes. "You are not from these parts."

"I grew up on a farm near the South Woods." Eolyn fought to control the tremor in her voice.

"And where are you going?"

"To the Town of Moehn. Then perhaps to the King's City."

His eyebrows lifted. "You have a long road ahead of you. What would compel a young lady like you to undertake such a journey alone?"

"My father passed away, leaving me with the farm. It's too much to manage on my own, so I'm going to Moehn, as I have family there. If they cannot help me, I will continue to the King's City, where I have a friend who I hope can find me employment."

"Employment!" He laughed. "You'd have better luck finding a husband, I think. Women in Moisehén have not sought employment since the time of the magas."

"I see." His response disconcerted her. What did the disappearance of the magas have to do with the practice of employing women?

"What is your name, child?" the man asked.

"Dhana."

"Nice to meet you, Dhana. I am Mage Echior. Welcome to our humble village." He gestured toward the revelers. "I cast the circle for this couple. May their life together be long and prosperous."

Eolyn watched the villagers, longing to indulge in the magic of their dance.

"You may join the celebration if you like," Echior said.

"No." Eolyn shook her head, uneasy. "I should be on my way."

"It is too late to make it to the next village before night fall."

"I wish to advance toward Moehn as quickly as possible. I'll make camp along the road if I must."

"It is not safe." Echior's tone became serious. "Especially for a young woman traveling alone. I would counsel you to stay in the village tonight. I can assist you in finding a bed."

"I appreciate your concern, but I must continue." Eolyn bowed and took her leave, skirting the edge of the celebration as much as she could. Despite her attempts at invisibility, her passing did not go unnoticed.

"Now there's a pretty one," a man said.

"Where ye be goin', m'lady?"

"A dance, love?"

"Now, why are ye in such a hurry?"

She felt pursued by a pack of dogs. When at last she cleared the crowd, her heart was racing. She walked away from the village as quickly as she could.

"Dhana!"

Eolyn clenched her fists and fought the impulse to run. She turned to see Mage Echior hurrying toward her. He moved much faster than she would have expected for a man of his age and build.

"Yes, Mage Echior?" She replied with forced calm.

"If you are going to Moehn, you should ask after Corey's Circle."

"Corey's Circle?"

Mage Echior wheezed and clutched at his ribs. "Corey is a mage, and the Circle is a spectacle that travels around the kingdom. They are often in Moehn this time of year."

"A spectacle?" The word was unfamiliar to Eolyn.

"Performers. They dance, sing, do stage illusions. Anyway, it is said he offers employment to women and…" Echior took a deep breath. "…that he treats his people well."

"Thank you very much, Mage Echior. I will look for Corey's Circle as you suggest." In truth, she had no intention of doing anything of the sort, but the sooner she appeased this man, the sooner she could be on her way.

Echior laid a heavy hand on Eolyn's shoulder. It was all she could do not to flinch.

"May the Gods protect you, Dhana," he said.

Night fell too soon, forcing Eolyn to make camp long before she had reached a comfortable distance from Echior's village. She settled well off the road, next to a small stream. After gathering dry wood, she lit a fire and prepared a dinner of hot tea and nut bread.

"The food is getting monotonous," she confessed to the crackling flames. "I should have asked Mage Echior for some stew."

The fire hissed a cheery response. Overhead soft blue clouds floated against a half moon. The tension of the encounter with Mage Echior began to fade. Eolyn hummed a quiet tune, adding her melody to the songs of frogs and the rhythm of the stream.

The air felt cool and promised a sleep of meaningful dreams. Eolyn would have prepared her bed right then, had not the smell of an intruder assaulted her senses. A twig snapped in the darkness. Eolyn stood and pressed her feet firmly against the ground. Her hand sought the hilt of her knife.

"Show yourself," she demanded.

The intruders—Eolyn detected at least two—paused. The scent of their hesitation wafted toward her. With a measured crunching of grass, two young men appeared at the edge of the firelight.

Eolyn recognized them from the village, a pair of boys whose auras were tinged with malevolence. She had not liked the oily feel of their gaze then, and she did not care for the predatory nature of their approach now.

"Are you lost?" she asked.

"Nah, m'lady." The one who responded was tall and lanky, with narrow eyes and numerous freckles on his long boorish face. He puffed himself up like a simp lizard on the first day of courtship. "But it seems ye might be."

He sauntered over to the fire and sat down, exchanging a repulsive grin with his partner.

Eolyn despised them both. "I am not lost, and I have not invited you to sit at my fire. You and your friend may leave now."

The boy found a rock and threw it idly into the flames. "Don't think we'll be goin' m'lady. Not 'til you show us some courtesy."

With that, they sprang on her.

Eolyn had no chance to think. She felt a soft mass of flesh give way to the strike of her knee, heard a bone crack under her fist. Her blade assumed a life of its own, hissing through the air and coming back into focus stained with blood. At the sudden release from their rough grasp, she stumbled back.

One of the boys lay on the ground moaning with an injured groin and a broken nose. The other stood in front of her, his eyes wide with shock, one hand pressed against his cheek. When he lowered his fingers they were slick with blood. Eolyn's knife had left a long gash.

"Leave me now or I will kill you both." She had never heard that tone in her voice, low and fierce. Everything went silent except the rhythm of their breath. The two men watched her like hawks.

The surest cut is across the throat, Achim had once said. *But in a direct confrontation you may not get an opportunity to do that.*

He had stuffed burlap sacks with dry leaves and tied them to trees. Then he had mapped out sternum, ribs and abdomen. *Send the knife in low, angling upward. If you aim too high, the blade will skip off the ribs. Put the weight of your body into the thrust. Don't depend on the strength of your arm. That's it. Now twist the blade, or draw it across the gut to finish the job. Never leave an opponent half dead, Eolyn, or he'll come back at you like an injured boar.*

Of course, it was one thing to send her knife into a sack of dry leaves. The thought of plunging her blade into the quivering stomach of one of these boys sickened her. But she would kill them. By the Gods, she would kill them both if they took so much as one step toward her.

A scuffle against dirt broke the silence. The boy with the injured groin scrambled to his feet and disappeared into the darkness. The other spat into the fire.

"Witch!" he said. "We'll come fer y' soon enough. You'll be on th' pyre by morn'!"

Then he turned and fled.

Only when the sound of their running faded did Eolyn let down her guard.

Violent shivers coursed through her body. The knife slipped from her fingers. She pulled her cloak tight about her, trying to warm the chill in her veins. She was not sure what upset her more, their perverse attack or the daunting power of her instinct to kill.

I cannot stay here.

She had perhaps an hour—at most two—before whatever story they invented reached Mage Echior and the search for her began.

Grounding her shaken spirit into the earth, Eolyn called the night air back to her lungs. She lifted her hand toward the shadows and sang a quiet invocation. In a matter of moments she heard the voice of a nearby fir. The tree was young, but its branches held enough strength to be endowed with flight.

Returning to the fire, Eolyn retrieved the requisite herbs from her belt and steamed the branch as long as she dared. By the time it began to pull toward the sky, her keen ears picked up shouts in the distance. She doused the flames, gathered her things, and concealed the evidence of her campsite.

Then she took off in a low and desperate flight, pushing as far toward the north as she could.

CHAPTER FIFTEEN

Corey's Circle

EOLYN DID NOT INTEND TO LINGER in the Town of Moehn, but curiosity detained her, and the swirl of noise and activity lent a comforting sense of invisibility.

Bright shop signs hung from houses of heavy timber and white plaster. Farmers lined the narrow alleyways, their stalls filled with the first harvests of the season. The people conversed in jovial voices and greeted each other with broad smiles. Children ran rosy-cheeked and capricious through cobblestone streets. Eolyn found herself mesmerized by pungent aromas of smoked meat and rotting fruit, by the ear-piercing laughter of children, and by the thundering clatter of horses and wagons.

The sun already floated high in the midday sky when a new sound caught Eolyn's attention, a low pulsing resonance that seemed to carry her name. People around her stopped their labors. Many started toward the source of the strange music. Children ran ahead of the gathering crowd.

Eolyn followed them toward the town center, where she caught sight of an elegant procession. Rhythmic drums interwove with the seductive refrains of flutes, bells, and other instruments unknown. Women in fine gowns lent rich voices to the music, while others danced in graceful circles marked by flowing veils. Several members of the procession passed on horseback and one of them, a beautiful woman with dark flowing hair and sun-warmed skin, spoke words in a strange tongue, her voice swaying with the cadence of the drums.

In the midst of their slow march, one man stood out. He wore robes of charcoal gray and carried a false staff that appeared to move with a will of its own. He stood as tall as Achim, but was much leaner in build. His movements were quick and nimble, and his coloring unusual, with fine hair cropped short and silver-green eyes set in a pale face. He brought to mind images of Dragon: the translucence of her scales, the creamy line that stretched down her throat toward her underbelly.

With a resounding voice, he invited everyone to the show, a show for young and old, a spectacle of illusions created especially for the fine people of Moehn.

"That's him!" A child next to Eolyn bounced up and down, clapping his hands. "That's Mage Corey! Quick now, maybe he'll give us some sweets!"

Led by the boy, a pack of children charged into the parade. Their rambunctious courage was rewarded with a shower of candy from Mage Corey's sleeve. In this moment, Eolyn realized how close the mage had wandered. She stepped aside to disappear in the crowd, but it was too late. Mage Corey caught her movement and set his silver-green gaze on her.

Eolyn tensed under his focus.

His face filled with a disarming smile.

He strode forward and improvised a fool's dance around her, finishing with an exaggerated bow. When she responded with laughter, Mage Corey produced a lily from his sleeve.

"My personal invitation to a beautiful woman," he said. "Present this at the entrance, and you pay half price, five pence instead of ten. A fine bargain for a show you will not forget."

"But I don't have any—" Before Eolyn could finish, Mage Corey moved on.

Money.

With a disappointed sigh, Eolyn tucked the flower into her belt. Ghemena had warned her about money, strange metal objects that appeared when people exchanged goods or services. Eolyn had never touched a coin and therefore could not visualize one. For this reason, she wanted to secure employment, but employment would not come soon enough to pay her way into Corey's Circle. And she dearly wished to have more knowledge of this 'spectacle'.

The heat and heavy step of a large animal interrupted Eolyn's thoughts. One of the pageant horses paused next to her, its rider a handsome man with thick black hair secured loosely at the nape of his neck. A curious expression passed over him, as if he recognized her, though Eolyn knew they had not met before this moment.

"What is your name, my lady?" He pronounced his words carefully, with a melodious accent that inspired images of wind moving across open plains.

"I am Sarah of South Moehn."

He smiled as if she had let him in on an important secret. "I am Tahmir of the Syrnte."

Tahmir reached forward. His fingers passed over her temple and descended in a gentle arc behind her ear. The gesture sent a shiver of sparks through Eolyn. She would have jumped back were it not for the

88

tranquilizing effect of his touch.

"Will you come to the show this evening?" he asked.

"I would like to, but I can't. Not until I..." She stopped short when Tahmir produced a single coin from behind her ear. He tossed the five pence into the air, compelling her to catch it.

"I cannot accept this," she said instinctively. Ghemena had warned her about accepting gifts from men, though at the moment she could not for the life of her remember why.

"Nor can I give it," Tahmir replied. "How can I give that which is not mine? And by the same token, how can you accept something as a gift if it is already yours?"

Eolyn closed her hand over the coin and studied the hazel eyes of her benefactor, trying to assess his intentions.

"So we will see you at the Circle then?" he asked.

"Yes. I suppose you will."

With a pleased nod, Tahmir of the Syrnte continued on his way.

Corey's Circle was set up just outside the town walls, a cluster of benches and galleries surrounding a central open space. Eolyn arrived as the sun hung low over the horizon. Already the place was overcrowded. Boisterous children elbowed each other for a spot in front. Others climbed onto the shoulders of their parents.

Just as Eolyn managed to find a place on one of the hard wooden seats, Mage Corey opened the show. He cast a circle and invoked the blessing of the Gods. As soon as he finish, acrobats bounded into the space with all manner of leaps and jumps, warming the crowd into smiles and applause. Syrnte riders followed, brandishing flame tipped swords and inspiring cries of wonder and delight.

As twilight gathered, Mage Corey reappeared for an act of illusions, skillfully delivered, though Eolyn could not help but notice he tended to cheat with real magic. Corey went from one trick to the next with bold jokes and parodies of grim old mages, evoking roars of laughter from his audience.

Just as twilight faded into darkness, a singer they called the Mountain Queen appeared. She was a tall woman with striking features and snowy blond hair cropped short. As the townspeople cheered, she beckoned to her companions, the beautiful dark-haired woman who rode in the procession and nine female dancers. A small group of musicians took their place at the edge of the Circle.

When the enthusiastic welcome of the audience melted into anticipatory silence, one of the musicians intoned a single note. Upon this, the Mountain Queen layered her full voice, calling forth the other instruments. She took the hand of the dark-haired woman, whose song wove deeply into her own. Together they brought the music into a crescendo that set the dancers in motion.

Eolyn caught her breath. During the years of her apprenticeship with Ghemena, she had studied Primitive Magic and applied its principles to sacred holidays and spells. Yet it was not until this moment that she understood the true power of this most ancient and least understood form of magic. The performers captured the spirits of wind and forest and transformed them into something even more sublime.

The people of Moehn connected their hands. Voices and bodies swayed in a single whole. Three times the Mountain Queen led them through the melody, each reiteration more intense than the last, until the harmonies hit an impassioned climax and then diminished, leaving a hushed and reverent crowd in their wake.

A moment of rich silence passed before the people burst into thunderous applause.

Eolyn recalled Ghemena's words. *You will recognize them by their unique magic. They are hiding in visible places.*

Could these be the friends her tutor had promised?

She dared to hope they were.

After the crowd dispersed, Eolyn ventured into the cluster of tents where Corey's people had retired. Calling on Fox for stealth, she moved in silence among the shadows.

A vibrant energy hummed about the place as equipment was cleaned and stored, and costumes exchanged for simpler robes. Easy chatter filled the air. Somewhere just beyond the tents, the musicians had regrouped to improvise lighthearted tunes with the help of a few pints of ale.

Eolyn's careful ear located Mage Corey's voice, sharp and agitated, in one of the larger tents. She slipped through the entrance and saw him seated at a small table. In front of him stood a sour-faced man wearing the brown robes of a Middle Mage. The fabric was of a finer make than Mage Echior's, and trimmed in gold. Upon seeing them, Eolyn hesitated.

"I assure you, Mage Melk," Corey insisted, "there was no unauthorized magic in tonight's show."

"But those women—"

"Dancers and singers, nothing more."

"And the lights!"

"All managed mechanically or with the intervention of my own magic," Corey assured him.

"But the *music*, Mage Corey! No music like that has been heard in this land, not even in the time of the magas. Surely you realize it was far too powerful for a humble audience such as ours."

"We have already discussed this, Mage Melk. My musicians come from all corners of the known world, from places you have probably never heard of. I brought them together to craft entirely new kinds of melodies. Am I to disband them now for having met my expectations?"

"If their work inspires subversive magic? Yes."

"There are no magas in this show."

"How can you be certain?"

"Because the magas were destroyed, my friend." Corey spoke as if explaining to a small child. "There are none left."

"Master Tzeremond does not share your optimism."

"Well perhaps he should. It might help him relax a bit."

"I must also object, Mage Corey, to the very vulgar jokes you made in reference to our most revered Master."

"Oh, for the sake of the Gods!" Corey threw his hands in the air. "Are you so incapable of understanding humor?"

"When it comes to matters of serious importance, yes. You must understand I will send a full report to the King's City tomorrow."

"Send your report. The Council will judge it a waste of their time, much as this conversation has been a waste of mine."

The Mountain Queen swept into the tent just then. She strode past Eolyn without as much as a sideways glance. During the performance, she had worn a stunning winter blue gown that sparkled with silver embroidery. Now she was dressed as a man, with a simple tunic and a plain colored cloak.

"Hello, Corey," she said warmly. "I see you have a visitor."

"This is the Magistrate of Moehn. Mage Melk, I present to you the Mountain Queen. You may question her directly if you like."

Mage Melk responded with a curt nod and exited the tent in silence.

"He's a friendly one." The Mountain Queen spoke with a curious lilt.

"They won't talk to a woman if they suspect she's a maga," Corey said. "They fear her witchcraft will seduce them."

"All the better for me I suppose. But how do they ask questions during a trial if they can't talk to the accused?"

"They bring in a High Mage to do their dirty work." Corey produced a small silver flask. "It's a nasty business, and I'd rather not discuss it tonight. What an insufferable fool! His title alone is a joke: Mage Melk, Magistrate of Moehn. It makes my teeth itch."

"With all due respect, Corey, you take a lot of risks the way you speak with these magistrates."

"I know very well the risks I take."

The Mountain Queen shrugged, drew an apple from her cloak, and took a crisp bite. "Have you not noticed the beautiful woman waiting in your door way?"

Corey focused on Eolyn. The tension departed from his shoulders. He opened a flask and poured himself a drink of crystal clear liquid, the stinging scent of which reached Eolyn several feet away.

"I've left you waiting a long time, haven't I?" he said. "Come into the light where I can see you."

Eolyn stepped forward.

Corey's eyes narrowed. "You look familiar. Where have we met before?"

"This afternoon, in town. During the pageant, you—"

"Ah, yes, I remember now. How may I assist you?"

"I came to thank you for your invitation. The spectacle was enchanting, and..." Eolyn shifted on her feet. "I thought there might be an opportunity for employment with the Circle."

"I see." Corey downed his drink. "Though if I had a job for everyone who came asking...Come closer, so I can have a good look at you."

Eolyn approached until she stood in front of the table. Corey took his time assessing her, from head to foot and back again.

"Well," he concluded, "you're pretty enough, and we don't have anyone with quite that tone of fire in their hair. What can you do?"

"Do, sir?"

"Can you play an instrument? Dance?"

"No, I don't play any instruments. I have danced, but I don't have the grace of your dancers."

"Can you sing?"

"A little, but my voice is not nearly as spellbinding as the women who sang tonight."

The Mountain Queen arched her brow. "You certainly know how to boast your talents."

"Young lady." Corey's impatience returned. "If you can't sing, dance, ride a pony, or juggle fire, we have no place for you here."

Eolyn bit her lip. Had she been wrong about Ghemena's prophecy? She had none of the talents Mage Corey demanded, unless...

Ignoring every cautious instinct, Eolyn stepped up to the table and showed Mage Corey her palms. Just as he had done during his act, Eolyn folded one hand over the other in a brief but complex choreography that ended with the revelation of a single coin at her fingertips.

She let the five pence piece drop onto the table in front of him.

Corey and the Mountain Queen stared in stunned silence at the bit of copper. The mage picked it up and examined it carefully.

"Now, that is convenient trick," he said, his tone dubious. "You produce a few thousand of these, and we could close up the show and go home rich."

"I cannot do that, Mage Corey. This is the only coin I have, which is why I need employment."

The Mountain Queen snatched the coin from Corey's grasp and held it up to the torchlight. "Hire her, Corey. She looks unassuming, but she's all a rebel inside. I think she'll fit in quite nicely."

Corey's brow furrowed. "What did you say your name was?"

"Sarah."

"Sarah, are you aware that a trick like this can put you on the pyre?"

"They could burn me, but not legally. What I did was not true magic. It was merely sleight of hand."

The Mountain Queen laughed. "Listen to her, Corey! She sounds just like you."

"I can't put you in the Circle doing this! Illusion or not, they'd set fire to you without trial." Mage Corey's rebuke rang harsh and final.

Eolyn lowered her gaze in disappointment. "I see. Thank you for your time, Mage Corey. I will not trouble you again."

"I did not dismiss you."

Leaning back in his chair, Corey poured himself another drink. He studied Eolyn, a thoughtful expression on his face.

"I might be able to get away with making you my assistant," he said. "You wouldn't perform any illusions yourself, but you'd be next to the 'magic'. I've been looking for a woman to accompany my act, but the girls of Moisehén won't let themselves near magic anymore, not even the illusion of it. You wouldn't be afraid, though. Would you, Sarah?"

Eolyn's heart leapt. "No, I would not."

"We could call you 'the last Maga of Moehn'. That would work Mage Melk into a fury."

"With all due respect, Mage Corey, I think the use of the word 'maga' in connection with my person would be too risky."

"I agree." He eyed her now with suspicion. "You don't have a husband, do you? A father or a guardian? Someone who might come after me with a knife if I let you stay with us?"

"No. I am alone in the world."

He nodded as if he expected this answer. "So you are. Alone, and unique."

Eolyn glanced away, disconcerted. Had he noticed the instantaneous release of her ward in the moment she produced the coin?

"It's decided then," Corey announced. "You may stay with us."

The woman extended her hand in welcome. "Congratulations. My name is Khelia. I'm from the Paramen Mountains, though I am not a queen. I hope that doesn't disappoint you."

"No." Eolyn frowned. "Should it?"

Khelia shrugged. "It disappoints me. If I were queen I wouldn't have to scrape out a living singing songs for this old miser."

"Old?" Mage Corey said, indignant.

"I was born and raised with the Mountain People, but my mother grew up in Moisehén," Khelia continued. "That would make you and me sisters, after a fashion."

"She must have a good instinct about you." There was an undercurrent of warning in Mage Corey's tone. "Only a handful of people know that story."

Khelia held Eolyn's gaze. Her eyes were mesmerizing, a stunning shade of ice blue. After a moment, she released Eolyn's and said, "I'm off, then."

"Who's going with you?" Mage Corey asked.

"Rohnan and Kahlil. The rest will stay."

"Thank the Gods. Last time you nearly killed the show with all the musicians you took. And your supplies?"

"Everything is ready." She skirted the table to kiss Mage Corey on the cheek. "Gods protect you from the wrath of the magistrates. And be kind to this woman. I like her."

Khelia departed, leaving Mage Corey and Eolyn to watch each other under the flickering torchlight.

After a long moment, Corey rose to his feet. "I suppose we should get you settled, then."

To Eolyn's horror, the mage took the coin she had visualized and slipped it into his purse.

"If it pleases you, Mage Corey." Eolyn struggled to keep the tremor out of her voice. The visualized coin would fade within an hour. If Corey were to notice, he would know for certain what she had done. "That coin is all I have. May I keep it?"

"No. I need this to help cover your expenses until you start earning your keep."

Eolyn opened her mouth to object but thought the better of it. To insist might arouse suspicion, and she had taken enough risks for one evening. She sent a silent prayer to the Gods, hoping that the disappearance of one coin among many would go unnoticed.

CHAPTER SIXTEEN

Sarah

AFTER A FEW WEEKS in the Town of Moehn, Mage Corey packed up his show and headed toward the province of Selkynsen. The Circle's long caravan snaked northwest through a gently rolling landscape laid out in verdant crops and adorned by scattered hamlets.

In some of the villages, Corey arranged simple shows for smaller, less privileged audiences. Farmers arrived in loose flocks, whole families crowding into creaky wooden carts drawn by stolid oxen.

When they descended through the narrow Pass of Aerunden, Corey wondered, as he often did, why the noble houses of Moehn had never fortified this access point. Well defended, it would have made Moehn nearly impervious to attack. Yet Moehn was the easiest conquest of the old kings of Moisehén, falling under their control long before Selkynsen or Selen.

Corey had often commented on this in the presence of Lord Felton, the patriarch of Moehn. The old man always responded in the same fashion, laughing in his humble, self-effacing way. "What can you expect from a province of farmers?"

"You underestimate your importance, Lord Felton," Corey had replied. "The fertile lands of Moehn feed the rest of the kingdom."

"Moisehén lives on the power of its magic and might of its kings," Felton declared quietly.

At times, Corey could not tell whether the patriarch was naïve or prudent. Were Moehn ever to wake up to its own power, it could become a force to contend with overnight. For this reason, Corey kept a close eye on the province, as he did on many things.

Once they cleared the pass, the Circle set up camp in the Valley of Aerunden, a narrow stretch of grassland between forested hills. Corey decided to linger a few days. He liked the magic that hummed under this valley, and he thought it wise to drink his fill before continuing on to Selkynsen. For all its wealth and elegance, the eastern province offered

95

pitifully few wellsprings of magic.

As Corey anticipated, his people were grateful for the break.

One afternoon, he returned from a lengthy walk through the summer woods to find Renate at work with her dancers.

That woman does not understand the concept of rest.

Not that Corey minded. Hawk-faced Renate kept the show crisp and his people in check with her tireless discipline. She was advanced in years, her raven hair streaked with gray, but no one was more dedicated to the Circle, and few kept Corey better company.

The mage paused on a small knoll to watch their practice. From this vantage point, he had a clear view of all the women, including the girl of most interest to him now, the intriguing Sarah of Moehn.

Renate made the poor girl suffer more than the others, with constant rebukes and scolding. This was the way of things for any new member of the Circle, but in Sarah's case the challenge was multiplied by the girl's utter lack of experience. Corey would no doubt get an earful about it this evening, but Renate had no grounds for complaint. She had brought this upon herself.

"Have you gone completely mad?" Renate had cried, bursting into Corey's tent the day after he hired Sarah. "Putting that girl in your magic show?"

"I've been seeking an assistant for some time," Corey had replied evenly.

"She'll be on the pyre within a week, and the rest of us may very well burn with her."

"She will not do any magic."

"Even the illusion of magic could—"

"She will not perform any illusions."

"Curse you, Corey! I am so weary of the risks you take."

"You are free to withdraw from the Circle any time you please, Renate."

Renate had set her lips in a thin line. Corey knew well the terror he invoked whenever he suggested she leave. Nothing waited for Renate outside the Circle, save solitude and fear, the unending torment of all her ghosts from the past.

Renate's tone softened. "Corey, please. She's just a child. Don't make her your toy in this."

Toy? Was that what Renate thought?

"I can't imagine what you expect to gain from this folly," Renate insisted, "but that girl, that beautiful, innocent girl, could lose her life. Is that a fair price for your amusement?"

He could not very well argue with that.

Well, he could, but why upset Renate more than necessary?

They came to an agreement that Sarah would perform in only half the shows as Corey's assistant. Otherwise, she would occupy a more benign role as a dancer. In truth, Corey thought this would do little to lessen the risk for young Sarah, but at least Renate's temper was soothed.

Several men of the Circle were gathered to watch the women practice. They sat or stood on the grassy slope, linen shirts open to the golden sun, their chatter low and jovial. Under other circumstances, Corey might have indulged their idleness, but today he had questions, and he wanted answers.

"I don't pay you to sit around gawking like fools while the women work," Corey barked. "Why don't you follow their example and do something useful?"

The men responded with guffaws and rolling eyes, but they heeded his rebuke. One by one, they rose and headed back toward camp, all of them save Tahmir, who remained at Corey's signal.

"What do you think of our new acquisition?" Corey nodded toward the young women, who held poses while Renate corrected their lines.

"She works hard," Tahmir said. "And she is not unaccustomed to criticism. I doubt she will ever acquire the skill of our better dancers, but she will hold her own. I suspect she'll be ready when we reach Selkynsen."

Corey agreed. The girl had a natural grace about her, the reflection of some animal spirit. A fox perhaps, or a lynx. "Tell me something I don't already know. Something your famous Syrnte sight has shown you."

Tahmir closed his eyes and lifted his face to the breeze. An unnecessary show, really. Those gifted with Syrnte sight saw past, present, and future as readily as they breathed. Yet like all Corey's people, Tahmir had a natural inclination toward drama.

Or perhaps he is merely considering his words.

"Her true name is not Sarah," Tahmir said.

Corey lifted his brow. It had not occurred to him the girl might have reason to use a false name. "What is her name, then?"

"I cannot say."

Cannot or will not?

"She has a gift with animals," Tahmir continued. "She took to riding very quickly, as if she understood the language of horses. As if she could speak to them, and they to her."

The riding lessons had also been Renate's idea. *So she can make her escape swift as an arrow, should there be any trouble.* Corey, mindful of his battles, chose to indulge his dance mistress in this as well. Tahmir had been assigned the task of teaching Sarah horsemanship, a duty he had accepted with discrete enthusiasm.

Stepping aside from the group, Sarah removed her worn tunic to continue practicing in her chemise. Corey noted a flash of light just above her elbow. He narrowed his eyes.

"That armband she wears," he said. "What is it? Have you seen it?"

"No, but my sister Rishona has commented on its workmanship. It is a jewel of solid silver, etched with the images of many animals strung together into a single serpent."

By the Gods. Corey's heart paused in disbelief. He checked his thoughts and covered them with words, hoping Tahmir would not notice the deeper question that now troubled him. "Where do you suppose a peasant girl would get a hold of something like that? What else has Rishona gathered from the women's tent?"

"Nothing that you don't already know," Tahmir replied. "The stories Sarah shares with the women differ little from what she has told us. Indeed, she has spoken very little about herself, preferring instead to ask questions about Moisehén. Its people, its king…and you."

"Me?" This amused Corey. "She suspects I pose a danger to her, then."

"She's been assured you bear no love for Tzeremond."

"If she's wise, that will make no difference in her suspicions. What else have they told her?"

"She knows about your blood ties to the Clan of East Selen, and to the royal house of Moisehén through Queen Briana. And she's heard many greatly embellished stories of your travels to the southern kingdoms."

Corey grimaced. "Nothing too scandalous, I hope."

"Nothing you would not want her to hear. She is very curious about magic."

"Indeed. She shows far too much curiosity in that respect. It's not normal for a girl of Moisehén."

"Perhaps she is one of your magas, returned from the world to which they were banished."

Something in Tahmir's tone gave Corey pause.

"That would be quite impossible, my friend," he said carefully. "All the magas of the Old Orders were dead by the time she was five. And Moehn has no tradition of magic, no hope of producing something as sophisticated as a maga. It's almost an insult to propose a maga could spring out of those muddy fields of oats and barley."

"Yet you share my suspicion."

Corey cast Tahmir a sideways glance.

"When she did the trick that got her this job, yes, I suspected, but I have found no evidence of a ward since. Still, it's clear she knows something. How much is anyone's guess."

"You don't need any more evidence to turn her over to the magistrates."

A witch to burn. That might earn him some favors.

"I prefer to keep her with us, for the time being," Corey said.

The mage turned his back on Renate's dancers and started toward the tents. Tahmir followed suit, keeping pace with Corey.

"I want to see how she responds to the Circle," Corey said. "Perhaps she will let down her guard. Perhaps she will tell someone what she is, and whether there are more like her hidden away in Moehn."

"She is a careful woman," Tahmir replied. "Slow to friendship, even slower to intimacy."

Corey shrugged. "How many careful women have succumbed to your admirable charms, Tahmir? Make use of your Syrnte skills. Convince her of your friendship, and let me know what you find out."

CHAPTER SEVENTEEN

A Special Interest

THE TOWN OF SELKYNSEN stretched along the west bank of the Furma River, which separated Moisehén from the neighboring kingdom of Roenfyn. Thick walls of yellow stone enclosed the city center. Shops and vending stalls crowded the narrow streets and winding alleys. Along the riverfront, there was a constant rush of activity as ships and ferries unloaded goods in exchange for the diverse products of the kingdom.

Eolyn's ears rang with rhythmic shouts of vendors and the avid chatter of hagglers. The smell of rotting fish, stale urine, and spilt ale buffeted her senses and made her eyes water. Buildings crowded over them, cutting off the expanse of the clear summer sky. She clung to her companions, Rishona and Adiana, and wondered whether Achim's 'stone forest' would be as chaotic and rancid as all this.

"I've never seen so many people in one place," Eolyn said.

"All the better for the Circle." Rishona offered a warm smile to a group of men. They paused in their conversation to watch the raven-haired beauty pass. "The more active the markets, the more generous our audience."

"What was it like growing up here?" Eolyn asked Adiana. "I can't imagine living in such a place."

Adiana lifted her chin. "Selkynsen is the center of the kingdom. Where else would anyone want to live? The life, the commerce, the culture. The King's City may be impressive, with its grand buildings and noble history, but all the real activity is here."

Eolyn shook her head. How could one live in a place without trees? The earth's magic ran in such insipid streams under the province of Selkynsen. She already felt the drain on her power.

"In truth," continued Adiana, "I only spent part of my childhood here. My parents were merchants and patrons of the arts. They recognized I had a gift for music when I was very young. They wanted to place me with an instructor, but with the purges gaining momentum, no one would accept a girl for fear of accusations of subversive magic. So my parents sent me downriver to New Linfeln. I lived there with my mother's cousin and studied music for nearly eight years."

"What brought you home?"

"Mother and father stopped writing, and then stopped sending money. I thought..." She shrugged and glanced away, tucked a loose strand of golden hair behind her ear. "I thought they'd forgotten about me. I spent everything I had left to come home. I was only fifteen at the time, and very angry at my parents for their neglect. I was going to give them quite a scolding, you know. But then I found out Mother and Father hadn't forgotten at all. They had died."

Eolyn's heart twisted at the memory of her own loss. "How?"

"Mother was burned for witchcraft." Adiana's voice took on a bitter edge. "And father was executed on charges of harboring a witch."

"Your mother was a maga?"

Adiana shook her head. "It's not very likely. Selkynsen never had much of a tradition of magic. Our strength is in commerce, music, and art."

"Art is magic," Eolyn said. "So is music. It's all Primitive Magic. The Old Orders considered Primitive Magic the most sacred of all."

Adiana laughed. "You've been spending too much time with Mage Corey. You should watch yourself, you know. It's not wise for a woman to speak as if she knows of these things."

Eolyn bit her lip. She hadn't considered the ease with which she spoke about magic. How many times had she made similar comments in front of Renate or Tahmir or even Mage Corey?

"Anyway, I'm not talking about Primitive Magic," Adiana continued. "I'm talking about mages and magas and the like. Very few of them ever came from Selkynsen. Yet during the purges more witches were burned here than anywhere else in the kingdom. How do you explain that?" Her eyes rested sharp on Eolyn, though the challenge seemed intended for someone else.

"I don't know," Eolyn confessed.

"Mother and Father died because others wanted what they had. Many families were brought down during the purges, and new empires built on their graves. Father's conviction allowed his entire estate to be confiscated by the magistrate."

"But their property should have gone to you!"

"A girl?" She let go a harsh laugh. "An orphan? No, I had no rights to anything, and no money left to get me back to New Linfeln. In a public show of mercy, the magistrate offered me a place as a servant in his household, but I could see that held no future for me. He was a perverse old man. Rather than submit to him, I ran away, thinking to find employment on the piers. By then, women weren't hired for much of anything. For a while I tried singing in the taverns, but the men…"

Adiana paused. She studied the cobblestones at her feet and wrapped her arms around herself. When she returned her gaze to Eolyn, her expression was forced somehow; light-hearted, but with tension upon her brow. "They always wanted more than a song, you know. They paid better if I obliged them, and became cruel if I did not. Still, I was lucky. Father's steward came after me before I wandered too far down that path. He took me in as one of his family."

"How was it that you came to join the Circle?"

"That happened much later. I kept my instruments hidden a long time, out of shame I suppose, or fear. Then one day, Corey's Circle appeared, with women creating music alongside men. I simply knew I had to be a part of it." Adiana took Eolyn's arm in hers. "Mage Corey has admitted you to a sacred place, Sarah. A world where you can be a little more yourself. This is what he gives to everyone who joins the Circle. You'll find we are fiercely loyal to him because of it."

Rishona interrupted their conversation with a gasp of delight. She rushed over to a vendor whose rickety table was filled with dried herbs and flasks of colored powders.

"Your people call these 'spices'," Rishona said as Eolyn and Adiana caught up with her. "They are from my homeland. We use them in much the same way you use herbs. They give excellent flavor to our food."

At the vendor's invitation, Eolyn reached for a flask containing powder the shade of oak leaves in late autumn. Just as she was about to open it, Rishona stayed her hand.

"Not this one, Sarah. Allow me to show you." The Syrnte woman removed the cream colored scarf she wore wrapped it around Eolyn's eyes, leaving her with the sensation of floating inside a bright cloud.

"This is the sea," Rishona said.

Eolyn sensed the flask under her nose and felt the warm rush of a salty breeze.

"These are the high plains of my homeland."

The maga's senses filled with the golden caress of sun-warmed grass.

"The night."

Eolyn detected an aroma at once ephemeral and intense, so sweet it left her heart aching.

"The fire that warms our hearths."

Beckoning Eolyn to part her lips, Rishona touched her tongue with a substance that flamed through her sinuses and burned down her throat.

"You put this in your *food*?" Eolyn gasped.

Rishona set her breath upon Eolyn's lips, generating a soothing frost that spread over the path of the fire spice. "That was to open your senses. What I am about to show you is far more subtle."

The Syrnte woman said no more, allowing Eolyn's imagination to play over the aromas and tastes that followed: of reeds growing on the edge of a placid lake, of damp leaf litter and fruit-laden trees, of the sun setting over a bright sea.

After many such journeys, a new aroma came to Eolyn that slowed her breath and quickened her heart. She inhaled her own perfume, a heavy, intimate spice that emanated from the heat of her hands and the soft contours of her breasts. She tasted the honey that spread across the inner curve of her thighs whenever she entered into ecstasy under a full moon.

Startled, Eolyn pulled back, but the scent of a man's desire halted her retreat and wove through her own fragrance. She had encountered this heady aroma once before, fleetingly, the day she said goodbye to Achim. It was not Achim, however, who anchored himself to her as their passion took flight.

Abruptly Eolyn tore off the scarf.

A heated flush overtook her cheeks. Rishona's gaze was cool and impassive. The maga felt certain the Syrnte woman had seen the vision. What she could not tell was whether Rishona had also crafted it.

"That is enough." Eolyn's voice was rigid. A tremor invaded her tone. "Perhaps you can show me more another day."

Rishona accepted the scarf, a faint smile playing upon her ruby lips. She turned to the stall keeper to place her order.

Adiana drew close and wrapped her arm around Eolyn's waist. "If I didn't know better, I'd say she's cast a spell on you."

"I think she did."

Adiana clucked her tongue. "Not possible. They wouldn't have let her into Moisehén if she were a witch. Rishona always plays the spice game when there's a new member. I think it amuses her to see our mundane senses confused by the aromas of her homeland."

But Eolyn was not about to dismiss the incident so lightly. Rishona had entered Moisehén at Mage Corey's behest. The suspicion that he might have hired a Syrnte witch with the full knowledge and support of Tzeremond's Order troubled her.

The vendor charged a premium price for his goods, and though Rishona managed to bargain him down, she left a large sum in exchange for tiny amounts of the precious imports. With a look of satisfaction, the Syrnte woman tucked the spices into her purse.

"My brother will be upset that his monthly allowance for wine has been spent." She lifted her dark eyes to Eolyn. "Though it will please him to know his meals will soon have more flavor."

"Enough dawdling!" Adiana declared. "Let's have a look at some fabrics."

She took Eolyn's hand and led the way to the textile shop, a cramped space with bolts of cloth stacked to the ceilings. The shopkeeper was a thin old man with a balding head and complacent smile. After laying out multiple silks and brocades, he left them to attend other customers. Rishona bade Eolyn to make her choice, but the variety overwhelmed the young maga.

"You must help me, both of you. You know better what would work for the show, and what would fit within the allowance Mage Corey gave us."

"We should choose a color that offsets the lovely tone of your hair," Adiana said. "Perhaps one of the greens."

"Green is the traditional color of High Mages," Eolyn objected. "It's too risky."

"Perhaps blue, then," Rishona suggested. "Not the ice-and-silver blue of Khelia's gown. Yours is a richer blue, the warm blue of a river on a summer day."

Rishona separated a sapphire damask with gold threads woven in loose diamonds. Eolyn ran her fingers over the extraordinary weave. She could not imagine herself in such fabric. It was so foreign to anything she had ever known.

"Well?" Rishona prompted.

"I don't know. It's too soft, I think."

Adiana giggled. Rishona called the shop owner and instructed him to cut the fabric. She then had him set out several bolts of simpler cloths before turning back to Eolyn.

"You are to choose something else," the Syrnte woman said.

"Another dress?" Eolyn asked. "Why?"

"It is a gift from Mage Corey, something to wear when you are not performing."

"A gift?"

"I overheard him just yesterday." Adiana said with a conspiratorial grin. "He thinks you look charming in those homespun russets, but he wants to see you in something more suited to your place in the Circle."

"My *place*?"

They laughed.

"It seems you have inspired some generosity among the men of the Circle." Rishona's words sent a burning flush through Eolyn's cheeks. She turned abruptly away and set her focus on the textiles.

Adiana drew close. "You should be pleased, you know. It's unusual for Mage Corey to take a special interest in one of the women under his employ."

"Special interest indeed." Eolyn did not bother to hide her annoyance. "Though it is not of a romantic nature."

"What other kind of special interest is there?" Adiana teased.

Eolyn drew a breath and searched for an appropriate response. She could not deny Mage Corey's vigilance of her, his ample attentions, his calculated kindness. But Corey did not seek her heart. He sought proof of her magic.

"There is a resonance in your spirit that reminds Corey of someone he lost, someone very dear to him," Rishona said.

"Rishona, I will not show Mage Corey disrespect by denying this gift, but nor will I suffer any more talk of his romantic intentions."

"Then perhaps we can talk about the song Nathan dedicated to you last night!" Adiana suggested. "I'll wager his caress is as sweet and sincere as his voice."

"We could also discuss the coin my brother offered you in Moehn."

"That doesn't really count," Adiana objected. "Tahmir's always handing out coins to women in those processions."

"He's done that before?" Eolyn asked.

Adiana shrugged. "It's brought more than one willing partner to his bed after a show."

Eolyn's heart sank. She had spoken little to Tahmir outside of her riding lessons, but she could not deny the attraction she felt for him. His dark gaze unsettled her, and he moved with a raw sensuality reminiscent of Lynx. Already there had been moments, a brush of his hand over hers, a meeting of eyes across the evening fire, in which she found herself thinking that perhaps he felt the same. To learn she was one of many disappointed her somehow.

"The point is," Rishona was saying, "Tahmir has a special interest in Sarah."

Adiana twirled a lock of golden hair around her fingers. "It must have been quite the blow to Tahmir's pride when you went searching for Corey after the show instead of him."

"I had no need for a lover that night," Eolyn snapped. "I needed employment."

Not a single statement Eolyn had made during this discussion was intended as a joke, and she could not comprehend why her companions kept bursting into laughter.

"And when you need a lover," Rishona asked, "whom will you choose?"

Adiana gave an exaggerated sigh. "Rishona already knows the answer to that question. She's seen all of our futures."

"That's not true," Rishona said.

"What I want to know is who you've been with. You speak as if you've long since entered into these pleasures, Sarah. Tell us about your lovers." Adiana said the word 'lovers' as if she were biting into a honey cake.

"I have not yet experienced a proper awakening of *aen-lasati*, but my grandmother instructed me in these arts. She explained what to expect and taught me the importance of...preparing myself."

"You have not *experienced a proper awakening?*" Adiana mimicked Eolyn with amusement. "You did grow up on the periphery of the kingdom! Nobody talks about it that way anymore. It's all about *losing* now. You can lose your virginity or you can lose your innocence or you can lose your lily. In the process, you will lose your reputation or at the very least you will lose respect. And it's always the women who seem to be losing. Nowadays the men are born without anything to lose at all. It's enough to make a woman lose her mind, if you ask me."

"Renate told us that in the time of the Magas, the women of Moisehén were better instructed in the arts of love," Rishona observed. "Your grandmother must have been of that generation."

"Indeed she was." Eolyn fell pensive at the invocation of her tutor's memory. For a moment she was back in the South Woods, working side by side with the old maga in the garden.

"Tell me, Sarah," Rishona's voice fell to a murmur. "Did your grandmother also teach you how to reject a man's seed when you so desire?"

This was a dangerous question, and Eolyn knew it. But the day had left her unsettled, as if a fence were being drawn around her. She felt the need to defend something of herself. If she could not yet defend her right to magic, then at least she would defend her right to intimacy. "Of course. I carry the appropriate herbs with me always."

Adiana sucked in her breath. "You know the old medicines of women?"

Rishona hushed them at the turn of the shopkeeper's head.

"You *must* teach me," Adiana insisted in a fierce whisper. "You must teach us all!"

CHAPTER EIGHTEEN

Subtlety of Judgement

ALTHOUGH EOLYN'S APPEARANCE in Mage Corey's act of illusions brought more than a few angry mages to Corey's tent, show after show passed without incident. Indeed, every audience received her with adulation. No one came to arrest Eolyn, and little by little the young maga felt more at ease in the company of the Circle.

Rishona and Adiana remained her faithful companions. Eolyn gained respect among the women with her knowledge of plants and traditional medicines. Through their travels, she learned much about her homeland: the elegance of Selkynsen, the rich veins of magic that hummed under Selen, the song of metal that reverberated over the ruling province of Moisehén.

When autumn began to fade toward winter, Eolyn's spirit dimmed under a growing suspicion that their season might pass without Mage Corey's caravan ever reaching the King's City. She had hoped to find Achim before year's end, and to abandon the Circle for his protection.

All her fantasies of encountering Achim were happy ones. Eolyn imagined him essentially unchanged from the boy she once knew, and her heart glowed at the thought of rediscovering their friendship. Achim would keep her safe and give her a new home. Together, they would find a way to restore the Old Orders.

A few days before the autumn festival of Samhaen, the Circle gave its last show in the town of Selen. Eolyn's companions celebrated the High Holiday with customs meant to honor the dead and bright revelry dedicated to bidding farewell to fellow artists and good friends. The Circle would lose more than half its company during the winter months, as many members returned to their homes and families for the off-season. Those remaining, including principle figures such as Mistress Renate, foreigners like the Syrnte siblings, and others who no longer had a family such as Adiana, would retire together to Mage Corey's estate in East Selen.

The afternoon before their anticipated departure, Eolyn took her customary walk accompanied, as she often was, by Mage Corey. The scent of winter had just begun to permeate the air. Dry leaves rattled as wind shook them from the trees. Eolyn remembered the day her village fell, and an involuntary shiver ran through her shoulders.

"Are you all right, Sarah?" Mage Corey asked.

There was no detail he did not notice.

"There's a chill on the air." Eolyn would speak no more of the raid on her village. She had already endured countless questions about it. "It's too late in the season for me to be using a summer cloak."

"We can go back if you like."

"No. Autumn is fading already. I wish to enjoy it as much as possible."

Corey paused, removed his cloak, and set it about Eolyn's shoulders. The intimacy unnerved her.

"That's not necessary," she said.

"I know." He fastened the clasp at the base of her throat. It was a beautiful jewel of solid silver, intricately etched with images of Dragon. For a moment he allowed his hands to rest on her shoulders. "Is that better?"

"Yes," Eolyn admitted. Already warmth was penetrating her limbs. The wool cloak was impregnated with a comforting aroma of pine and winter winds.

Mage Corey stepped away and they continued their walk.

Although he always requested Eolyn's permission to accompany her, the maga understood she had little option but to accept. She chaffed under Corey's vigilance, yet found some pleasure in his charismatic presence. She admired Corey's easy jests and natural attention to the details of the landscape: a winter hawk gliding in the distance, a fallen leaf painted in stunning colors, the harvested field illuminated by auburn rays of a chilly afternoon sun.

"I have heard many legends of East Selen," she said. "I look forward to seeing your home."

"I look forward to showing it to you, though I will not be able to for many weeks yet."

"What do you mean? I thought we were leaving tomorrow."

"You and the others depart for East Selen at dawn. I must journey to the King's City."

"Why do you not take us with you?" Eolyn's disappointment spilled out unhindered. She bit her lip, already regretting her outburst.

Mage Corey cast her a sideways glance. "This trip holds no interest for you or any other members of the Circle. There will be no performances, and I will be locked up in meetings with the Council—

which will put me in a very foul mood, I might add. All the more reason why I should go alone."

"But I would like to see the King's City, the Stone Foundation of Vortingen, the great castle of the warrior kings. My grandmother told me wonderful stories about it."

"It is a place of grandeur, though many who knew it before the war say it has lost much of the magnificence it once had."

"Why did you not take the Circle there this past summer?"

"The City of Moisehén is a difficult place. One sour-faced High Mage can kill the show. And of course, it means more work for me, managing the visits and discussions of the countless mages who reside in the city. On top of all this, we've put you in my act of illusions. I could not bring that to the King's City, not yet. Though I am certain your place in the show has been reported in full by the magistrates. I will spend a good deal of time defending that decision."

"What will happen if you are unable to win the Council's support?"

"I will have their support in everything by the end of my visit. I always do. It is simply a matter of persuasive argument."

Eolyn turned this statement over in her mind, her fingers passing idly over the cool metal clasp that secured Corey's cloak. She had seen him go head-to-head with almost every magistrate of every village they performed in. Always the mages challenged him with the same arguments, and always they threatened to report him to Tzeremond. Yet the Circle continued unhindered, and Mage Corey's confidence in the security of his endeavor never faltered, not even now when he talked of defending his actions before the Council.

"It is not just persuasive argument, is it?" she ventured, casting him a careful glance. "You are never truly concerned about the magistrate's accusations, and you are always certain of the Council's support. Why is that?"

Mage Corey's smile faded. He paused in his stride and furrowed his brow, as if struggling with the thread of a new idea, or coming to terms with some quiet revelation.

Eolyn wondered if she had been too bold.

"I perform a service for the Council." Corey resumed his pace, keeping his gaze fixed on the path ahead. "The Circle is not simply a show. It is a laboratory, of sorts, invented to study alternative forms of magic."

Eolyn's feet rooted into the ground beneath her.

Mage Corey continued a few paces before he turned and focused his silver-green gaze on the maga.

"For what purpose?" she asked.

"Master Tzeremond and the King fear the manifestation of a new class of magic, something beyond their ability to detect or control. So they have launched a great project to try to understand the magic of foreign lands, of the Syrnte, the Mountain People, even the Primitive and Simple Magic that persists in the hearts of the women of Moisehén. The Circle is part of that project. My work is to observe the ways of our members and to study the effect of their magic on the people of Moisehén. The purpose of my yearly visits to the King's City is to report everything I learn to the Council."

"And you do this for them?"

"It is what they expect of me."

"But the magistrates and all the others…the threats they make to the Circle…?"

"The magistrates understand nothing of the true nature of this endeavor. Only the Council knows, and the King."

"And the members of the Circle?"

"Each person under my employ knows what I judge necessary for him or her to know."

Eolyn wanted to resume her pace, but her feet clung stubbornly to the ground. It was a maga's reflex, this anchoring of one's spirit deep into the earth when confronted with fear. Eolyn hoped Mage Corey would not recognize the technique.

"You must understand that you are not to discuss what I have revealed with anyone," he said.

"Why are you telling me this?"

Mage Corey closed the distance between them. His magic spread in a hush through fallen leaves, surrounding her, cutting off all retreat, and daring her to defend herself with a counter spell. He stopped just in front of her, his face a breath away.

"Because, Sarah," he murmured, "sometimes I like to imagine you and I live in a world where we do not feel compelled to keep secrets from each other."

Eolyn's throat went dry.

"Indulge me in this fantasy," he continued, "and tell me: Why do you desire so much to go to the King's City?"

Eolyn willed her eyes to remain on his. When she spoke, her voice was steady. "It is a child's wish. I had a friend growing up. I believe he lives there. I wish to find him. That is all."

Mage Corey studied her for a moment. Then he stepped away and continued his walk. The autumn earth released Eolyn's feet. She quickened her pace to catch up with him.

"A friend," he asked, his voice a mask of idle curiosity, "or a lover?"

"A friend. We were only children when we knew each other."

"I see. I am sorry, Sarah, but I cannot take you to the city, not because I object to you finding your friend, but because I am averse to leading fawns into nests of vipers. Though having you there would be worse than that. Vipers at least have some sense of who their true enemy is. Too many mages of Tzeremond do not possess subtlety of judgment. They do not have the patience to distinguish a true threat from a false one. That place is not safe for a woman of your...qualities. And I will be far too busy with the Council to look after you."

"I understand, Mage Corey." In truth, Eolyn was now quite relieved she would not be accompanying him.

"Still." Corey stopped to face her once more, his expression thoughtful. "I know many people in the City of Moisehén. If you give me the name of this friend of yours, perhaps I could..."

Eolyn's expression put a stop to his words.

"I see I am pressing too hard," he said. "Very well, Sarah. We have had a fair exchange today: one truth for one truth." Touching Eolyn's chin, Corey brought her gaze back to his. "Perhaps we can continue this conversation when I return to East Selen."

Eolyn nodded, though she was already reconsidering her decision to spend winter with the Circle.

"I'm pleased you will accompany us, you know." Corey released her chin with a subtle caress. "I expect your presence will bring much warmth to the cold nights ahead."

CHAPTER NINETEEN

Midwinter's Eve

EOLYN WOULD HAVE ABANDONED the Circle forthwith were it not for one consideration: Running away would only confirm Corey's suspicions. Staying, on the other hand, might confuse his pursuit. Surely he would not expect her to remain if she had magic to hide. So after much deliberation, Eolyn chose the known risk of Corey's vigilance over the unknown consequences of facing winter alone. She resolved to leave the Circle at the first thaw, make the journey to the King's City on her own, and at last find Achim.

By the time the caravan reached East Selen, autumn had painted the trees in deep shades of copper and burgundy. Dry leaves lay in heaps along the ground. The wind had stilled in preparation for the arrival of the first frost.

For centuries, the lands of East Selen had been controlled by a single extended family that produced some of the greatest mages and magas in history. Though the clan perished under Kedehen's wrath during the war, Eolyn felt their spirits wandering the hills. There was a haunting joy to their presence, a community lost in time and yet preserved by the landscape.

Corey's guests were housed in a rambling, semicircular manor with thick timber supports and thatched roofs. The interior was broken into cozy apartments with multiple hearths. A single large hall situated at the center of the manor provided the setting for evening meals and social gatherings. In front of the hall stood a giant fir planted by the first mages and magas to settle in the area. The entire construction rested in the shadow of a dense forest, the magic of which reminded Eolyn of the South Woods, though it seemed darker in aspect.

When the first snow fell, Mage Corey appeared, wearied from his journey yet infused with the energy of contentment that accompanies any true homecoming. Upon his arrival, preparation for the Winter Solstice began in earnest. Mistress Renate oversaw the casting of bayberry candles and the baking of nut cakes and sweetbreads. Hunting expeditions were organized to secure fresh venison, allowing Rishona to demonstrate her exceptional abilities with the bow. Abundant branches of pine, holly and mistletoe were harvested to add fragrance and color to the dining hall. For his part, Mage Corey spent hours wandering the forest, often inviting Eolyn to accompany him, until this year's Yule log revealed itself to his discerning eye.

The frenetic energy of her companions disconcerted Eolyn. Although she grew up with stories of the boisterous feasts of old, her childhood celebrations of Winter Solstice had been dependably simple and quiet.

Days before the feast, the women began airing, brushing and retouching their finest gowns. Eolyn, who had but two simple woolen dresses to keep her warm during the winter months, now wondered whether it would be appropriate to attend the midnight festival in such plain robes. Rishona resolved this dilemma by appearing one afternoon with another expression of Mage Corey's special interest: the loan of an exquisite forest green, fur-lined gown. It had once belonged to a woman of his clan.

"I told Corey you are not partial to wearing green," Rishona said, "but he thought you might make an exception this time."

At sunset on Midwinter's Eve, Mage Corey's guests gathered in the dining hall illuminated by countless brilliant candles. The tables were amply spread with roast goose and venison, herbed vegetables, sweetmeats, and breads. The Yule log carried the warmth of the sleeping sun in its yellow flames, and the heady scent of pine and bayberry intoxicated the celebrants long before anyone started pouring the wine.

Mage Corey occupied the head table, accompanied by Mistress Renate, Rishona, and Tahmir. All the other guests took their seats at two long tables facing each other across the modestly sized hall. Ample room was left between them, space that would fill with dancers as the night wore on and the wine took effect.

The feast was well underway when Khelia burst through the heavy double doors in a thick swirl of snow, followed by several companions with musical instruments. Delighted by her unexpected appearance, the guests applauded and cheered. Mage Corey crossed the dining hall to embrace her, and she assumed a place by his side at the table.

The celebration flourished on animated waves of laughter until at last the music started, and dancers invaded the floor. Khelia took her leave of the main table and moved toward Eolyn, indulging in lively conversation with anyone who crossed her path.

"I'm glad to see you're still here." The mountain woman greeted

Eolyn with a warm embrace and a kiss of friendship. "Corey's been kind to you, then?"

"Yes. A little too kind, actually."

Her eyes sparked in amusement. "Well, he does have a bit of a romantic side, though one would find it hard to believe at first. Don't worry if he's started showering gifts on you. He expects nothing in return, really, except perhaps a bit of honest friendship."

"I know."

"Though it's difficult for a true woman to be honest these days in Moisehén." Khelia's eyes moved across the crowd of dancers. "It's quite a dilemma, don't you think? One can be true, or one can be honest. Which do you prefer, Sarah?"

She turned her attention to Eolyn, as if to cut a clear path to the maga's heart with those ice blue eyes.

"I prefer to be true," Eolyn said.

Khelia smiled and lifted her cup. "So I suspected. I hear you're quite the hit throughout the land, with your magic act."

"It is Mage Corey's act, and it is an act of illusions."

"Yes, well, it's all the same now, you know. They haven't threatened to burn you yet, have they?"

"No, not yet."

"That's good news. Corey will probably keep it up for at least another season then."

Eolyn decided it was time to change the subject. "Where have you been, Khelia? I thought for certain you would perform with the Circle again before the season ended."

"Why?" Khelia flashed Eolyn a daring smile. "Did you miss me?"

"I had hoped to have the opportunity to get to know you."

"Get to know me?" Khelia's pale brows lifted. "Well, it's difficult to know anyone inside the Circle, but we may have other opportunities if the Gods are willing. In the meantime, I suggest you do not ask where I have been, or where I am going, for that matter. Some questions are better left unanswered."

Eolyn's annoyance at this relentless game of hide and seek was beginning to break through her reserve. Every member of the Circle, it seemed, guarded some secret or worked toward some private objective. In the middle of it all stood Mage Corey, weaving all their disparate threads into a single shadowy net. She wondered what stories the mage had told Khelia. In which of Corey's realities did the mountain woman live?

Khelia laid a hand over Eolyn's. "Don't let my evasions upset you. They are but the momentary price of having a true friend, instead of an honest one."

114

At this Eolyn's mood softened. She returned Khelia's gesture with a squeeze of her hand.

"Come and dance, Sarah," Khelia beckoned. "This is not a night to be thinking so much. Renate tells me you've quite a gift for movement."

"She said that?"

"She always hands out compliments when she's had too much to drink."

Eolyn laughed and followed Khelia to the floor. They danced until her muscles filled with sweet fatigue and the roots of her hair were damp with sweat.

As midnight approached, the musicians quieted their instruments. Mage Corey's guests convened in a circle at the center of the hall. This was the most sacred moment of the year's longest night, marking the farthest reach of the sun into the great void of the Underworld. All across Moisehén, from the hearths of its peasants to the King's great hall, the sun's descent would be received with reverent silence.

Moving his hand in a slow arc, Mage Corey dimmed the candles until only the flickering flame of the Yule log illuminated the room, casting such shadows that Eolyn imagined the Guendes slipping out of the woodwork to join them.

Closing her eyes, she caught sight of the sun, a dim star in a cold black sea, a hesitant glimmer almost lost to the night. The vision ignited a deep ache in her heart, an irresistible desire to sing as she always had with Ghemena. So she lifted her voice in an ancient melody that once belonged to the magas of Moisehén, a poem of love composed for a single purpose, to bring the sun back to the world of the living.

Adiana was the first to join her. She took Eolyn's hand and graced the melody with the weave of her fine voice. Within moments, the other women of Moisehén accompanied them. Even Renate tried to enter the chorus, though some unseen power choked her back into quiet tears. The verse ended in resonating silence.

When Eolyn opened her eyes, Mage Corey was watching her, his expression unreadable amidst the shadows.

He raised the lights of the bayberry candles and turned his attention to the musicians. At his bidding the music resumed, but the circle did not break. This new melody, though unfamiliar to Eolyn, evoked a sense of deep memory.

Rishona and Mage Corey moved to the center of the floor, where they danced around each other, giving dimension to the space between them with elegant movements of their hands. The exchange was subtle yet sensual. The air became so charged Eolyn felt her skin tingle. They repeated the pattern three times before bringing the movement to a breathless finish.

Rishona withdrew, and Mage Corey extended his hand to Eolyn.

Instinct compelled Eolyn to step away, but Adiana reversed her momentum with a firm hand against the small of Eolyn's back.

"Mage Corey, I don't know this dance," Eolyn said as she stumbled forward. "I can't do it."

He took her hand and drew her close. His voice was low and infused with such confidence it sent a shiver through her. "This dance is in your blood, Sarah. It is as old as the land to which we were born. All you need do is follow the music with your heart."

Just as Mage Corey promised, Eolyn remembered. The steps returned to her, carried somehow on the fluid waves of rich music, on the slow heartbeat of the cold winter earth, on the sharp fire of Corey's essence, on the whispering spirit of the dead magas.

Eolyn's interpretation of the rite, though not nearly as skilled as Rishona's, carried a natural expression of their faith. The movement settled comfortably about her, like a favored old cloak with soft, warm folds.

In another age, Corey and Eolyn might have engaged in similar rites on countless occasions, he as Mage and she as Maga. Now everyone who watched thought magas no longer danced in Moisehén. Yet Eolyn sensed she had finally, completely exposed herself to Mage Corey, and she discovered she did not care. It seemed a small price to pay in exchange for this moment, for the sense of shared magic at her fingertips, for the steady heat of his silver gaze, for the fleeting vision of how he might respond to her caress.

When they finished, Eolyn withdrew, and Khelia joined the mage as his third and final partner. Although Eolyn had not witnessed the dance before this night, the maga knew it would end here with Khelia next to him, sparkling as she did like the stars against a black winter night. The last notes of the song resonated against the windowpanes. The lingering heat of the dance rose about Corey and Khelia like a bright cloud. They finished with an impassioned kiss.

The people broke into applause and laughter and loud demands for more music. When the musicians obliged, the guests reclaimed the floor. Mage Corey took Khelia's arm in his, and they departed for the night.

"What do you say now about his 'special interest'?" Eolyn asked Adiana, watching them leave.

Adiana shrugged. "Their union tonight is an offering of pleasure meant to give thanks to the Gods. It's not the same as falling in love. Not the same at all."

Eolyn drew an annoyed breath, but subdued the impulse to correct

Adiana. The time for thanksgiving would come in the morning, when the pale light of dawn announced the return of the sun. The communion shared by Khelia and Corey, if indeed sacred in aspect, would serve a different purpose altogether, helping illuminate the sun's path during its perilous journey back home.

But why argue about the nuances of the old rites? Her friend's words may have triggered Eolyn's anger, but Adiana was not the source of her discontent.

Adiana joined the dancers and beckoned Eolyn to follow, but the maga desisted. Restlessness had invaded her evening. Everything felt out of place, including her own person. Calling upon Winter Fox for invisibility, Eolyn retrieved her cloak and slipped out the door, hoping the familiar company of the forest would afford some peace.

The night received Eolyn with a frigid embrace. A handful of stars pressed through the clouds overhead. Fresh snow hushed her steps and muffled the sounds of celebration, bringing back memories of peaceful midwinter nights with Ghemena.

How remarkable, Eolyn now thought, that the company of one woman was more than sufficient for so many years, while the company of all these people left her feeling alone and incomplete.

Eolyn passed the Old Fir. A frosty breeze rushed through its high branches, stirring up the sharp aroma of its verdant needles. The tree spoke in a dialect Eolyn could not place, until she realized with great surprise it was whispering the language of metals.

The armband given to her by Achim responded with a silver hiss.

Eolyn gasped as the jewel uncoiled and traveled in sinuous spirals toward her wrist. The silver dragon emerged from her sleeve and came to rest in a loose coil in the palm of her hand. It lifted its head toward the tree as if in silent expectation.

They spoke at length, the Old Fir and the silver serpent, but Eolyn could not understand them. Despite her skill with the knife, she had never really mastered the language of metals.

Lowering its head, the bracelet flattened into a three-tiered coil, at the center of which emerged a single point of light. The jewel then slithered up past her elbow and coiled around her arm, coming to rest in its customary place.

Eolyn cupped her hands around the bright gift it left behind, her surprise transformed into awe. Many months had passed—indeed for her it felt like an eternity—since she held a white flame of magic in her hands. She brought it close to her lips and whispered, "Indulge this fantasy of mine."

Ehekaht, naeom aenthae.

She nurtured the fire with her breath until it shone like the morning star. Then she willed the glowing orb into the highest branches of the Old Fir, where it burst into a thousand tiny flames that settled twinkling among the snow draped branches.

Ehukae.

Eolyn savored the beauty of the sparkling tree, and the rich sensation of magic flowing through her veins, for longer than was perhaps prudent.

Snow began to drift down from the sky. Icy fingers of winter penetrated her cloak. Reluctant to let go of the magic, Eolyn nonetheless allowed the white flames to fade.

When she turned back toward the amber glow of the dining hall, her heart stopped. The shadow of a man stood in her path.

"Tahmir," she said. "How long have you been here?"

In a few paces he closed the distance between them, hushing her with the touch of his fingers upon her lips. With a soft snap of his fingers he ignited a warm orange glow in the air, a floating light reminiscent of the lanterns of the Guendes.

"Show me your hands," he said.

Fascinated, Eolyn brought them out from under her cloak. Tahmir pressed the orb against her palms until it penetrated her skin and filled her body with the warmth of the midsummer sun. Eolyn had never encountered magic like this, and she watched her hands in wonder as the glow faded and its essence spread through her.

"You cannot tell Mage Corey what you saw me do," she said, returning to the concern of the moment.

"You have nothing to fear from him."

"He sent you after me, didn't he?"

"I do not watch you at Mage Corey's bidding. I watch you because it gives me pleasure to do so."

Eolyn could not help but smile. Such comments were so very typical of Tahmir. He never lost the opportunity to remind a woman of her beauty. "But Mage Corey asked you to keep an eye on me."

He measured his words with care, as he always did. "You unleash something in your people. Especially in your kinswomen. The effect was subtle at first, but it grows. Corey has noticed this and wishes to understand it."

"And he solicited your assistance in the task." Anger rose inside of her. Why did no one respond to her questions with a straight answer? "Don't you tire of it, Tahmir? After all, you are under his vigilance too, you and your sister Rishona. We are all watched by Mage Corey. We are all played by his hand."

She could hardly see Tahmir in the dark but she felt his response, the curious raise of his brow, the puzzled frown on his sensual lips.

She folded her arms and turned back to the Old Fir. "It was a mistake for me to overwinter in East Selen. Mage Corey will win this game, for I do not even know what he is playing at."

"What game would you play, Sarah, if the rules were yours to craft?"

Tahmir shared this gift with Rishona, this ability to speak a truth so sharp one did not feel its quick descent into the heart. In an instant he had laid open the source of her discontent, and foreshadowed the path she would take because of it.

He will arrive not with the spring rites of Bel-Aethne, Ghemena had once promised, *but in his own time and of his own accord. He will carry the summer in his caress. He will bring companionship to your longest night.*

Always she had imagined *he* would be Achim, but now she was not so sure. Ghemena had not prepared her for uncertainty. Eolyn's longing for the old rites had never been stronger than on this night. She wanted real masks, not metaphorical ones. She wanted the intimate support of a true coven, not the distant song of dancers and musicians.

"You have told me that your people celebrate the same holidays we do." Her voice echoed calmly against the night.

"We honor the phases of the moon and the cycles of the sun, though our seasons and our harvests are laid out differently against the year."

"Do you observe the practice that was once the tradition of our mages and magas, an offering of pleasure given to the Gods?"

In the months since they first met, she had posed many such questions to Tahmir, hoping to better understand his people. So she knew her words could lead to a lengthy conversation about the nature of Syrnte rites, the high festivals during which they were observed, and their interpretation in the context of his faith. She felt a small surge of relief when he chose the simplest of all answers.

"Yes."

"Then make this offering with me tonight." Her voice held steady, surprising given the sudden pounding of her heart. "Help me guide the sun back to Moisehén."

Tahmir did not hesitate, nor did he rush. He stepped forward, drew back her hood and sent his long fingers into the thick tresses of her hair. He tilted her face and set his lips upon hers.

Raised as a maga, Eolyn knew her body well, having explored its contours and recesses in midnight communion with the Spirit of the Forest. But she had never been touched like this by another, not since her farewell to Achim, and that exchange was abrupt, plagued by the

Karin Rita Gastreich

awkwardness of recently discovered passion.

In contrast, Tahmir drew her to him as if he had decided long ago exactly how to kiss her when given the opportunity. Eolyn savored her response, the thin sheen of sparks that leapt upon her breath, the arch of her neck as it ceded to his exploratory descent, the shiver of pleasure ignited by the touch of his tongue upon her skin, the white-hot shaft of heat that shot from her core into the snow covered earth below.

Eolyn lost her balance. Catching herself against Tahmir, she spread her fingers over the resonating plain of his chest. She recognized his intoxicating aroma. It was the same rich dance of spices Rishona had given her when they visited the market that first day in Selkynsen.

He caressed her with the heat of his breath. "This decision must be yours. It must be freely made."

"It is." She drew his lips back to hers. "This is my choice."

CHAPTER TWENTY

Eostar

AFTER THEIR FIRST MIDWINTER'S OFFERING, many nights came to pass where Eolyn sought the warmth of Tahmir's bed. Each encounter revealed another undiscovered path across the solid contours of his body. Eolyn delighted in the response of his sun-warmed skin to the curve of her palms, in the silky fall of his black hair between her tapered fingers, in the sensual pull of his lips upon her breasts, the curve of her abdomen, the sacred mystery of her sex. Over and over she cultivated the flame of his desire and lost herself to the pleasure of his strength, until the ecstasy of the gods bound them and abandoned them, leaving her nestled against him in sweet, satiated exhaustion.

Her magic took root in their passion and grew with a ferocity she found difficult to contain. At first she was certain this sudden expansion of power, building like a hot current inside of her, would not escape Corey's notice. Yet the mage, who had shown unrelenting curiosity about every other aspect of her life, expressed no interest in her relationship with Tahmir. This surprised her, and then fueled her wariness. She took care not to repeat any acts of magic in Tahmir's presence. Nor did she speak with him about the truth of her training. Despite their intimacy, Eolyn could not wrest from her imagination the thought that anything revealed to Tahmir would eventually be known by Mage Corey.

Spring announced its arrival in East Selen much as it always had in the South Woods, with the crystalline shower of ice melting from tree branches, the tentative song of the first arriving wood thrush, and fresh blossoms of rose aethne suspended low over newly exposed leaf litter.

With the Circle's new season set to start after Eostar, rehearsals increased in frequency and intensity. Tents were checked for wear and damage, equipment repaired, and costumes aired, washed and mended. The celebration of Spring Equinox, though undertaken with the same enthusiasm the Circle dedicated to all its festivals, proved a less sumptuous affair than Winter Solstice.

Karin Rita Gastreich

This was a time of mixed emotions for Eolyn. Even as she prepared for the journey to the King's City, the thought of saying goodbye to Tahmir and other friends she had made in the Circle filled her with a strange melancholy.

A couple weeks after the equinox, as crates were packed and carts loaded, a sickening rumble sounded from deep inside the earth. Eolyn, whose senses had not detected such terrifying movement since the day the Riders destroyed her village, mounted the first horse within reach. She would have fled into the forest without looking back had Tahmir not caught the horse's bridle and stopped her flight.

"It is only the King's messenger," he assured her. "Come, let us see what news they bring."

Subduing her panic, Eolyn dismounted. Tahmir took her hand and walked with her to the front of the manor, where everyone was gathering. A small company of men bore down upon them. Armor flashed under the spring sun. Purple and silver flags snapped in the wind. Hooves kicked up clumps of dirt.

When the men drew to a halt in front of the manor, Mage Corey stepped forward to greet them. The messenger did not dismount but turned to all assembled and announced in a cry fit for a city square:

"The King is dead!"

The words knocked Mage Corey back a few steps. In the year since Eolyn had known him, she had never witnessed such an expression on Corey's face, such blatant acknowledgement of the entirely unexpected.

After a moment of stunned silence, Mage Corey regained composure. He turned to his people and led them in the only response acceptable under the circumstances.

"*Long live the King!*"

It was well known in Moisehén that practitioners of magic, if the Gods favored them with a natural death, lived to be very old. Indeed, their age proved difficult to calculate because youth clung to their features. This was not due, as many might have imagined, to secret spells, magical elixirs or pacts with supernatural forces, but to the simple fact that mages and magas did not live in terms of days, months, and years. For them, life flowed in immeasurable waves of experience. Thus, the demise of Kedehen during a period of relative peace came as a surprise to all the people of Moisehén, including his son and only heir, Prince Akmael.

The accident occurred in the days preceding Eostar, when the King hosted traditional spring tournaments. The finest warriors gathered from the four provinces, their armor a blaze of silver over heavy warhorses.

Long wooden galleries were erected outside the city walls for the nobility of Moisehén, who sat resplendent beneath the bright banners of their houses. Gold chains glinted upon the men's velvet doublets, and women's veils fluttered in the wind.

Honoring the custom of his ancestors, Kedehen opened the tournament by accepting a ceremonial challenge from one of the recently sworn knights of the provinces. The identity of his opponent was determined by chance, and on that sunny morning, Sir Borten of Moehn was drawn. A tall, lean youth with just a hint of a beard, Borten was the youngest man to ride that day.

As Borten mounted his horse, the crowd mocked him. Moehn was not known for the skill and valor of its fighters. Yet Borten held his head high and refused to play the coward.

Admirable, Akmael thought, as the knight accepted his shield and balanced his lance, for the young man had little chance against the Mage King.

Akmael had heard the thunder of his father's horse plowing down the length of the lists countless times. He had seen Kedehen unseat every man who ever challenged him, and the King had killed more than a few.

Yet today as the horses approached each other, the tremor of the earth beneath their hooves took on an unsettling rhythm. A slip on a stone perhaps, or a hidden muddy spot, interrupted the cadence.

When they met, the King's lance glanced off the knight's shield, eliciting a roar of surprise from the onlookers. Borten's weapon drove into the King's helmet with a harsh splintering rasp. Wood shattered against metal as the lance tip broke. The knight's horse rushed passed the King and reached the end of the run, where Borten turned his steed, dropped the broken lance, and lifted his visor.

The crowd was silent. Kedehen's horse slowed to a stop just after the impact. The King wavered in his seat. Long howling cries rose from the galleries as ladies and lords realized what had happened. Akmael ran toward his father. Just behind him he heard the heavy pounding of Sir Drostan's feet.

Kedehen fell as they reached his horse. With Drostan's help, the prince caught the regent and lowered him to the ground.

The impact of the lance had bent and lifted Kedehen's visor. Blood flowed freely from a twisted knot of wood and flesh that had once been his eye.

"My Lord King," Sir Drostan prompted.

The regent said nothing, but drew a slow ragged breath.

A mage warrior of the Old Orders, Drostan had served the House of Vortingen faithfully since the time of Akmael's grandfather, Urien.

Though strands of gray ran through his red beard, his strength seemed undiminished by time. The man was built like a bear. He laid his powerful fingers next to the wound and then looked up at Akmael. A furrow settled upon Drostan's brow, and a slight tremor invaded his voice. "It has driven deep, my Lord Prince."

Akmael understood at once his world was about to change.

Sir Borten approached and fell to his knees a few feet away. The knight covered his face with gloved hands and wailed supplications to the Gods.

"Fool!" Lord Felton came up behind Borten and struck him on the head. Not once had Akmael witnessed the congenial Felton lift his hand against another man, but that day the patriarch of Moehn drew his sword and might have run the knight through, had not the King lifted a trembling hand.

"Wait." Kedehen's voice rasped like dry leaves.

"Lord Felton, stay your hand!" commanded the prince.

Felton paused, his bushy white brows crouched low over angry blue eyes.

"It is my father's wish," Akmael said.

The portly man sheathed his sword. By now, several others had approached, including Lords Herensen of Selkynsen and Baramon of Selen.

Kedehen laid a hand on the prince's forearm. "Let him be, Akmael. Let the boy go."

It was an inexplicable request from a King who had rarely shown mercy during his reign.

"He dealt a...fair blow." Kedehen exhaled a long shaky breath. "The will of the Gods...Do not send him to the Afterlife, he might cause me more trouble there." Kedehen let go a hoarse chuckle, perplexing Akmael even further. The prince had never seen his father so much as smile. "Pardon him. Bring him to the City. He is a knight to have at your side."

"My Lord Prince, if you would allow me." The court healer, High Mage Rezlyn, appeared at Akmael's side. His dark beard was streaked with red and silver, his hazel eyes filled with anxiety.

Akmael stood and turned the King over to Rezlyn's care. Kedehen closed his good eye. His breath continued shallow but even. Rezlyn's aged fingers traced the wound with great care.

Borten remained hunched on his knees, his blond hair casting a thin shadow over a smooth face. Sweat ran in rivulets down his neck.

Though Kedehen had commanded Borten be spared, to pardon a King's assassin in front of the assembled nobles of Moisehén would give the appearance of weakness, something Akmael could not afford in this of all moments.

"Arrest him." Akmael nodded to the King's guard. "We will see to his fate once we have attended to my father."

In the sanctuary of Kedehen's chambers, High Mage Rezlyn removed all he could of the splintered wood. He washed the wound and applied fresh poultices every few hours. He varied the portions of yarrow, vervain, tormentil, john's wort and fox's clote to fight infection, and added fennel and elecampane so that the delicate tissues of the eye might heal. He administered cowbane in hopes of abating the agony.

Despite Rezlyn's tireless efforts, within days the flesh surrounding the wound began to rot. Puss flowed in a sour mass from the ruined socket. The King's chambers filled with the stench of death.

Reluctantly, medicinal herbs and healing ointments were replaced by abundant winter sage and lavender. Thick midnight blue candles were lit in preparation for Kedehen's passage to the Afterlife.

Many nobles and mages requested a final audience with the King, but he would receive no one except his healer and his son. Even his lifelong mentor, the wizard Tzeremond, was driven from the room with mad shouts and curses.

The King was losing his mind as well as his life.

Prince Akmael remained at his father's side from the time of the accident until the moment of his death. Those unfamiliar with the ways of the royals might have interpreted this as an expression of love, but theirs had never been an affectionate relationship. Still, Akmael felt a profound sense of loss at Kedehen's departure. Since the day Queen Briana had brought him into this world, Akmael had been prepared to assume his father's place. Yet no one warned him of the heavy sense of solitude that would descend upon him in this moment.

"Akmael." It was the seventh morning following the accident when Kedehen called to his son one last time. The pale blue light of predawn filtered through the narrow windows of the King's chambers. "Are we alone?"

Akmael glanced up at High Mage Rezlyn, who had kept vigil with him these seven days. With a reverent nod, the healer departed.

Kedehen opened his feverish eye and fixed it on his son. The flickering light of the candles cast his image in shades of gray and yellow. One side of his face had bloated under the pressure of accumulated rot, the other had sunk into a landscape of dark pits and hollows. His mouth was slack and exuded a foul air. Still Akmael leaned forward to hear his words. He took his father's burning hand in his.

Kedehen's voice came hoarse and strained. "You found one, didn't you? One that you never told us about. Clever, treacherous boy."

125

"Found what, my Lord King?" For days now his father's ravings had confused Akmael. He wondered if he, too, would lose all sense of reason when his time came.

"A maga," Kedehen hissed. "You found a maga."

Akmael withdrew in surprise, though he did not release his father's hand.

Eolyn.

It had been years since the Prince had known anything of his friend from the South Woods, though the Gods knew he had tried to find her. In all this time he had not spoken of Eolyn to anyone.

"The Queen calls to me from across the Plains of the Dead," Kedehen said. "She has whispered your secrets to me."

"You can hear Mother?"

"Deadly witch, that Briana…" A retching cough overtook Kedehen. Akmael brought a flask of herbed wine to his lips. The King drank and wheezed. "By the Gods I loved her…love her still. She'll try to kill you."

"The Queen?"

"The maga."

"She does not know how to kill."

"The sword she speaks to does."

"The girl understands too little of swords to—"

"She is no longer a girl. This weapon loves her. It will do as she asks." More nonsense. A blade could no more love a woman than a horse could fly, and Eolyn had never mastered the sword. "Take great care with her. Keep her alive. Seduce her, or she will destroy you."

Akmael shook his head. His father could not be speaking of his childhood companion. There must be someone else, another maga in the kingdom who posed a threat.

"Seduce her, Akmael. Convince her to bear your sons. Destroy any sisters she has…Do as I did. Only then will your power be absolute."

Kedehen tried to inhale, but his body revolted at the effort. Violent convulsions shook him. When at last the seizures stopped, his grip on Akmael's hand relaxed. His ashen lips curved in a thin smile as he released his final words.

"I knew the Gods would save one for you."

CHAPTER TWENTY-ONE

A New King

PRINCE AKMAEL ASSUMED the Crown of Vortingen on the twelfth day after his father's death. The ceremony took place on the Stone Foundation of Vortingen, a smooth outcrop of granite just north of the castle walls.

Sir Drostan stood alongside eleven other members of the Council of High Mages. Opposite them were patriarchs of the provinces, Lords Herensen, Baramon, and Felton among them. A grim magic floated on the morning mist, as if the surprise of Kedehen's death had not yet worn off. Low thunder and dim flashes of lightning crowded the northern horizon. Careful expressions of sorrow and regret masked the noblemen's thoughts, which Sir Drostan imagined laden with treacherous possibilities, now that Kedehen's iron hand had been obliterated.

The natural contours of the Stone Foundation mimicked the shape of the lands of Moisehén: the plains of the north, the wide river of Selkynsen to the west, the rolling hills that gave way to mountainous terrain toward the south and east. This was the place where Dragon granted the crown to the ancient warrior chief Vortingen. With each passing generation, the castle he built grew until it became the formidable complex that now occupied almost half the hillside.

Master Tzeremond presided over the ceremony, offering the silver circlet in solemn song to East, South, West and North, before placing it on the young royal's head. Standing tall in his flowing robes, the wizard raised his staff high and invoked the sacred name of Dragon.

Ehekatu naeomed ahmuni ay des Vortingen!
Ehekatu naeomed ano Kaht, Akmael!

In a single movement, mages and nobles knelt before their new regent.

Afterwards, the King descended from the castle and passed through the city streets on horseback. Tzeremond rode at his right hand with the High Mages behind them. The attending nobles and knights of Moisehén followed.

Despite the damp air, people came out in great numbers. Women threw lilies in their path, a symbol of hope for a renewed and peaceful realm. People sang and danced. Still, the reception paled in comparison to Sir Drostan's memories of the ascent of King Urien some two generations before.

A mere boy riding on his grandfather's broad shoulders, Drostan had watched Urien progress through streets filled with colorful banners and boisterous song. Couples danced in his path, and children ran laughing among the plodding horses. Behind the King, mage and maga warriors marched some three thousand strong, their flaming staffs held high and their skillfully handled swords shining in the summer sun.

For young Drostan, the knights of Vortingen had seemed a dreary complement to the charismatic power of those mages. That was the day he had declared, with the pure enthusiasm of a very young child, "I want to be a mage warrior, too!"

It sobered him now to remember the naïve hopes of that little boy. He never imagined it his destiny to see those gifted men and women tear each other apart on the battlefield. Nor had he expected his oath would obligate him to take the great tradition of Caedmon, once shared by thousands, and entrust it to the fate of a single prince.

Only a few hours had passed after Akmael's coronation when Sir Drostan received his first summons from the new King. The knight arrived at the council chamber to find the regent deep in conversation with Master Tzeremond. They sat at a long table made from a single panel of solid black oak, the same place where Kedehen had met with his Council and made the most important decisions of his reign.

Military and magical artifacts adorned the room. Large windows along the southern wall afforded a strategic view of the rolling plains below. Like all the chambers of the King's apartments, it had been cleaned, aired and laid with fresh rushes. Yet Drostan could not rid his senses of the rot that had destroyed the King's face, and he felt Kedehen's ghost lingering in the shadows.

The guards who admitted Drostan closed the doors behind him. Akmael beckoned him to approach.

"Master Tzeremond has informed me of the elaborate project undertaken at my father's bidding to better understand foreign and exotic forms of magic," Akmael said as Drostan took his place. "It seems to me a lot of effort for a threat that is at best suspected."

"The shadow of the magas clings to this land." Tzeremond's lips were drawn, and his bony hands worked against his rowan staff. "Despite our most diligent efforts at eradicating them, there are murmurings in

Selen of a snow witch who inhabits the eastern forests. And last summer just outside Moehn, we had a confirmed report of subversive witchcraft. A woman traveling alone tried to seduce two boys. When they resisted, she shape shifted into a lynx and attacked them before disappearing into the night."

While Tzeremond spoke, Drostan kept a careful eye on his new liege. The young King had inherited all the hard lines of his father's face, but had not yet mastered the use of that stony countenance. Something flickered behind his dark eyes at the mention of the witch from Moehn, though it was gone before Sir Drostan could capture its essence.

"Two witches do not comprise an armed rebellion." Akmael's gaze turned to Sir Drostan, inviting the knight to speak. Was this why he had been summoned, to mediate in the first disagreement between King and wizard? The thought did not please Sir Drostan at all.

"My Lord King, as you know, I leave the question of how to find and exterminate subversive magic to Master Tzeremond." Sir Drostan directed a respectful nod toward the wizard. "Though I agree it is an uneasy peace your father achieved. The possibility of an armed rebellion can never be taken lightly, especially at the dawn of a prince's reign. As Master Tzeremond may have informed you, this past fall border guards intercepted a small caravan filled with arms. What they carried was not much, but it was meant for battle. We cannot tell how many more of these shipments have entered our lands unnoticed during recent years."

"Did you question the drivers?"

"There were only three men who accompanied the carts. All of them tried to escape, and just one was apprehended alive."

"The King turned him over to us for questioning," Master Tzeremond added, "but he perished before revealing anything."

"Perished, Master Tzeremond?"

"My Lord King, as you are aware, the more stubborn the criminal the more rigorous the techniques applied. High Mage Baedon oversaw the process personally, prolonging the interrogation for weeks, but in the end the prisoner did not last long enough to give us the information we sought."

"What your father and the Council suspected was an armed movement organized through the use of primitive and foreign magic," Drostan said. "The integration of such forces, if not stopped in time, could pose a serious threat to the peace of the kingdom."

"Why was I not informed of this while my father was alive?"

The question generated an awkward silence. Sir Drostan inadvertently met Tzeremond's gaze. Kedehen held no one above suspicion of treachery, except perhaps this wizard who once sat at his right hand.

"He thought I might be involved." Akmael spoke as if realizing it for the first time. "He suspected I might use this movement to betray him!"

"My Lord King," Tzeremond responded smoothly, "your father bore you great respect. In his heart, he did not wish to believe you capable of treason, but any prudent King would take similar precautions when it comes to his closest heirs. It is not wise to let pride or affection cloud one's judgment when defending the Crown. Your father understood this, as must you."

"I see." If the King found Tzeremond's paternalistic tone insulting, he did not reveal it. "Very well. Any grievance I have with my father will have to wait until the Afterlife. Master Tzeremond, you will keep me informed of your findings. I would also have an audience with High Mage Thelyn, and any other mage involved in this project."

"As you wish, my Lord King."

"Sir Drostan, we need to increase our vigilance along the borders and monitor the activity of our blacksmiths. You will also report back to me with a full assessment of the defenses of this city and our readiness in the event of an uprising."

Sir Drostan nodded. He had much to say regarding their readiness in the event of an attack, though little of it could be spoken in front of Tzeremond. The Crown of Vortingen commanded foot soldiers and knights aplenty, and the fortress was as impenetrable as it had ever been. But the class of mage warriors was near extinct. Master Tzeremond had anointed only a handful of High Mages these past twenty years, and just one of them, Akmael, had been trained in the arts of war. The prince had grown into an accomplished fighter under Sir Drostan's tutelage, but the legions that once defended the heart and soul of Moisehén were gone.

"May I suggest, my Lord King," Tzeremond said, "that it would be useful at this early stage in your reign to organize a progress by the Riders, so the people might be reminded of the price of treason?"

Just what the wizard would recommend. A band of knights without honor to ravage the countryside. Kedehen would not have hesitated at the suggestion, but Akmael paused. His jaw worked against some unspoken thought.

"My Lord King?" Tzeremond prompted.

"No, Master Tzeremond. No. I would have the Riders disbanded."

Sir Drostan's breath stopped short in surprise.

"That was my father's way. It is not mine."

"My Lord King," Tzeremond stammered, "I do not think it wise."

"I have not solicited your opinion, Master Tzeremond. This is a military matter, and the King has decided. Sir Drostan, see that it is done."

"Yes, my Lord King." Drostan could taste Tzeremond's fury like a stinging mist. The wizard was not accustomed to having his opinion overlooked by the King of Moisehén.

"There is another matter we have not yet settled, Drostan," the King continued. "Regarding Sir Borten. We will respect my father's wishes. The man is not to return to Moehn. Keep him here for one year and have him perform whatever service you deem appropriate in support of our men-at-arms. At the end of that period, if he has served well and proves worthy, we will consider incorporating him as a Knight of Vortingen."

"My Lord King." Sir Drostan nodded. Though less pleased by this command, he was bound by duty to obey.

Tzeremond moved as if to speak, but Akmael raised his hand and dismissed them both. "That will be all."

Though the wizard held his tongue as they departed, Drostan was not fooled. Tzeremond would seek a way to make the King's will reflect his own, and he would not rest until he succeeded.

CHAPTER TWENTY-TWO

Summons

SOON AFTER COREY'S CIRCLE set up in the town of Selen, High Mage Thelyn paid them a visit. The Council Member arrived on horseback with a small escort of men-at-arms bearing the colors and crest of the royal house of Vortingen.

Dressed in attire that accrued to his station, Thelyn dismounted with easy grace. A square cap sat upon his head, and he carried a staff of polished cherry wood. His forest green cloak hung in long, loose folds. Tall and well groomed, Thelyn wore this uniform very well.

Mage Corey greeted Thelyn warmly, glad to see his old friend. Corey and Thelyn were of a similar age and had studied magic together in the King's City. Though Thelyn did not share Corey's natural talent, he had a higher tolerance for Tzeremond's character and an innate skill for the political maneuvers necessary to excel in his Order. He commanded an impressive knowledge of Primitive Magic, and had supported the unique work of the Circle from the very beginning.

Together they retired to the privacy of Mage Corey's tent. Their meeting, conducted in quiet tones, extended for over an hour. When the two finally emerged, Mage Corey called Rishona and asked her to oversee the preparation of Thelyn's tent. Then Corey sent for Mistress Renate.

He moved straight to the point as soon as Renate appeared. "You are summoned to the King's City."

She froze a few paces short of the chair he had set out for her, face white as a lily.

"In truth, we are all summoned," Corey said, "but your summons is immediate. You will depart with High Mage Thelyn tomorrow."

"Tomorrow?" Renate's usually sharp voice came small and weak. "Why? What have I done?"

"You have not done anything, dear Renate." Mage Corey took her hand and guided her to the chair. He poured a drink and insisted she take it. "At least, Thelyn is not here under the open pretense of arresting you.

132

Somehow he has managed to convince Master Tzeremond and our new King that it would be appropriate, in the spring of this great reign, to resurrect some of the old customs. To recreate, as it were, the former glory of the High Festivals of Moisehén."

"But what does this have to do with me? Why should their plan obligate me to return to that place?"

Corey drew a slow breath. It pained him to ask this of Renate. On the few occasions the Circle visited the King's City, he had always given the mistress leave not to accompany them. She despised returning to the place where she had abandoned her magic and watched her sisters die.

"Thelyn needs a woman to help him. Someone who remembers the role of the magas in the old festivals. Someone capable of constructing the image of those rituals within appropriate bounds, as determined by the enlightened era in which we now live. He believes your work with the Circle makes you just the person for the task."

"It is one thing to choreograph a few dances for the Circle, but what he is asking cannot be done. We can imitate the old rites, but without true magas…" Her voice broke off and her face twisted under the burden of unspoken thoughts. "It cannot be done."

"I am afraid you have no choice. Thelyn carries orders from the King. You must assist him, whether or not you think the task is possible."

Renate lifted the cup to her lips, gaze focused on some inner world. "Which festival are we talking about?"

"Bel-Aethne."

"I see." She lowered the drink and met his gaze. "They can't do it without representation of Aithne. And how can they represent Aithne without reminding our people of the magas?"

"That, dear Renate, is precisely your task."

"Very well. I will do this thing you ask of me, Corey. But you must tell me what this is really about. They don't have to resurrect Bel-Aethne. They could just as easily wait until Summer Solstice."

Corey considered his response. "I confess, Renate, I am not entirely certain what they are up to. I do know the rest of the Circle will follow you soon. Thelyn expects to incorporate our people fully. Artists and mages are being brought from all over the kingdom. Some have even been invited from neighboring territories. The people of Moisehén will flock to this event. Perhaps all the Council seeks is to consolidate the power of the new King under a spirit of celebration. Yet knowing Master Tzeremond, I believe there is a deeper objective. I suspect he is planning his own assessment of the status of magic in Moisehén."

"And a well-constructed Festival of Bel-Aethne would be excellent bait for women of special ability," Renate realized. "A true homage toward Aithne under a new King might be just enough to cause suspected witches, and their supporters, to let down their guard."

Corey chose to neither confirm nor deny her conclusions.

"Did Thelyn speak to you of this?" she asked.

"Not explicitly. He appeared caught up in his enthusiasm for the project—and for the opportunity to work with you, I might add. But he is a member of the High Council, and he knows every decision they make has a dual purpose."

"Thelyn has always been a friend to us. I would not be here, working with you, if it weren't for him. Even so, to arrive unannounced and force me back to that place under these circumstances…Anything could happen to me in the City."

"High Mage Thelyn assumes personal responsibility for your safety. He has given me his word you will come to no harm. You will stay with him as his guest until the rest of the Circle arrives, at which time you will be free to join us again."

"As his guest or as his prisoner?"

Corey leaned forward and refilled her cup. "For a woman of your talent, dear Renate, it is all the same."

The morning of Renate's departure dawned gray and without spirit. Though everyone turned out to wish the mistress a safe journey, their mood was as colorless as the sky. Only High Mage Thelyn acted with enthusiasm, but his cheerful words did little to return the blood to Renate's cheeks.

The old mistress held each member of the Circle in a lengthy embrace. When she released the last of her students, tears sprang from her eyes.

Mage Corey helped Renate onto her horse. He pressed her fingers between his palms and tried to reinforce her courage with his magic, but Renate's lips remained tight and her face ashen.

"After Bel-Aethne, everything will change," Rishona said, as they watched the travelers depart down the long road to the King's City. "We must enjoy the days that are left to us, for we will not be together like this again."

During the days that followed, the Circle chased away their melancholy with vibrant performances and spontaneous post-show festivities. Mage Corey did his best to join these efforts, but the forced joviality failed to dispel the weight inside his heart.

Restless visions invaded his sleep, of black shadows and violent explosions, of his father's face when the soldiers burst into their home, of the tortured screams of Corey's mother on the night she died.

Briana leapt out of the shadows like a hunted animal. She grasped

Corey's small hand and dragged him into the forest. They fled toward an ever-deeper night until they were lost in suffocating darkness. Still they ran, as fast as they could, but it was not fast enough. Swords found them, spinning through the sky. Corey felt the cold cut of steel as it drove hard into his flesh. He heard their metal voices ring with the triumph of death.

The mage woke with a start. Sweat trickled down his neck. He glanced around the dark tent.

Someone is here, watching me.

Corey's hand found the knife under his pillow. With a snap of his fingers he set a nearby lamp aglow.

"Show yourself," he demanded

A hooded figure moved cautiously into the light.

He recognized her at once and sighed in relief. "Khelia. You should not have come."

With the grace of a cat, she extinguished the lamp and knelt beside him. "It is time."

"Khelia…"

"We are not as prepared as we would have liked." She spoke as if anticipating his objections. "But you know what is said of this new King, of the magic he commands. We cannot hesitate. We must strike now, before he consolidates his power."

"They have Renate."

She responded with a sharp intake of breath. "What? How?"

"Thelyn came unannounced and took her just a few days ago. She is to assist him in organizing the High Ceremonies of Bel-Aethne. We have been ordered to follow, and will set out for the King's City tomorrow."

"Thelyn knows the affection you feel for Renate." Anxiety sharpened her voice. "He holds her hostage to guarantee you will do as he asks."

"Of course he does."

"You put the entire Circle at risk if you take them there!"

"I'm afraid I have little choice."

"And what of you, Corey?" She rested her hand on his. "What if they are after you? We lose everything if we lose you."

Her words moved him deeper than she could know. "That is not true, Khelia. I am but an instrument in a much larger process. This does not depend on me. Not anymore."

The mountain warrior lapsed into troubled silence.

Corey heard soft sounds of field crickets and the quiet rush of a starlit breeze. Somewhere outside, moonflowers were blooming. Their sweet aroma reminded him of the nights he had shared with this beautiful and spirited warrior.

Karin Rita Gastreich

When he spoke again, it was in reassuring tones. "Don't worry about me, or Renate, for that matter. I have always turned Tzeremond's plans to our advantage, and this will be no exception. Tell Ernan to wait until we've finished with Bel-Aethne. I will use the festival to assess the strengths and weaknesses of our new King. After that, we will decide upon our next move."

Khelia nodded and kissed him on the lips. Then she slipped away without a sound.

Letting go a long, slow exhale, Corey reclined on his bed and stared into the darkness.

An accursed mess, that's what this is.

A simple trick of fate had converted all his elaborate schemes to rubble.

There was a time, not too long ago, when he might have put a stop to their plans with a few pointed conversations. Not anymore. This movement had assumed a life of its own. The best he could hope for now was to navigate the coming chaos without getting himself killed.

Just play the game carefully, as you've always done.

He shifted his position and bade himself to sleep.

It's not that bad, after all. You still have Sarah, and that is no small thing.

He smiled and surrendered to the tide of his dreams.

The Gods could not have given him a better prize with which to negotiate his fate.

Chapter Twenty-Three

Sedition

EOLYN COULD NOT CONTAIN her joy at the turn of events. At last, she would visit Achim's home! And she did not have to give up her place in the Circle to do so.

Her excitement did not diminish her sensitivity to the mood of her companions, all of whom perceived the King's City as a dark cloud on their collective horizon.

Mage Corey, in particular, had never been so distracted. His vexation broke to the surface constantly. He had grown cross and impatient. He even retreated from his incessant vigilance of Eolyn.

Though she appreciated the unexpected freedom, the maga soon discovered she missed Corey's company. One afternoon, feeling the landscape somehow incomplete without him, Eolyn sought out the mage and invited him to join her walk.

Corey hesitated. For a moment, Eolyn thought he would refuse. But then he grinned and threw a cloak around his shoulders. "It's not every day you step forward with an invitation, Sarah."

Spring had advanced into early summer, with warm southern winds pushing back the cold breath of the north. Cultivated fields adorned the fertile hills in sunlit shades of green. Apple and cherry trees shed their fragrant blossoms to begin the slow swelling of flowers into fruits. Songbirds worked tirelessly at feeding their nestlings, and dragonflies buzzed low over sparkling streams.

"You must be pleased we are visiting the City of Moisehén," Mage Corey said. "Perhaps you will find your friend."

"I have many friends now, Mage Corey. The finding of this one does not carry as much weight as before." Eolyn spoke truthfully. She had put off her departure for weeks now, not because she feared traveling alone, but because she did not want to say goodbye. For all its mysteries and deceptions, the Circle had become her home. "But yes, I am pleased. Even if I don't find him, at least I will know the home of his youth."

Karin Rita Gastreich

"Is he a mage, this acquaintance of yours?"

"He had just finished his studies of Middle Magic when we last saw each other."

"Did he plan to continue under Tzeremond?"

"I don't know." Eolyn hedged on the truth. She knew where Corey's questions were leading. Only a small number of students completed their training in High Magic under Tzeremond. If Achim was ever anointed High Mage, Corey almost certainly knew him.

"The study of High Magic under that wizard changes a man," Corey said. "He will not be the boy you once knew. You must be very careful, Sarah. Do not be too quick to trust him."

The frankness of his tone disturbed her. "We were close as children. I have faith he remembers our friendship well."

"If he mastered magic as taught by Tzeremond, he will find the seam of your ward and unravel it for all to see."

Eolyn's words caught in her throat. For several moments, the only sound was the rhythm of their feet against gravel.

"I don't understand what you are talking about," she managed to say.

"Sarah." Mage Corey placed a hand on her arm, forcing her to stop and look at him. "In a matter of days we will enter the citadel of military and magical power in this kingdom. Every member of the Circle understands the dangers of that place except for you, and I understand the unique risk that will accrue to each person who follows me, *except for you*. That you have some ability is obvious, but it has been impossible for me to assess the extent of your gifts. I would much rather leave you behind, for I do not tolerate unknown risks. Yet Thelyn has inventoried all of our members. During his visit, he wrote each face upon his memory. So the face that does not arrive with us in the City will be the first one he looks for when the new purges begin. I will not abandon you to that fate, but I must know who it is I have taken under my wing before we enter that place."

Eolyn searched Corey's expression, the fine lines of his face. Though she sensed sincerity, she did not dare trust him. "I am Sarah of South Moehn, just as I told you. I know a few tricks that my grandmother taught me, and nothing more."

Corey's features hardened, but then something broke behind his expression. What Eolyn saw in that moment caught her off guard: sadness, coupled with the realization of what it might mean to him to lose her. Unsettled, she averted her gaze.

Mage Corey touched her chin and brought her eyes back to his. "The problem is this, dear Sarah: Just the sight of you inspires images of the Magas of Old."

"They cannot burn me for my appearance."

"You do not know what they can do. They will stop at nothing in their quest to extinguish all memory of that noble and ancient line of witches." He released her and turned away.

Confused by the mix of signals that just passed between them, Eolyn let him to retreat into pensive silence.

The sun lay low on the western horizon, casting an auburn glow over trees and fields. A cool breeze penetrated her summer cloak, making her shiver.

Mage Corey extended his arm and bade Eolyn to come to his side. He placed a firm hand on her shoulder and pointed to the crystalline surface of a nearby stream. "Do you see how the dragonflies move across the water? The pair of them there, locked together in flight?"

"Yes, Mage Corey."

"That is how we will be in the City of Moisehén. You are not to leave my side during the time we are there. You will not perform with the rest of the dancers in the Ceremony of Primitive Magic, and you will stand with me, in representation of Aithne, during the Fire Ceremony. As for all other events, public and private, you will accompany me unless otherwise instructed. I will not take you to the city unless you give me your word on this."

Eolyn's anger at this ridiculous proposition was tempered only by the nascent realization that perhaps Mage Corey truly desired to protect her. Still, she would have thrown these terms in his face and marched off on her own, had not a clear advantage of his plan occurred to her.

Achim, she thought. *Mage Corey can lead me to Achim.*

"Very well," she said. "It will be as you wish."

The caravan departed Selen and snaked its way westward through verdant hills. Woodland birds followed their progress, darting with eager chirps between scattered trees and groves. Sporadic, lazy showers drifted over the landscape, leaving in their wake a golden light that illuminated the wet earth with crystal colors of Dragon. At nightfall, the company made camp beside clear brooks, and the musicians brought out their instruments to complement the subtle sounds of twilight.

Mage Corey paced their travel so that on the morning of the seventh day, they crossed the final ridge of Selen and began their descent toward the low undulating plains of the ruling province of Moisehén. From a distance, the city and fortress of Vortingen shone like a polished stone over grazed and cultivated fields.

As the caravan drew near, the city grew into slated rooftops and stone spires. The castle occupied a ridge above, its fortifications built

139

upon sharp cliffs that descended from the flat summit. Only the northern face of the mountain remained free of construction.

Eolyn suspected this was the sacred site Ghemena had told her about, the Stone Foundation where Dragon had crowned the warrior chief Vortingen and charged all his descendants with the protection of Moisehén. She asked Mage Corey if her excursions with him would include a visit to the Foundation. He found that very amusing, the thought of a woman setting foot in such a sacred place.

When at last they arrived at the city wall, High Mage Thelyn rode out to meet them accompanied by Renate, who no longer exhibited the frightened pallor that had consumed her in Selen. The Council Member escorted them to a campsite set aside for the Circle, complete with its own water well and recently supplied firewood. Located just outside the main gates, the site provided ready access to the city, as well as easy vigilance of the Circle for anyone who might care to watch from the high ramparts.

Soon after the Circle set up camp, Renate met with the women in their tent. Savoring the stiff, peppery tea Rishona had prepared for the occasion, Eolyn listened enraptured as Renate told them elaborate stories of her stay in the King's City. The mistress spoke at length about the complicated preparations for the festival of Bel-Aethne, describing with some pride the many debates that went into resurrecting the different stages of the festival.

"It has been a difficult task, but we managed to organize almost everything in keeping with the most important customs of old." A faint smile touched the corner of her lips. "The Fire Ceremony of the Middle Mages inspired the most discussion. I could hardly envision it without direct representation of Aithne, and even Tzeremond acknowledges she had some role in bringing the sacred flame to our people. In the end, we decided to use nine women dancers, each paired with one of the Middle Mages. Several of you will participate."

"We are going to invoke the sacred fire?" Milena's hazel eyes went wide.

"No, Milena. You hardly have the skill to do such a thing. You will dance. Then you will stand next to the mages when the sacred fire is invoked, just as Aithne stood next to Caradoc in support of all his endeavors."

"But Aithne didn't just stand there," Eolyn interjected.

Everyone's attention turned to her. She faltered under the sudden scrutiny.

"What I mean is, all the legends concur," she said. "Aithne and Caradoc created the sacred fire through their act of perfect union. It was the magic of both—not one or the other—that brought light and warmth to our people."

Adiana's pale brow lifted in amusement. "So you want an act of perfect union during the Fire Ceremony? Tahmir will be rather upset. I've heard you're to dance with Corey!"

A hot flush rose to Eolyn's cheeks.

"Adiana." Renate's admonishment fell ineffective against the women's laughter. The mistress turned on Eolyn with a severe expression. "Sarah, you would do well not to voice your unusual interpretation of Bel-Aethne in this place. The wizard's spies are out in force, as I am certain Mage Corey has informed you."

"Well if there's to be no perfect union during the fire dance, how about during the High Ceremony?" Adiana said. "I've heard that in the old days, the Third Night of Bel-Aethne was a riot of sensual indulgence."

"For the love of the Gods, Adiana," Renate said, "where do you find your stories? In the great tradition of the Old Orders, the third night of Bel-Aethne was the climax of an elegant ceremonial cycle…"

"There, you see?" Adiana's blue eyes flared in triumph. "The *climax*."

Renate raised her voice over everyone's renewed laughter. "And we will repeat this cycle just as the Old Orders did. We will begin with the rites of Primitive Magic on the first day and proceed to the Fire Ceremony of the Middle Mages on the second day. On the third day at midnight, the Celebration of High Magic will be completed with the union of two partners in the white light of passion—"

"*Two?*" Eolyn's indignation was lost among the cheers and applause led by Adiana.

"An act that invokes High Magic because it transcends time," Renate insisted, her shoulders as stiff as her voice, "yet remains Primitive because it is accessible to all regardless of training. The King will stand in representation of Caradoc, and the High Mages will choose his Aithne."

"Oh." Adiana's playful grin fell into exaggerated disappointment "Well *that* sounds rather boring, unless…" An easy smile spread through her rosy lips. "Unless one of *us* gets to be Aithne. They say he's handsome, you know. The most powerful mage and king to ever walk these lands."

"Does that mean he can go all night?" one of the women quipped.

"Sounds like a perfect union to me!" another replied.

"How do you think we might get on that list, Renate?" Adiana asked.

"I doubt you'd qualify," Milena interjected. "Tzeremond's mages will pick a virgin for sure."

Adiana shrugged. "Well, it'll be his loss then. No virgin of Moisehén can entertain him as well as I can."

"I can't believe you are discussing this as if it were some kind of jest!" Eolyn's anger cut harshly through their banter. "The third night of Bel-Aethne should commemorate one of the greatest mysteries of our faith! In the old days, every man had the opportunity to become Caradoc, and every woman Aithne, and the fire of their love was renewed a thousand times over to illuminate this land. But Tzeremond..." She thrust her finger in the direction of the castle. "Tzeremond would have all of this erased from our memory! Now only one bed will be illuminated, and poorly at that. The Gods will not be pleased."

Eolyn's outburst ended in surprised silence. Even Adiana, who never lacked for a clever retort, only opened her mouth and then shut it again.

"In the traditional rites of Bel-Aethne," Eolyn continued, "the magic of our mages and magas was turned over to our people. Everyone was allowed to taste the passion that bound Aithne and Caradoc. Everyone felt the joy of magic running through their veins. But Tzeremond and his mages do not want us to remember this. They will not tolerate a living reminder of Aithne's power. This is why they deny the sacrament to all but the Mage King. They seek to transform one of our greatest traditions into nothing more than a ritual seduction, at best. Quite frankly, it's disgusting."

They all stared at her, stunned looks on their faces.

Renate shifted in her seat and took a pensive sip from her tea. "So then, Sarah, what do you suggest?"

The prompt startled Eolyn. Too late, she realized what she had just said. Did Renate truly expect her to propose a course of action? Or was the mistress simply seeking to close the trap?

Retreating from Renate's discerning gaze, Eolyn studied her hands. Her tapered fingers, trained since childhood for sorcery, had lain useless now for more than a year. Since she joined Corey's Circle, not a single invocation had been crafted through them, except on Midwinter's Eve.

She realized how tired she was of standing still, of waiting until she found Achim, of expecting the world to change of its own accord. She could not continue like this any longer. She had to do something, and she wanted to do it here.

Drawing a shaky breath, she lifted her gaze to her companions. "Well, I do have an idea. There exists a simple, very subtle form of Primitive Magic that we have already exercised within the Circle, though not with the focus required for the task I have in mind."

"Are you suggesting we invoke magic?" Milena asked. "A bunch of women? Inside the King's City? You must be mad."

"It sounds deliciously risky," Adiana countered, "and far more entertaining than watching the King have his pleasure with someone else."

"The High Sacrament will be conducted in private," Renate said pointedly.

Adiana rolled her eyes. "By the Gods, they really do want to take *all* the fun out of it, don't they?"

"Sarah," Renate said. "Please, continue."

"In essence, what it involves is capturing a thread of desire that runs hidden in the fabric of Moisehén. We have all felt this thread, a longing in the hearts of our people, during every one of our performances. We can take their dream and weave it into movement and song."

"So." Adiana's brows furrowed in doubt. "You want us to do another dance?"

Eolyn looked to Renate. A tremor had invaded the young maga's hands. She felt she could not continue unless Renate gave a clear signal as to where her loyalties lay.

"I know this magic to which you refer." Renate set the tea down in front of her. "It is the power to reflect and amplify a dream by transforming thought into movement and letting movement flow into thought. I have taught all of you how to do this, though I have not revealed to you the many potent ways in which it can be used."

"Sounds like a dance," Adiana said.

"If it were invoked during the celebration of Primitive Magic, it would be just another dance," Eolyn conceded. "But we are meant to accompany the Middle Mages during the Fire Ceremony. If we implement this magic then, it will mingle with the power of those mages, be strengthened and reflected back to the people with greater force. Each person will be visited by a vision. Collectively, they will remember the ignored powers of Aithne, and they will see the magas as they once were."

There. I've done it.

Although Eolyn claimed the spell was Primitive Magic, Renate would know only a High Maga could weave such disparate forces into a single potent image. Eolyn kept her head bent, afraid of what she might see in the mistress's gaze. If Renate betrayed her trust now, Eolyn would be on the pyre by morning.

"I don't like it," Milena decided. "What you describe sounds far too obvious to go unnoticed by the High Mages."

"Therein lays the brilliance of it." Rishona spoke for the first time. "It will culminate in an ephemeral instant, hardly distinguishable from a collective memory. Syrnte witches practice a similar magic."

"Nothing more will happen," Eolyn assured them, "except that an image will be sealed into everyone's minds. Against that image, the High Ceremony and the Midnight Sacrament, even if managed entirely by Tzeremond's mages, will simply not make sense. Their interpretation of the rite will have no meaning for our people."

"Tzeremond and his mages would not detect the coming of this spell, nor would they recognize it while implemented." Renate's gaze, dark and full of caution, remained steady on Eolyn. "But if effective, they will know what happened afterwards, and they will hunt down the perpetrators."

"I don't care," one of the women said. "What do we really have to lose at this point? The Circle will be disbanded after Bel-Aethne. Rishona has foreseen it. And when that happens, our place in this kingdom will be lost. If we do not take our risks now, while we are still together, then when?"

"I, for one, am tired of whispering in fear," another agreed. "If I have this power to which Sarah refers, I wish to exercise it."

"Could we also make the King impotent?" Adiana asked. "I mean, now that it's clear I won't get to sleep with him."

"We will not stop the High Ceremony," Eolyn replied firmly. "We will only render it meaningless."

Adiana sighed. "What good is magic if you can't make a man impotent?"

"No more jesting," Eolyn said quietly. "This is very serious. We must all be in agreement if we are going to do this. And we must have Renate's blessing."

The announcement of this final condition generated an expectant silence. All eyes now turned to the mistress.

Years ago, it was said, Renate had betrayed her sisters to save herself. Eolyn had no doubt she was capable of betraying the women assembled here. But if the mistress chose to walk down that path, Eolyn would not let her do it without giving her this burden, without forcing her to remember that it was her assent that led them to the pyre.

Renate pursed her lips and gave a quiet nod.

CHAPTER TWENTY-FOUR

Bel-Aethne

DURING THE DAYS BEFORE BEL-AETHNE, Mage Corey attended a string of engagements. True to his word, he kept Eolyn at his side. Only on two occasions did he leave her in Tahmir's care, once when he met with Master Tzeremond and again for an audience with the King.

Eolyn soon learned that gatherings of mages were governed by unspoken rules. Wizards of equal rank were kept together. Women, while present, were shielded from any meaningful discussion of magic, commerce, or other affairs of the kingdom. Eolyn never deciphered how they communicated the appropriate moment, but no sooner would Corey bring his lips to Eolyn's ear with a reminder to watch her tongue, than she would be herded away with the rest of the women, often by the perfumed consort of the highest ranking mage.

Thus Eolyn came to know a very different community of 'daughters of Moisehén', bred to serve the needs of their mages and purged of all desire for a magic of their own.

By the eve of Bel-Aethne, Eolyn had met a number of men from Tzeremond's Order, yet Achim did not appear among them. She began to suspect he never would. Perhaps he had not completed his training, though it was difficult to imagine. Perhaps he had traveled back to the South Woods in hopes of finding her, though surely he would return for this important event. Perhaps he had passed prematurely into the Afterlife. Yet Eolyn could not help but believe she would have sensed his departure. The mystery occupied her thoughts, sometimes keeping her awake at night.

A crescendo of activity filled the final days before the great festival. In the central square, carpenters worked in a constant clatter to erect galleries from which the King and his attendants would observe the ceremonies. The people of Moisehén flocked from the farthest reaches of the kingdom, crowding inns and setting up camps outside the city. Avenues and alleys filled with the pungent aroma of roasted meat and fresh ale. Vendors sang like summer frogs, peddling traditional adornments of the season: white lilies, fragrant pine branches, decorated masks, and hooded cloaks. Laughter and chatter rolled freely through the streets.

On the second evening of the three-day festival, people packed the city square in anticipation of the Fire Ceremony. Men and women wore colorful cloaks and decorated masks. They held lilies and pine branches in a sea of white and green. Children darted among the adults, pushing and shoving for favored spots next to the single promenade that connected the palisade on the north with the tent from which mages and dancers would emerge on the south. The low platform led to a sacred circle cast the day before, during the celebration of Primitive Magic.

As the afternoon sun slanted golden red against the high rooftops, trumpets sounded, indicating the opening of the castle gates. The winding path from the fortress was long and steep, so several minutes passed before the King and his retinue completed their ritual descent. They rode into the square on magnificent horses, much heavier in build than the sleek runners Corey owned. Each mage wore a forest green cloak richly embroidered with gold and jewels. They did not cover their faces with common masks, but used a play of shadow and light that blurred their features as well as their auras.

Spying the scene from the entrance to their tent, Eolyn wondered whether the spell that created those masks bore any resemblance to the invocation of a maga's ward.

Adiana pressed her warm cheek against Eolyn's.

"We cannot see the King's face," she said, "but look at his bearing. He wears power with absolute confidence, even in these early days of his reign. What they say about him is true. He is the worst kind of king, the handsome kind, the charismatic kind. They will love him even as he exploits them all for his own gain."

People parted to allow passage of the royal procession. Eolyn sensed gray tendrils of fear curling up from the onlookers, a shimmering mist that drained in a constant stream toward the King and his High Mages.

Tzeremond's students do not simply harvest the energy of the earth, she realized.

They fed on fear and used it to enhance their power. Ghemena had warned her about this. Kedehen had cultivated terror among his people during long, brutal years. Now the new king enjoyed the fruits of his father's labor. Bel-Aethne was but a temporary salve on this ever-open wound, a momentary distraction from the corruption that consumed the once splendid traditions of Moisehén.

As the King took his seat, Adiana drew Eolyn into a tight hug. She kept her voice low. "Are you certain you want to do this?"

"Yes." Eolyn had never been more certain of anything in her life.

"Then I am with you." With a brief kiss, Adiana slipped away to join the musicians.

Eolyn checked the intricate lacing of her mask and pulled her burgundy hood over her head. Adiana's song already floated clear and high when she took her place beside Corey. A thrilling sense of purpose rose inside her. The women had followed her lead. Renate had kept their secret. Eolyn felt as if all the events of her past had conspired to create this moment, in which she would at last crack open the door of lasting change.

As Corey took up her hand, a spark passed between them. He stiffened and cast a glance toward her. Despite the mage's mask, Eolyn saw tension behind his silver-green eyes.

Doubt clouded her resolve. Corey had never been anxious before a performance.

"Is something wrong?" she asked.

He did not respond, but studied her as if considering some difficult decision. A knot took hold of Eolyn's heart.

Did Renate tell him?

If she did, why had he not intervened?

Before Eolyn could shape her misgivings into words, Corey tightened his grip and escorted her out the tent. They followed the others in procession, keeping stride with Adiana's song.

Love that burns in my heart
Night no longer grows dark
Come, my Aithne, my Caradoc
Embrace me

Eolyn and Corey fell into a complex choreography, where the interaction of each couple merged into the seamless pattern of the whole. Eolyn had planned to invoke her subtle magic here, early in the dance, but she hesitated, wary of what she sensed in Corey's demeanor.

The people crowding the square joined their voices with Adiana.

See the white moon shining
Hear the black sky in song
The raging love of a river's passing
The warmth of a sun that has not gone
Our union illuminates the midnight sky
Conquering eternity with this eternal moment...

Caught by the spontaneous power of those voices, Eolyn and Mage Corey paused in their dance. Magic surged through the crowd, dissolving the mist of fear and leaving in its wake a bright solidarity. They raised their blossoms and pine branches high, moving them back and forth in unified rhythm.

Though she could not see the High Mages, Eolyn sensed the pallor that descended over their muted auras. A shadow of foreboding deepened about Master Tzeremond. Only the King's colors remained unchanged. If the response of the people moved him, he did not reveal it.

Mage Corey touched Eolyn's hand in a subtle signal to continue.

"What is happening?" she asked.

Corey drew her close and murmured into her ear. "This is the magic of the people of Moisehén. A sleeping river that binds them. A power that has not stirred for decades." They spun away from each other and came close again before he added, "Tzeremond will not be pleased."

Adiana brought the hymn to a close. The mages and dancers formed two concentric circles, with the men on the inside. Rishona's rich voice now rose into the air. The mysterious language and sinuous melodies of her people evoked a sense of deep longing in Eolyn's heart. It had been bold of Renate to propose that a Syrnte woman sing during the Fire Ceremony. Yet Eolyn could not imagine another person who matched so well the essence and majesty of the Sacred Fire.

As the music gathered force, each mage sent an arc of bright flame from the palm of his hand into the center of the circle. They integrated their powers into a single swirling core of light. The whirlpool spread swift upon the ground before contracting into a glowing pillar that billowed high above the square, evoking cries of wonder from the people.

In the gathering twilight, the mages crafted an awe-inspiring choreography, splitting the brilliant light into multicolored images that portrayed the many legends of Aithne and Caradoc. The mythical lovers danced through flames and unveiled the mysteries of magic. They fled from Thunder, responded to the call of Dragon, and forged their passion into a thousand fire-bearing branches.

Eolyn scanned the faces of the entranced onlookers.

Now is the time.

Between the dancing flames of the Middle Mages and the deep imagination of her people, she began to work her spell in the silent tongue of Dragon.

Ehekaht.

Naeom veham.

Naeom eh nom zehlam.

Ehukae.

Spreading outward at her bidding, the magic of dance wove into the hidden dreams of the audience. Eolyn felt the vision take shape. Swaying robes of deep burgundy. Healing hands and graceful limbs. Flowing hair and hawk-like eyes. Indomitable freedom and fearsome magic.

The fleeting mirage captured the old rites, in which the Fire Ceremony was invoked by a balanced coven of men and women, lending a rich texture to the sacred flame that for all the skill of the mages present, could not be produced without women's magic.

The spell faded. A low shudder coursed through the column of fire. Eolyn opened her eyes, troubled by the ominous rumble.

The character of the shifting light altered, becoming more ardent. Mage Corey's shoulders tensed. The other mages exchanged nervous glances. Several tried to pull away without success. Eolyn caught her breath as she realized the flame was holding them against their will.

Without warning, the red-hot core exploded upward. A rush of hot air threw the mages violently to the ground. The Sacred Fire roared into the shape of a flaming dragon, arched its burning neck, and bore directly down on Mage Corey.

Eolyn had no time to consider her actions. She flung her arm forward and shouted,

Ehekaht, faeom aenre dumae!

Magic surged through her feet and burst from her palm in an arc of clear blue light. The indigo flame intercepted the dragon's head not more than a few inches from Corey's face. Flaring up, it engulfed the red serpent and consumed its writhing neck. The creature was transformed into a nebulous ball of blue and red flame that imploded with a thunderous bellow and then faded into a single dying spark.

Absolute silence followed.

With horror, Eolyn realized what she had done and where she had chosen to do it.

Mage Corey removed his hood and mask in a single motion, his expression incredulous.

Though she dared not raise her eyes, Eolyn knew the King had risen to his feet. She sensed the acid gaze of Tzeremond. She understood there would be no escape.

"Bring her to me, at once." The King did not raise his voice, yet the command was heard by everyone.

A shuffling murmur took hold of the crowd. Some pushed away from the square. Others stood frozen in place. But most strained forward to catch a glimpse of the hooded and masked woman who through some miracle had acquired the gift of magic.

Guards materialized out of the shifting mass of people. They surrounded Eolyn, their unsheathed swords hissing with death.

Mage Corey scrambled to his feet. "Fools! Those blades won't do you any good."

He forced his way through the guards and grabbed hold of Eolyn, one hand firm on the back of her neck and the other palm hard against her forehead. Eolyn struggled against the uncomfortable grip, but he held fast and forced her gaze to meet his. *"Ehekahtu naeom maleh."*

She went still with surprise. His invocation made no sense.

"There you are, men," Corey said. "I've bound her magic."

Yet he had done no such thing.

Corey slipped his hand around Eolyn's arm in a grip so tight it hurt. "You'll want me by your side, however, if you plan to make it to the castle alive."

The captain cast a nervous glance toward Eolyn. Sheathing his sword, he gave Corey a curt nod. "Very well, Mage Corey."

The King had already departed the square on horseback with his attendants, leaving the guards to navigate the restless crowd as they tried to open passage for the new prisoner. Their efforts fell impotent against the will of the onlookers, who pressed ever harder for a glance at the maga.

Eolyn had never been surrounded by such a mass of people. Their faces blurred. The heat became suffocating. Just as she was certain the crowd would overwhelm the handful of armed men and tear her apart, a chill rippled through the square and silenced their clamor. A path opened, snaking toward the rise of the castle road. At its center, not more than ten paces in front of Eolyn, stood an ancient woman with wise eyes and a toothless smile. She held a single lily in her hand, which she set carefully on the ground before vanishing altogether.

Eolyn did not know if anyone else saw the apparition, but in the old woman's wake, everyone released their lilies. Flowers showered in from all directions and accumulated in a heavy, scented snow at her feet.

The guards gave Eolyn a violent shove and ordered her forward.

Chapter Twenty-Five

Vortingen's Keep

The fortress of Vortingen loomed unnatural, with massive gates and impervious walls. Ominous shadows clung to its edges. The maze of corridors induced a sense of confinement and anxious disorientation. Weapons hissed and babbled, their metallic tongue unintelligible to Eolyn.

Corey's grip on her arm tightened as he pulled her close. "Do not let them intimidate you. Their power lies in your apprehension. Whoever instructed you must have given you techniques to control your fear. Put those lessons to use now. Our future depends on it."

Our future.

This simple expression of unity placed a terrible burden on Eolyn's heart. For all she knew, Corey might burn with her on the morrow. "Forgive me, Mage Corey. I didn't think—"

"No, you did not." Anger colored his tone. "For the moment I will thank you for saving my life, though you may have rendered it forfeit by doing so. There will be time for explanations and apologies, if we live to see the sun."

They continued in silence. Eolyn could sense Corey sifting through different versions of their history, searching for a story that would explain her actions without sending them both to the pyre. His anxiety unnerved her, then filled her with indignation.

What have I done to deserve this?

As a child, she kept every secret taught by her mother. As a girl, she grew up hiding in the misty heart of the South Woods. Ever since her return to Moisehén, she had concealed the truth of her power and refrained from all overt acts of magic, starving her spirit in the process. Now in a single careless moment, she had used her gift for the presumably noble act of saving a mage's life.

And this is how they reward me.

"That's better," Mage Corey said.

Eolyn stiffened, unnerved by the impression that he had read her

151

thoughts.

"Now you must calm your anger," Corey said. "Do not speak to them, Sarah. Focus on subduing your emotions. I will manage the rest."

They arrived at a small antechamber dominated by two great wooden doors carved with the dragon crest of Vortingen. More guards stepped forward to surround them. The heavy doors swung inward, and they were escorted into the presence of the King.

Eolyn had never seen so much space enclosed in one room. Thick pillars reached up like great stone trunks, their branches dividing in clean arcs high overhead. Tall windows, black against the gathering night, lined the long hall. Thick torches illuminated the polished floor, chasing shadows to the far corners. The magnificence of this place reminded Eolyn, oddly enough, of the South Woods. Taking some comfort in that thought, she drew a breath and straightened her shoulders.

The High Mages were assembled on either side of the King, whose face remained hidden behind the spell of his mask. At the King's side stood Tzeremond, assaulting Eolyn with the deep cut of his amber gaze. Eolyn hesitated, but Mage Corey placed a strong hand on her shoulder. Together they moved forward until the guards signaled them to stop.

The King studied her, expression unreadable behind the shifting light of his mask. The silence grew long and uncomfortable. Tzeremond's glance strayed toward the King, as if prompting him to speak, but the regent suffered no distraction in his assessment of Eolyn.

She lifted her chin and held his gaze. Some unspoken question took shape between them, hanging like a loose mist in the flickering light.

"Who will speak for this woman?" The King demanded.

"I will, my Lord King," Mage Corey replied.

"I will speak for myself," Eolyn said.

The mages murmured in indignation.

"Please, my Lord King." Mage Corey said quickly. "Have patience with her. She is but a peasant from Moehn. She knows nothing of the ways of court."

"Though she knows something of the ways of magic," the King replied. "What is her name?"

"Sarah," Eolyn said.

Corey lanced her with his gaze.

"Remove your mask, Maid Sarah," the King instructed. "I would see your face."

"I will be pleased to remove my mask when you remove yours," Eolyn replied.

The torches dimmed at her insolence.

The King sat back in his throne. Disapproval spread from his feet and flowed down the steps like a deadly mist.

"Leave us," he commanded.

The High Mages bowed and drifted toward the antechamber in a low rustle of robes. Tzeremond remained next to his King, and Corey stood firm beside Eolyn.

"You are dismissed as well, Mage Corey," the King said.

Corey hesitated, then drew a quiet, decisive breath. "Have mercy, my Lord King. What happened today is not her fault. I assume full responsibility. I taught her tricks no woman should know, out of my own curiosity and pride. She comes from a sheltered background. She knew little of our laws when I met her and lacked that innate fear of magic shared by so many of the women of Moisehén. I wished to test how far she might journey into darkness. But her magic has never been employed outside the Circle or in public until today. It will not happen again. You have my word."

"Mage Corey, you have heard my command. You will wait in the antechamber until I have finished with this witch."

Eolyn felt Mage Corey's spirit hit the floor.

He placed his hand on her shoulder once more, transferring what he could of his strength and magic before departing. She understood the flavor of his resignation. *Corey believes he is saying farewell.*

"Master Tzeremond, you too are dismissed," the King said.

"My Lord King, I thought I could be of some service in questioning this woman."

"I will call upon your services soon enough. You will wait with the others until summoned."

With a clipped bow, Tzeremond departed. He swept past Eolyn, searing her senses with the acrid sting of his aura. The doors shut behind him.

An unnatural silence followed, the deep quiet of a mountain fortress; a terrible emptiness uninterrupted by the song of warblers or the chirp of crickets. A cold stillness never penetrated by the rush of a spring river or the soft wind through high firs.

The King drew himself to his feet. "How long have you been with Mage Corey?"

"Just over a year."

"A year?" He descended from the throne and approached her in measured steps. "That is not much time to learn a trick like the one you did today."

Eolyn considered her response with care. The blue flame she crafted represented very advanced magic. The King had every reason to question whether Corey could teach an uninitiated woman how to invoke it so quickly. If she answered honestly, she would expose Corey as a liar. Yet out of respect for Ghemena, she could not play accomplice to his story.

"Corey is a gifted mage," she said.

The King nodded. An amused smile touched his lips. "That he is, but he did not train you."

He stood a couple paces in front of her now. Eolyn's instinct registered a disturbing familiarity in his stance. He reminded her of Lynx in the moment just before she pounced. But the appetite was different. Darker, deeper.

Still, Eolyn did not fear. She had shape shifted into both sides of the predator-prey game often enough to know the prey almost always won. She sent the roots of her spirit deep into the earth and kept her gaze steady on his.

"There was another act of magic today," he continued, "a subtle but powerful spell invoked during the Fire Ceremony. Did you do that as well?"

The question caught Eolyn by surprise. She drew an uncertain breath, fighting back the slight tremor that invaded her hands. The decision to save a mage's life was defensible, worthy of the King's mercy, but the vision she had invoked during the Fire Ceremony was treason.

"I did not induce our people to sing," she said. "That impulse arose of its own accord."

"I do not refer to the song, but to the image our people were given during the rite. A vision of the Magas of Old. It was very well done. Exquisite. Almost imperceptible."

Eolyn's blood ran cold. His words were snaking around her like a tether, cutting off escape routes, pulling her toward condemnation. The pleasure he drew from seeing her cornered was palpable.

"It is said there are many ways to subdue a witch." The King paced a slow circle around her. Eolyn forced her heart to steady as he approached from behind. "How would you have me tame you?"

"I would not be tamed, sir."

"Indeed." He removed her hood and began to undo the lacings of her mask.

The touch paralyzed Eolyn. She wanted to run, to take the form of Night Hawk and escape through the high windows. But her feet clung stubbornly to the ground. The power of shape shifting eluded her.

He lifted the mask away, exposing her face to the stone-chilled air.

Then he stepped very close, so near she could feel his heat reverberate against her back. His powerful hands found the base of her throat. Her nose tingled with the pricks of tiny needles. A bitter metallic taste filled her mouth.

Eolyn recognized the signs of *Ahmad-melan*, the curse mages used to induce frightening hallucinations in their victims. She carried none of the known remedies with her, except the ability to control her fear, and an invocation in the tongue of Dragon.

The King's hands closed around her neck.

Ehekaht, faeom, Eolyn prayed. *Ehekaht naemu.*

His grip became unbearably painful, as if he were trapping a rock inside her throat. Eolyn's lungs, instantly aware of the crisis, convulsed.

Veham-mehta. Ehekaht.

She closed her eyes, bade her lungs to be still, her heart to remain calm. Her body could not panic. She could not let it panic.

Ehekaht, faeom. Ehekaht naemu. Veham-mehta. Ehekaht.

The vision faded. The bruising pressure disappeared. Eolyn gasped as air rushed fresh and cold back into her lungs.

"Well done," he said. "Very well done, indeed."

The admiration in his voice sparked her anger, but she subdued the impulse to strike back. She understood this game. Losing control of her emotions would only make her more vulnerable.

Pulling the folds of Eolyn's cloak off her shoulders, the King traced the line of her arm until he found the place where Achim's armband rested beneath her sleeve. At his touch, the metal recoiled and hissed.

Startled, Eolyn jumped, but the King trapped the bracelet against her skin, his grip sending a sharp shaft of pain through her arm. Eolyn went still as a rabbit in the jaws of a wolf.

He knew the bracelet would be there.

The Mage King caressed her ear with his breath. "What you did today was reckless, *Eolyn*."

The invocation of her true name hit hard. Eolyn's eyes stung with the impact. A mist of fear rose about her feet.

He knows my name. He knows of Achim's gift to me.

What then did he not know?

And what had they done to Achim?

"I do not recognize that name, my Lord." But Eolyn's voice shook and her throat had gone dry.

The King inhaled the scent of her hair and withdrew.

"Then perhaps you will recognize me." He completed his circle to face her and allowed his mask to dissolve.

Eolyn did not at first recognize him. Not because his countenance had changed, but because nothing had prepared her to connect the boy she befriended in the South Woods with the feared and hated King of Vortingen.

"It's not possible," she whispered.

She stepped forward and lifted her hand to his face, searching for some hint of an illusion, some spell invoked to trick her, though she knew of no magic that would allow one mage to shape shift into another. He responded to her touch, but the press of his lips against her palm felt perverse, and she withdrew her hand as if it had been seared.

"Where is Achim?" Her question was directed not so much to the King as to the extraordinary powers that had brought the boy into her life, only to let him become lost inside this stranger.

Eolyn stepped backwards, her dreams of the past crumbling into the void of her future. The boy she had trusted, the name upon which she built her hopes, was nothing but a cruel illusion crafted by the man who stood at the very center of the system that would see her destroyed.

"To what twisted end did you cultivate my affection?" she said, bewildered.

An intense pain ignited inside her head. The walls spun, the very foundations of the castle seemed to shift. A tremor shook the hall, sending the King stumbling away.

Eolyn sank to the floor. Spreading her hands upon its polished surface, she drew deep and ragged breaths. At last the world became still again, but her head still ached and her spirit had been drained away. She felt like a cup emptied of the wine that had once given it meaning. When she spoke, her voice was broken and subdued.

"Have mercy, my Lord King. I have tried to respect the laws of this land. I departed the forest a year ago because my guardian passed into the Afterlife. I returned to Moisehèn to find..." Her heart stalled. *To find you.* "Mage Corey took me in. He gave me haven, an income, a new family. But he knew nothing of my ability, for I did not practice any magic at all. When I saw the fire go out of control and the red flame bearing down upon him, I had to intervene. I could not let him perish, knowing it was in my power to save him. It will not happen again."

Somewhere beyond the pounding in her ears, she heard him invoke her name. But was it the Mage King who called, or her ruined memory of Achim? The confusion between past and present, between hope and disillusion, was tearing her apart. She felt his hand on her shoulder and flinched away.

"Please." A sob broke through her voice. "Let me leave this place."

Eolyn spoke against hope. She let her pounding head sink into icy hands.

I should have listened to Ghemena. I should have never trusted him. In my foolishness, I have failed them all. My people, my dead sisters, Dragon, the very Gods themselves.

From the beginning, he had meant to claim her, just as Kedehen had claimed Briana, her life subject to his dominion, her magic used for his ends.

There would be no return of the magas, no restoration of the honored traditions of her people. She had fallen into the Mage King's trap, and now there would only be him, the true son of Kedehen, fueling his magic through the shattering of all her dreams.

CHAPTER TWENTY-SIX

Flight

A TREMOR SHOOK THE ANTECHAMBER, throwing Corey off his feet and sending a wave of panic through the High Mages. Only after the movement of the earth subsided, did the mages regain their composure. Meaningful glances were exchanged, nods of satisfaction expressed.

The last maga of Moisehén is vanquished.

The thought sank like a stone in Corey's heart.

Akmael's staff sounded three times from inside the throne room. The heavy doors opened. Abandoning all protocol, Corey pushed ahead of the rest. He stopped short when he saw her, like a wild rose crumpled against the unyielding floor.

The King sat upon his throne, face as expressionless as the walls of his fortress. "You see, Master Tzeremond? She can be taught humility when handled properly."

Then Akmael settled a black gaze upon his cousin. "Mage Corey."

"My Lord King." Corey's voice was a smooth river of contempt.

"Take this woman from the city, and do not return until she has unlearned the tricks you taught her."

Shock rippled through the High Mages.

In an instant, Corey was at Sarah's side. Her hands felt cold as death, and her skin was a sick tone of gray, but she stirred when he touched her.

She is alive! Thank the Gods, she is alive.

"My Lord King," Tzeremond said, "I do not think it wise to—"

"Drostan," the King said, "see that these two are escorted to the castle gates."

The knight stepped forward and offered his assistance to Sarah, but she shrank from his touch. Corey wrapped his arm around her and pulled her up from the floor. They had advanced only a few steps when she doubled over and vomited a pool of bile right at Tzeremond's feet. Heart racing, Corey half-carried, half-dragged her out of the throne room, anxious to avoid the wizard's curse.

A small group of guards assembled around them. Drostan led the way. They walked in silence, hurried steps echoing against torch-lit walls. At the castle gates, Corey and Sarah were released without ceremony into the night beyond.

Corey paused and gathered his breath, Sarah sagging against his shoulder.

A cascade of stars shone over the city.

The silence was unnerving.

What just happened?

Sarah should have been possessed on this night, her remains burned on the morrow. What impossible turn of events had caused the King to set her free?

Gently, Corey used his magic to prod Sarah's spirit, trying to assess what Akmael might have taken, what he had left behind. Beneath the terror and despair, everything seemed intact.

Everything except her heart.

That had been shattered in a way that could only mean…

Corey shook his head. *No.*

The serpent bracelet on her arm stirred as if in answer to his question.

But how?

A shadow moved on Corey's left, and Tahmir slipped out of the night. Sarah moaned as the Syrnte warrior drew her away from Corey and into his embrace. He pressed his lips to her forehead and murmured words of comfort.

"Where is Renate?" Corey asked. With any luck, there might still be time to get her out of the city.

"Thelyn sent her away after the Fire Ceremony," Tahmir replied. "He urged her to flee, but she came to the Circle and refused to go anywhere until we had news of you and Sarah."

Tahmir lifted Sarah off the ground and carried her as they began a swift descent toward the city gates.

"He let her go?" Corey said, surprised. "We may still have a friend on the Council, then. Tahmir, when we get to the city gates I want my three fastest horses ready, with Renate on one of them."

"Rishona will be waiting with everything you need."

Sarah murmured against Tahmir's chest. Corey had to lean close to hear her.

"My satchel," she was saying, "and my walking stick. They must go with me."

"My sister has already retrieved them for you, dear Sarah," Tahmir replied.

Karin Rita Gastreich

She responded with a sharp inhale, as if her spirit were returning to her body. Sarah stirred in Tahmir's arms and looked up.

"I can walk now," she said, though her voice was weak. "Tahmir, I want to walk."

He set her down and took her hand in his. The three of them continued together, footsteps tapping against cobblestones. Mournful silence permeated the midnight mist. Even the bars and taverns had shut their doors.

"Where is everyone?" Corey asked. "Bel-Aethne is not a festival of silence. These streets should be filled with revelry."

"A crowd gathered outside the castle gates after Sarah's arrest, anxious for another glimpse of the maga. When the tremor hit, they scattered in terror, thinking the King and his mages had destroyed her. The city is in mourning now."

"Well, isn't that ironic," Corey said. "After all those years they spent under Kedehen, watching without protest while he bled this kingdom of their magas."

"They were trapped then by their fear."

"Fear. Greed. Madness. Whatever it was, I'm glad it's gone. Would that I could be here tomorrow, when news of her release spreads like wildfire through these streets."

Rishona met them outside the city gates. She embraced Sarah and gave her a flask of minted water to wash the bile from her mouth. The Syrnte woman had selected three animals with silvery gray coats that would blend well with the moonlit fields. She also produced translucent riding cloaks for both Sarah and Corey.

Renate sat on her horse, ready for travel.

"Curse this waxing moon," Corey muttered, "and the clear sky that allows it to illuminate the land."

"These colors will help conceal your retreat," Rishona assured him, fastening his cloak and giving him a brief kiss.

"All the same, let us hope the King does not change his mind."

Sarah donned her cloak and climbed up on her steed. Tahmir handed her the staff and satchel, then caught her hand in his.

"Ride swift," he said. "Do not look back."

"Why are you not coming with us?" Anxiety filled Sarah's voice.

"I will follow, soon."

"Follow us now!"

"We do not have time for romantic interludes," Corey snapped.

"The smaller your group, the less likely your passing will be noticed," Tahmir told Sarah. "It is better this way."

"No." Sarah clung to his hand.

160

"We will be together again." The Syrnte warrior pressed her fingers to his lips. "Until then, listen to your dreams. Look for me there."

"Everything connected with her must be destroyed," Corey said to Rishona as he mounted. "Costumes, bed sheets, combs. Everything."

"Adiana is taking care of it," Rishona assured him.

Corey's horse pranced restlessly beneath him, its breath a fog against the night air.

"It is over," he announced. "Disband the Circle tonight. Those who understand who we are know what to do. As for the others, use your judgment. If they are ready, let them make their choice. If not, pay their severance and thank them for their services on my behalf. No one is to linger. I want this camp abandoned within the hour."

"Consider it done," Tahmir promised.

With a short nod, Mage Corey signaled the horses and they took off, a moonlit cloud of dust rising in their wake.

CHAPTER TWENTY-SEVEN

Tzeremond's Counsel

AKMAEL SENT TZEREMOND AWAY with the High Mages, instructing them to resuscitate the stalled festival of Bel-Aethne.

Once alone, Akmael assumed the shape of a gray owl and departed through one of the high windows. With the warm evening air flowing over his wings, he directed his flight toward the ramparts and settled in a whisper of feathers just above the castle entrance.

Twilight had thickened into night. The waxing moon cast broad shafts of silver across the cobblestones below. Mage Corey and Eolyn emerged from the gates, the maga leaning on the mage.

A Syrnte man slipped out of the shadows and wrapped his arms around Eolyn. Akmael's feathers ruffled as the stranger pressed his lips into her thick copper tresses. The man gathered Eolyn up and carried her away, Corey at their side.

Uncertainty plagued Akmael. He fought the impulse to follow them. He had entrusted Eolyn to Corey, but on what grounds? The devotion of the mage to her defense? The blood of East Selen that bound Corey to Akmael?

Despite their conversations in recent days, Akmael was not convinced of his cousin's loyalty, but Tzeremond would return soon, and he could not linger. Mage Corey would have to be contacted—and the Syrnte interloper dealt with—later.

With a lift of powerful wings, Akmael took flight and veered back toward the castle. He descended into the throne room and assumed his human shape just as the guards announced the return of Tzeremond.

"The festival will continue as planned, my Lord King," Tzeremond reported. "It is fortunate the High Mages were set to preside over the third day. Few changes will be required."

"I am pleased to hear it."

Tzeremond stepped forward, eyes aflame with urgency, knuckles white against his staff. "My Lord King, that witch must not be allowed to escape."

"Before we speak of that woman," Akmael replied, "you will tell me who made the attempt on Mage Corey's life today, and by what authority."

Tzeremond retreated a step, then drew a breath and said, "I invoked the Dragon. Although, as you undoubtedly noticed, the spell was crafted to make it appear as if the Middle Mages lost control of the fire."

Akmael studied Tzeremond's unwavering gaze. Clearly, the wizard believed he could undertake such an act with impunity. Kedehen had granted Tzeremond full authority for administering justice in crimes of magic. Still, certain protocols were expected.

"Who presided at his trial in my place?" Akmael asked pointedly.

"My Lord King, as you know Mage Corey visits us once a year to report on his work with foreign and unusual magic. We take advantage of these meetings not only to learn from him, but to assess his loyalty to the Order and to the Crown, a loyalty that has always been under suspicion, as you are aware, given the fate of his clan. Recently we have come to believe his work has led him astray. There are indications he has assumed a key role in the nascent rebellion about which Sir Drostan and I informed you."

"Why did you not tell me this before?"

"Mage Corey is a delicate target. He has garnered great popularity with the people, with many important families and a number of mages. And though you no longer sustain a close relationship with him, he is your cousin. We had hoped this festival would bring more evidence to light, allowing us to arrest him without controversy. But during today's Fire Ceremony, I realized we had waited too long. A vision was sent to our people, a perverse image of magas creating the sacred fire alongside the mages. The only person in the ceremony skilled enough to attempt such a manipulation was Corey. So, I decided the time had come to eliminate him."

Akmael took a moment to absorb these words. *Would my father have condoned such an act?* "A trial would have been more appropriate."

"In this case, perhaps not. Given his reputation, and the infancy of your reign, it would be more prudent to avoid a messy arrest and trial. Better he fall victim to an accident."

How many of Tzeremond's rivals had fallen victim to accidents over the years? "Mage Corey was not the only one with the ability to craft the vision to which you refer."

Tzeremond gray brows furrowed. "It is a mistake to let her go, my Lord King. And to allow Mage Corey to escape with her."

Akmael took a few paces away from his mentor and placed a broad hand upon one of the many pillars that supported the throne room. He noticed a hairline crack, evidence of the tremor she had just invoked.

Father was right.

Eolyn was no longer a girl. The maga commanded her own authority now. Indeed, she was a vision of magic reinforced by spellbinding beauty. The scent of the South Woods hovered about her like a bright cloud. Her very presence had filled his heart with an unbearable need, igniting a desire more intense than he thought possible. He had come close, dangerously close, to satiating the darkest of appetites.

Even now, Akmael could not say what stayed his hand. The rich flavor of Eolyn's magic lingered on his tongue and nourished the flame in his breast.

"Her power is extraordinary," he murmured. "She moved the earth, Tzeremond. And then bade it to be still."

"The maga did that?" The wizard's voice shook.

"Yes, though it seemed she was not entirely cognizant of the magic she invoked. I find it curious that whoever trained her did not open her awareness to this gift, this ability to set the deepest powers of the earth into motion."

"Only her ability to unsettle the ground has been proven, my Lord King."

"That, and her capacity to stop a death flame invoked by a master." Akmael's hand drifted away from the pillar. He turned back to Tzeremond. "A power like that could be harnessed, could it not? A power like that could be made to serve me, just as Briana's magic served my father."

Tzeremond went still as an arrow poised in its bow. A glow of trepidation filled his amber eyes. "That was a unique situation, my Lord King. One I would not recommend repeating."

"But it could be done."

"Yes, it could be done, though it is not necessary. You have no need of her power."

"I am no longer your student, Tzeremond. It is my decision what I need, what I do not need, and what might serve my purpose whether I need it or not."

"I only offer the advice I think best, my Lord King. The appearance of this maga has caused confusion among our people. The guards report they threw lilies in her path. They need a clear act of justice from their new King, or this one incident could very well undo the life's work of your most honored father."

"Their desire for the magas is like a forgotten river threatening to burst out of the earth," Akmael countered. "We cannot subdue their longing indefinitely. Perhaps it would be better to let it emerge into the daylight, where we can see it and keep it under control."

"There is no controlling the magas! Five years of war they brought upon Moisehén. They turned our people against each other, cursed us with division and bloodshed. They burned fields, ravaged towns, and left countless orphans in their wake. And for what purpose? So that your father could not wear the crown the Gods had clearly destined him to wear. You are bound by duty to your people, and the memory of your father, to keep this land free of the magas' poison."

"My father eliminated all but one. He kept Briana for himself."

Tzeremond held Akmael's gaze for a long moment. Then he let go a quiet sigh. "I will not stand in your way, my Lord King, if you decide to attempt such a thing, just as I did not stand in your father's way, when he took Briana of East Selen. If you desire her magic, then claim it."

Akmael's glance strayed toward the high windows where he had just escaped as Owl.

They will be at the city gates by now.

Eolyn, Corey, and that Syrnte thief.

Tzeremond stepped close and spoke in low tones. "She need not live in order for you to make use of her power. Bring the woman back, possess her, and send her remains to the world of the dead."

Yet Akmael did not want to subdue Eolyn in the way Tzeremond had taught him. He did not want to feed on Eolyn's fear or break her body or even expropriate her extraordinary magic. The thought of Eolyn disappearing in a flash of violence, never to be enjoyed again, filled him with disgust.

"Or keep her if you must," Tzeremond added, "in the East Tower, just as your father did."

No.

Akmael desired something else from her, something deeper and more powerful. Something he could not yet name. "She cannot be brought to me by force. Briana trusted my father, if not with everything, then with that which was most important to her. So it must be with this maga. I would have her return to me willingly, and surrender her magic without reservation."

"You deceive yourself, my Lord King," Tzeremond said. "A maga does not surrender her magic. You must imprison this woman, or you must kill her. There is no other choice."

CHAPTER TWENTY-EIGHT

Refuge

EOLYN, COREY, AND RENATE RODE south over open fields for hours. Only when the gray light of predawn filtered into the sky did Corey slow their pace. He guided them toward a thick stand of trees and turned their path toward the east. As rays of sun began to penetrate the green canopy, Corey bade Eolyn and Renate to dismount by a small brook, so their horses might rest.

Muscles stiff with exhaustion, Eolyn led her horse to the stream. She dropped to her knees, refreshed her face with cool water, and wet her parched lips. Closing her eyes, she inhaled the rich aromas of the forest, of wet loam, fallen nuts, and crushed leaves. Her heart ached for the South Woods, for its beauty and peace, its safety and power.

Withdrawing from the stream, she took a weary seat beside Renate on one of the large, smooth stones. Only Mage Corey remained restless. His feet marked agitated paths through the leaf litter. His face reddened with anger. Swearing harshly, he hurled a shaft of bright flame at a nearby boulder, splitting it in two.

"Do you take me for a fool?" He turned on Eolyn. "A few *tricks* from your grandmother? You put us all at risk! The entire Circle could have perished—may still perish—thanks to your lies and your deceit!"

"That is enough, Corey!" Renate shot back. "You have no right to attack her like that! Did you ever give her reason to trust you? Did you ever tell her who we really are? What we really do? Even if you had, what evidence would you have offered to support your story? What proof could you have given to convince her you were not just another clever spy of Tzeremond? She did exactly what a woman of her power needs to do to survive in this kingdom. Indeed, she did exactly what you would have told her to do, had you known the truth. *She trusted no one.*"

Eolyn looked up at the mistress. "You told him nothing?"

"No," replied Renate. "I did not reveal your secret, Sarah. I am not the scared girl I was twenty years ago. I know now how to protect my

166

own, although until this moment I have had none of my own to protect."

"Tell me what?" Corey demanded. "What else did you not tell me?"

Renate regarded him with a cool gaze. "That question is for Sarah to answer, if she so chooses."

Corey drew a deep breath and exhaled in resignation. His temper faded, though his eyes remained weary with frustration.

He approached them, took a seat facing Eolyn, and said quietly, "I hope by now you understand I mean you no harm. Please tell me who you are."

Tears spilled unbidden onto her cheeks. Eolyn wiped them away, frustrated by the evidence of her vulnerability. "My true name is Eolyn. When I was a child, my family perished during a raid of the King's men on my village. I fled into the South Woods, where an elder by the name of Ghemena took me in and cared for me. She trained me in the ways of the Old Orders and anointed me High Maga before passing into the Afterlife."

"Ghemena?" Renate's eyes widened in astonishment. "Do you mean Ghemena of Berlingen?"

"She spoke often of Berlingen, yes."

"But that abbey was destroyed," the mistress objected. "They said everyone perished. No one survived!"

"Ghemena escaped, aided by a nephew who happened to be with her at the time."

"So, you are a High Maga." Corey's tone hung between doubt and hope.

"Trained by one of the greatest Doyennes of my generation," Renate said.

"Who would have thought such a discovery still possible?" Corey asked.

"You speak of me as if I'm a relic," Eolyn said.

"You are," mage and mistress replied in unison.

A smile broke through Corey's weary expression. Laughter crept into his voice, growing in intensity until it broke full over the forest glade. "Imagine, Renate! I snuck a High Maga into the King's City, right under Tzeremond's nose! I introduced her to half the mages in the kingdom, and no one detected her! That old wizard must be out of his skin with fury! You should have seen his face when the King set her free."

Corey's laughter stopped short, and his shoulders tensed.

In a sudden, impatient move he rose and started pacing again. "I thought we had lost you when I saw you on the floor of the throne room. I thought he had possessed your magic and left you for dead."

"Possessed my magic?" This phrase made no sense to Eolyn.

"Tzeremond's mages know how to separate magic from a maga's spirit and claim it for their own," explained Renate. "A perverse and violent practice that arose during the purges."

That was what I sensed, Eolyn realized. The malevolent hunger she felt in his presence, the attempt to invoke hallucinations through *Ahmad-melan*, the use of her own name to break her.

By the Gods, what has he become?

"What I don't understand is why he set you free." Corey said. "What counter spell did you use to stop him?"

"No spell." Her heart contracted painfully. "I have no spell against what he wanted to do. But something happened...I'm not sure what. I recognized him, and everything changed."

"You *recognized* him?" Corey's impatience flared again. "What kind of maga's riddle is that? Of course you recognized him, he is the King!"

Eolyn's head sank into her arms, not because Corey's challenge distressed her, but because in that moment she realized Achim...No, Akmael, the Mage King, had kept her mask. With but a hair or an eyelash or even her essence extracted from its fabric, he could find her.

Or worse.

"Corey, I think we can do without your sarcasm and even suspend the questions for at least one day," Renate admonished. "Let her rest for pity's sake. She's been through enough."

But Corey did not move.

Eolyn kept her face hidden, but she felt the intensity of his gaze as he worked through some unspoken question. Just as she thought a new barrage of words would take shape on his lips, the mage turned abruptly away. After a few moments, the shifting of his footsteps against the leaf litter ceased. She heard the soft whisper of his cloak as it fell to the forest floor.

"Come, Maga Eolyn."

She raised her tear-stained face.

Mage Corey stood with his hand extended toward her. Shafts of morning light painted his hair in soft shades of gold.

"You must rest," he said. "We will take but an hour here. Renate and I will wake you when it is time to continue."

Relieved, Eolyn accepted his invitation and laid her aching limbs against the soft folds of his cloak. The musk of leaf litter wafted up through the fabric. Though grateful to lie down, Eolyn was certain she would not sleep for a moment.

Then Mage Corey knelt close and set his hand upon her forehead in a firm yet gentle hold. At his touch, the anxieties that plagued Eolyn fled into nothingness. She sank at once into a deep and dreamless slumber.

They traveled under the cover of forest whenever they could and by night when they could not. No path marked their circuitous route, yet Corey appeared to know it well. The few times his memory failed, or some change in a landmark confused him, he consulted the trees or passing animals.

Eolyn made no inquiries as to their destination. Emptied of all sense of purpose after her disillusion with Akmael, she wrapped herself in a deep need to leave the decisions to someone else. The turning of their path under the summer sun indicated they progressed roughly in the direction of Selen. In time, encounters with open fields ceased and they continued through narrow corridors between ancient trees.

One afternoon, they arrived at a small stand of birch. Corey bade his companions to halt. Sunlight filtered through shifting branches, illuminating scattered patches of forest herbs. Insects chirped softly. A faint scent of open fires floated on the wind.

After a few moments, Eolyn detected the soothing call of the firhawk, a skilled imitation that few would recognize as human-made.

"They have seen us," Corey said. "It is safe to proceed."

The three of them continued in silence, crossing two low ridges before coming to a large flat area. Here, the underbrush had been cleared away and replaced by clusters of tents. A village of cloth-draped poles and open hearths stretched so far that Eolyn could not determine its limits.

As they approached, men and women paused in their routines and emerged from the dwellings. Armed with bows, knives, axes, and swords, they gave an intimidating display of arms that might have turned many away. Mage Corey, however, dismounted and engaged in hearty greetings with them. Renate followed and was embraced as their sister.

Disoriented by the mass of strangers, Eolyn remained on her steed until a wisp of memory startled her. Searching the crowd, she noted a movement among the tents, a parting of bodies that indicated the approach of a person of importance.

In an instant, she slipped off her horse. Heart racing, Eolyn pushed impatiently past numerous surprised faces, breaking through the barrier of bodies until at last she stood before a man who stopped as if a wall had been thrown into his path.

His face was long and aged before its time. A deep scar stretched down the length of his cheek, disappearing into his auburn beard. He watched Eolyn with the clear green gaze of their mother, his expression hovering between doubt and astonishment.

"Eolyn?" he whispered.

"Ernan," she replied in disbelief.

A murmur rippled through the crowd, bringing conversations to a halt and evoking curious gazes. Eolyn held steadfast, afraid any movement might break this illusion.

It was Ernan who reached out first. He touched her cheek, and then threw his arms around her, crushing Eolyn to his chest. He kissed her face over and over, his eyes damp with tears. His aroma, though dominated by aggression and bloodshed, retained nuances of Eolyn's deepest and dearest memories: of dark and fertile earth, of pumpkins in the fall and apple blossoms in the spring, of adventures with their mother in the South Woods, of the embrace of their father at sunset.

All the best moments of their shared childhood resurfaced in one miraculous moment. Eolyn cried out for joy and wrapped her arms tight around her brother, who had returned from the dead.

Ernan took Eolyn's hand and placed one arm over her shoulder. Maintaining this protective embrace, he led his sister to his tent.

While Ernan set out dark bread, Berenben cheese, and fresh ale, Eolyn observed his large collection of weapons. She found spears, swords, and knives of all shapes and sizes. They were adorned with feathers, tassels, jewels and strange symbols. Their blades sang with voices as fresh and sharp as the first ice of winter.

"Where did you get all this?" she asked in wonder.

"I have traveled far, learning the arts of war in foreign lands. This collection is but one of the many fruits of my studies."

Eolyn ran her hands over the long, smooth shafts of his spears and the intricately worked surfaces of his shields. Then she turned to study her brother.

War had drawn a brutal map across his face. Indeed, the boy she once knew was all but gone. She lifted her hand to touch his scar. Ernan smiled and caught her fingers in his rough grip before pressing them to his lips.

"You have grown into a beautiful woman, dear Sister."

"I cannot believe you are standing before me," she exclaimed. "All this time I thought you were dead! I *buried* you, Ernan."

"Buried me?" The thought seemed to amuse him.

"When I left the forest, I passed what was left of our village. I found the remains of a child in the cellar of our home. I thought it was you. I put him to rest where we used to harvest pumpkins."

"A child in the cellar?" His lips compressed in a frown.

"Perhaps it was one of our friends."

"Gavin, maybe."

"Or Dels." Images of their childhood companions returned as if everything had happened only yesterday. Eolyn saw Gavin's shy smile and freckled face. She heard Dels shouting across the field about the flipp toad he had just caught by the brook. As a girl, Eolyn wasn't supposed to like toads, but Dels always caught the biggest and ugliest, and Eolyn could never resist his call to see them.

"Perhaps he came to the house just as the Riders set upon the village," Ernan said. "Father must have hidden him in the cellar before running off to look for you and me."

"But what happened to you? That dark hole you pushed me into was awful! I saw *everything* just as if I were in the middle of it." For the first time it occurred to her that Kaie must have left a spell on that place, though what invocation might have allowed such visions she could not imagine. "It seemed impossible that you could have survived. Then night fell and morning came, and you did not return."

Ernan's face clouded. "I am sorry, Eolyn. I never made it back to the village. I had almost cleared the woods when a stranger caught me and kept me from advancing further. The Gods gave him inhuman strength, for I struggled like a wild animal. Yet he subdued me, bound me with a rope, and hauled me up a tree. He stuffed me into a hollow and kept me there until it ended. From that high perch we were invisible to the King's men, but I saw what they did. The Riders slaughtered everyone, men, women, and children. They set fire to all the homes. They slew our father as he retreated toward the woods, and our father, Eolyn…He could wield a sword. Did you know that?"

Eolyn shook her head. She remembered very little of her father, except his smoky aroma and dark complexion. It saddened her to realize this. Why did her mother's image remain so vivid in her dreams, while her father's memory had all but faded from her heart?

Ernan guided Eolyn to the table, where he had laid out food and drink. He poured a mug of ale and offered it to her. Accustomed to the sweeter taste of wine, Eolyn thought the yeasty brew somewhat bitter.

"There was much they kept from you, many things I was forbidden to speak about. Father fought in the war, side by side with our mother. The day the Riders attacked our village, he defended himself well, sending several of the King's knights into the Underworld before him. But there were too many of them, and in the end they cut him down like all the rest.

"For three nights the stranger held me until the last of the Riders, satisfied their bloody work was finished, took the road north and disappeared. Only then did the forester untie me. I practically flew out of the branches, so great was my haste to return to you, but you'd already departed."

Ernan's jaw clenched, old frustrations smoldering in his eyes. "We tracked you for days, Eolyn. We followed whatever traces you left behind. The deeper we ventured into the woods, the more difficult your trail became. It was as if the Guendes themselves had taken to covering up your path. Then we came to a river filled with large boulders, and the man would go no further. He said the forest across the river was enchanted, that no one who wandered in there ever returned. He said if my sister crossed the river, it meant the forest had claimed her for its own and there was naught to be done. Furious, I tried to continue without him, but he knocked me down and dragged me away once again.

"For a long time I hated him. I blamed him for your disappearance and called him a coward. But as it turned out, this forester was a good and valiant man. He took me in as one of his own. He had been a Knight of Vortingen, trained under King Urien. He served Kedehen's brothers and finally Kedehen himself until the war ended and the purges began. Then he deserted, taking refuge deep in the South Woods. His name was Varyl, and in time he taught me everything he knew."

"Varyl?" Eolyn repeated in astonishment.

Ernan's gaze locked onto hers. "You have heard this name before?"

"Varyl was the forester who brought us supplies twice a year. The river you came to must have been the same one I crossed. The Guendes appeared to me on the other side. They led me to the cottage of Ghemena, a maga of the Old Orders. I lived with her from that day forward. She taught me everything she could before passing into the Afterlife."

"And you knew Varyl?"

"He never spoke to me. At first, Ghemena was going to send me back to Moisehén with him, but then she changed her mind. They argued bitterly about it. She must have demanded he never tell anyone, not even you."

Ernan's gaze turned inward and he went very still. Unsettled by his response, Eolyn leaned forward to offer a comforting touch. Without warning, he flung his mug into one of his shields, making her jump back. Clay clattered against wood and metal. Reddish brown liquid splattered everywhere and then dripped onto the ground.

Eolyn held her breath, uncertain what to do.

"Curse him!" Ernan exclaimed. "Why didn't he say anything?"

"He must have done it to protect us," Eolyn replied quietly. "To protect me and Ghemena."

Ernan lifted his face. "You are the maga discovered at the festival of Bel-Aethne, the one Corey spirited away from the King's City."

"Yes."

An odd fire ignited in his eyes. "Then it is my own sister who commands the magic of old! Your appearance is a great sign, a testimony to the worthiness of our cause. With you at my side, we can defeat the

Mage King and put an end to the evil that possesses our land."

"What are you talking about?"

"All the people you see here, Eolyn. They are my army."

"You intend to bring war upon Moisehén?"

"War is already upon us! Our people have been brutalized, our women denied of their magic. I do not intend to start the war, I intend to finish it. And now with you, my own sister." He drew a sharp breath and rose to his feet. "Already my people have repeated the story of your escape a thousand times. At last, a High Maga has come to us! A woman who can confront and defeat the heir of Kedehen."

"Confront him?" Hollow pain flared in Eolyn's heart. "I cannot confront him. He is a mage warrior. I know nothing of war."

"Yet already you have outwitted him."

"The King set me free." A mystery that disturbed her deeply. "He could have kept me prisoner, had it been his desire, but he set me free and entrusted me to Mage Corey."

Ernan leaned forward and took both her hands in his. His palms were hot. The smell of ale permeated his breath. "Don't you see, Eolyn? It's as if our destiny were written from the moment our village was destroyed. I was given to the care of a Knight of Vortingen, and you to a Maga of Old. We have each learned the skills necessary to avenge our parents' murder, the destruction of our village, and the oppression of our people. We are meant to do this together, you as maga and I as warrior."

"Our mother's battles were her own." Ghemena's words sounded shaky on Eolyn's lips. "Who are we to resurrect them?"

Ernan's brow furrowed. He sat down, heavy, in front of her. "How can you say that, Eolyn? After everything Kedehen took from us, everything he destroyed. Does it mean nothing to you, that Mother and Father were murdered, that the innocents of our village died, that you've lived your whole life in hiding just to be who you are?"

"I..." Eolyn shifted in her seat, uncertain. "I'm sorry, Ernan. It's not that I don't believe in your cause. It's just that my magic is not meant for war. Ghemena would never forgive me for putting my gifts to such use. And Kedehen is dead. The man who took everything away from us is gone. We have hardly given his son an opportunity to be King. What if he is different?"

"Did your encounter with him give you reason to believe he is different?"

"No," she admitted. "It did not."

"Eolyn, do you know how our mother died?"

His tone ignited a current of dread inside of her. "Why do you ask?"

"She died at his hands. Kaie left us to go to the King's City, hoping

173

to set the Queen free. But when she tried to escape with Briana, Prince Akmael intercepted them. He killed them both."

Eolyn stood and stumbled away from her brother, knocking the table and sending more ale to the ground. "But he was only a child at the time! Surely he did not have the power to defeat a maga warrior *and* a witch of East Selen!"

A memory broke through her words, an image of a day long past, when the boy Achim took shelter with a girl named Eolyn in the musty hollow of a large beech. Heavy summer rain poured down, hiding the world and leaving them trapped near the heart of the old tree.

That was the day Achim told Eolyn the story of his mother's death, of the stranger who called her 'friend' and then tried to kill him. Had that, too, been a lie? In her heart, Eolyn believed it was not. The tears Achim had entrusted to her, his surrender to her consoling embrace, the exposure of his vulnerability. All of this testified to his sincerity.

"That's not how it happened." Eolyn returned to her seat, truth spreading through her like the bitter essence of crushed rue. "Kaie tried to eliminate the prince. Briana died defending him. It was Kedehen who struck down our mother when he came upon them, though he did not kill her. He turned her over to the mages, to find out where she came from and what else she was hiding before her execution."

Eolyn's throat was tight with sorrow. For the first time, she comprehended the absolute remorse her mother must have suffered in her last days. The brutality of the mages, the flames that choked out her existence, the pending fate of her family, all of this would have paled next to the devastating burden of having killed one of her own sisters.

"How do you know this?" Ernan's tone was sharp, his eyes narrow.

Eolyn detected the zealous flare in his heart. Instinct told her he would not respond well to the statement *the King and I were close friends as children, and he told me all about it.*

"My tutor, Ghemena, used her divinatory tools to determine the fate of our mother," she said.

"I see." He studied her with care. "But it changes little. If our mother sought to destroy the boy, she must have known and feared what he would become. The magic of East Selen cannot remain in the line of Vortingen. The Mage King must be stopped before he consolidates his power."

Ernan rose and went to his collection of arms. Eolyn noted the height of his body, the breadth of his shoulders, the weight of his step. She wondered how many men he had killed, and how many more he would bring down before confronting the one upon whom he hoped to exact his final vengeance.

"I have something to show you, Sister." He returned with a weapon wrapped in well-oiled leather. A hissing ring cut through the air as he withdrew the sword from its resting place.

Eolyn's heart went still. She had seen this blade. She recognized its silver white glow and mysterious voice from a dream granted to her as a child, a nightmare of blood and fire. She had watched Akmael die beneath this sword.

"This was my prize from the battle of Darya," Ernan said. "This, and the scar you see on my face."

Ernan proffered it to her.

Eolyn set her fingers upon the cool silver blade. The hilt was ivory in color and without adornment. Though the weapon appeared newly forged, it whispered with the blood of the many it had slain, peasants and knights, princes and kings.

"This is Kel'Barú," Ernan said, "the sword of the Galian wizard Sapoc."

Ghemena had mentioned the fire wizards of Galia, but Eolyn knew little of their sorcery.

"How did you come by it?" she asked.

"I killed its master. It was my final victory before returning to Moisehén. When I captured Kel'Barú, I knew the time had come to confront the Mage King, for this is a blade worthy of a wizard's blood."

Eolyn hardly heard her brother's words. She sank to her knees and set her ear against the flat surface of the blade. A tremor invaded her fingers.

"You understand it," Ernan realized. "You can hear its voice!"

Eolyn closed her eyes against the sting of tears. Already Kel'Barú had learned her name.

Eolyn, it sang. *Eolyn, Eolyn, Eolyn.*

"I have heard the mages of Moisehén can speak to metals," Ernan continued with excitement, "but Corey insisted this sword was unintelligible."

"I have not understood the voice of any sword until this day," Eolyn confessed. *Why*, she wondered with a breaking heart, *would this, of all swords, speak to me?*

"Sweet sister." Ernan took the blade from her and sheathed it. Setting his strong hands on Eolyn's shoulders, he brought her to her feet and enclosed her in his solid embrace. "Do not weep! Can you not see the herald of our destiny? You can speak to this sword. I can wield it. Together, we will use Kel'Barú to destroy the Mage King! Together, we will bring the days of our exile to an end."

CHAPTER TWENTY-NINE

Kel'Barú

WITHIN A FEW DAYS of Eolyn's arrival, Khelia and several of her companions returned from a hunting expedition, laden with venison, rabbits, and wildfowl. Cheeks flushed and eyes shining, Khelia greeted Eolyn with happy laughter and a full embrace.

Khelia, it turned out, had known Ernan for many years and even fought multiple battles with him. The Mountain Warrior witnessed the confrontation between Ernan and the Galian wizard Sapoc in the Battle of Darya, and she relished telling the tale over and over, each version somehow more bloody and violent than the last. She stood on equal footing with Ernan in the planning of the rebellion. Indeed, their army included a large number of warriors, men and women, who had followed Khelia from the Paramen Mountains.

Eolyn was truly happy to see her. In short order, the women developed a custom of seeking each other out in the afternoons. Distancing themselves from the encampment, they would engage in a game of throwing knives, or simply converse while enjoying the forest. Though Ernan's army was located well inside the heart of the ancient woodland, there was a patch of young trees nearby, full of birch and alder that stretched in thin columns toward the azure sky. Their soft trunks made for excellent targets.

"We could not have asked for a clearer sign from the Gods," declared Khelia during one of these outings. "That they should deliver you, a High Maga, into our company at precisely this moment."

"You speak like my brother." Eolyn sent her blade singing into a pale trunk. "I've told him already. I can't help you with this campaign. Ghemena taught me nothing about war."

Khelia flung her blade to meet Eolyn's. "You have been underestimating your abilities from the day we first met! You stopped a red death flame in its path without as much as a staff in your hand. I think that would be a very useful ability to have on the battlefield."

"I know a handful of flames for ceremonial purposes, a couple for self-defense. I have some talent with the knife, and I fight well enough to scare away ill-intentioned village boys. That is all."

"We have no one else with your skills in magic."

"What about Mage Corey?"

"Corey has exceptional gifts for his rank, but he does not command your breadth of knowledge." Khelia's voice lost all undertones of amusement. "We need you to win this war, Eolyn."

"An entire Order of Magas, with an army of maga warriors, opposed the House of Vortingen once," Eolyn countered. "We know where that left them: scattered and destroyed. My life as a refugee is testimony to their extermination. If you choose to lead your people to a similar fate, you cannot expect me to take part in it."

Khelia extended her arm toward her knife, sitting snug inside the trunk of the young birch.

Ehekaht, she murmured. *Naeom denae.*

The handle shivered, and the blade worked its way stiffly out of the wood before flying back to Khelia's grip.

Eolyn stared at her, astonished. "Where did you learn to do that?"

"My father was a Mountain Warrior who descended from our lands with his comrades to assist the magas against Kedehen. That is how he met my mother, who was an initiate when the war began. Afterwards, they fled to the mountains to escape the purges. I was born among the Mountain People. My mother taught me the traditions of Moisehén, and my father, how to use the sword. I figured out for myself how to integrate the two."

Eolyn studied her friend, a glimmer of hope in her heart. Khelia knew something of the craft. She had not been educated under the strict traditions of the Old Orders, but she was a maga nonetheless, and a warrior at that.

Extending her arm, Eolyn called her own blade. As it flew into her grip she cast Khelia a sideways glance. "Who taught you how to sing?"

Khelia laughed. "The whole village! That is the tradition of our people."

"And your mother anointed you High Maga?"

"No. She never completed her own training. I learned much from her though, and I also sought instruction from our Wissens, but Mountain Magic is very different from the sorcery of Moisehén. So I have an odd combination of gifts, being adept at some things and useless in others. Master Tzeremond and the Mage King won't know what to expect from me. That is one of the reasons why I believe we have a chance."

"Yet by the same argument, my participation would be a liability, for

I was trained in the old ways. They will know exactly what to expect from me and how to counter it."

"Perhaps," Khelia conceded, throwing her knife to a new mark. "Although, when you were brought before the Mage King, he encountered something unexpected, something so surprising it made him lose his bearings and set you free."

The observation subdued Eolyn, turning her thoughts toward the true dilemma of her heart. She could not tolerate the idea of confronting Akmael on the battlefield. She could not envision using her magic to kill him, no matter what he had become.

"As for Tzeremond," continued Khelia, "our greatest strength now is his fear of you."

"Fear of *me*?" Now it was Eolyn's turn to laugh. "He hates me, but he does not fear me. Far from it."

"Corey said the stench of his fear filled the throne room."

"The air in that place was rank, but not with Tzeremond's dread."

"Your apprehension must have inhibited your ability to detect it."

With a slight shrug, Eolyn whispered to her knife before sending it toward the new target. It sank into the bark with a satisfying thunk, right next to Khelia's blade.

Khelia clapped her hands in delight. "Excellent throw! You do have some talent. Do you know how to handle the sword?"

"I learned a little once." *From a boy I trusted, with a blade Dragon destroyed.* "I was never very good at it. I don't like swords."

"You like Kel'Barú."

Eolyn could not argue with this. Something about that weapon had captured her heart. The way it hummed in Ernan's grip, the way its long silver face reflected all the colors of the forest.

Years ago, Akmael had told her magic could not be used to forge weapons, but the Galian wizards had apparently found a way.

"You should give Kel'Barú a try," Khelia said. "It's meant to be wielded by a sorcerer, not by common soldiers like us."

"Ernan handles it well enough."

"It only performs in his grip when you're around. If I didn't know better, I'd say that sword is in love with you."

A shiver passed through Eolyn. She did not want to wield that sword, lest it slay Akmael while in her hands. "My skills are not worthy of such a weapon."

Khelia flung her blade anew, giving its flight an elegant arc and landing it at nearly twenty paces. Visibly pleased, she set her hands on her hips and cocked her brow at Eolyn. "Well then, we'll just have to practice, won't we?"

Despite Khelia's insistence, Eolyn did not for a moment entertain the thought of expanding her meager knowledge of weaponry. Ghemena's abhorrence of warfare had long since turned her away from this path. If she was to restore women's magic to Moisehén, she wished to do it on her own terms and with her own gifts.

Still, Kel'Barú called to her.

With Ernan's permission, she began to take the sword on long walks. She wandered deep into the ancient forest with the blade strapped to her back, drinking up the rich magic of those verdant corridors, until she found a clear and peaceful brook by which to rest. There, she would unsheathe the blade and set it next to her against the solid trunk of a beech, oak, or willow.

Sun filtered through the canopy. Trees whispered on the wind. Kel'Barú sang songs of another world.

On the western shores of Galia, fire springs from the earth and flows in burning rivers to the sea. It is from this union of earth, fire, and water that the Galian wizards draw their power.

Ghemena had told Eolyn these stories, years ago in front of the hearth in their cottage.

There was a time when Galian wizards visited Moisehén. They were comrades of our mages, and they loved our magas, taking many with them as consorts. But the rise of Kedehen put an end that friendship. The Galians were not pleased by the war and the persecutions that followed.

Kel'Barú's smooth hum reflected the liquid melody of the brook. It told her of its birth many generations before, of battles it had fought and warriors it had killed. The more time Eolyn spent with Kel'Barú, the more she felt drawn to its compelling voice.

"I would have liked to have met your former master," she murmured one day. "He must have been a noble wizard, for you are a noble weapon."

Kel'Barú beamed at this compliment, catching the sun's reflection in its silver blade.

"Do you not resent my brother, at least a little, for having slain him?"

At this Kel'Barú's glow dimmed. The sword sank into a deep silence, the heavy quiet of the center of the earth, a sad stillness only metals could achieve. When at last it spoke, its voice was subdued. *Sapoc was not my master.*

Surprised by this response, Eolyn reached out and set her tapered fingers upon the blade, cold to the touch despite the afternoon sun.

"I'm sorry, Kel'Barú," she whispered. "I think I understand something of your grief. I, too, have lost many who were dear to me, a warrior and wizard among them."

"And I, it seems, have lost the woman I love to a piece of forged metal."

Startled by the man's voice, Eolyn snapped out of her trance.

Tahmir stood over her, his dark eyes filled with amusement, his silky black hair flowing free about his broad shoulders. She had not even heard his approach.

"By the Gods, it's good to see you!" Jumping to her feet, Eolyn flung herself into his embrace. The rich spice of his aroma inundated her senses. "What of Rishona and Adiana? What of the rest of the Circle?"

"We abandoned camp the night you left. Rishona and Adiana arrived with me today. The others travel by their assigned routes and should join us soon."

"Have you any word of the King?"

"Your appearance at Bel-Aethne caused a great stir. The people of Moisehén say it is an omen. Tzeremond's mages are mad with rage. The purges have been renewed."

"Purges?" Eolyn withdrew in alarm. "But there is no one left to purge!"

"They take whomever they can, girls with an unusual look, spirited women, widows who prospered after their husbands' deaths. It does not matter anymore whether the magic is real."

"And the King does nothing?"

"What would you expect him to do?"

Tahmir's discerning gaze unsettled Eolyn. Ghemena had told her the Syrnte could hear thoughts, and that time bent around their magic in strange ways. She now realized the full implications of this. How many of her thoughts had he heard during these past months? How much did he know of her past, and what had he seen of her future?

"A great unrest is spreading through Moisehén," he said. "Your people are tired of the Mage King. The appearance of a maga has renewed their courage. The moment is ripe for your brother's rebellion. With you at his side, there is little now that can stop him."

"When I was a child, I was told to run and hide from men-at-arms," Eolyn replied. "Now I am told I must run to meet them."

Tahmir took her hands and brought them to his lips. "Ernan and Khelia are skilled warriors, but they need you at their side if they are to succeed in this campaign."

"Are you here to convince me, as well?"

"No. This is decision is yours alone to make."

Eolyn's eyes narrowed and she withdrew. "You knew Ernan was my brother all along, didn't you?"

Tahmir hesitated before admitting, "I recognized you as Ernan's sister the moment I first saw you."

Eolyn could hardly believe her ears. *Is this how all men responded to the gift of a woman's affection, with lies and deceit?* "When were you planning to tell me?"

He studied her with a frown. "It is not prudent to reveal everything I see. If I caused distress by keeping your brother's existence from you, I apologize. It was not my intention. The window in which you were meant to confront this truth had not yet arrived."

Anger rose to her cheeks. "And the window in which I get to confront the truth about you? When will that appear?"

Tahmir drew a slow breath and looked away. "I believe you know the answer to the question you ask."

"Well yes, as a matter of fact I do. Corey told me about your place among your people. But I had rather hoped to hear it from you."

His expression hardened. "There was much you chose to keep from me."

"What interest does a Syrnte Prince have in the provincial conflicts of Moisehén?"

"I am here to avenge the death of my eldest sister, Tamara."

Eolyn checked her anger. This Corey had not mentioned. "You have another sister?"

"Had. Tamara was the wife of Feroden, the third son of Urien."

"There was a marriage between the royal houses of Moisehén and the Syrnte? I've never heard of such a thing."

"It was not widely known. Feroden thought he would never be called to wear the Crown of Vortingen. He traveled far outside Moisehén and eventually reached my homeland, where he became enamored of our way of life and won Tamara's hand in marriage. Then word arrived that his second brother had perished and the Crown awaited him. Feroden did not wish to leave the Syrnte. But his loyalty to the bloodline of his fathers prevailed. He knew his younger brother could not assume the crown, having chosen the life of a mage. He offered Tamara the opportunity to divorce him with honor and remain with her people, but Tamara would hear nothing of it. She vowed to accompany Feroden to the end of her days, and found her vow fulfilled much sooner than anticipated."

"What do you mean?"

"Feroden's caravan was attacked on the way to Moisehén. No one was spared, and the many generous gifts of my father were plundered. It was only through the good grace of a forester who happened upon the scene afterwards that my sister's remains were returned to our family. My father cursed the instigators of this crime and vowed before the Gods of our land that our family would avenge it."

"And you are bound to carry out his oath? You couldn't have seen more than a few summers when all this came to pass."

"It is our way. Years later, Rishona received a vision in which she saw the perpetrator of this disgrace, the man who gave the orders to murder Feroden and all who accompanied him."

"The Mage King?"

"No. Kedehen had no knowledge of the plot to take his brother's life. It was Master Tzeremond who dispatched the assassins."

"Tzeremond." The name fell from her lips in a soft hiss.

Eolyn turned away from Tahmir and drifted to a young oak at the edge of the stream. She laid a hand upon the rough bark and stared into crystalline waters running over smooth pebbles. "Always Tzeremond. And you would kill King Akmael to get to him?"

"I will do what I must do."

Eolyn's heart sank under the revelation of this circle of vengeance, marked while one man was a boy and the other not yet born. "How the threads of the past have come together, only to cast shadows on the future. What does your Syrnte awareness tell you now, Tahmir? What direction must I take from here?"

"You know I will not answer that question."

"Tahmir, I can't…" Her voice trailed off in confusion. She looked to him for help, but Tahmir's expression was firm, impassive.

How little I know of him, she realized.

How very little he had allowed her to see.

Eolyn sank to the ground, supporting herself against the solid weight of the young oak. "I can't."

What was it she could not do? Touch Tahmir as she had before? Seek the warmth of his company under the midnight moon? Drink the wine of his pleasure with the same abandon? Stop loving him altogether? She did not know, for she could not see beyond this moment, in which the fabric that once bound them was being torn asunder.

Tahmir approached and knelt beside her. He pulled her into his warmth. He caressed her face with tender kisses. His hands traced the curves of her body, reviving memories of pleasures they had discovered in each other's arms.

But Eolyn could not respond. The river of her passion had run dry.

With a quiet sigh he relented, wrapping his arms around her and simply holding her close.

"You need not give up all your dreams, my love," he murmured. "You must only discard the illusions that no longer serve you."

CHAPTER THIRTY

The Hunt for Eolyn

AKMAEL HAD NOT SEEN TZEREMOND dedicate such zeal to a task since he destroyed the last belongings of Queen Briana. His mages ravaged the camp abandoned by the Circle, but found no remnant of the maga's passing—no comb, no veil or purse that could be connected to her. The Master set his best diviners to work with the finest seeing wells, but no trace of the witch was revealed. Thick branches of fir were imbued with the power of flight, facilitating prolonged forays over the landscape by the High Mages, but to no avail. Middle Mages were instructed to question the plants and animals, the rivers and stones, but everything responded with silence.

When Sir Drostan informed Akmael that Tzeremond's rage had spilled over into renewed purges, the King openly rebuked the wizard for the first time. Their impassioned disagreement played out in front of the Council, providing Akmael a useful opportunity to gauge the loyalties of the High Mages. The court physician Rezlyn, the diplomat Tzetobar, Sir Drostan, and Thelyn refrained from falling in line behind Tzeremond. Of these, only Drostan inspired Akmael's complete trust.

In the end, Tzeremond yielded to the King's will, but the damage was already done. Wearied by the reign of Kedehen and disheartened by the violence under their new King, the people of Moisehén simmered in discontent. Akmael hoped to quiet their fury and avoid an outright rebellion by securing Eolyn in the coming weeks. If they were not appeased by seeing her at his side, at least he could use her power to subdue them.

In either case, he intended to find her before Tzeremond. Of late, the wizard's prudence was too easily blinded by dogmatic wrath. Akmael feared for Eolyn's safety, should she fall first into Tzeremond's hands.

It was late at night, and more than half a moon had passed since Bel-Aethne, when Akmael retreated to his chambers and retrieved the silver web from its hiding place. Not more than a year before, he had nearly

183

destroyed the gift of his mother, enraged because it had failed him. Instead of carrying him back to the South Woods and Eolyn, the medallion had flung him across the provinces of the kingdom, landing him in a dozen small villages, none of which bore any sign of his childhood friend.

Akmael now believed Eolyn's ward must have deflected the seeking power of the web, causing him to miss her in space and time. Perhaps with some minor interventions, the problem could be fixed.

He set the jewel on a polished oak table, next to the ceremonial mask he had confiscated from Eolyn when they had brought her to him as a prisoner. The silver web sparkled under the flickering light of the torches, and the folds of her mask seemed to waver with the shadows. After a careful search, Akmael found what he sought: a coppery strand of Eolyn's hair, glowing with magic and still bearing traces of her exquisite aroma.

With a quiet invocation to Dragon, he wove the hair into the heirloom of his mother, snaking it tightly through the intricate mesh. When he finished, a sudden white glow flashed through the medallion, fusing the strand of hair to the web and rendering it indistinguishable from the other threads.

Satisfied, Akmael stood and lifted the circle by its silver chain. He drew a breath and began a new incantation, one he had worked meticulously by integrating the lullaby of his mother with a spell designed to separate the seam of a maga's ward.

Ehekahtu
Elaeom enem, eleaom enem
Sepoenem fae
Elaeom enem, elaeom enem
Renoenem mae
Ehukae

As he repeated the verse, the stone walls melted around him and soft loam rose to his feet.

The web had taken him to a forest, ancient in aspect though different from the South Woods. The pale light of the new moon filtered through the canopy. A breeze shifted restless against the trees. He thought he could feel Eolyn's essence on the wind, but she was nowhere to be seen.

Disappointed though not deterred, Akmael lifted the medallion to try again. Just as he spun the web to begin his invocation, a soft rustle in the underbrush detained him. Eolyn appeared a few paces away in the shape of Wolf, her true identity betrayed by the full spectrum of her magnificent aura.

Akmael caught his breath. The Gods must have favored him, for she did not detect his scent. Stepping into the clearing, she searched the leaf litter with her snout, her awareness focused on some favored smell emanating from the damp earth. Her coarse gray fur blended into the shadows. The faint moonlight glinted against her black eyes. She continued oblivious to him, until in a sudden shift of attention, she paused and looked up. She sniffed at the air, and her muscles tensed. Her ears turned in Akmael's direction.

Then she growled and bolted into the forest.

Calling upon the shape of Wolf, Akmael charged after her.

Eolyn hurtled through the bushes, managing with nimble turns a rough terrain unknown to Akmael. Branches caught at his fur and scratched his snout. Tangled roots threatened to trip his paws. More than once, Eolyn gained enough distance to lose sight of her, yet Akmael kept tight upon her scent and did not give up.

His muscles began to burn. His tongue hung limp from his jowls. Panting hot clouds into the air, he pushed his limbs to move faster.

Without warning, the undergrowth disappeared. Akmael skidded into a small clearing. The she-wolf paced a confused circle in front of him, her whimpers soft and high pitched. A steep wall of rock had cut her flight short. Upon sensing Akmael, she swung around to confront him and bared her fangs in a vicious snarl.

They stalked each other, heads low and tails ominously still, quiet growls and sharp barks building in a tense duet. Eolyn sprang first, striking Akmael's shoulders and digging her claws deep into his fur. Her teeth sought his neck. Akmael twisted his throat out of reach, forcing his snout underneath her muzzle and leaving her snapping at his ears instead. Again he ducked his head, barely avoiding the tear of her canines.

He had never seen Eolyn so intent on drawing blood. Wedging his paws up through her hold, he pushed against her muzzle and spread his claws over her face. With a sharp yelp, Eolyn stumbled back, breaking their grapple. Recovering her balance, she lunged low, fangs flashing in the moonlight. Just as her jaws snapped shut, Akmael reared up on his hind legs, leaving nothing for her to take hold of. Coming down upon her back, he caught the nape of her neck with razor sharp teeth and forced her decisively to the ground.

Eolyn went very still, though her muscles remained rigid. After several moments she tried to shift her position, scooting a few inches along the ground. He tightened his grip with a low growl, sending a clear signal that the strength of his muzzle could break her neck.

Again she paused. He felt her pulse against his jowls, rapid and strong. The intensity of their conflict had left her fur warm and damp at the roots. Her rich musk rose about him in waves, saturating his senses to the point of dizziness. His loins tightened with need. Every instinct of Wolf was urging him to claim her, right then and there.

Was such a thing possible?

Did the mages and magas of old partake in the pleasure of the Gods even when they shape shifted?

Eolyn's muzzle sank between her paws. Her ears twitched and she whimpered quietly. Her pulse slowed. The tension drained out of her haunches and into the midnight earth.

Interpreting this as a sign of submission, Akmael loosened his hold and stepped away.

In an instant, Eolyn rose to her feet, resumed her human form, and kicked him full in the stomach. The force of her strike surprised Akmael. He hit the ground with a yelp, and the shape of Wolf deserted him. His hand went instinctively to where the blow burned against his side.

"You have lost nothing of your strength and skill," he said, "but don't you think that move was a little unfair?"

"You lied to me!" she shot back.

Akmael could not help but smile. "I did not lie."

"You said—"

"It is not what I said." Akmael pushed himself to his feet, feeling the sting of the scratches she had left. She had given an excellent chase and a worthy fight. He was lucky his ears were still intact. "It is what I did not say—what I never told you—that has infuriated you."

"All those times you tried to talk me out of studying magic when you knew someday you would be King and with a wave of your..." She moved her hands through the air as if searching for the proper word. "Your *scepter* you could bring down the laws of this land and create new ones!"

"It is not that simple."

"Of course it's that simple!"

"I am a mage, not a seer. I had no way of knowing under what circumstances your abilities would come to light. My father would have suffered little debate in sending you to the pyre. Indeed, they would have transformed you to ashes before I knew you had been apprehended. Even if I did hear of your arrest, I could not have impeded the course of events. As a prince, my will counted for nothing."

"Well, as King, it counts for everything."

"The power of the Crown is inextricably bound to Tzeremond's Order. This is the legacy I inherited from my father. It could take years for me to unravel."

"So you were impotent then and you are impotent now."

"That is not what I said."

"I don't believe you Akmael! How do you expect me to believe a word you say after what you tried to do to me in the city?"

Akmael hesitated. He could not deny the hunger he had felt, the dark intentions that had risen in his heart. "I am sorry, Eolyn. You must understand; I have lived all my life in a place where shadows were confused with light, and light with shadows. I misinterpreted what I felt when I saw you. I was a student of Tzeremond. How else could I have reacted in the presence of a woman of your power?"

"Did you do the same to the girl they brought you on the third night of Bel-Aethne?" she countered. "Did you strike terror in her heart before forcing her into your bed?"

"No." He had cast a temporary illusion over that girl, giving her red hair and earth brown eyes. But she had been no substitute for his Eolyn. "It was not like that."

Eolyn lunged at Akmael, hand raised to strike him. He caught her wrist in a vice-like grip that gave pause to her fury. In the silence that followed, Akmael measured the heat under Eolyn's skin, the rhythm of her pulse, the condensation of her breath against the cool night air.

"Eolyn." He did not bother to hide the note of surprised hope in his voice. "Are you jealous?"

She wrenched free of his hold. "Your magic is a disgrace! You have allowed your abilities to be twisted to foul ends. Dragon did not grant us these powers to invoke fear or take advantage of those weaker than ourselves. And our festivals are meant to celebrate the heritage of Moisehén, not to reinforce your authority, much less your sexual prowess."

"That may be the case, but your question about the third night of Bel-Aethne...It did not arise out of concern for the proper interpretation and practice of magic. Did it?"

Eolyn lifted her chin. "There is no place for jealousy in a maga's heart."

Akmael caught her lips in his. In an instant the spark granted to them as adolescents was reignited. He wrapped his arms around her, inhaling her honey and wood aroma, intertwining his fingers in her silky hair, exploring every delicate contour of her face and throat. The force of his passion pushed her back against the raw trunk of a large tree. His hands traveled insatiable over the landscape of her body, at once familiar and new.

A broken sob escaped her lips, followed by a soft moan. She sought his kisses and drank with abandon. Her breasts rose toward his touch, straining against the confines of her tunic. Akmael wanted nothing more than to tear through that thin fabric, to bind her to him in intimacy and release himself inside her earthy heat.

His lips came to rest against her forehead, his breath hot upon her skin. He could hear the blood rushing through her veins. She remained quiet in his embrace, her breath deep and steady, her aspect one of uneasy resignation.

"If you truly remember our childhood friendship with fondness," she murmured, "you will release me from this spell you have cast."

"There is no magic in Moisehén that can invoke this." She had to acknowledge that in this much, he spoke the truth. The mages of Moisehén had recognized long ago the impotence of their magic in matters of the heart. "Spells of passion and desire are the domain of the Gods, to be crafted only by them. This feeling that binds our hearts is their gift. To deny it would be an insult."

"Then how do you propose we accept it?"

He lifted her face to his. "Come back with me."

"As your prisoner?"

"As my Queen."

Sadness filled her aura. "Don't you see, Akmael? It's the same thing."

He released her and stepped away.

"Corey told me how your mother lived," Eolyn continued, "how she died. Confined to the East Tower, locked behind doors sealed by magic. Was it to keep her in, or to keep Tzeremond out?"

"My father cared for his Queen. He never allowed any harm to come to her. It was a maga who killed her in the end, not the Mage King, or the wizard whom you so detest."

Eolyn stiffened and cast her gaze toward the forest, arms folded tight across her chest. "He would have destroyed her, if the maga had not come. And he destroyed what he could afterwards. Corey said Tzeremond burned everything she left behind, that none of her magic survived."

Akmael clenched his jaw. "What, precisely, is the nature of your relationship with Mage Corey?"

"What?" Her eyes snapped back to him. "What does that have to do with anything?"

"And the Syrnte man who greeted you at the castle gates? Who is he to you?"

"Is that what this is about, Akmael?" Her anger flared anew. "Do you think by seducing me you can win me over to your side? Those people are my friends! They took me in when I had no place to go, no one to turn to. Their leader is my brother."

Akmael drew a sharp breath. "Your brother? You said he was dead!"

"I thought he was. I have only learned since Bel-Aethne that he lives. A forester rescued him the day our village was destroyed, a man trained as a knight under your grandfather. He taught my brother everything he could, and when Ernan was of age, he traveled to distant lands to learn more about the arts of war. My brother's entire life has been driven by a single purpose: to confront and kill the Mage King of Moisehén. Now that your father is gone, his obsession turns to you."

Akmael considered her words in silence. "I have a formidable rival, then. With access to the secrets of the Knights of Vortingen, and a High Maga at his side."

Eolyn averted her gaze.

"Is this what you want, Eolyn? To make war upon me?"

She shifted on her feet and looked up at him. "You know very well Ghemena left me ill-disposed toward this bloody sport, but I understand what they will face in you, in your army, and in Tzeremond's mages. I will not leave them alone. I will stand with them, even if the only service I can provide, in the end, is to ease their passing into the Afterlife."

Akmael clenched his fists. It was not possible she would refuse him for a band of common rebels. Her destiny was greater than that. "I am bound by the blood in my veins and the vows I made to my fathers to defend the Crown of Vortingen. I will show no mercy to those who try to wrest it from my stewardship, not to your friends, not even to your brother."

Eolyn's voice turned bitter. "You must, of course, defend the Crown as you deem best."

In a matter of moments, the few paces that separated them had expanded into an impassable chasm.

She will not come with me tonight, he realized.

At least, not willingly.

A shadow rose inside of him, dark and foreboding.

All I need do is reach out and take her.

This game would end, and his hunger would be satiated. Eolyn's magic would be his forever. But she would be gone.

"Akmael." Her hand touched his, tentative and warm. "It does not have to come to war. If you would only—"

"Go," he commanded, all his will focused on subduing his appetite. "Leave me before I take you by force."

Eolyn hesitated, but only for a moment. In a flash of white light she assumed the shape of Owl, fleeing from him on silent wings.

CHAPTER THIRTY-ONE

Premonition

EOLYN TOLD NO ONE of her encounter with Akmael. After all, what would she say? That the Mage King could find her whenever he pleased. That he toyed with her like a cat with its prey, capturing her, seducing her, setting her free on the threat of trapping her again.

That his kiss lingered on her lips, taking her into her dreams at night and bringing her back to sensual awareness with the dawn.

That she longed and feared for his return.

Why did he let her go? Why did he not empty her of her magic and end this torture?

She bore her doubt and confusion, her desire and dread, in agonized solitude, for if Ernan or anyone else knew, they might cast her aside as a traitor. Who among them would understand this insidious flaw of her heart, this debilitating need to see in Akmael the man she had hoped Achim would become?

In the weeks before Summer Solstice, Ernan's and Khelia's army emerged from the forests of East Selen. Their march reverberated through the earth, making the very trees tremble.

As the rebels muddied rivers and trampled fields, the trepidation of the peasant farmers floated toward them like thin smoke, sharp and compelling. When Eolyn inhaled their fear, it settled at her core, fueling the fire of her heart with a disconcerting power. For the first time, she understood the temptation of that dark wine, imbibed all too often by Tzeremond and his mages. The realization she shared something of their thirst did nothing to soothe her troubled heart.

Winning Selen was expected. The province had never pardoned Kedehen for annihilating the Clan of the East and demolishing the magical stronghold of Berlingen. The leading nobles recognized in the rebellion an opportunity to recapture the glory lost so bitterly during the war. For years, they had cooperated with the movement, concealing its growing army in their dense forests and managing multiple supply lines.

190

When Ernan's troops arrived at the Town of Selen, the gates were thrown open to the rebels. The ruling families greeted them with much ceremony, their patriarchs embracing Corey and Ernan, their youngest daughters filling Eolyn's arms with fragrant wildflowers.

The overlord, Meryth Baramon, approached Eolyn with reverence, taking her hands in his with a deep bow. He was a tall man whose chestnut beard had begun to gray. His hazel eyes were somber yet kind. Eolyn noticed a certain resemblance to Corey in the length of his nose and the set of his jaw, although the mage had insisted he held no blood ties to the surviving nobles of Selen.

"We bid you a most joyous welcome, Maga Eolyn," he said. "May you always find home and hearth in Selen."

"Thank you, Lord Baramon." Eolyn bowed in return. "I am honored by your kindness."

"Baramon," Corey appeared at her side and greeted him with a hearty embrace. "It is good to see you again."

"And you, my friend. We have a special gift for you and the maga."

"I hope it involves much food and wine," Corey said.

Baramon laughed. "Yes, much food and wine, and the detained mages of Selen."

Corey lifted his brow. "You have all of them?"

"A few slipped through our grasp, but those who did not flee west were easy enough to round up. There weren't many here, as you know, and they are Middle Mages all, but students of Tzeremond nonetheless. We can watch them burn on the morrow, if you like."

"Burn?" Eolyn frowned. "What do you mean, 'burn'?"

They looked at her, Baramon's expression one of puzzled surprise, Corey's predictably unreadable.

"Surely you are jesting?" she prompted.

"Maga Eolyn," Baramon replied, "these are the same men who burned your sisters. They would see you on the pyre given the opportunity."

"They are sons of Caradoc just as I am a daughter of Aithne," Eolyn countered. "To kill them would accomplish nothing except to bleed Moisehén further of her magic. We cannot take what little is left of our heritage and simply convert it into ashes." She looked to Corey. "Surely you cannot agree with this proposal. You must know these men."

"Yes, I do. For that reason, I'm inclined to agree with Baramon."

"If they are Middle Mages, it means Tzeremond judged them unworthy to study High Magic," Eolyn pointed out. "He would not have judged them unworthy had they accepted his doctrine in full."

"That is a dangerous assumption to make," Corey replied. "Many were turned away from High Magic because Tzeremond judged their indoctrination incomplete, but many more simply did not have the skill, whether they accepted his teachings or not."

"Then we must at least make an effort to distinguish between the two. We cannot simply burn the innocent with the guilty."

Corey considered her words. "Well we could, in fact. It's been done before."

She drew an angry breath at his tactless humor, but Corey raised his hands in a conciliatory gesture.

"Perhaps she has a point, Baramon," the mage said. "Those who are not a threat could be useful allies if we spare them."

The lord glanced uncertainly at Eolyn. He stepped close to the mage, his voice low and strained. "Ernan will not delay his campaign while we hold trials for these men, and keeping them imprisoned with their magic unbound is no small matter. Already I've tripled the guard. I cannot sustain this situation indefinitely."

Corey frowned and met Eolyn's gaze. "Perhaps the maga would be willing to accompany me to the dungeons this afternoon. Together we can bind their magic, rendering them no different from any other prisoner."

Eolyn could imagine a hundred ways she would rather spend her afternoon, but if it meant saving the lives of some of these mages, then descend into the dungeons she would. "Of course, Mage Corey."

"How long would the binding last?" Baramon asked.

"On a Middle Mage?" Corey shrugged. "Until Maga Eolyn or I choose to release them."

Baramon studied them both and gave a curt nod. "Very well. We will do as Maga Eolyn suggests."

He took his leave to speak with Ernan.

Corey drew close and murmured, "How does it feel, Maga Eolyn, to hold the power of life and death in your hands?"

Eolyn recoiled. "You know those men don't deserve to die without a trial."

"Do I? You'll find, in times of political turmoil, that what one deserves and what one gets are often very different. Trials do little to change that."

"You object to sparing their lives?"

"No." A percipient smile invaded his expression. "Quite the contrary. This is a welcome omen of things to come. They'll call you Queen before this all ends, Eolyn. And I daresay, you will rise to the title."

She paled at the disturbing prophecy, but Corey did not seem to notice. With a subtle wink he left her alone to join Baramon and her brother.

192

The day after their entry into the Town of Selen, Ernan called his war council. They met in a room set aside by Baramon. Wine, ale, dark bread, and cold meats were laid out in generous portions. Khelia, Mage Corey, and Rishona sat with Ernan and Lord Baramon. Tahmir did not join them, as he had taken a more discrete route through the southern forests, accompanied by a small retinue of Syrnte cavalry.

Eolyn, averse to the confines of stone walls, took a place next to a large window overlooking the tile roofs of the town below. It was a bright day, and the streets were full of activity. Summer flowers adorned amber colored homes. Over the fields just beyond the city wall, she spotted a hawk in flight. The fear of peasant farmers could not be felt here, and Eolyn was glad for it.

"I say we march on the King's City." Ernan's passionate declaration reminded Eolyn of their mother. "Draw him out of his fortress, and vanquish him on the plains below the Stone Foundation of his fathers."

"We aren't ready, Ernan," Khelia objected. "We must reinforce our army before meeting him. Our first step should be to seal our alliance with Moehn. Then we must negotiate with Selkynsen."

"Moehn is a province of farmers," Ernan said. His disdain surprised Eolyn. Moehn had been their home, after all. "They have no military tradition. Even if we drag them out of their reluctance toward warfare, training their peasantry would take too much time."

"It was a knight from Moehn who killed Kedehen," Corey pointed out.

Ernan scowled and waved away the comment.

"It's not the skill of their fighters that would help us," Khelia insisted. "Moehn is the source of food for the entire kingdom. All we have to do is cut off the pass of Aerunden, and Moisehén will be brought to its knees."

"If we wish to move this war to a rapid conclusion, we should leave Moehn to its farming and secure the support of Selkynsen," Corey said. "Selkynsen controls the kingdom's supply lines, and it has the largest military force next to the King's."

"The Lords of Selkynsen will not be easily swayed," Baramon cautioned. "They prospered under Kedehen. They were the first to bow to Tzeremond, purging magas and all other dissidents. Indeed, the most successful merchants of the province built their fortunes on the ashes of the purges. They have no reason to rebel."

"Their submission to Tzeremond was driven by practical concerns," Mage Corey said. "They would have followed any mage—or maga—who happened to have the King's ear at the time."

"Well, we can't offer Selkynsen the King's ear." Khelia flashed a clever smile. "Except perhaps on a silver platter, when it's all over."

"If persuasion is not an option then we could try to invade the province," Ernan said. "Conquer the lords and bring their levies into our service."

"The price of invading Selkynsen would be too high," Khelia countered. "We'd lose more than we could ever gain."

"Have you so little faith in our people, Khelia?" Ernan said.

"All I'm saying is that we have one chance to make this work. We must play our strengths with utmost care. Time our strike with the patience of a lynx."

"There is no need to invade." Mage Corey folded his hands on the table and leaned forward. "We laid a strong foundation in Selkynsen during our years with the Circle. Their conversion may not be as difficult as you think."

"You can't possibly believe they would risk open rebellion?" Baramon's doubt showed in his frown.

"A broader vision has been visited upon Selkynsen since we began our work there. They are no longer driven solely by their pocketbooks, or even by the security of the existing order." Corey made eye contact with each of them as he spoke. "With a few more seasons, we might have converted the entire province. But even now we have powerful friends. We have Lord Herensen, who governs nearly half the province and holds considerable sway over the rest. It would be prudent to talk to them before we invest our efforts in anything else."

"You are thinking to undertake this task yourself?" Ernan said.

Corey nodded. "I am."

"No." Eolyn's interjection brought all eyes to her. "It's too great a risk, Corey. If something should happen to you…"

Corey gave her a warm smile. "I am moved by your concern, Maga Eolyn, but there is no need. I will contact Lord Herensen directly. He knows who can be trusted and will arrange the appropriate meetings."

Biting her lip in doubt, Eolyn turned back to the view of the city.

Something's not right.

Shadows lurked behind Corey's words, a troubling premonition just beyond her grasp.

"How many of our people do you need?" Khelia asked.

"Two companions," Corey replied. "No more. We must travel with discretion."

"Even if we cannot sway all the Lords of Selkynsen, dividing them would make a difference." Khelia nodded, thoughtful. "It would make a very great difference, indeed."

"Camron and Sael will accompany you." Ernan stood as if preparing to close the meeting. "They will be ready at the first light of dawn."

"I will accept these escorts, Ernan," Corey said graciously, "but we will not leave until after Summer Solstice."

"But that is days away! We've no time to waste, Corey."

"The observance of our High Holidays is not a waste." Eolyn felt Corey's silver-green eyes settle upon her, though she kept her back to the company. "Nearly a generation has passed since I've seen a High Maga at Summer Solstice, and I am not about to pass up this opportunity now."

CHAPTER THIRTY-TWO

Summer Solstice

AS AFTERNOON RAYS spread over the fields, Corey and Eolyn led the people of Selen to the edge of nearby woodlands. There, they laid out generous gifts for the Guendes and lifted their voice in song. They invited the forest spirits to feast and asked them to use their magic to turn the sun back toward the Underworld, so its cycle might be completed.

Under the gathering twilight, mage and maga returned to the town square to cast the sacred fire, which would burn through the brief summer night. Their duties fulfilled, they then let their magic rest out of respect for the Guendes, who on this one night of the year assumed dominion over all powers of invocation.

After parting from Eolyn's company, Mage Corey visited many fires, spending time with Baramon and his family, Ernan's followers, and Khelia and her Mountain Warriors. He found warm welcome everywhere, enjoying hours of companionship and many cups of wine, before wandering to the place where former members of the Circle filled the night with song and laughter.

Calling upon the spirit of Fox, Corey kept his distance at first, hidden in the shadows as he watched them dance. It pained him to think that his time with these artists and musicians had all but ended, that their joyous lives might soon come to a bloody and gruesome end.

Eolyn sat quietly on the periphery of the festivities, a cup of wine cradled in her tapered fingers. Orange flames illuminated her thoughtful face and left her back cloaked in shadows. She seemed out of place, with her somber expression and quiet demeanor.

Letting the spirit of Fox fall from his shoulders, Corey stepped forward. His presence was noted immediately. The Circle welcomed him with raucous shouts and hearty embraces.

Eolyn blinked and looked up as if returning from a trance. A smile spread through her dark eyes, and she rose to meet him. For the first time, they embraced as friends. Her aroma of honey and wood felt familiar

196

somehow, like an unexpected homecoming. Mage Corey pressed his lips to her forehead and took Eolyn's hand in his, noting it cool to the touch.

"You have not yet danced," he said, "and there is little time left before the sun is due to rise."

She shrugged. "The sun has returned every Solstice for a generation now, with or without the maga's dance."

"That's not true. Briana danced during the reign of Kedehen, and when she died we had Ghemena, though nobody but the sun, the moon, and the Guendes knew. Soon after that we had you. I imagine the sun has delighted in your dance since you were a little girl. He will be very sad indeed, if you abandon him now."

"My dancing would not please him even if I tried, for it would be forced and without passion."

Such a grim set to her jaw.

Touching Eolyn's cheek, Corey brought her eyes to his. "When we first arrived at Ernan's camp, I anticipated his mission would bring you hope. Then he turned out to be your lost brother, and I thought this would give you joy."

"It has," she said, though her tone was unconvincing. "What greater joy can there be than to have my family returned to me?"

"You are serious of late," Corey insisted. "You sing only when your duties require. You do not dance. You have even withdrawn from Tahmir."

She glanced away, blinking. "That's not true, Mage Corey. Tahmir rides south, while we remain here. How can you expect us to share intimacy across such distances?"

You could have asked to go with him.

Corey would never have allowed it, of course. But she could have asked.

"I do not refer to the miles that separate you now," he said. "You have not touched him with the same affection since we left the city."

"Corey, I don't—"

"I am not questioning your decision. I only mention it out of concern for you. You cannot refrain from Primitive Magic indefinitely. You know the consequences of such abstinence. It will only weaken your powers."

"How can one dance and sing?" Her voice stiffened into a challenge. "How can one seek the pleasure of the Gods, on the eve of war?"

"There is no better time to remember why we enjoy being alive."

"Ghemena never approved of war," Eolyn said. "It would displease her to no end that I am supporting my brother in this endeavor."

"You are a High Maga in your own right now. It is one thing what

Doyenne Ghemena taught you, quite another how you to decide to use your gifts."

"Did you say the same thing to your cousin Briana, when she laid her magic at Kedehen's feet?"

Stung, Corey took step back. Eolyn had struck low and hard, at the most vulnerable of all his wounds.

He took a drink from his wine. "Well. You are in a serious mood tonight."

An uncomfortable silence followed.

Eolyn withdrew and sat on a nearby log.

"I am sorry, Corey," she said. "I am not myself of late."

"Indeed, as I was saying."

"It was wrong to speak ill of your family." She extended her hand in a gesture of friendship. "I'm sorry."

He nodded and took a place next to her. "Many have spoken ill of Briana, but she was not ambitious, or drawn to power, or seduced by dark forces, as your beloved tutor might have told you. She was a skilled witch, one of the greatest of her generation. She would have led our Clan, were it not for the war. But the war happened, and Briana did what everyone else did in those times. She made the choices she thought best under the circumstances."

"How did she come to be his queen?" Eolyn asked.

"That is hardly a topic for Summer Solstice."

"If not now, then when? Soon you depart for Selkynsen, and we will continue our march. I cannot..." She frowned and glanced away. "I can't meet him in battle, unless I understand something of what happened before."

Corey drew a deep breath. The air smelled of smoke and fire and betrayal, and it did nothing to alleviate the pain flaring inside his chest. He might have shared many tales with Eolyn tonight, but this one he preferred to leave buried in the dust. There was too much of Eolyn's future in Briana's past. And fate had handed him too great a role in both. Hearing the story of his long dead cousin would not ease Eolyn's struggle, but Corey sensed the weight on her shoulders as he studied her hopeful expression. He did not have the heart to deny her.

"I was a small boy when the war started," he said. "I saw little of it before it ended. Most of the fighting happened on the western frontier of Selen, or in Moisehén and Selkynsen. The Clan of the East was divided during the conflict, but enough of our people opposed Kedehen to incite his rage and suspicion.

"The war had scarce ended when the King came for us. It happened just days after Midwinter's Eve, a time of year when no one would have expected a battle. As was our tradition, the entire Clan had gathered for the festival. People thought we had achieved peace, and it was the most beautiful, celebratory Midwinter's Feast I remember from my childhood. We were not prepared for an attack. Our minds were as far as they could be from conflict and war.

"Kedehen's men came at night. They dragged my people out of their beds and murdered them on the doorsteps. Men, women, and children. No one was spared. I woke up, and then I kept trying to wake up. I thought I was trapped in a nightmare. My mother…" Corey paused and cleared his throat. "My mother suffered much before she died. My father was hacked to pieces in front of my eyes. To this day I do not know what miracle took me away from them, what shadow rendered me invisible to our attackers.

"I escaped our house and ran, but everywhere I went there were swinging blades and exploding flames. Then Briana appeared out of nowhere, stumbling over me. She looked ragged and frightened, like an animal cornered in a hunt. She caught my hand in hers and took me running deep into the forest.

"I slowed her down. My legs were too short to keep up. I tripped and screamed and bawled like the pathetic child I was. She should have left me behind and secured her own escape, but she picked me up and kept running as best she could.

"A mage warrior intercepted us. He tore me out of Briana's arms and raised his weapon to end my life. In that moment, Briana produced a night shade mushroom—"

"A night shade?" Eolyn said in disbelief. "In the dead of winter?"

"I don't know how she found it, but there she was with the poison on her tongue. She threatened to kill herself if he did me any harm. Just that was enough to stop him. He bound us both and took us to the King."

"He had orders to capture her alive?"

"Yes. It was a coincidence of fate that I was with her when she was apprehended. A coincidence that saved my life."

"Why did Kedehen want her?"

"I do not know. Perhaps he planned to possess her magic, though the practice was not yet widespread. Perhaps they had shared in the pleasure of the Gods during some festival, and he desired her still. She was stunningly beautiful, Eolyn, with ebony hair and the silver-green eyes of our people. Her magic preceded her everywhere. One simply knew she was about to arrive and anticipated her appearance with great joy.

"When they brought us to the Kedehen, his eyes burned with triumph. I don't think he even noticed me at first. His tent was filled with armored men and mages and servants. One bark from him, and they all disappeared.

"There was a strange magic between him and Briana, something darker and deeper than anything I had experienced in my short and sheltered life. I clung to my cousin, my runny nose buried in her skirt, my eyes swollen with tears. She placed her hand upon my head and did not waver. She held her chin high and kept her voice steady, even when the King stood no more than a breath away. She asked only one thing of him that night. She asked him to spare my life."

"And he granted her request," Eolyn whispered.

"The Mage King had many vices, but he was true to his word. I was removed from their presence and taken elsewhere. Strangers gave me food and told me to sleep. But I knew my family had been obliterated, and young as I was, I understood the exact nature of the bargain struck on my behalf. I did not sleep that night, or for many nights thereafter."

"Oh, Corey." She took his hand in hers.

They sank into a pensive silence.

Lighthearted music filled the air. Dancers swirled and laughed around the fire.

Curse it all, Corey thought.

They should be getting drunk and celebrating the Solstice, not dragging out this wretched story to be picked upon by the dogs of the night.

"You thought it a very high price for her to pay?" Eolyn asked.

"Well." He gave a rueful smile. "I suppose no price is too high for this mage's life, though I have met many since who would argue otherwise."

A tender smile touched her lips.

"What I mean is, do you think it was the sacrifice it appeared to be?" Eolyn appeared to be choosing her words with care. "For Briana, I mean. Do you think she acted entirely against her will, when she submitted to the King?"

Corey let go a slow breath and tasted his wine once more.

Well I knew that was coming, didn't I?

"I don't pretend to know the heart of any maga," he said, "even Briana who, although my cousin, was many years my elder and moved in a world very different from mine until the night we were thrown together in flight. I do not know what she felt for her King."

"And Kedehen? Did he...?" Eolyn's voice faltered. She looked away.

Corey lifted his cup to his lips, only to find it dry. Scowling, he flung it into the fire. "Did Kedehen love Briana?"

Eolyn did not respond, her focus intent on the flames. By the Gods she was beautiful. Too beautiful, even for a King.

Corey leaned forward and took both her hands in his. "Eolyn, look at me."

She consented, her dark eyes sincere and expectant. Long had he admired her innocence. Too long had he indulged it.

"No King of this land has ever loved or will ever love a woman," he said. "The capacity for love was bred out of Vortingen's line long ago. Royals fear love and the treachery they believe it brings to their games of power.

"A King seeks many women for pleasure, and he will choose one of suitable lineage to bear his heirs. On very rare occasions this woman of lineage will also ignite his passion. This is the closest they can come to the experience we call love—desire mixed with respect for the mothers of their sons. Perhaps this is what Kedehen felt for Briana."

Eolyn took a moment to absorb his words. Something faded behind her eyes, a lingering hope perhaps. A childhood fantasy. Whatever it was, Corey was glad to see it go.

"It would not have been enough for her," Eolyn said. "It would not be enough for any maga."

"It was sufficient to bear Kedehen a son."

"You resented her for that?"

"No. No, I did not resent her. Briana was not the sort of woman who could ever inspire resentment. Her child was like a brother to me during those first years, although there were times when I could not look at him without remembering the death of my parents."

"Does it not trouble you now, to make war on your cousin?"

"You are as much my family as he is, perhaps more so." Corey reached for her forgotten cup and raised it to her lips. "I sense your curiosity for this topic runs deep, but I have grown weary of this conversation. Soon I embark upon a mission from which I may not return. I would see you dance before I go."

At last she allowed herself a short laugh. "You will only sadden me further with such talk."

"That I would see you dance?"

"That you may not return." Her expression grew serious again. "Corey, I meant what I said the other day. I don't want you to go. I have a very bad feeling about this."

"You are a maga, not a Syrnte witch, so I am disinclined to listen to your premonitions."

"But Corey—"

"I am exaggerating the peril of my adventure in a pathetic attempt to convince you to take pity on me and warm my night with a little of your magic," he said. "I would not have suggested speaking with Lord Herensen if it were unlikely to work. You know me, Eolyn. I do not take foolish risks. Unless, of course, they are forced upon me by clever magas."

She laughed again.

Thank the Gods.

Corey proffered his arm, and she accepted his invitation.

Together, they entered the circle of dancers.

"We have only a few hours before the dawn," he said, pulling her close. "We must make the most of what time remains to us."

CHAPTER THIRTY-THREE

Betrayal

EOLYN AWOKE WITH A START, heart pounding, sweat trickling down her neck.

A humid breeze lifted the skirt of her tent, revealing a flash of silver light that heralded an approaching storm. Shivering, she wrapped her blanket tight around her shoulders.

A shift of eyes. The flash of a blade.

The dream slipped away with her sleep, leaving only scattered images that evaporated like mist when she tried to grasp them.

A spray of blood. The cracking of ribs.

Rising, Eolyn lit a candle, found her water basin, and refreshed her face. Something called her, a howl trapped inside the rising wind. She considered escaping into the forest, into a world without war, as Owl or Lynx or Deer. But the last time she shape shifted Akmael had found her, and she dared not risk encountering him again.

She pulled a simple dress over her nightshift and put on her cloak. Leaving her tent, she greeted two guards Ernan had posted. At times, it seemed she had escaped Corey's vigilance only to be subjected to her brother's less subtle approach. She bade them not to follow, assuring them she would not wander far.

An army was never quiet, as she was learning, not even during the dark hours of the night. There was always movement and voices: mocking laughter beyond the next tent, brutal swearing, an unexpected clash of metal, the heavy stamp of horses. Rough grunts of men and stifled moans of the girls they bedded. Eolyn wondered if she would ever grow accustomed to it. She hoped she would not.

Drifting unseen through shadows, she watched men-at-arms drink and gamble at the edge of their fires, soldiers she did not know, men who would risk their lives for her freedom.

A shattering of glass. A room with no escape.

A sudden grip on her wrist startled her. She looked up into black eyes, saw ebony hair drawn into a braid, felt a curved dagger at her throat. Recognition, then astonishment, flashed across his rugged face. He released her and stepped back.

"Maga Eolyn." The Syrnte warrior gave a nod of respect. "My apologies. I did not recognize you."

She had walked to the far side of Ernan's camp, where a small cluster of gold and burgundy tents marked the dwellings of Rishona and the Syrnte soldiers who accompanied her. Their camp was quiet, with but a couple torches illuminating its edges.

Rishona's men wore little besides their breast plates and weapons, leaving their powerful arms and muscular legs exposed. This one smelled of sweat and night and the spices of his homeland. He made her heart ache for Tahmir. What she would not give to have him beside her now, to know the comfort of his strength.

A flash of pain behind the eyes. Darkness.

"I am here to see Rishona," she realized. "Please, tell her I have arrived."

"Let her pass, Rahim." The Syrnte princess melted out of the shadows, fastening her cloak with a jeweled brooch. When she took Eolyn's hands, her touch burned.

"You skin is ice, *samtue!*" Resting her palm against Eolyn's cheek, she searched the maga's eyes. "The Ones Who Speak tried to reach you. Did you hear them? Do you know what has happened?"

Confused, Eolyn looked from Rishona to her guard. "No. No, I do not know."

Rishona drew a hesitant breath and then said with quiet resolve, "Corey has been betrayed."

Eolyn's heart constricted. Her balance faltered, but Rishona caught and steadied her. They walked arm in arm to Ernan's tent, as fast as their feet could carry them. Her brother's guard left them waiting outside while he announced their arrival.

Eolyn heard a muffled protest. Within moments a girl appeared at the doorway, slender with brown hair that fell in tangled curls to her waist. Without a sideways glance, she dropped a few coins into her purse, adjusted a cloak about her shoulders, and continued on her way.

Eolyn fought the flush of indignation that rose to her cheeks. She could tolerate such behavior on the part of Ernan's men, but in her own brother, it seemed unacceptable.

The pleasure of the Gods is not to be bought and sold in the marketplace, Ghemena had taught her.

But then, Ghemena had said many things that no longer seemed to have a place in this world.

Ernan appeared and ushered them inside. Upon hearing their news, he sent at once for Khelia, who arrived with Adiana on her heels. Eolyn listened in horror as Rishona described her vision of Corey's arrest, while Ernan paced about them, the scar on his face white with fury.

"Why did you not foresee this?" he demanded when Rishona had finished.

"I do not choose which visions come to me or when," she replied.

"Selkynsen is lost." He shook his head, his eyes fixed on the floor as if divining a message from the earth itself. "We must march toward the city at once."

"That decision is not yours alone to make," Khelia objected.

"I don't see how we have a choice, Khelia." He met her gaze. "We must strike quickly before reinforcements arrive."

"What about Corey?" Adiana asked.

"We do not know who betrayed Corey or why," Khelia insisted. "The province may yet be divided."

"Lord Herensen betrayed him," Rishona said.

"But Corey left certain of their friendship!" Eolyn exclaimed.

"The King's messengers reached Herensen first. The patriarch of Selkynsen has judged our cause too risky, and saw a need to reassure the King of his fealty. It was not his intention that Corey be mistreated, but once they arrested him, the situation passed beyond Herensen's control."

"If we have lost Herensen, we have lost the province," Ernan maintained. "We must march before it is too late."

"Why does nobody answer me?" Adiana demanded. "We must do something about Corey."

Ernan studied her with a puzzled frown. "There is nothing to be done."

"Nothing to be done?" she repeated, incredulous. "They will torture him, execute him even, if we do not act quickly."

"If we are lucky, they will kill him before he reveals too much."

"You can't be serious." Adiana looked to the others for support. "We can't abandon him just like that. He is the thread that holds us together. None of us would be here if it weren't for Corey."

"Adiana is right," agreed Khelia. "We cannot simply sit here while he perishes at their hands."

"Marching on the King's City is not sitting here." Ernan's voice was thick with impatience. "We have this one opportunity and we must seize it!"

"Let me go for Corey," Adiana insisted. "Give me half a dozen men and women. We will find a way."

"They intend to take him to the King's City," Rishona said.

"There you see? I know that road. I can walk it in my sleep. There are two passes, both excellent for an ambush, and a third that could work if the others fail."

"They will expect you in all those places," Ernan objected.

"I don't care. We must at least try to save him."

"Adiana." Ernan placed his hands firmly on her shoulders. "I cannot sacrifice any of my warriors to this mission you propose. We need every last man and woman if we hope to bring down the Mage King."

"I can send some of my people with you, Adiana," Khelia offered.

"And I, some of the Syrnte," Rishona added. "They are fighters of great stealth, and their magic may be of use to you."

"Has not the obvious occurred to you?" Anger flashed in Ernan's clear green eyes. "Do you not see the possibility that is we who are betrayed?"

Stunned, Khelia took a step backwards. "You can't possibly mean that."

"Why not?"

"Corey started all of this," Khelia replied. "He would never lie to us. Not like that."

"Mages of Tzeremond don't lie. They simply avoid telling the whole truth." Ernan turned to Eolyn. "What say you, sister? Is there anything Mage Corey has said or done that might be inconsistent with him being a spy of Tzeremond?"

"He hates Tzeremond," Eolyn replied. "He spits that name out as if it were venom. He refused to study High Magic because of Tzeremond."

"Did Corey tell you that, or are you simply repeating one of the many rumors he has allowed to flourish around his person?"

"Ernan—"

"He gives the appearance of a Middle Mage, but you told me that in the King's City, he kept company only with the High Mages."

A grain of dread settled in Eolyn's heart. Ernan had a point. Corey had always seemed far too influential for his rank. He never wore the colors of a Middle Mage. And yet in the city, the High Mages had received him as one of their own.

"His life was built on duplicity," Ernan continued. "His cousin betrayed her clan. Who are we to presume she did not teach him by her example?"

"I *saw* him arrested by the Lords of Selkynsen," Rishona said. "His magic was bound, and he was beaten. My visions do not lie."

"How long has he studied your Syrnte ways?" Ernan countered. "The mages of this land can plant visions in the minds of our people. Surely by now Corey knows how to plant visions in your mind, as well."

"That kind of spell can only be cast at close range," Eolyn objected. "And there are clear symptoms. The victim cannot tell, but those around him can. We would know. I would know."

"Would you, sister?" Ernan turned on Eolyn, hands flexing at his sides. "What transpired between you and the Mage King in the moments you spent alone with him?"

A chill passed down Eolyn's spine. "I told you what happened."

"No, you did not," Ernan said. "You have kept something from me, something important. I feel it simmering beneath your reserve, goading you with every moment that takes us closer to battle. The Mage King set you free and entrusted you to Mage Corey, who brought you to us. Why? To force our hand? To bring us out before we were ready?"

Ernan seized Eolyn's arm in a painful grip.

"Will you betray your kin, Eolyn," he growled, "as Briana betrayed hers?"

Eolyn froze at this unfathomable accusation. She felt the eyes of Khelia, Rishona, and Adiana upon her. Silence hung stiff as a hot summer cloud.

"Oh, for the love of the Gods!" Khelia's powerful voice cut through the tension. "If there is no one in this room you can trust, Ernan, we may as well pack up our weapons and go home now. Adiana, you will have three of my best warriors to accompany you to Selkynsen."

"And three of the Syrnte," Rishona said.

"I too would like to go," Eolyn said.

This announcement was met with silence.

"There will be mages to contend with," Eolyn reasoned. "You need someone who knows how to confront them, who can release Corey's magic."

"Now that I cannot permit," Khelia replied.

Ernan lifted his hands to the heavens. "Thank the Gods we are at least in agreement on this!"

"If we lose you in addition to Corey, we have no hope," Khelia said. "I cannot ask my warriors to march upon the Mage King without a High Maga at their side."

"I could fly back here once we are done."

"And risk a High Mage trapping you along the way?" Ernan objected. "Never."

"Well which is it, Ernan?" Eolyn's own temper flared. "Am I strong enough to defeat the Mage King, or too weak to contend with one of his mages?"

Ernan's jaw clenched. His face hardened in distrust.

"Or do you think I wish to abandon this rebellion and run away with

Mage Corey?" Eolyn said.

"Eolyn, we do not question your abilities or your loyalties," Khelia interjected, though a glance at Ernan betrayed her flicker of doubt. "This is not about you, it is about our own sense of hope and purpose. You have become the symbol of our struggle, the promise of our success. Our people see you, and they are motivated to attempt the impossible. If you disappear on the eve of our confrontation with the Mage King, the effect would be devastating. You must stay here. Adiana will find a way without you."

But how could Eolyn remain behind? For if Ernan was wrong, then Corey must be saved. And if he was right...

If he's right, I want to hear it from Corey's own lips.

That he had deceived her with his friendship. That he had set her up as the unwitting instrument of her brother's doom. That he had used her, right from the very beginning.

Rishona placed a comforting arm about her shoulders. "His arrest was sent to your dreams, Eolyn, but that does not mean his fate is in your hands. You must let Corey go. It is your destiny that requires your attention in this moment, not his."

CHAPTER THIRTY-FOUR

Mage and King

COREY HIT THE GROUND with a harsh thud. Shadows blurred about him, men silhouetted against a twilight that was unbearably brilliant after so many days in the dark.

Aromas of summer grass and night blossoms filled the air, yet did nothing to alleviate the stench of blood and sweat that clung to Corey's clothes. He recognized Thelyn's smooth baritone, along with voices of three other High Mages.

By Thelyn's command, Corey was wrapped in a coarsely woven net of Lievian spider silk. Every time they moved him, pain shot through his limbs. Just as his vision began to clear, he was lifted off the ground, suspended in the net between flying staffs. They rose high and carried him swiftly over a rolling landscape illuminated by a silver moon.

Night air refreshed his face, and trees met his passing with shifting words of encouragement, but every muscle throbbed in protest. Every thought echoed with regret. What he wouldn't give for a hot bath, a mug of wine, and the songs of his people under a starry sky. What he wouldn't give to meet the Solstice Dawn at Eolyn's side once more, to enjoy her light-hearted laughter, to feel the heat of her hand in his.

If he could turn back the days, months, and years, he would see things done differently the second time around. But then so would everyone else. The resulting mess would be just as dismal. In all likelihood, Corey would still have finished here, a sack of bruised flesh carried upon the wind toward certain doom.

But I would have kissed Eolyn. I would have known the bittersweet taste of a maga's lips.

Below them, the King's City appeared, blanketed in shadows of gray and midnight blue. They landed in one of the lower courtyards, slamming Corey's battered body against the flagstones. The net was sliced open. Rough hands grabbed him and dragged him off.

They descended into the labyrinth of shadows beneath the fortress.

209

Karin Rita Gastreich

Corey had thought the dungeons of Selkynsen miserable, but here the darkness was absolute. The only sound was the musty heart of the mountain, beating slow and cold.

No food or water was brought to him. For what seemed hours, he sat in the company of his aching body, wondering who would arrive first, Tzeremond or Baedon. Perhaps they would come together, magical instruments in hand, eager to play their games of torture and intimidation.

At last he heard footsteps and voices, the turn of the massive lock, and the screech of dry hinges. The heavy door was shoved inward. Torch light blinded him. Guards stepped into the cell, followed by King Akmael.

Surprised and wary, Corey watched his cousin through swollen eyes. Briana's son stood tall, somehow at home in that dark place, his face as expressionless as his father's had once been. The guards set the torches high and ensured the steadfastness of Corey's chains before retreating from the cell. For several moments, king and mage studied each other in silence.

"I sent instructions regarding your care," Akmael said at last. "It appears they were not heeded."

Corey shrugged, though his shoulders winced at the movement. "They would have had my head on a pike and thrown my flesh to the vultures had High Mage Thelyn not intervened. I am as he found me."

"We will have to work with what is left, then," Akmael replied. "There is much I would learn from you, Mage Corey."

"My Lord King." Corey drew a wheezing breath and met his cousin's gaze. "As I once told you, what humble knowledge I command is intended for your service, for the good of our Clan, as was sworn to your mother and my protector, Queen Briana. Ask what you will, I will respond truthfully."

"So you say, but I am told you revealed nothing to the inquisitors of Selkynsen."

"I do not know who pays the inquisitors of Selkynsen. My secrets are meant only for my Lord King, to be heard and acted upon by him alone."

Akmael lifted his brow in doubt. "You would have died at their hands rather than speak?"

"Yes."

Akmael studied the stale air for a moment, then returned his gaze to Corey. "Why did you deliver the maga to the rebels?"

"It was the safest place I could think of outside this citadel. What happened to me in Selkynsen would have happened to her—and worse—had I attempted to hide her in any other corner of this kingdom."

"You knew her brother was their leader?"

210

"No." Corey frowned. How had the King come by this information? "That was unexpected, and unfortunate. The maga would not have been so keen to support their cause, were it not for him. She loathes the very thought of war, but she loves her brother and will not abandon him."

"I see."

Corey studied his cousin, but to no avail. The mage could read the face of Master Tzeremond himself, but these accursed Kings of Vortingen never let a thought slip past their eyes. Of one thing he was certain: his fate would be decided within the next few minutes.

"I wanted to smuggle her out again," Corey said, "but it seemed too risky on all accounts. In any case, the current situation may well be to our advantage. Her presence has mobilized them, brought them forward before they are ready. Ernan's forces cannot hope to match yours, and they will find no support in Selkynsen, as Herensen remains loyal to you. They've no choice but to confront you with what they have."

"She is the only one left to us, Mage Corey. She cannot be lost."

Corey cleared his throat. A difficult point, that one, but he had done what he could. "Her brother will not allow any harm to come to her. As an additional precaution, I have left the maga with annals of war time magic pulled from the libraries of Selen. Old techniques used by mages with no training in weaponry. It's no guarantee of course, but it should keep her out of harm's way when they meet you in battle."

The King did not respond.

"It would be prudent for our mages to use similar techniques," Corey added, to fill the silence. "Otherwise she might conclude I have deceived her."

Akmael nodded, though his expression remained unchanged. "The seals on the East Tower have been broken. A room is being prepared for you there."

The significance of this declaration was not lost on Corey. The East Tower had not been opened since Briana's death. "How long will I be detained?"

"Until we crush this rebellion," Akmael replied.

Or until the King decides whether he has any further use for his cousin.

Tension faded from Corey's muscles. He had been granted time and words. With enough of both, he might yet secure his future.

"Sir Drostan will see you on the morrow. You must treat his ears as mine, Mage Corey. I will not indulge you with another private audience until your loyalty is beyond doubt."

The mage nodded. The weight of regret and relief brought his aching head to his bruised hands.

"You will be moved before sunset." The King turned to take his leave.

Corey drew another painful breath. His ribs pinched his lungs. "That armband she wears. You gave it to her didn't you?"

His words brought the Akmael's smooth retreat to a sudden halt. "She told you about that?"

"No. She speaks to no one of you. I recognized the Silver Dragon as an heirloom of East Selen. When I first saw it..." How long ago was that? A year perhaps, under a late spring sky on the grassy knolls of Aerunden. Eolyn was no more than a peasant with a curious gift then, an unassuming girl of little significance. "I suspected she had met some lost cousin of mine. It was easier to imagine another member of the Clan surviving, than to conceive of a manner in which you might have known her." Easier, and somehow more bearable. "But then the pieces of her story came together, and they all pointed to you."

"It was an improvised present," Akmael spoke to the door, "from a self-centered boy with neither the foresight nor the imagination to craft a gift worthy of her friendship."

His words fell like pebbles into a deep well, disappearing as soon as they were uttered. Corey would have thought he had imagined them, were it not for the resonance they left, waves reverberating against the dank air. "You invoked an ancient tradition of our Clan when you honored her with that jewel."

Akmael turned to his cousin with a puzzled expression. "The armband was mine, a present from my mother. She said nothing of the Clan when she gave it to me."

"It makes no difference whether you understood its significance. It was the Silver Dragon that chose Eolyn, not you."

"Chose her?"

"That jewel came from the heart of East Selen. It is an invitation to join the Clan, to be a part of its legacy as much as any person who carries the blood of our ancestors."

"And Eolyn knows this?"

"No." Corey shook his head. "To speak to her of it during these days would have been imprudent. She must be told, however, and she must decide whether to accept."

The King took a moment to absorb this. A smile curled his lips, and he nodded. "Then we may yet make her ours, Mage Corey. We may yet make her ours."

CHAPTER THIRTY-FIVE

Revelations

"They head southwest, my Lord King," Sir Drostan reported. "Their numbers are reinforced by about four hundred men from Selen."

"Cavalry?"

"Fifty, at most. The rest are foot soldiers. Mage Corey suspects they intend to reunite with Syrnte riders, secure the Pass of Aerunden, and recruit additional support from Moehn before marching toward the King's City."

The knight waited as his liege considered the news.

Tzeremond stood with them in the council room, bony hands working against his rowan staff.

The King took his time, back turned to his advisors as he looked out the window and surveyed the broad expanse of land toward the south. An undulating landscape shone green and gold under the summer sun. In the distance, a dark blue smudge indicated the low mountains that bordered Moehn.

"Very well." Akmael turned to face them. "We depart at dawn. Send immediate word to Herensen and the lords of Selkynsen. They are to meet us at Rhiemsaven in three days' time."

"With all due respect, my Lord King," Tzeremond said, "I think it unwise to act upon information given to us by a traitor and a heretic."

"I understand, Tzeremond, and I agree. But Mage Corey's words are corroborated by what we have gathered from our own scouts and spies. We must respond accordingly. We cannot simply sit here until the enemy knocks at our gate."

"Of course, my Lord King." Tzeremond nodded respectfully. "Then perhaps it would be wise, before we march, to settle the matter of how best to dispose of the maga."

"That question has already been settled," the King replied, "as you should remember. She is not to be disposed of. She is to be captured and brought to me, alive and whole."

"But if we allow them to meet us in battle, with her power at their disposal—"

"Her power is inconsequential to the outcome of this conflict."

"You underestimate her abilities, my Lord King. A mistake your father would never have made."

The King turned his black gaze upon the wizard. Hairs rose on the back of Drostan's neck. Had Tzeremond lost all sense of discretion, comparing the King to his father and finding him wanting?

Tzeremond lifted his chin, lips tight and shoulders set. "I speak frankly, my Lord King, for your good and for the good of this kingdom."

"Master Tzeremond," the King spoke through clenched teeth, "she is but one maga. My father destroyed an entire Order of her kind."

"Your father sent whatever survived of that rabble to the pyre because he knew one maga is enough to bring down a kingdom." Master Tzeremond's amber eyes burned in defiance. "One is certainly enough to bring down an army. You have not confronted a maga in war, so you do not know the spells they can cast. We must destroy her before we meet them if possible, and early in the battle if not."

Sir Drostan cleared his throat. "Even by our most generous estimates, the rebel army cannot number more than half of the King's fighting force, especially once the lords of Selkynsen join us. We have twelve High Mages, a Master, and several mage warriors still fit for battle. We have our most worthy Mage King. One maga cannot contend with all of that. The decision of the rebels to take the Pass of Aerunden is clever, but it will accomplish little in end. This dispute will be short lived, no matter where we meet them in battle, no matter what the extent of her powers."

"She stopped a red flame without a staff in her hand!" Tzeremond shot back. "She made the very foundations of this fortress tremble. No mage or maga of this land has ever accomplished such a thing."

"She may have unusual powers," the King conceded, "but she has no training in warfare. She cannot craft a death flame or manipulate fear or invoke any of the techniques we use to vanquish our enemies. She can use her skills only in self-defense. It has long been a limitation of her training."

Tzeremond snorted, "You speak as if you know her. None of us know her. We've had no luck tracing her past."

The King paused before announcing pointedly, "I do know her, Tzeremond. I have known her for years."

Astonished, Sir Drostan stared at his King. Tzeremond lost his color. The flames of Dragon himself could not have broken their stunned silence. The old wizard's breath seemed to catch on his tongue. One hand moved restlessly through the air as if in search of something to support his shock. With visible effort, he pushed a single word out of his throat.

"*How?*"

"By the will of the Gods, Master Tzeremond."

The old mage blinked like a confused child.

"This is indeed fortunate." Sir Drostan interjected with care, uncertain whether it was wise to speak at all. "We have direct knowledge of this woman's abilities, then. It will save us much time and unnecessary preparation."

"Who trained her?" Tzeremond's voice was hoarse. Drostan had the distinct impression the old wizard was no longer aware of his presence.

"One of the Doyennes of the Old Orders," the King said, "a hag by the name of Ghemena."

"*Ghemena?*" The wizard hissed. His staff nearly slipped from his hand. "You knew Ghemena?"

"I never met her, but the young maga spoke of her often."

"That's impossible!" Tzeremond exploded with rage. "Berlingen was destroyed! Everybody perished. Sir Drostan, you gave me your word no one escaped!"

Drostan's heart skipped a beat under Tzeremond's sudden focus. The knight managed to hold his voice steady, but only with tremendous effort. "We intercepted no one that night. Perhaps the Doyenne found a way to slip through our nets unnoticed, though it is more likely she left before the raid started."

Tzeremond retreated into a lengthy silence. A summer breeze shifted through the southern windows. From the western tower they heard the rhythmic calls of the changing of the guard.

At last Tzeremond raised his amber eyes. His expression softened, and he adjusted his grip on the staff. "If it was Ghemena who taught her, then you are correct in your assessment of her powers, my Lord King. I knew that Doyenne well. She was incapable of training any maga in the noble arts of war. If you will...If you will excuse me, I would share this information with the High Mages. As Sir Drostan has so wisely acknowledged, it will make an important difference in how we prepare for this battle."

The King narrowed his eyes. "You are under oath to do her no harm, Tzeremond. If you defy my orders, you shall pay for it with your life."

"My Lord King." Tzeremond's tone was subdued and humble, his gaze direct. "I would never betray you or this kingdom. My long years of service to your father demonstrated that."

Akmael studied the wizard's face before conceding. "Very well,

Master Tzeremond. You are dismissed."

With a deep bow, the wizard turned to leave. Sir Drostan moved to follow, but the King bade the knight to remain with a subtle gesture of his hand.

As soon as the doors closed behind Tzeremond, Akmael approached Sir Drostan, his voice low, his expression severe. "For the moment, dear knight, I will not question your decision to lie in the presence of Tzeremond, but nor will I tolerate any attempt to deceive me. You will tell me the truth of what happened in Berlingen, and you will tell me at once."

Unnerved, Drostan shifted on his feet. Ever since his induction as a Knight of Vortingen, he had prided himself in being an honest and loyal warrior. But once, a long time ago, he deceived his liege, and now that transgression had returned to condemn him, just as he always feared it would.

"My Lord King," he said. "I have served the Kings of Vortingen faithfully all my life, and with your father made no exception. I followed him into war and defended the Crown to the best of my ability. Even so, with all due respect to our dead King, I have always believed the war he asked us to fight, the war brought upon us by the magas, was a war without honor. We slaughtered our brothers and sisters on the battlefield, and extinguished the brilliance of our heritage with the blood of our kin."

Sir Drostan paused, confounded by his loose tongue. What did his thoughts on the war have to do with Berlingen? Indeed, what did it matter whether he agreed with the war or not? A knight's duty was to follow his king.

He searched his liege's face for some sign of judgment, but Akmael's expression remained impassive. The King nodded, bidding the knight to continue.

"The Abbey of Berlingen was not a military target. It was a retreat for the oldest and wisest of mages and magas, an unrivaled storehouse of magical knowledge. We were sent to Berlingen on the pretense of evacuating those revered men and women to a safer place. But when we arrived, the seal of the King's orders was broken and the true objective of our mission revealed. The soldiers sent with us, men selected for their eagerness to kill, set upon the abbey, burned everything to its foundations and cut down everyone within. The mage warriors took posts in the surrounding terrain, under orders to kill anyone who tried to escape.

"I intercepted Doyenne Ghemena quite by chance. The knight Sir Varyl accompanied her. I did not know how he came to be there, for he was not among the company sent to execute the raid. When he saw me, he unsheathed his sword to defend her. Varyl was a skilled fighter, but he was not a mage warrior. I could have defeated him easily, yet what would that have left me? I trained to be a warrior in the tradition of Caedmon, a knight of the House of Vortingen, not a thief in the woods and murderer of old women. So I let them pass, and I never reported their escape."

The King's brow furrowed. "You did not know what happened to Doyenne Ghemena after that?"

"No, my Lord King. Not until today."

Drostan felt Akmael's senses upon him, measuring the pulse in his temples, the lines of his face, the shift of his eyes.

"Why did you remain in the service of my father all these years, if you felt so strongly about the war?" the King asked.

"When I spared Ghemena's life, she entrusted something me, a tiny purse meant for your mother. I was but a knight then, and even when granted a place on the Council, I had few chances to see the Queen, much less deliver such an incriminating gift. But eventually I succeeded, and after that she…Well, she was kinder to me. The Queen told me I would one day regain my honor, but only if I continued to serve the Kings of Moisehén."

"And was her promise fulfilled?"

Sir Drostan drew a shaky breath. "My Lord King, forgive my boldness in saying so, but I have always believed you have the makings of a great ruler. It is in serving you that I have hoped to recuperate my honor."

"I see. Yet I, too, am leading you into war against your own people."

"Ernan's followers are nothing more than mercenaries and dishonest men. Even if he recruited some of our own, the people of Moisehén who march with him do not fight against you, they fight against the memory of your father. Moisehén suffered much under the war and the purges that followed. There is a desire among the people to play out their vengeance. They have yet to separate you from our dead King."

Akmael's lips compressed into a puzzled frown.

Sir Drostan lowered his gaze. Years had passed since he had spoken so frankly, and a great weight now lifted from his shoulders. Still, he expected the worst. His disobedience in Berlingen was an act of treason, punishable by death.

The King broke the heavy silence with an abrupt laugh.

Sir Drostan withdrew a step, surprise mingling with trepidation. He had not seen his prince so much as smile since the days of Akmael's youth.

The King's hand fell upon Drostan's shoulder with a heavy clap.

"Do not worry, loyal knight," Akmael said. "I will not punish you for disobedience. I need your head firmly on your shoulders if we are to succeed in this battle, for we will be fighting on many fronts."

CHAPTER THIRTY-SIX

Tzeremond's Torment

TZEREMOND STRODE DOWN the castle corridors, dark robes flowing behind him, magic crackling through his staff. He did not acknowledge the guards who saluted his passing. When he arrived at his quarters, he sent his chamber servants away, shut the door behind them, and leaned against the solid oak. His hands trembled, and his breath came in wheezing gasps.

Drawing air deliberately into his lungs, Tzeremond stood, steadied himself on his staff, and continued through the maze of small chambers that led to the heart of his apartments.

He reached a place sealed by magic and accessible only to him. A dark, windowless sanctuary illuminated by gray candles, littered with secret books and parchments, and adorned with numerous magical objects.

Opening a small box of ironwood, Tzeremond pulled his most treasured tool from its resting place among sheets of black silk. The polished crystal stared back at him, a faint glow in its black heart.

Divination is a reckless form of magic.

He jumped at her voice, glanced around, but saw nothing.

Sending a soft curse into the shadows, Tzeremond sat at one of the cluttered tables. He shoved aside papers, books, and instruments. Then he laid the crystal sphere in front of him. Closing his eyes, he spread his long fingers over its smooth face.

Ehekaht, naeom veham
Renenem pelau
Erenahm uturm se sepuenem eom

She laughed at him. "You can't see the future in a rock, my love."

"I saw our future well enough!" he spat back.

"Did you, Tzeremond?"

That voice, its sad lyrical beauty, like a knife through his heart.

Tzeremond looked up, and there she stood. Young and beautiful,

218

just as she was so many forgotten years ago. Her eyes shone gray like the autumn dusk, her platinum hair ran in a silky river down her back. Her fine linen gown was drawn loose about pale shoulders. A melancholy smile graced her lips.

"One day that toy will mislead you," she said, "and you will regret it."

"It was you who misled me!" he cried "That is the only regret I have."

She lowered her eyes, and her image dissolved like a mist.

Tzeremond returned to the cloud-filled crystal and repeated his spell. The device may have failed him these past weeks, but by the Gods, it would not fail him now.

He focused all his will on its smoky depths, until images began to dance through the glass. For hours he sat deep in concentration, combing the past in search of a connection he had missed, a critical thread he had failed to cut.

As the candles burned low, he found her: a child racing into the woods. Her laughter mocked the autumn wind. Her magic was still too weak to be detected under the cover of that ancient canopy. Tzeremond watched as Riders ravaged her village. He saw the Guendes lead the girl away and take her across the river, through an enchanted forest that parted like a curtain to reveal the lost home of a woman he once believed dead.

Ghemena.

With an unnatural roar, Tzeremond took the crystal and flung it against the wall. The smooth glass shattered into a million indigo flames that flared and dissolved like quicksilver. Light faded into darkness. Tzeremond let his weary head sink into his hands, clutched at his graying hair, and wept.

They outwitted us.

Somehow, the dead magas had lifted spells out of their graves with their cold, charred fingers. They had saved Ghemena. Then they had delivered to her a girl who could corrupt a prince.

How very clever their ruse. How innocent the young maga must have appeared! How ingenuous the boy who found and befriended her.

No wonder the problems with Akmael persisted after the death of his mother: the insolence, the barely concealed skepticism, the arrogant insistence on questioning the obvious. A student of similar temperament but different breeding would have been barred from further training, but this was Kedehen's only son, destined to become High Mage and King.

For years, Tzeremond had tried to convince Kedehen to take another queen, but to no avail. With a second prince, the future of

Moisehén might have been secured and the scourge of female magic forever extinguished.

But the Gods had not willed it so. They had left Moisehén at the mercy of this insipid King, a man who pardoned his father's assassin, set a maga free at Bel-Aethne, and treated the heretic Corey like an honored guest.

And now he wants the maga for himself.

It could not be allowed to happen. Kedehen had the strength to resist the darker influences of Briana, but his son was of a different constitution. This witch would be Akmael's ruin, and with him the ruin of an entire kingdom.

With weary determination, Tzeremond recognized the path before him. Redeeming the young King would be difficult, a complex and delicate undertaking. It would require much of the wizard, perhaps the rest of his life and magic. But the Gods reserved the greatest tasks for their most dedicated servants, and Tzeremond resolved to accept this challenge with gratitude and humility.

The future of his people depended on him.

Filling his lungs anew, Tzeremond dried his tears and lifted his head. He extended his hands to the candles, restoring them to their full height and steady glow.

Much of the night would pass before he found the curse he sought among the stacks of books and parchments. It was an ancient spell, meant for the most troublesome of enemies, so powerful he would need assistance to control it. But Tzeremond knew who among the High Mages were loyal. He copied the spell faithfully and tucked the parchment into his robe.

When he extinguished the candles and returned to his bedchamber, dawn's pale light was just beginning to filter through tall windows.

"Ghemena," he whispered, lifting his face to the new day. "You have played your last hand. Now watch as play mine."

CHAPTER THIRTY-SEVEN

Ahmad-kupt

THE MARCH FROM SELEN to the Pass of Aerunden proved arduous. Ernan's column snaked forward at a tedious pace. The stink of urine and manure followed them everywhere. The longer Eolyn rode at her brother's side, the greater her distaste for this endeavor the Gods had handed her.

Ernan's men took what they wanted from fields and farmers, filling wagons with grain and slaughtering pigs or cattle wherever they pleased. Girls showed up from villages, bartering pleasure in exchange for food or coin. When Eolyn asked Ernan to put a stop to these practices, he laughed, though not unkindly.

"I cannot ask my men to fight on empty stomachs," he said. "And if they have other appetites that need filling before they confront their fate on the battlefield, who am I to stand in their way?"

"At least pay the farmers for their food," Eolyn insisted.

"Their liberation from the Mage King will be payment enough."

With that, her brother turned his attention to other matters.

They were still a couple days east of Aerunden when Renate caught up with them, one afternoon.

Some weeks before, the mistress had retired to Corey's estate, claiming she was too old to lend further service to the rebellion. Eolyn had tried to convince her otherwise, but without success.

Renate's unexpected arrival sent a wave of excitement through the camp. The mistress had undergone a visible change. The lines of her face no longer ran so deep, and the silver gray of her hair had given way to intermittent strands of charcoal. She wore midnight blue colors of a Middle Maga.

Overjoyed by this transformation, Eolyn greeted Renate with a full embrace and a kiss of friendship. Together, they retired to the privacy of the High Maga's tent.

"I departed East Selen as soon as word of Corey's arrest reached me," Renate said as they sat down. "It is a tragedy, Eolyn. A tremendous loss for all of us."

"We cannot give ourselves over to mourning just yet. Rishona's dreams indicate Corey is alive, and his injuries have been attended to."

"But I have heard rumors." Renate's hands worked nervously in her lap. "It is said he abandoned the rebellion and swore fealty to the Mage King."

"I know." Eolyn did not like to be reminded of this. "Do you think it's true? That he would betray us?"

Renate shook her head. "I have considered Corey my friend too long to rid myself of the habit of believing him. But he was a student of Tzeremond, and he is cousin to the King. I suppose it will be revealed, before this has all ended, where his loyalties lie."

Eolyn sat back and bit her lip. Uncertainty weighed heavy in her heart. She rose to her feet, retrieved the tomes Mage Corey had given her in Selen, and set them in front of Renate.

"These are the only annals I have of wartime magic," she said. "They all came from him, from Mage Corey."

Renate took one of the volumes and leafed through it.

"Are they authentic?" Eolyn asked. "Do you think they'll be useful?"

"I don't know. I had no training in this kind of magic."

"But you knew people who did. Do you remember anything?"

Renate set the book on the table. "They used sacred circles used to channel courage to the warriors, and different sorts of flames and curses. *Ahmad-melan*, for example, and—"

"*Ahmad-kupt?*"

"Yes. The death charge." Renate frowned. "You found that spell in these books?"

"I think this is it." Eolyn reached for another volume and drew a small slip of paper from inside the cover. "It was inserted between the pages, as if someone had left it there by mistake. The bound volumes don't contain any spells for war flames and similar curses, or if they do I haven't found them."

Renate murmured the first word of the curse as she read. An icy shiver ran down Eolyn's back. The mistress bit her lip and examined the rest of the invocation in silence.

"Such violence in those words." She set the paper down carefully. "May the Gods save you from having to use them."

"So it's the death charge?"

"That, or something very similar. You must take great care with that curse, Eolyn. It could kill you just as easily as your enemy."

"Ghemena told me as much, a thousand times it seemed. Sometimes

222

I'd like to curse her for leaving me so ill-prepared." She let go an exasperated sigh. "I need at least another year to understand all this, to practice. I try to tell Ernan, but he is too bent on defeating the Mage King, too convinced our destiny is at hand. Or perhaps too distrusting of me to listen to my council."

"Distrusting of you?"

"He thinks I might be under a spell of the Mage King. He's said nothing more of it since Selen, but I see it in his eyes often enough. And he will believe his suspicions confirmed when he sees how miserably I perform in battle." Eolyn rubbed her forehead, trying to alleviate the tension that had lodged there. "This is hopeless, Renate. What am I to do?"

"I'd hardly say it was hopeless. I've seen hopeless, you know. They said none of us would survive, and yet here we are still."

Eolyn tried to smile, but tears stung her eyes.

"I have a gift that may brighten your spirit, Eolyn. Wait here."

Renate left the tent and returned with an oblong cedar box that she set on Eolyn's lap. An exquisite image of Dragon was carved upon its face. Her long tail and powerful limbs intertwined with the thick branches of an ancient oak.

"Open it," Renate said.

Eolyn undid the seal and lifted the lid. A burgundy robe lay inside. She ran her fingers over the soft fabric, sensing the magic embedded in its ruby threads. "Where did you find this?"

"We have kept it hidden in Corey's estate for years. This used to be mine before the purges began, before I surrendered my magic and allowed my staff to be destroyed."

"But they would have burned your robes at the same time."

"I was not wearing the robe when they apprehended me."

Eolyn stood to lift the dress out of the box. She draped the garment over one arm and studied the elaborate motifs embroidered on its surface. Ghemena had taught her the intricate spells, secret fibers and special dyes used for the robes of a High Maga, but without a complete coven of twelve, it was impossible to craft one.

"It is too great a gift to accept," she murmured.

"You must wear it when you confront the Mage King," Renate replied. "It will enhance your power, and protect you, should the Gods require you to invoke a curse like *Ahmad-kupt*."

"Then I will wear it only for this campaign, and return it to you when we are victorious."

"I have no more use for it."

"But you will," Eolyn said. "When Dragon grants you a new staff."

Renate's complexion lost its color. She looked away. "Do not jest about such things."

"It is no jest."

"A staff, once destroyed, cannot be replaced."

"Why not, if the Gods will it?"

Renate shook her head. "Dragon would punish me for such arrogance. I surrendered my magic, a faithless coward, and watched without protest as all my sisters burned."

"The Gods have a different way of judging our transgressions." Eolyn returned the gift to its box and took Renate's hands in hers. "They interpret our acts across a grander expanse of time and consequence."

"More words from your Doyenne."

"No," Eolyn realized. "Those words are mine. What I mean, Renate, is that perhaps you were meant to give up your magic then, so you could recuperate it now, at a time of greater need, and greater hope."

Renate choked back a sob and hid her face behind shaking hands. Sensing the upheaval that moved toward the surface, Eolyn wrapped her arms around the mistress and drew her close. A shudder went through Renate's shoulders. She clung to Eolyn and wept long and hard, releasing all the tears denied during the interminable years since the last of her sisters had perished.

CHAPTER THIRTY-EIGHT

Prophecy

THE MORNING AFTER ERNAN AND KHELIA'S forces arrived at the pass of Aerunden, Tahmir appeared in front of Eolyn's tent with a fresh pair of horses. The sun had not yet risen over the eastern hills, and the maga's muscles ached after the long journey from Selen, but Tahmir's company renewed her spirit. They mounted the horses and retreated from the broad expanse of tents that now comprised the rebels' war camp.

The pass of Aerunden occupied the southeast apex of a long valley that stretched north until it opened abruptly onto rolling plains. A verdant forest cloaked the surrounding hills. Upon their arrival, Ernan had remarked with satisfaction how the trees would conceal their scouts and archers. But all Eolyn could see was sweet magic flowing from the living woods. Just above the entrance to the pass rose a low ridge capped by a flat grassy knoll. Eolyn planned to cast her sacred circle there, should the King meet them here in Aerunden.

"All the windows of Ernan's destiny are converging," Tahmir said as he rode next to Eolyn. "He will confront the Mage King in this valley."

"When?"

"Soon. You will hear the movement of the royal army, even before your brother's scouts report their approach." Tahmir scanned the surrounding hills. "Where would be the best place for Tzeremond to cast his circle?"

Eolyn closed her eyes and listened to the trees. After a few moments, she nodded toward a low rise on the northern side of the valley. "That will be his first choice. Magic runs from the heart of that mound into the valley, and it provides a view of the entire field of battle. We should inform Ernan. He can set up a guard to defend this hill and impede Tzeremond's access."

"No." Tahmir shook his head. "Better that we know where he will be."

"If you plan to fulfill your father's oath during battle, you won't be able to do it there. The mage's circle will be well defended. In the tradition of Moisehén, the moment the circle is broken, the battle is lost. The King will place all of his lines in front of it, and a special guard around it. It will be impossible to reach Tzeremond."

"My warriors and I will find a way. Would you accompany me up that slope, Eolyn? I want a closer look, to know all the details of how his circle will be cast."

They dismounted at the base of the hill. Tahmir sent the horses back to camp.

"We will descend on the other side, and mark a path behind the ridge on foot," he said. "That will be the surest route for approaching him once the battle begins."

They took their time, weaving back and forth across the face of the small mountain until the Syrnte warrior felt confident in his knowledge of every tree, bush, and stone. A morning mist clung to the herb-littered floor, and the leaves hung thick with the sweet aroma of late summer. A chorus of birds floated on the air; angry squirrels chucked from safe perches. These melodies made Eolyn's heart burn with the desire to return home, to the safe places and carefree adventures of her childhood in the South Woods.

"Do you remember, Tahmir, when you first taught me to ride?" she asked. "I was so afraid then. I thought that in any moment I would be found out and my life would end in flames. Now I look back, and the troubles of the Circle seem trivial compared to what we face today."

"Your burden has never been trivial." He took her hand in his as they walked.

"I remember every detail of those afternoons: the slant of the sun across the fields, the smell of tilled earth, the heat of the horse's bodies. I wish those moments had lasted forever."

"Your people speak of time as if it can be sliced up and eaten like bread. For the Syrnte, time is not that way. We experience no beginning and no end. We have only the now, and our shifting visions of past and future."

"Yet you know birth and you know death. If I ask you to tell me about the first time we met, you would speak of the pageant in Moehn."

"Perhaps. Or perhaps I would speak of the first dreams I had of you, or of the first afternoon we rode together, or of the first time we made love. I could even speak of moments we have not yet lived, and in the end I would confess that until an eternity has passed, I will not truly have known you at all."

Eolyn paused, troubled by his words. "So have we loved each other, or not?"

Tahmir smiled and took her face in his hands. His dark eyes, rimmed by thick lashes, harbored tiny flames of the golden sun. "What would your Doyenne say?"

"She would say love is not bound by time."

He brought his lips to hers in a gentle kiss. "So it is with us."

When they reached the summit, Eolyn paced the grassy clearing until she located the primary conduit to the heart of the mountain. Removing her shoes, she pressed her bare feet against the damp earth and focused on the steady pulse emanating from the core far below. Had she brought along her staff, she might have dared a descent into the darkness to explore the ribbons of magic that radiated toward the battle field, but without oak and crystal to anchor her spirit, the risk was too great.

Eolyn opened her eyes. "If I have understood the annals correctly, Tzeremond will stand here. The magic is not as strong as on the southern side of the valley, but for him, it will be more than sufficient."

"Who will be with him?"

"Eight High Mages, one at each of the cardinal points, twelve paces from Tzeremond's position."

A shadow crept into the edge of Eolyn's awareness, faint yet unbearable. Her senses filled with an ephemeral mist that smelled like blood. Cries of anguish rose from the empty field. Eolyn covered her face to shut the vision out.

"I am a fool to have come here," she said. "We are leading these people to disaster."

Tahmir approached and placed a steady hand on her shoulder. "They would have met their King in battle, with or without you at their side. Your foolishness, as you call it, is their hope, even for those destined to die. You presence will ease their passing."

"Not if Tzeremond—"

"You need not worry about Tzeremond. He will have journeyed into the Underworld long before he has the opportunity to break your circle."

"Is that what your visions tell you?" She did not hide the challenge in her voice.

"Battles are difficult to divine," Tahmir admitted. "Too many windows intersecting at once. But my heart assures me Rishona and I will not fail in this task to which my father appointed us."

Tahmir pulled her close. Eolyn had always found refuge in his heat and strength, and today was no different. She rested her head against his broad shoulder. The voices of fear dissolved. In the valley below, the long grass bent in undulating waves, its color deepened by passing shadows of white clouds. A small winding stream glinted under the rising sun.

"I must let the creatures of the water know," she said, "so they have

227

time to evacuate before the battle begins."

"Eolyn." Tahmir's voice reverberated inside his chest. "When this war is over, I want you to come back to my homeland with me."

His invitation moved her deeply. Nonetheless, she said, "I can't do that."

"If you will not come out of love for me, than do it for yourself and your people." Cupping her chin in his hand, Tahmir brought her eyes to his. "There is a wind in my country called 'Saefira', the breath of the sun. Every year at the First Equinox, she appears from the east. When our children are of age, we take them to meet this wind, and she awakens their powers. Saefira would awaken you, too. You have abilities the rigid traditions of Moisehén have not allowed you to discover. My sister has foreseen this. Your power is greater than you imagine, and the Syrnte can show you how to use it."

Images, beautiful and seductive, filled her mind: of vast plains and wide rivers, colorful caravans and vibrant people. She saw them dancing under the bright sun and chanting by the silver light of stars. The haunting rhythm of their music filled her ears, weaving a dream of endless nights at Tahmir's side, of the eternal pleasure of his touch, of the protective heat of his embrace.

"I would give much to follow you to your homeland, Tahmir," Eolyn said. "But when I accepted my staff, I made a vow to bring the traditions of the magas back to this land. If we defeat Tzeremond and the King, the most important part of my work will have only just begun. And if we lose…Gods help us if we lose, but if we lose then I must find some way to start over. In either case, I cannot leave my people."

He pressed his lips against her forehead. She responded to their searching tenderness, melting into his embrace, returning his caress with her unspoken assent. They would make love on the way back to camp in some unexplored corner of these peaceful green woods, invoking the spirit of the forest and offering their shared ecstasy to the Gods.

"There are many paths to your destiny," Tahmir murmured. "Not all of them are confined to these hills."

CHAPTER THIRTY-NINE

Invocation

THE DISTURBANCE STARTLED EOLYN out of her sleep. A massive movement of horses and soldiers was upsetting the pulse of the earth. The air rang with the metallic chorus of their weapons. A deep ache ignited behind Eolyn's temples and spread to the back of her head.

Fighting the sour pit that took hold in her stomach, Eolyn rose, dressed, and sought out her brother.

Hours later, Ernan's scouts, sent out days before, appeared to confirm that the King's army marched toward Aerunden. They had two days, perhaps three, at most.

While Ernan and Khelia set their people to work readying their weapons, Eolyn enlisted Rishona's help for her own preparations. They made extracts of horehound and laurel to mitigate curses of *Ahmad-melan*, and crafted amulets of houseleek and vervain to blunt the enemy's blade. They gathered white willow and mandrake to ease the pain of the wounded, and laid wood for the sacred fire of Eolyn's circle: Oak for strength and endurance, Rowan for control and victory, Alder to give guidance to those destined for the Underworld.

Late in the afternoon on the following day, the first of the royal troops appeared at the far end of the valley, purple banners snapping above a cloud of dust. With the sun descending rapidly in the west, they halted their advance at some distance, setting up camp while the rest of the column arrived. Even as night fell, the King's men continued to file into Aerunden, a long river of bright torches that fed an ever-expanding pool of shimmering light.

Accompanied by Ernan, Khelia, Tahmir, and Rishona, Eolyn climbed the southern ridge to cast the first sacred circle she had ever dedicated to war. Calling upon the power of the earth, she ignited the wood and fed carefully measured portions of juniper, rosemary, and winter sage into the flames. She invoked the memory of her mother and Ghemena to give strength to her magic and peace of mind in the face of

229

death. Kneeling before each of her companions, she painted their hands and feet with dyes prepared from night berries and blue iris root, meant to ward off their enemies in this world and the next.

Ehekaht, Ehekahtu, she sang, *Naeom cohmae, faeom denae, naeom dumae.*

As the ritual drew to a close, the people retired to their tents. Only Ernan lingered, standing beside his sister in silence as they watched the King's army fill the valley beyond.

He placed a hand on her shoulder and said, "It is not unlike the nights we used to stay up on the farm, searching for falling stars in the moonless sky."

"There you are wrong, dear brother," she replied quietly. "This is not like those nights at all."

He stiffened and withdrew his hand. When he spoke again, his voice was hoarse. "I thank the Gods every day that you were returned to me, and not—as you might have imagined—because of the victory you can help us achieve, but because I missed you, Eolyn, from the moment you were lost."

She tried to swallow, but her throat was tight. "I missed you too, Ernan, more than you can imagine. Every year after the raid, I stayed up late on Samhaen, hoping to catch a glimpse of your spirit. I left out as much sweetbread as Ghemena would allow, because I remembered how much you liked it, and every morning it was gone. Who could have eaten it, I wonder? It must have been the Guendes. But I thought it was you. I always believed it was you."

She paused, embarrassed to speak of such childish memories in such a grave moment. But then she felt him smile in the dark, and it brought her comfort.

"Well," he said, "if the Gods call me home tomorrow, you must lay out sweetbread again. And a mug of ale, while you're at it. I've heard there's no good drink to be found in the Afterlife."

"Don't jest about that, Ernan. I lost you once. I can't bear the thought of losing you again."

He stepped close, catching her off guard with the sudden awareness of his ephemeral warmth. "Eolyn, if I do not survive tomorrow—"

"You will survive. Don't even suggest you won't."

"If things go badly for us," he insisted, "if you see my lines break, you must take your horse and ride as fast as you can to the head of this pass. Tahmir has several of his riders stationed there. They will escort you to safety."

"Tahmir?" An odd anxiety crept into her heart.

"The Syrnte know a way through the South Woods, a little traveled path that skirts the western flank of the Paramen Mountains and leads to their homeland. You will go with them, and you will not return."

"You and Tahmir agreed to this plan without consulting me?"

"Promise me you will put yourself in the care of his men."

"No! No, I will promise no such thing, because I will not abandon my people, and you will not fail."

Ernan drew a long breath and turned to the valley, one hand gripping the hilt of his sword. She wanted to remember this image forever, the cut of his profile against the shadows, his scent of leather and summer grass. She hardly knew her brother, and now he threatened to leave her again. Something deep inside rent in two. Eolyn stifled the sob that rose in her heart.

Ernan glanced upwards as if searching the stars. Then he set his gaze upon her. "Eolyn, dear sister, if I said anything in these days past that offended or upset you, I apologize. I know where your loyalty lies. I know what you want for yourself and for our people. I have never doubted you, or the destiny that brought us here. Not for a moment."

Eolyn understood her brother was not being entirely honest, but it did not matter. Tomorrow he would march toward fields of death with her memory in his heart. He would seek out his vengeance, thinking to honor her, hoping to venerate their mother. He needed this reconciliation, and she would not deny it to him.

"I know, brother," she said. "Nor have I ever doubted you. If it is within my power to bring you to victory tomorrow, then I will see it done."

Ernan nodded. Unsheathing Kel'Barú, he proffered the blade to her. "I would be greatly honored, Maga Eolyn, if you would speak to my weapon tonight, and keep it by your side while you make your final petition to the Gods."

This was an old tradition on the eve of battle in Moisehén. In all probability, Akmael was offering his own sword to Tzeremond at this very moment. Eolyn accepted Kel'Barú with a bow of respect. "The honor is mine, brother. I will care for your sword and commend it to Dragon."

Ernan embraced her and departed.

Kneeling at the center of her circle, Eolyn laid the sword in front of her. Kel'Barú's pale blade reflected the river of stars that illuminated the clear sky. The grass felt cool and soft against her knees. Evening songs of frogs and crickets floated out of the trees in a soothing cadence. Under any other circumstance, this night would have inspired the tranquility of the infinite. But the sun would set over bloody fields tomorrow, and the moon would rise over ravens and wolves.

On the north side of the valley, Eolyn could see the purple blue flames of Tzeremond's fire. She imagined the old wizard kneeling beside it, observing the same rites and invoking the same spells as she, honoring the same traditions shaped by so many generations before them.

How can a people with so much in common be so divided?

Akmael would be making his way down that hill now, his expression severe, his dark gaze focused. Upon entering the camp, he would greet his men with words of encouragement, perhaps an occasional handshake or clap on the shoulder. Before retiring to his tent, he would look toward the northern ridge and observe the fire where she knelt. He would wonder if she were blessing the sword intended to kill him.

A deep shudder took hold at the base of Eolyn's spine and traveled up through her shoulders. She covered her face with her hands.

"I cannot do this, Kel'Barú," she confessed in tears. "I cannot ask you to slay Akmael."

The blade shifted as if moved by some unseen hand.

"But if I do not ask you to slay him, I may be sending my brother to his death."

The wizard's weapon lay in silence. For all its enchantment, Kel'Barú was more a loyal dog than a sentient being. It could not give advice or comfort. It could only wait to hear her bidding while humming quiet songs of warriors killed and battles won.

Eolyn drew a shaky breath and took the sword in her hands. The magic of the weapon shifted, connecting to her spirit and will. She pressed the flat of the blade to her lips, then raised it toward the heavens.

Kel'Barú's song grew more complex, reaching toward the stars, culminating in a spellbinding cadence of joy and valor. Captivated by its power, Eolyn responded with her own voice, offering Kel'Barú everything she could: her love, her fear, her gratitude and resentment, her hopes and disappointments, her uncertainty and her conviction.

Ehekaht, she prayed, *this is my petition to the Gods. Bring victory to Moisehén. Whatever the path, whatever the cost, whatever the price you require in blood, return the magic of our ancestors to my people.*

Hear the plea of your servant.

Help me fulfill my vow.

CHAPTER FORTY

Ahmad-melan

EOLYN CUT A FINE FIGURE as she rode out to meet the King, her hair spun red-gold by the cool breeze. She wore a burgundy robe and held her polished staff high. The crystal head shone in the gathering light, a bright reflection of the rising sun.

Akmael felt an unexpected surge of pride as he watched her, accompanied by an undercurrent of desire. Once again, he resolved to have her—woman and maga—before the sun set on the valley of Aerunden.

Beside her rode the man Akmael assumed to be her brother, and next to him a woman with the look of a warrior from the Paramen Mountains.

Khelia, perhaps.

Corey had mentioned her.

Behind them, the rebels were organized into four companies that spanned the width of the narrow valley. Their right flank appeared restless and ill-armed, with pitchforks and hoes. Next to them stood the Mountain Warriors, their lines steady under the constant flutter of sky blue banners. Akmael could feel their predatory gaze from across the field of battle, but lacking spears, they would be easy prey. To their left, under flags of dark green, were several rows of spearmen donated by Selen, a grim reminder of the seditious lords that had turned against him. When this was finished, their years of stewardship over his mother's land of birth would come to a bitter end. The last company, on the rebel left, was tight knit and just as solid as the Mountain Warriors. Akmael suspected these were Ernan's own, experienced men who had fought many campaigns together.

A small group of horses, no more than fifty, were stationed to the rear. If Corey were to be trusted and the estimates of the royal scouts correct, that left around five hundred men unaccounted for, in addition to an unknown number of Syrnte cavalry.

No doubt Ernan had concealed archers in the forest, a move Akmael had anticipated. Two companies of his own footmen were positioned to go in after them during the first charge. A second line of horsemen would follow the vanguard to challenge the Syrnte should they appear, or to assist in the rout if they did not.

Assuming Ernan had no real surprises to offer, this battle might well be over by midmorning. And if a thousand mounted men-at-arms were not enough, Akmael had spearmen aplenty to bring into the fray. Either way, victory would be his. If Eolyn's brother had any sense, he would recognize this and desist in his madness.

With a nod to Tzeremond and Drostan, Akmael advanced his horse. They emerged in front of his army to receive the rebel's challenge.

Ernan and his companions halted a few paces before them.

The King studied them in silence, his eyes lingering longest on Eolyn. One remarkable maga arrayed against him and his mages. It was, perhaps, Ernan's greatest folly to place so much faith in her magic. But his folly had been transformed into her valor, and she held the King's gaze, her dark eyes resolute, her expression impenetrable.

As if we had not known each other before this day.

"Ernan of Moehn." Akmael turned to his opponent. He noticed something familiar in Ernan. The fire behind those green eyes troubled him, stirring some dark shadow lodged deep inside his heart. Like a bad dream that struggled to be remembered. "I have heard much of your skill and experience. Surely you recognize the impossibility of your situation. If you lay down your arms now, I am prepared to accept your surrender on generous terms. Your people will be granted my pardon and allowed to remain in this kingdom in peace, except, of course, for your mercenaries and foreign allies, who must depart my lands at once."

Eolyn drew a breath of surprise. Akmael caught her gaze in his.

Furrowing her brow, she glanced away.

"You have expressed a clear interest in Selen," Akmael continued, returning to Ernan. "I can grant you a portion of the lands in the east, from the Furma River south, and west to the Maeskon Hills, to be kept by your family and their descendants. Your sister," he nodded toward Eolyn, "will remain a maga, by my leave. I suggest you accept my terms, so that we can desist from this bloodshed and go home."

"Ernan," Eolyn said. "Perhaps we should consider—"

"We will not surrender." Her brother's resolve at once impressed and dismayed. Akmael thought it unfortunate that this man, who might have made a worthy ally, was so bent on being his sworn enemy. "The line of Vortingen has betrayed our people. We have come to avenge the corruption of this kingdom, to end the rule of you and your fathers, and to restore magic to all the people of Moisehén."

"You have no case for vengeance against me, and you cannot win today. If you fight, your people will fall like summer rain. Their blood will drench this valley. It is within your power to avoid this tragedy." Akmael shifted his focus once more to Eolyn. "Surrender, and accept the promise of my protection."

Ernan brought his horse forward to block the King's view of Eolyn. Tension took hold of the rebel leader's shoulders. Waves of heat rose off his armor, though the dawn air remained cool.

Akmael noted a disturbing change in the rhythm of Ernan's breath. Instinctively, the King's hand went to the hilt of his sword, but Ernan did not attack. He sat as still as stone, green eyes smoldering beneath red brows. He looked not upon the King but upon something seen only by him.

A metallic odor pricked Akmael's senses, and realization dawned on him. He glanced at Tzeremond, but the wizard's amber eyes were fixed upon Ernan, who now turned to his sister and said to her in a low growl, "On this day, you will perish upon my sword."

Ernan spurred his horse back toward the rebel army.

Face filled with alarm, Eolyn spun her mare to follow.

Khelia, visibly disconcerted by their sudden retreat, trailed behind at a gallop.

Akmael had to fight his impulse to take off after them. Anger spilled out in a vicious rebuke. "It is too early in the day for such curses, old wizard!"

Tzeremond lifted his brow in mild surprise, but nodded in deference. "Forgive me, my Lord King. I thought you would be pleased. Surely you saw he was not inclined to accept your terms, and there is more than one way to avoid bloodshed."

Akmael subdued his temper. "That was a dishonorable move, and the threat to his sister is not a good sign."

"I assure you, my Lord King, he will be too disoriented to raise his sword against anyone."

Unconvinced, Akmael gripped his reins and slowed his breath. Corey had once assured him Ernan would never allow harm to come to his sister, but the thought did little to comfort him now. Even the greatest bonds of love had been known to shatter under the terrifying frenzy of *Ahmad-melan*.

About fifty paces before reaching their line, Ernan veered away from his fighters and sped to a temporary refuge under an isolated tree. Eolyn, still some distance behind him, pulled her horse to stop.

Khelia came up behind her, anxious and perplexed. "What in the name of the Gods just happened?"

Eolyn kept her gaze fixed upon Ernan. "Khelia, go to our people. I must speak with my brother."

Leaving the mountain warrior behind, Eolyn approached Ernan and dismounted under the shade of the spreading branches. She drove her staff into the earth.

Ehekaht
Naeom veham
Leanom enem
Ehukae

The air shimmered, and the valley blurred. Only her brother remained in focus. He stood with his back to her, one hand upon the hilt of his sword, the other gripping a low strong limb. The heat of his rage reverberated in tight waves off his back.

Eolyn drew a deep breath, trying to control her apprehension. Cautiously she stepped toward him. "Ernan."

"Get away from me, witch," he growled. "I've had enough of your spells and deceptions! You convinced me once you were my sister, lost and returned to me. Now I see you are nothing but a whore of the Mage King!"

Eolyn braced her heart against his insults. Ernan was not himself, and if she did not break this curse, the anger that burned in his veins would drive him mad. The battle would be lost before they had even begun.

"Ernan—"

"*Do not provoke me!*" Unsheathing his sword, he lunged at her.

"Ernan!"

His blade halted just short of her throat. Eolyn heard the metallic sob of Kel'Barú as it strained against Ernan's will.

"I am Eolyn, your sister and High Maga of Moisehén. You will hear me and see me. Now."

Rivulets of sweat coursed over Ernan's temples. His eyes twitched and dilated.

"Sister?" He choked as though it took all his strength to speak. Kel'Barú broke free of his grip and tumbled to the ground. Ernan sank to his knees under the force of the fever. "What has happened to me? I am overcome with the desire to kill you."

Tears escaped his eyes. Eolyn moved quickly lest rage sink into inconsolable despair.

"It is *Ahmad-melan.*" She retrieved an amulet from her belt and broke it open, releasing a copper dust into his face. "Breath, Ernan. Breathe deep."

His head shot back with the sting of the antidote. Stepping behind him, Eolyn placed one palm against his damp forehead and the other upon his throbbing chest. Closing her eyes, she sought the roots of the curse and pulled them out with force.

Ehekaht,
Naeom denae daum
Erenahm rehoernem ekaht
Behnaum enem

Ernan keeled over and vomited sour bile upon the grass. The fever departed, leaving him shivering in its wake. Kneeling, Eolyn gathered him into her arms and brought a flask of minted water to his lips.

"It is over." She assured him quietly, encouraging him to drink. "You will recover your strength in a few moments."

"I saw you embrace him." Ernan's voice shook. "You surrendered everything and laid your power at his feet. You betrayed me to my death. It all seemed so real."

"It was a vision, a reflection of your deepest fears. Tzeremond, or perhaps the King." Her voice faltered at the thought. "One of them found your fear and manipulated it against you. Forgive me, Ernan. I had not thought them so dishonorable as to attempt such an attack before the battle began. I will not fail you again, and I will not betray you. Not today, not ever."

He pushed away from her and steadied himself on his knees.

"Our people." He glanced in the direction of the rebel lines. "I drew my sword against you. What will they think?"

"They have seen nothing. I invoked a vision ward. They are watching us, brother and sister, warrior and maga, as we pray to the Gods for victory."

"Victory," he repeated as if trying to remember where he was and why he had come here. "Yes. Victory."

Ernan struggled to his feet. He retrieved Kel'Barú from where it lay and extended his arm to Eolyn. The madness in his eyes had faded. His expression was once again calm, his voice resolute. "Come, sister. We have a battle to win."

Eolyn accepted his hand and stood, but her relief was short lived. As they approached their horses, Kel'Barú startled her with a silver hiss.

He turned me against you.

She paused, fear threading through her veins. *He was not himself. A curse took hold of him.*

He meant to kill you.

Before she could respond, Ernan sheathed the blade and mounted

237

his steed.

"Brother," she said, "you must choose another weapon for this battle."

He laughed. "I have no finer sword, Eolyn."

"Please, Ernan. Something's not right with Kel'Barú."

Frowning, he withdrew the sword from its sheath and held it in front of him, gauging its balance before sending a few clean slices through the air. The blade shone brilliant as ever, its song smooth and confident.

Ernan shrugged and smiled. "Kel'Barú has always danced for my sister, and today will be no different. This sword was meant to taste the blood of wizards, Eolyn. It will share in the glory of our victory over the Mage King, else why would it have come to me?"

With that, he spurred his horse toward his men.

Akmael's grip on his reins relaxed when Eolyn emerged from the vision ward with her brother, the two of them united and ready for battle. He even allowed himself a smile at Tzeremond's sharp hiss of frustration.

Truly she was gifted, having undone the curse of a master with such ease. How many times had he tried to persuade her to abandon High Magic? If she had listened to him, she would have betrayed her very essence. Yet in choosing that path, she had embarked on an inevitable confrontation with forces that would deny her this privilege. Akmael was born to those forces, and he could no more escape his heritage than she could her destiny.

For what purpose, then, had the Gods allowed their short-lived friendship in the South Woods? Perhaps those lost years would grant some redemption for the blood to be shed on their behalf today.

Or perhaps the Gods were simply cruel.

Ernan galvanized his men, his sword shining silver-white under the rising sun. His followers responded with thunderous shouts and raised arms, invoking victory in Eolyn's name. Like a crimson flame, she rode the length of their forces and passed through her people's midst, her touch a source of courage and resolve. She ascended the southern ridge behind their ranks, and assumed her position as High Maga.

Akmael turned back toward the royal army.

"None of them are to survive this day," he reminded Drostan. "Make certain the men understand. I will suffer no prisoners, except for the maga. She is to be brought to me alive and whole, untouched by any blade."

CHAPTER FORTY-ONE

Aerunden

AS THE KING'S GUARD ADVANCED, nostalgia caught in Sir Drostan's throat, a longing to see an army of magas arrayed before him.

He remembered the exhilaration of facing those worthy opponents: the brilliance of their armor, the sharp snap of their burgundy flags, the high pitched fury of their battle cries. They had met Kedehen's army with well-forged swords and power-laden staves. Their flames had scorched the battlefield, leaving smoldering earth and burnt flesh. Their death charges had thundered through the ranks of the King's men, killing all who did not have time or skill to deflect their deadly curses.

But the royal army withstood their attack. Drostan had slain every one of his own adversaries—men with whom he had studied, women to whom he had made love, friends and colleagues turned enemies of the King and therefore of Moisehén.

He did not mourn them until long after the war, when he found time and quiet and secret places in which to grieve. Once his regrets were spent, he did not think of them again. Not until today, when their memory emerged like a glittering mirage over the humble valley of Aerunden.

Ehekahtu, he murmured, *Sepuenem al melan dumae, Erehai abnahm al shue.*

The distance between him and his opponents was still too great for *Ahmad-melan* to take effect, but Drostan never entered a battle without invoking its protection. Once the fighting started, it was much more difficult to cast such spells.

At the King's command, Drostan reined in his chestnut horse, slowing to a trot with the rest of the line. By now, he could see the faces of the rebels, not more than a hundred paces away, like hawks caught on the ground. Fear rose in smoky wisps off the ill-formed right flank.

Already the magic that ran beneath the field of battle was palpable. The chants of Tzeremond's mages faded, fell back, and surged forward

239

again. Maga Eolyn defended her own, raising barriers against Tzeremond's curses as she reinforced the courage of her foot soldiers. Not one sword had clashed, and yet the battle had already begun, wrapping around them in an invisible cloud, running beneath them in tightly held ribbons of magic.

A long shout was heard from the King's lead archer. Shafts of ash sped in a high arc toward the rebel's right flank. As they paused at their zenith, Drostan sensed the indecision of the maga, and he held his breath.

She is new to war, and she is only one.

She could not weave spells of valor and deflect arrows at the same time.

In the instant she made her choice, the tide of magic beneath the right flank receded. A burst of wind issued from the southern ridge. She had responded just as they had hoped. Arrows scattered and missed their targets, but the second volley came on the heels of the first, straight and swift, giving her no opportunity to intervene. Bodkin points pierced arms, shoulders, legs, and faces. Cries of pain and panic filled the air.

"Forward!" Akmael cried, and the horns sounded the charge.

Drostan sprang ahead with his liege's men. They formed an impenetrable wall of horses and metal. Nostrils flared. The odor of fear and sweat filled Drostan's senses. The power of Tzeremond's mages carried them forward.

They charged into the ranks of the Mountain Warriors. Men on either side of the breach buckled back. Uncertainty rippled through the front lines. Drostan lifted his sword high and brought it down on the first rebel within reach. He felt the satisfying crunch of metal against bone. The blade released a spray of blood, and the man crumpled to the ground.

All around, foot soldiers cried out under swords and hooves. Drostan allowed himself a grim smile as he hacked another mercenary into the Underworld. There would be no need for magic here. They had breached Ernan's lines with ease, and soon the second charge would join them.

This slaughter will be over within the hour.

A vicious blow knocked the wind from Drostan's lungs and sent his mount screaming to the ground. The knight landed hard, one leg pinned under his flailing horse. A mind-numbing roar thundered through his head. Heart racing, he shoved back his visor, struggling to regain focus.

Drostan watched, incredulous, as a wild cat ripped through the neck of his mount. Almost as large as the horse, the savage creature had snow white fur and gray stripes. It lifted its bloody jowls, roared, and set ice blue eyes upon Drostan.

Before the knight could retrieve his sword, the cat sprang. Giant claws scraped at his armor. Fangs slashed at his face. Drostan wedged a mailed forearm into the beast's throat, in a desperate struggle to hold it off. His free hand searched for a weapon, any weapon.

His grip closed around the haft of a discarded axe, which he brought full force against the side of the creature's head. The impact reverberated through his arm, but the cat did little more than pause in annoyance. The creature's weight was crushing him. Drool dripped hot onto his face.

Adjusting his grip, Drostan drew the weapon back and struck again, driving the metal blade into the animal's skull. The creature's sharp howl of pain sent shivers through the knight. He wrenched the axe away and struck again. The cat stumbled back. Drostan struggled out from under his horse and lunged forward, hitting the beast over and over. Blood sprayed everywhere, until at last the giant feline collapsed into a heap of blackened, sodden fur.

Exhausted, Drostan sank to his knees, oblivious for the moment to the battle that raged around him. As he reached forward to touch the animal, it transformed in front of his eyes, leaving in its place a man, his flesh ripped open and covered with blood.

Stunned, Drostan turned the body over. The height, the features of the face, the color of the hair and eyes were all unmistakable. His opponent had been a Mountain Warrior. But how, in the name of the Gods, had he learned to shape shift?

The knight pushed himself to his feet. Pain burned raw through his thigh. The tiger's claws had punctured his arm. He tested his weight on the bruised leg and grunted in satisfaction. The wounds were deep, but he had suffered worse.

Recovering a sword from the ground near his mutilated horse, Drostan straightened and scanned the melee around him, eyes narrowed and muscles tensed. A legion of snow tigers assaulted the royal army. Fangs and claws flashed in dust raised by the battle. A handful of mage warriors, old men like Drostan, had shape shifted into bears to counter this new threat. They rose high on sturdy hind legs. Their deep bellows rumbled across the battlefield. Giant cats rushed at them in a vicious blur. Men and horses caught between the shape shifters were being torn apart.

Torturous moments passed while Drostan searched the chaos, apprehension mounting as he realized he had no answer for the one question that mattered most.

Where was the King?

TAHMIR HAD STARTED UP THE NARROW VALLEY with a handful of Syrnte warriors before dawn. They moved like shadows through the misty forest, invoking powers of stealth embodied by great predators that ruled the plains of their homeland. As the sun warmed the high branches, they climbed the rear of the hill. The few guards they found before reaching the summit were easily silenced.

Signaling his men to fan out near the edge of the clearing, the Syrnte Prince concealed himself behind a small cluster of saplings. Master Tzeremond had cast his circle just where Eolyn anticipated. He stood in dark undulating robes, the smooth melody of his spells contrasting with the chaotic clamor in the valley.

Rishona's impatience echoed inside Tahmir's head. She waited with a small company of horsemen, hidden in the woods behind Ernan's lines. Tahmir could feel the quick pulse of her heart, the sweat of her palms inside leather gloves. She was anxious to charge forward, to defend the many she had come to love, to win the crown she so desired.

Patience, dear sister. Our destiny is at hand.

Tahmir drew the arrow meant for Tzeremond from its resting place. He had fashioned the shaft from a smooth branch of young ash and balanced it with tail feathers from the hawk of their mother, Tamara. Rishona had imbued it with complex spells designed to cut through the formidable defenses of a mage's sacred circle. The tip was bathed in venom. They had brought the arrow from their homeland, and during their time with Mage Corey, they had guarded its existence in absolute secrecy. On the eve of the battle, they had removed the arrow from its finely carved case and ignited its sleeping magic.

Setting the arrow on his bow, he drew the string taut and waited for the currents of time to slow. Eddies settled, and the window to Tzeremond's death came into focus. Tahmir sent the arrow hissing toward the wizard. It sank into his back like a knife through soft butter. Passing directly through the old mage, the arrow continued in a smooth arc toward the ground and skidded out of sight.

Tahmir caught his breath.

The window of chance twisted and then vanished.

Time resumed its flow. Tzeremond remained standing as if nothing had happened, his robes motionless in the wind. He ceased his song, then shimmered and disappeared.

Three of the High Mages vanished with him.

The voices of the remaining five faltered. One rushed forward to the place where their master had just stood, his expression incredulous. Another turned with deadly precision toward Tahmir's hiding place. Extended his arm, the mage shouted.

Ehekahtu, faeom
Re dumae!

Tahmir flung himself to the ground just as the flame hit. Saplings burst into flames overhead. He rolled to his feet and raced downhill, ducking out of the path of a second shaft that singed his shoulders and hair. All around, his men perished with agonized cries. The stench of burning flesh filled the air.

Just ahead, Tahmir saw himself glance over his shoulder as a low rumble rose from the summit. Tahmir skidded to a stop, merging with his own image as past met future. He turned to look back, and light ripped open the forest. Heat scalded his face and enveloped his body. Death burned through his lungs. Fire consumed flesh, melting skin and muscle into a bubbling, blackened mass.

For one excruciatingly painful moment, Tahmir saw every path he had lived and would not live. He remembered music, passion, and dance. He heard his sister's laughter and saw the sunlit plains of their home. He reached out to the many he had loved, and mourned the one he had forever failed.

Eolyn.

Darkness claimed him, and all awareness slipped from his grasp.

AKMAEL'S DESTRIER REARED, throwing him to the ground as a tiger tackled the horse and ripped open its neck. The King struggled to his feet under a fountain of blood.

Ehekahtu, faeom re dumae!

Magic surged through Akmael's feet and burst from the palm of his hand. The snow tiger fell convulsing as its head melted into blackened fur and ash-covered fangs.

Another tiger sprang through the smoke. With no chance to invoke a second flame, Akmael swung his sword. She ducked out of reach and caught Akmael's shin with her paw, knocking him off balance. Akmael regained his footing and spun to face her again.

The snow tiger crouched a few feet away, curved fangs exposed in a vicious snarl, the thrill of the hunt in her ice blue gaze. Roaring, she threw herself forward and crushed Akmael against the earth. His sword slipped from his hand. His helmet was torn away, and his vision blurred. Then her teeth came into focus, gleaming inside an ebony mouth.

An explosion of fur swept her away. Gasping, Akmael pushed himself up and reached for his sword. A massive bear had tackled the female and now grappled with her. Claws tore at fur, jaws snapped at limbs. Akmael recognized the reddish hue of the bear's aura.

Drostan!

His relief palpable, the King drew himself to his feet.

An enemy horseman bore down upon him, cutting through enraged beasts and desperate foot soldiers. Akmael looked toward Drostan, but the bear now struggled against two of the tigers. He steadied his stance and waited, sword in hand, until the destrier was almost upon him. Then he drove his blade into the satin brown snout, parting skin, teeth, and tongue in a spurt of blood.

The animal screamed and reared back, throwing its rider. A hoof knocked Akmael in the chest. The sword was torn from his grasp and landed several feet away. Akmael stumbled back and reached for his blade as his attacker hit the earth.

Ehekahtu, naeom denae!

But his breath was short and his stance weak, and the weapon did not return to him.

His opponent rose to his feet. Akmael recognized him by his long sword, so pale it might have been forged from ivory. Ernan's blade sang with a voice unlike any Akmael had heard, a rich amalgamation of earth, fire, and air.

The rebel stepped forward and removed his helmet, letting his red hair fall wild over his shoulders. His pale green eyes narrowed. "Look upon me, son of Vortingen, and remember the one who sent you to the Underworld on this day."

Akmael had seen those eyes before, on the face of a woman, a maga and warrior. In an instant, Ernan's image faded and, the red-haired witch stood in front of him, implacable in her rage, the corpse of his mother reflected in her merciless gaze. She pointed her staff at him and cried, *This boy must die!*

The King staggered back, stunned.

Ernan, son of Kaie.

Ernan, brother of Eolyn.

Both of them spawned by the witch who murdered Akmael's mother.

Why had he not seen it before? The circumstances of Eolyn's childhood, the timing of the raid upon her village, the shade of her hair in late afternoon, the tone of her voice when she became angry.

Rage carved a jagged river through deep and forgotten places in Akmael's soul. It opened a black pit under his heart, and ignited a stormy wrath fed by long buried memories of what he had been forced to endure, powerless, as a child. Of what he refused to tolerate now, as a man and a king.

Eolyn's brother strode toward him, raising his long sword with both hands. His scar glowed white upon his flushed face. His eyes burned with bloodlust.

Akmael took his axe from his belt and gripped it with deadly calm. He steadied his stance, connecting his magic to deepest powers of the earth. "Come, then, Ernan son of Kaie. Your doom awaits you."

EOLYN CRIED OUT IN PAIN. She sagged against her staff and clutched at her breast, lungs burning inside her chest.

Tahmir.

She had seen the blinding light, felt the scalding heat, and sensed the terrible emptiness that followed. Across the valley, wisps of smoke rose from the summit occupied by Tzeremond and his mages.

What has happened?

Eolyn struggled for breath, trying to rise above agony and wrap her spirit around the moment at hand. Her staff took on an ominous hum. The image of Dragon glowed fiery red inside the quartz crystal. In the valley below, the two armies were tearing each other apart.

What have I done?

People she loved were dying. Killing each other, and for what?

A small flock of ravens landed in a nearby tree, their black wings fluttering and grasping at the air. The thin branches bent under their weight. With throaty cries, they summoned the scavengers of the forest.

So quickly they detect the smell of death!

More ravens would arrive before nightfall, along with badgers and wildcats. Wolves would follow, gnawing flesh off bones, fighting over limbs and entrails.

Will they feed upon me? Upon Ernan, upon Akmael?

Where is my brother? Where is the King?

She searched the valley and found them. Ernan was charging toward Akmael, Kel'Barú high his grip, its silver white blade the only bright point on the smoke-filled plain. Eolyn shivered, remembering this moment as she had seen it, in a vision years ago in the South Woods. Horror undermined her magic. Her breath stopped altogether, and the circle fractured.

I cannot let them die.

She called to her horse, resolved to descend from this ridge and come between her brother and Akmael. She would oppose their bloody game until they lowered their arms, or she would die trying to stop them.

But the mare reared and bolted. An ice cold wind hit Eolyn and flung her to the ground. Eolyn's staff skittered out of reach. Startled and bruised, she tried to get up, but a foot upon her back forced her into the dirt. Grit and blood filled her mouth.

"I expected more of a challenge from a student of Ghemena." Tzeremond spoke with deadly calm.

Three ravens landed close by and peered at her with obsidian eyes. In a flash of light they assumed their true forms, High Mages all.

Eolyn reached for her staff, but a thin tether snaked around her neck, cutting off her breath.

Tzeremond directed a white hot shaft of light into the heart of Eolyn's staff. The oak and crystal should have shattered under his curse, but it remained whole. Not one singe marred its surface.

The wizard spat and yanked Eolyn to her knees by the tether.

Eolyn's hands went to her throat, struggling to loosen his hold.

"Your mother was Kaie, wasn't she?" He murmured in her ear. "The witch who murdered her own sister."

Eolyn struck him with her elbow, but he only tightened the tether, making her choke.

The High Mages formed a triangle around them and began a slow chant in a language she did not recognize. A knot of terror took hold inside. What manner of curse could require so many mages?

Tzeremond gripped her chin and forced her gaze to the battlefield. "In truth, I am grateful to you, Eolyn, for you have brought us our final triumph. Today, all resistance to the Mage Kings of Moisehén will end, and the last of your perverse magic will be purged from our land. We have waited long for this day. We have crafted it with great patience. My Order, my King, and I."

She squeezed words out between agonized gasps. "I will not listen to your lies!"

"You are wise not to trust me, maga, but then why would I deceive you now, when our triumph is at hand?" He stroked her hair. "You remember the boy, Achim?"

Eolyn's heart faltered. Hairline cracks spread over its pulsating surface.

"Yes," Tzeremond said. "I see you do. Achim was not as naïve as you and your Doyenne assumed. He saw what you were from the beginning, and he understood how to use you for his purposes. He cultivated your trust because he knew, as all my students know, that the stronger the illusion of friendship, the more brutal the betrayal. The more shattered the betrayed, the greater the power we derive from their fall. The Mage Prince has only ever wanted three things from you, Eolyn. To avenge the death of his mother, to make your magic his own, and to put an end to the perfidious defiance of the magas. Today he will see his desires fulfilled. My King will slay your brother and slaughter your friends. Then he will come to possess you, to finish what he asked me to begin."

Eolyn fought to invoke a counter spell, but it was no use. Tzeremond had cut off her breath. What kind of fool was she, to have suspected nothing when she saw the ravens? To have dismantled her circle without as much as a glance at her back?

"Look at what is happening, *Eolyn*." Tzeremond spoke, but it was Achim's voice she heard upon his lips. "See this battle for what it is."

Eolyn's spirit was sucked into a screaming tunnel and thrown into the midst of the battle. Bears grappled tigers, knights hacked down foot soldiers. The air was murky with blood and dust. Men and women lay broken across the landscape. The stench of scorched fur and burning corpses stung her nostrils.

She heard Akmael's war cry before she saw him. He charged her brother, and they met in a horrible clash of metal upon metal, fiercer than any beast around them. Ernan's red locks whipped through the air. Akmael's curls lay matted against his brow. The King's face was dark, the magic that coursed through him ominous.

Ernan faltered before his adversary. The blade of the Galian wizard glanced off Akmael's armor and slipped against the King's axe. The weapon betrayed Ernan time and again, in subtle but crucial ways. With each swing, Eolyn's brother tired a bit more. Yet Ernan did not seem to notice. Lost in his obsession for vengeance, he was unable to recognize his dream unraveling.

And Akmael...

Akmael, Eolyn realized with icy dread, was toying with her brother, letting him stumble, fall and come back only to give him another debilitating blow.

Ernan staggered and leaned over, struggling for breath, eyes blinking rose colored sweat.

Kel'Barú slipped useless from his hands.

Eolyn let go a desperate sob.

The King moved in for the kill.

Eolyn cried out to Akmael to stop, but she had no voice. Such was the power of Tzeremond's curse. Eolyn saw, but could not be seen. She heard, but could not speak. She could not turn away or close her eyes.

The King drove a fist into Ernan's face. Her brother's head snapped back, burgundy streams flew from his lips. Again Akmael hit him. Armor and mail tore away strips of flesh. Ernan responded with a few blind swings, but his nose had caved in, and his cheeks were being transformed into raw pulp.

Stop it, Achim! Eolyn's heart collapsed into the pit of her stomach. *Stop!*

Ernan sank to his knees, keeled over, and lay on the ground, his breath reduced to a rasping gurgle.

The Mage King towered above him, shoulders heaving. His face was filled with contempt, his eyes black as a moonless night. He took the haft of his axe in both hands and brought the blade down upon her brother's throat.

THE SYRNTE CAPTAIN STUDIED RISHONA, a frown upon his face, his steed restless beneath him.

"My Lady," he said, "If we join the battle now, there may still be an opportunity to—"

"I said, go!" Rishona replied. "The windows have closed. My brother is dead, Ernan has fallen. The Mage King will have his victory, and there is nothing our warriors can do to stop it. Our time here is finished. There is nothing left in this place to die for."

He nodded his assent. "And you, my Lady?"

Rishona drew a shaky breath. *I do not know. Perhaps I have nothing left to live for.* "I will follow shortly. Let me say one last prayer for my brother, that he may find his way across the abyss in peace."

He signaled the men. They scattered silently through the woods, disappearing fast among the shadows.

Rishona watched them go with a heavy heart and broken spirit. She dismounted and paced circles among the trees, gloved hands clenched at her sides.

Oh, Tahmir.

Loss ripped through her soul. Tears streamed down her cheeks. Sinking against a tree, she struck the bark with her fist.

Beyond the woods, battle cries were undercut by the low thunder of a second charge, the charge she had intended to meet.

Regret closed tight around her heart. She looked in the direction of her warriors, but they were already well away.

Have I made a mistake?

For the first time in memory, she could not see a clear path to the future. She felt lost and alone, abandoned by all her guides and loved ones.

Gathering damp leaves in both hands, Rishona buried her face in the aroma of earth and water, of death and renewed life.

Of home.

Was that not what she felt when she wandered these hills? Rishona had always pretended to be a stranger from a distant land. Yet she belonged to this place of rich loam and wet forests, more than she had ever belonged to the desiccated plains of her grandfather's people.

Rishona was still at one with her mother, Tamara, when terror overtook them, when brutality invaded the once quiet place that was Tamara's womb. But Rishona had refused to die with her mother. She had fought and pushed, begged and pleaded, until Tamara used her last breath to force her daughter into a ruthless world. The babe Rishona had landed hard on wet leaves, ears ringing with the last agonized cries of her mother. Cold air had rushed into her lungs, bringing with it the smell of blood and sweat, of rotting earth and brackish water.

Even among the Syrnte, it was rare to remember one's day of birth, but Rishona knew it was her own wails that brought the forester out of the woods. When the man wrapped the orphaned babe in his cloak, the boy Tahmir had appeared as if out of nowhere, eyes wide with shock, lips trembling in apprehension.

"You're to take care of your sister now." The forester had placed her in Tahmir's arms. "She's to depend on you."

Ever since that day, Rishona had deferred to Tahmir, to his plans and judgement, to his caution and courage. And after all these years of pursuing a dream of justice, what had they achieved? Nothing.

"You spared me!" she cried to the heavens. "When assassins drove their knives into my mother's belly, you spared me. For what purpose, if not this?"

A whisper sounded beneath Rishona's knees. Sinister and primal, it rose from deep within the earth, like the hiss of a thousand snakes.

Have the Gods abandoned you, Rishona of Moisehén?

Rishona's breath stilled. Her heartbeat slowed. She knew this call well. She had heard it often in her dreams. With trembling hands, she pressed her palms against the earth.

Your destiny is not lost. Avenge him. Avenge them all.

Closing her eyes, the Syrnte princess summoned the Ones That Speak for guidance. They hung back, reluctant to shape the future under the brutal swirl of the present. In their silence, she found only remorse. The excruciating emptiness of her brother's death, the relentless shame of her own failure.

Rishona choked back a sob and wiped the tears from her face. Rising to her feet, she retrieved a crossbow and sent her gelding deep into the forest. Then she turned toward the hill where Tzeremond held Eolyn. With cold determination, she chose a path to its summit.

THE TETHER SEARED EOLYN'S THROAT as Tzeremond whipped it away. She crumpled to the ground, gulping air between bitter sobs. Pain clawed at her ribs, like a beast tearing her apart from the inside. She cursed the Gods for not letting her die as a child, for leading her to Ghemena, and then to Mage Corey. Most of all, she cursed them for delivering her to Akmael.

Tzeremond circled her. The ominous chant of his mages continued. Churning clouds blocked out the sun. Thunder sounded overhead.

"We defeated an entire army of your kind," Tzeremond said. "It was irresponsible of Ghemena to let you believe you could confront us alone."

Eolyn clung to the earth, seeking a comfort that could not be found in the cool and fragrant grass. Just over the pale green blades she saw the crystal glitter of her staff, a useless tool that had brought her nowhere. She was only a pawn in the end, a toy used by the Gods to finish what Kedehen had begun.

She shut her eyes against the truth, and heard an impossible sound: the laughter of a young girl. A blur of motion emerged from the trees and ran toward her. A child knelt and peered at the fallen maga. Dark red curls framed her round face. Her earth brown eyes sparked with curiosity.

I think it would be better to die with a little magic in me, she confided, *than to die without any magic at all.*

Eolyn managed a smile, and the girl faded. Images of the South Woods returned to her, of twisting corridors and endless adventures. She heard the trees and the animals, felt the warm embrace of Ghemena. She remembered the first time Achim ran with her into the cold river, and all the magic they discovered together, before the Gods set them on different paths, before fate goaded them into war.

Drawing air into her lungs, she anchored her spirit deep into the earth. She felt water flow through her veins and stoked the fires of her heart. When all the elements illuminated her interior, Eolyn rose to face her adversary. Calling her staff, she drove it into the ground and let the long forbidden curse burn over her tongue.

Maehechnam arrat saufini

Ehemkaht neurai!

Lightning shot down from the boiling clouds, tunneling into the root of her staff and crackling up its length. White fire whipped through Eolyn, straining her limbs and threatening to explode inside of her. Bursting from the crystal capped head, the bolt smashed Tzeremond into the ground. The wizard cried out, limbs flailing, and then lay motionless.

Eolyn drew a ragged breath. Her body ached and her ears rang. Her hands felt raw and blistered, but she was alive.

Yet so was he.

Tzeremond coughed and rolled onto his side. Trembling violently, he pushed himself to his knees, wheezing and clutching his stomach. His robes were scorched and his hands blackened. His face was chalky gray, but rigid with determination.

He reached for his staff and steadied himself against it. He did not stand, but pinned Eolyn with his amber eyes and lifted one shaking arm toward her. Extending his boney fingers, he cried out:

Saenau

Revoerit

Nefau

The ground lurched beneath Eolyn. Her staff slipped like quicksilver from her hands.

A frigid wind spread through her like a tumor, drying the blood in her veins and leaving them hollow. Desperately she tried to invoke a counter spell, but the elements deserted her. The earth crumbled into a vortex and sucked the churning black clouds toward its core. A current was dragging her down, and she found nothing to grasp that could stop her fall. Dirt clogged her throat, rocks battered her limbs. The weight of the mountain fell upon her and consumed her in darkness.

CHAPTER FORTY-TWO

Abyss

AKMAEL WRENCHED HIS BLADE FREE from the earth next to Ernan's neck. He stood over the rebel leader, one hand gripping his axe, the other clenched in fury.

Gods take her! What has she done to me?

No King of Vortingen could suffer such a man to live. Yet in the moment Akmael's weapon descended, he had seen Eolyn's face and heard her lament. He had hesitated, and his blade missed its mark.

For what?

So Kaie's son could drag himself off this wretched field and foment another insurrection? Ernan could not be spared. Not even for her.

Akmael lifted his axe once more, but a tremor passed through the earth and threw him off balance. He felt a part of his soul tearing away. His gaze snapped toward the southern ridge. Lightning wrapped a fine luminous net around roiling clouds that swirled and descended in a sharp funnel toward the heart of the mountain.

Eolyn!

Around him, the battle was fast drawing to a close. Rebels not yet slain were fleeing into the woods under the second charge of his men. Akmael seized the bridle of the nearest mounted knight. "Your horse!"

The man obeyed.

Taking the knight's long sword as well, Akmael leaped upon the animal and spurred it forward, cursing fallen bodies and discarded weapons that obstructed his path.

By the time he arrived at the summit, the storm had vanished and the sun warmed the grass once again. Baedon and two other High Mages attended Tzeremond, who sagged against his staff. Eolyn lay lifeless on the ground.

Akmael's heart spasmed as he dismounted and knelt beside her. There was no breath upon her lips, no pulse beneath her skin. An unnatural chill had overtaken her, deeper and more ominous than the simple cold of death.

"What happened here?" he demanded.

"We have succeeded, my Lord King." Baedon responded with a deep bow. "Albeit at great cost. Master Tzeremond has suffered a terrible curse—"

"Succeeded at what?"

"Why, my Lord King." Baedon sent a confused look toward the wizard. "Your orders were clear."

Tzeremond lifted a trembling hand to quiet the mage. His face was ashen, but his eyes glowed with relief. "We have cleansed her of her magic, in this world and the next."

His words struck harder than any weapon. Akmael's eyes stung with the impact. When he found his voice, it was hoarse. "Cleansed her?"

"*Ahmad-dur,*" Baedon said. "We invoked *Ahmad-dur.*"

"Against this woman?" Akmael bellowed. "For the love of the Gods! She was a maga, not a monster!"

Tzeremond subdued a rattling cough. "It was the only way to finish them, once and for all."

With a furious roar, Akmael charged them. He severed the neck of one mage and drove his blade through the gut of another. Only Baedon escaped, taking the form of Raven and soaring out of reach. Akmael let him go and thrust the point of his bloodied sword under Tzeremond's chin. "You dare disobey me?"

"You think I am afraid of death?" Tzeremond rasped. "I, who served the Gods faithfully all my life? I, who brought magic to the line of Vortingen? I do not fear death! I fear the wrath of Dragon should I prove weak against the whims of my misguided student!"

Akmael drew back his weapon and swung, but his sword was deflected by another blade. The clash of metal sent a shower of sparks into Tzeremond's face. The King's wrath turned to surprise when he recognized the man who had crossed swords with him. "Drostan?"

"Pardon me, my Lord King." The knight's voice was steady, his gaze resolute. "Tzeremond can do no more harm as he is, but if you slay him now, he may be waiting for you, where she has gone."

Air returned to Akmael's lungs, like the sharp breath of a winter morning. He stepped back and turned to where Eolyn lay.

"What...What are you saying?" Tzeremond's voice shook. "Drostan, this thing you propose...It is madness!"

"It's been done before," Akmael murmured.

By the wizard Tyrendel, and Master Eranon, among others. Akmael had memorized all the legends of descent after his mother's death, desperate to learn how to enter the Underworld and return with his spirit intact, hopeful he might one day find his mother and bring her home. That boyhood dream had long since faded, but perhaps those studies would serve him now.

Akmael drove his sword into the earth and began stripping off his breast plate.

"My Lord King!" Tzeremond cried. "The dead must not be brought back!"

"She's not dead," Akmael replied. "Not yet."

"But she is lost to this world! The curse of *Ahmad-dur* cannot be reversed."

Akmael knelt beside Eolyn. A frost had set upon her lips and lashes. A bluish sheen had spread beneath her skin. The chill of her fingers was like a knife through his heart. Eolyn's body now served as nothing more than an anchor for her spirit, tethered to the realm of the living and then cast into the Underworld. Thinking she was dead, the maga would try to cross to the Afterlife, but the tether would hold her back, trapping her among the Lost Souls.

"You will not find your way back!" Tzeremond pleaded. "Such skills vanished with the masters of old! You will fall prey to the Lost Souls, or be devoured by Naether Demons. They will destroy you, my Lord King, and with you the line of Vortingen. You cannot abandon our people!"

"Silence him, Drostan." Akmael kept his eyes fixed on Eolyn. For the first time, he realized how the mere knowledge of her existence had sustained him, whether they were together or apart, whether they stood as friends or enemies. He could not lose her. Not like this.

Opening his belt, Akmael withdrew all the winter sage he had.

Enough to guide a soul to the other side, but not sufficient to bring one back.

Spying Eolyn's purse, he reached toward it and then hesitated. The traditions of Moisehén forbade one mage to violate the medicine belt of another.

"Well," he whispered, loosening her belt with care, "I suppose you will think this the least of my transgressions, should you return."

He was relieved to find her purse abundantly lined not only with winter sage, but with the dry cottony fruit of white albanett, and several night shade mushrooms. Some instinct of hers must have anticipated this. She was not ready to leave them yet.

Dividing the herbs into nine bundles, Akmael set them in a circle around Eolyn. He called her discarded staff, laid it by her side, and placed her cold fingers upon it. Taking her other hand in his, he pressed his lips upon her forehead. Then he rested one palm over her heart and recited the verse of Tyrendel, memorized so many years ago.

Ehekaht Ehekahtu

Elaeom maen du
Sepuenem maene
Elaeom maen du
A nuhm moerte
A nuhm moerte a vaete
Faeom semtue
Ehekaht Ehekahtu

The herbs ignited. Bitter smoke stung his throat.

Akmael closed his eyes, drew a deep breath, and repeated the chant. His voice fell into a constant rhythm, his spirit focused on a single purpose.

The earth shifted. A thin rumble sounded beneath the grass as the trees sent their roots toward him. Shoots sprouted at his knees. Leafy tendrils crept over his torso, rough woody vines spread across his back. When they finished embracing his body, the fine limbs wove a winding path down his arm toward Eolyn. In the moment they touched her, the tender new buds withered and turned black.

Akmael felt the terrifying pull of the earth's core, a primeval force that strained his bones to the breaking point. Placing his trust in the plants that sustained him, he let his spirit fall into the abyss.

VIOLENT CONVULSIONS SHOOK EOLYN as spirit was wrenched from body. She fell weightless through a world without form, until blackness enveloped her in its soft embrace, and she understood the Gods had spoken.

The time of the Magas was ended. The Fates had set her free. The scent of winter sage drifted about her spirit in a wispy cloud. Refusing to succumb to sadness, she took heart in the thought that Ghemena waited on the other side, along with her mother and father, and Ernan.

Remembering what Ghemena taught her, Eolyn sang the song of passage. Her voice rose muted inside the thick darkness, nothing more than a murmur against an eternal night. She paused and listened to the silence. Soon the voice of Ghemena could be heard faintly across the void, followed by Eolyn's mother and father. Their melody floated on tendrils of light, weaving into a pale moon caught behind a mass of clouds.

As Eolyn drifted toward their song, the landscape took shape around her, a stone filled place where the air did not move. The ground spread into a path that wound against steep cliffs and over formless valleys.

The singing moon settled at the top of the next peak. Yet when she reached it, the voices receded and the light descended to the valley below. Though time no longer held her, the journey seemed without end, the ephemeral orb always escaping to the next horizon.

Doubt began to seep into Eolyn's heart. Anxiety quickened her pace. Finally, upon one rise, she succeeded in touching the orb, only to have it to vanish altogether.

Eolyn stopped and remained very still. Uncertainty crowded her spirit, worn thin by battle and death. Were her loved ones rejecting her? Had her failure condemned her in Ghemena's eyes? Had her weakness caused Kaie to turn away?

She attempted to begin her song anew, but the melody eluded her memory. A knot of fear took hold. She tried to loosen it, but there was no living earth in which to root herself, no air with which to fill her lungs, no fire burning in her heart, no blood rushing through her veins. The elements that empowered her in the living world could not be accessed here, not even to subdue her fear.

The Lost Souls, Ghemena told her once, *hear doubt like a soft bell calling them to the feast.*

An oily mist rose off the ground. Eolyn retreated in dread. She felt the dead slither down the passageways of her mind, spirits in various states of decay, anxious for the renewal she offered, hungry for the life force that would slow their inevitable decline into nothingness. Older souls flitted like shadows on the edge of her awareness, younger ones rose up as pale reflections of their human form. Together they advanced toward her. She could hear their longing, feel their desire to consume her magic in soft whispers drawn out slowly against the night.

Desperate, she ran. But what refuge could be found in the Underworld? What corner of her mind could shut them out?

Willing her path onto a wide plain, Eolyn instinctively sought the safe memories of her childhood: the village of her youth, the cottage of Ghemena, the deep folds of the South Woods. Every haven responded to her call, revealing itself in gray shadows, but the Lost Souls destroyed them all. They tore down her village, trampled Ghemena's garden, and felled ancient trees with slow sure strokes.

They surrounded Eolyn and crowded in on her spirit. They wrapped her in their embrace and dragged her down into their midst. The hooks of their hunger sank into her soul with the delicate pinch of tiny leeches. She tried to cry out, but no voice sounded in her throat. She tried to escape, but her limbs were paralyzed.

A sudden movement startled her out of her stupor. A blur of gray fur rushed past. She heard a low growl and saw eyes flash in the dark.

Recognizing Wolf, Eolyn broke free and scrambled after him. The animal led her back inside the forest, to the banks of a small stream where it vanished inside its den. Eolyn followed, sealing the entrance behind her with what little magic she had left. Though Wolf had already disappeared, relief renewed her. Shivering, she gave thanks. What better place to hide from darkness than in a dark hole?

A hollow scream sounded across the wastes outside, cutting short her respite. Something crashed against her hideaway. The sealed entrance shattered into a thousand smoky pieces that melted into nothingness.

Had there been a breath to hold in that place, Eolyn would have held it then. Before her, an unearthly creature swayed on long glowing limbs, its predatory eyes lost in gaping hollows, its sagging mouth an open pit. Assaulting her with an ear-piercing howl, the Naether Demon leapt forward, exposing long curved claws.

Eolyn jumped out of its reach and stumbled into empty space. A small passage at the end of the hideaway revealed itself to her. Overcome with terror, she fled into its depths.

AKMAEL'S SPIRIT TOOK ROOT in the void. The night was thick, the dead ominously still. He heard no song of passage floating across the abyss, saw no distant illumination that would indicate a maga's bright soul. Only desolation reached out, touching his heart and rendering it cold.

He could yet risk invoking more magic if he wished to find her.

Without the power of the living elements, Tyrendel had written, *a mage in the Underworld must expend his own spirit to cast even the smallest spell. This diminishes his chances of returning whole, and the magic awakens the dead.*

But to sit here without knowing when or if a path would be revealed, fearful that while he stalled she perished, was unacceptable.

Even as doubt crowded his thoughts, the Underworld responded. Faded faces emerged on the edge of his awareness and flowed past him. Akmael recognized the River of Hunger, of which Tyrendel had spoken. The dead were rushing toward a soul bearing light. Perhaps that soul was Eolyn's. Caught between hope and anxiety, Akmael let their impulse carry him forward, floating in their midst, his spirit as still as a midwinter night.

A pale star came into focus at the center of a vortex created by the Lost Souls. Akmael recognized Eolyn's aura, though much of the color had already bled out of it. He beat back the urgency that crept into his heart, for fear any strong emotion would be noticed as a sign of the living.

Amorphous tentacles of hunger had trapped her, but she broke free, dragged herself away from the frenzied mass, and vanished. The vortex lurched after her, sucking Akmael into its core. He crashed into the place where she had disappeared. An obsidian barrier shattered under the impact of his living spirit.

Just beyond his reach she cowered, her face pale, her eyes wide inside darkened hollows.

257

Eolyn, he called.

She backed away, stumbled, and fled.

A hungry murmur spread through the Lost Souls, like a violet shadow creeping across the evening sky. They had recognized his living soul, a fount that could satiate their hunger like no other.

Blinding them with a shaft of light, Akmael took off after Eolyn. Her diminished strength was no match for his speed. He descended upon her and invoked a ward to halt her retreat.

No! She pounded her fists against the invisible wall. *Ghemena, help me! For the love of the Gods!*

He reached out to calm her, but she scuttled away, convulsing in panic. Akmael steadied his spirit.

Eolyn.

Another seizure took hold of her. Trepidation weighed down his heart. She responded as if he were some creature of the Underworld, a Lost Soul or worse, a Naether Demon.

Eolyn, I am Akmael, High Mage and King of Moisehén. I have come to help you. See me now.

It was no use. The confusion of that desolate place had ensnared her. Like a caged animal, Eolyn flung herself against the confines of the ward. When they did not give, she wilted, her soul inundated with sorrow, her flame all but spent. Akmael's hope faltered. His own magic would soon fail. He could not bring her back if she did not overcome her terror and recognize him.

Behind him the vortex resumed its shape. The dead were returning. There was precious little time left. He spied the tether crafted by Tzeremond and grasped it with his spirit. If he could not recover her whole, perhaps he could break the cord and push her over to the other side.

He had known it might come to this, and yet he hesitated. To set her free would diminish his power and terminate any hope of returning to his own body. Nor could he follow her, as he had tethered his spirit to the world of the living before descending. A prisoner of the Underworld, he would perish here, becoming one of the Lost Souls, or worse.

It is the only way.

He pulled the glowing thread taught. The thought of letting her go, this time forever, rent through him, hollowing out his soul and shattering his heart. Retrieving one of the pulsing shards, he set its sharp edge against the tether.

Ehekahtu
Naeom denae daum
Erenahm rehoernem ekaht

Behnaum enem
Ehukae Ehekahtu

Magic flowed into the blade. Light sparked as he set the shard upon its mark.

Akmael.

Her voice stayed his hand.

Eolyn rose up and touched him, her spirit warm against the frigid night. *It's you.*

The dead paused in their approach.

A sapphire flame ignited between them. From what source, Akmael could not fathom. He watched, mesmerized, as Eolyn caught the dancing light in her tapered fingers. The Underworld trembled and the dead retreated while Eolyn coaxed the flame into a scarlet and purple blaze. Her aura ignited in blinding colors, wrapping Akmael in brilliance. A fountain of light escaped them, rushing into the black sky and rupturing the vault of the Underworld. Illumination flooded the landscape. The Lost Souls screamed and fled.

Eolyn faltered, as if overwhelmed by her own power. The vault began to close, heralding the return of the endless night. Akmael caught Eolyn and drew her close. Binding her spirit to his, he commanded the trees to pull them out.

Air rushed harsh into Akmael's lungs as the vines released him.

Eolyn struggled to her knees, only to be overcome by a hacking cough. She vomited fine white ice that melted into the sun-warmed earth. Sweat broke out upon her skin, and she shivered uncontrollably. Instinctively, she sought the heat of his embrace.

"Akmael," she whispered through chattering teeth. "What have you done? The dead are not to be brought back."

"You were not dead."

"The battle…"

"It is over."

"My brother." Her choked sob ended in a fit of coughing.

He hushed her and cradled her in his arms. "He is alive."

"I saw you kill him."

"I wanted to slay him." His voice was grim with the implications of the task he had left undone. With any luck, one of his men had finished it. "I should have. But I could not do it because of you."

Her breath steadied, and her fingers drifted to his face. She traced the line of his brow, his nose, his lips. "Akmael, are my eyes open?"

"Yes."

"The world is covered in shadows. I cannot see you."

"Your sight will return." He spoke with more confidence then he

259

felt. Blindness was one of many prices that could be paid for venturing into the Underworld. He caught her fingers and pressed them to his lips. "Rest, Eolyn. You are safe and cared for."

Placing his palm upon her forehead, he invoked an ancient spell of East Selen, one of the first taught to him by Briana. In an instant she fell asleep, releasing her limbs to his embrace. He gathered her in his arms and picked her up off the ground.

The Valley of Aerunden was quiet, battle cries and clashes of metal replaced by the moans of the wounded and dying. A handful of his men had gathered on the ridge. Covered with blood, dirt, and sweat, they stood waiting for his next command.

Tzeremond remained huddled on his knees, his hands now secured behind his back, Drostan's blade steady at his throat.

A rush of footsteps behind Akmael broke the quiet. Drostan cried out a warning. Akmael heard the crude sound of metal ripping through mail and flesh. He turned just in time to see Ernan collapse at his feet. The rebel leader's fine ivory sword fell from his grasp. A pool of blood spread quickly from beneath his body.

A soldier with thin blond hair withdrew his weapon from the corpse and knelt.

"Forgive me, my Lord King," he stammered, "for drawing my sword at your back. He intended to kill you."

It was Borten, the young man who had slain Akmael's father. With a mixture of relief and misgiving, Akmael looked from Borten to Ernan's corpse.

It is done, then.

Already he could hear Eolyn's lament. She could forgive him many things, he knew, but this she would never pardon. "Rise, Sir Borten."

The young man obeyed, sheathing his sword. *He is a knight to have at your side,* Akmael's father had said. And so he was. "It seems you have proven yourself worthy for the King's service."

"My Lord King." He bowed again.

Akmael could tell from Borten's expression how much the words moved him. "Take my horse, and deliver the maga safely to High Mage Rezlyn. Tell him she has returned from *Ahmad-dur.* He is to ensure that she recuperates in full. I will have no one else attend to her. And stay with her, Borten, until I arrive."

Borten nodded. Akmael entrusted Eolyn's exhausted body to him.

As the knight departed, fatigue overtook Akmael. Every muscle ached. His cuts stung and his bruises had begun to throb. He felt drained of strength and magic. Thank the Gods the battle had ended, and ended in his favor.

Bending down, he retrieved Ernan's sword. Corey had spoken of this weapon, a work of Galian wizards. In truth it was finer than he imagined.

Eolyn, it sang, sad and mournful. *Send me with Eolyn.*

He tested its balance and ran his fingers along the length of the blade. "We'll see about that, my friend. I've a mind to keep you for myself."

Tzeremond's high-pitched wail broke through Akmael's thoughts. A bolt had penetrated the wizard's torso.

A woman emerged from the forest—Syrnte, judging by her coloring. In an instant, three of Akmael's men were upon her, forcing a crossbow out of her grip. She struggled against their hold even as they drove her to her knees.

Achme talam nu! she cried. *Bechnem ahraht neme, Salahm machne du!*

The arrow in Tzeremond's chest ignited. The air filled with his agonized cries and the acrid stench of burning flesh.

One of the knights buffeted her across the face.

Mechahne! she wailed, tears and blood streaming down her cheeks. *Mechahne achnam! Talam nu ahram! Tzeremond!*

A muffled scream sounded from the heart of the mountain. A tremor passed through the earth. Akmael gripped his sword as a menacing shadow bloomed underneath the wizard. Tzeremond's eyes rolled back into his head, and he fell lifeless to the ground. As quickly as it had appeared, the dark stain upon the grass melted away.

The woman went limp and sank to the earth.

"Forgive me," she sobbed. "Mother, Father, forgive me…Death was not enough for him. It was not enough to for me."

CHAPTER FORTY-THREE

Recovery

SHADOWS DISSIPATED INTO A THIN GRAY MIST. Eolyn opened her eyes and saw a large room with stone walls and a vacant fireplace. Light from tall windows illuminated fresh rushes spread over a smooth floor. There was a long table laid out with herbs, tinctures, and candles bearing the scent of lemon grass, primrose, and sage. Warm linen sheets and summer blankets enveloped her. A familiar presence took shape at her bedside.

"Corey." She drew a careful breath into aching lungs. "It's good to see you again."

He started at her voice and looked up from a tome spread open on his lap. A smile filled his face, and his silver-green eyes sparked with relief. "It is good to know you can see."

He leaned forward to help arrange pillows as she pushed herself up to sit. She felt groggy, her muscles stiff and slow to move. "How long have I slept?"

"Seven days and seven nights, including the time it took to bring you here."

"Where is here?"

"The King's City. You came around occasionally to take infusions, but even then you were only half awake."

"I heard your voice when the wraiths appeared." She rubbed her forehead, trying to push away vestiges of terrible dreams that flickered like shadows on the edge of her awareness.

"I called you out of your nightmares," Corey said, "but I did not bring you back from the world of the dead. Do you remember what happened, Eolyn?"

"I think so." She took another breath, unsettled by the prickly feel of air against her ribs. "Where is Akmael?"

"Attending to the duties of a King, I imagine. I can send him word, if you like."

Eolyn shook her head. She was not ready for that. Not yet. "And

Ernan?"

Corey averted his eyes. His lips pressed into a thin line.

At once Eolyn understood. Black spots hampered her vision. The room wavered.

"Your brother is dead, Eolyn," Corey said quietly.

"That's not possible! Akmael assured me he had been spared."

"After you returned to the world of the living, Ernan attacked the King. He was struck down by one of Akmael's men-at-arms."

Eolyn sank back against the pillows, stunned. "It can't be."

Only a few weeks had passed since she had found him, this boy resurrected from the dead and transformed into a warrior. A stranger who shared her blood and swore no harm would come to her while he lived. Now, the knights of Vortingen had taken him away forever, just as they had her father. Her eyes burned with tears. "Akmael lied. He lied to me. Again."

"The King did not deceive you, Eolyn. Ernan was alive when you asked for him."

She pinned Corey with a hard gaze. "Ernan was my brother, and Akmael let him die."

"He hardly had a choice."

"He *always* had a choice!" That Corey would defend the Mage King appalled her. "He had a choice. In everything."

Corey frowned. He rose and prepared a mild infusion of chamomile and mint, warming the cup with a quiet spell.

Eolyn accepted the tea with shaking hands. "Why has he brought me here? Am I his prisoner now?"

His Briana?

"No. No maga will ever be held inside these walls against her will. At least, not under this King."

The mist cleared. Everything came into sharper focus. Eolyn studied Corey as a sick feeling spread through her stomach.

"The distance between you and Akmael has been bridged," she realized. "He is your cousin once more."

"I have had ample time to reflect on the circumstances of our past, and several opportunities to speak about the future with our King."

"Was this before or after you became party to Ernan's rebellion?"

If her bitter challenge surprised him, Corey did not show it.

"I will not ask you to understand," he said, "much less pardon me. I did what any mage must do to survive in this world. I made the decisions I thought best under the circumstances."

"And the others whom you betrayed, Corey? What happened to them?"

"I do not know the fates of most." His voice was grave but steady. "The only one they captured alive was Rishona. She killed Tzeremond, with an arrow through the heart and a nasty Syrnte spell. She summoned a Naether Demon to receive him in the Underworld."

"A Naether Demon?" The very word inspired terror. Eolyn had confronted one of them during her own descent, limbs long and glowing, claws slashing at her like obsidian knives. Insatiable hunger had flowed from its gaping eyes.

Or had it? From one moment to the next, the creature was gone, and there was only Akmael. She shook her head in confusion. Everything felt like a dream now, an illusion that sprang out of nothing.

"I thought no one could communicate with the Naether Demons," she said, "that their banishment put an end to all contact with the living world."

"Apparently the Syrnte have found a way." Corey did not appear pleased by the prospect. "But the curse left her bedridden, and I suspect it will go badly for her the day those creatures demand recompense."

Eolyn furrowed her brow. It seemed unthinkable to condemn anyone, even that old wizard, to such a malevolent end. What could have driven Rishona to employ such dark magic? Eolyn set her tea aside. "I want to see her."

"You cannot." The words were spoken quietly, but they felt like a slap in the face. "Rishona has been taken to Selkynsen, where she will be held until a Syrnte delegation arrives with a suitable ransom."

"Ransom?"

Corey shrugged. "Akmael thought to execute her at first, but given that Syrnte ambitions make them prone to war upon any excuse, we thought it best not to force hostilities."

"And Tahmir?" She dreaded the answer, but she had to know.

"No one has seen him since Aerunden. Rishona believes he is dead."

"I knew it," Eolyn whispered. "I felt something…in the battle."

Corey's expression softened. He left his chair and sat next to her on the bed. "I have burdened you with too much in the first moments of your awakening."

"All of my friends are gone. All of them, slain or scattered."

Corey took her hand gently. "Not all."

He drew back the loose fabric of her sleeve until his fingers came to rest on the intertwining images of Dragon wrapped around her arm. The intimacy unnerved her. She tried to pull away, but he held firm.

"We must speak about this," he said.

Eolyn averted her eyes, her body tense as a viper ready to strike.

"Akmael gave it to you, did he not?" Corey asked.

Angered, she wrested her hand from his grip and pulled her sleeve over the jewel with force. "*Achim* gave it to me. After I met Akmael, I tried to remove it with as many spells as I could invent, but it has not budged. I will find a way, though. I will not be bound to him or his murderous line of kings!"

"Did the jewel stir upon your skin during the months we spent in East Selen?"

"Tahmir told you about that?"

"Surely you do not still believe he was my spy?"

Corey's tone was calm and unflinching, and under his steady gaze the fire of her anger wavered.

What is the use of resisting anymore?

The rebellion had ended. Ernan and Tahmir lay dead. Her friends were banished. If she was not a prisoner now, they could declare her one whenever it pleased them. What difference would it make anymore, to conceal the truth?

"On Midwinter's Eve," she murmured. "At the foot of the Old Fir. It spoke with the tree of your ancestors, though they used a dialect I could not understand."

He nodded. "I am glad to hear it. The jewel is an heirloom of our Clan. Queen Briana entrusted it to her son before she died, though she did not tell him its meaning. And it does bind you to Akmael, although not in the way, perhaps, that you fear. It binds you to me, as well. It binds you to the entire clan of East Selen."

He paused a moment before adding, "All two of us, as it were."

"I don't understand."

"East Selen is not a clan of the blood," Corey said, "at least not entirely. If it were, we would be no different from the royals, plagued as they are by rivalries and intrigues, by the denial of love and passion, by betrayal and—"

"You haven't avoided any of that."

Mage Corey let go a sigh and retreated to his chair. "This period in which you have come to know us has not been the brightest in our history."

"So you understood the meaning of this jewel from the first time you saw it?"

"It is your invitation. The armband clings to you in silence because you have not yet made your choice. Should you accept, it will stay with you forever, reinforcing your magic and protecting you as one of our own."

"And if I decline?"

"It will return to the roots of the Old Fir from whence it came, until a new invitation is made to another."

"Then I decline." Eolyn pulled up her sleeve and spoke fiercely to the silver band. "I do not wish to be a part of it. Any of it. I decline!"

The jewel remained motionless against her arm.

After a moment, Corey cleared his throat. "It would appear she is not convinced of the conviction behind your words."

Eolyn cried out and drove her fist into the bed cushions. She wanted to fling herself upon Corey and claw out his eyes, but she did not have the strength. "Why do you do this? You betrayed my brother. You delivered me to Ernan *knowing* I would inspire him to march to his doom. Our friends are scattered and dead because of you, and still you insist on dragging me into your games. Why won't you just *let me be*?"

Corey remained still as a serpent on a sun-warmed rock. She was reminded of the first time they met, of the last time they embraced. What a strange bond the Gods had granted them, that this sense of mutual understanding should persist despite the many deceptions that marked their relationship.

When at last the mage spoke, his voice was subdued. "I hold on to you, Eolyn, because you give me hope."

CHAPTER FORTY-FOUR

Reconciliation

AS EOLYN RECOVERED, Corey remained at her side. He conversed with her in the evening, greeted her with breakfast in the morning, and administered her medicines under High Mage Rezlyn's strict instructions. The days of Corey's vigilance had returned, Eolyn realized, and she suspected his constant company was a manifestation of Akmael's will.

A few days after her awakening, Corey offered to escort Eolyn through the castle grounds. Her limbs were in much need of movement, and she accepted, resting her hand on his arm to steady herself.

The fortress of Vortingen bore little resemblance to the place she experienced only a few months earlier. Corridors that had once appeared an indecipherable maze of suffocating darkness now spread in broad promenades that wound patiently from one set of apartments to the next. Tall windows allowed light to play on the sun-warmed interior. Many of the inner courtyards supported dense gardens blooming with late summer flowers.

"This is not the castle you brought me to at Bel-Aethne," she told Corey. "Nothing looks the same."

"At Bel-Aethne, you came here by night, a prisoner in fear for your life. Now you walk freely by day, as the King's guest." He paused before acknowledging, "Though it is true that a shadow has been lifted from this place."

The King's guest. It seemed an unkind euphemism. Guests were not under constant watch. And if she were well enough to mount a horse and continue on her way, would they let her leave?

In quiet hours of the night, after Corey left Eolyn to sleep, her thoughts gravitated toward Briana of East Selen, confined to a single tower, slain at the hands of one of her own sisters. Would Akmael force her down a similar path? Was she his guest, or the prize of his victory?

One day, when her legs were sufficiently steady, Corey led Eolyn on a long climb up the winding stairs of one of the towers. The cramped

267

space and narrow windows generated a sense of confinement, and Eolyn breathed a sigh of relief when at last they emerged on the southern ramparts.

Below them spread a magnificent carpet of fertile plains and rolling hills. Toward the horizon, she saw a blue green haze that marked the border of Moehn. Longing filled her heart, an intense thirst for the forest that had once fueled her soul.

"Akmael has sent word to bordering kingdoms," Corey said. "He has asked the magas to return."

"There are others?" The thought surprised her, so accustomed was she to being alone.

"It is possible. Ghemena may not have been the only one to escape, and if others did, they may have acquired students. Those who accept the King's invitation will be allowed to practice all forms of High Magic, but they will not be permitted to learn or engage in the arts of war. And they will be watched closely. Any talk of the Mage King ceding his staff will be considered treason."

Eolyn looked at Corey, who kept his gaze fixed on the terrain below.

"Are you trying to warn me?" she asked.

"All I'm saying is that if you have any doubts about the matter, based on the teachings of your beloved Doyenne, you had best put them behind you."

She blinked and glanced away, uncertain how to respond.

A boy ran past, brushing her skirt. Startled, Eolyn watched him race to the highest point on the ramparts, where he climbed the wall and stood over the undulating plains, his arms spread wide.

"What is it, Eolyn?" Corey sounded anxious and far away. "Your face has lost its color."

She stepped toward the child.

Instinct told her not to call out to him. He bore a striking resemblance to the boy Achim, but his hair fell straight and shone a burnished brown in the afternoon sun.

"It is the young Prince Kedehen," she realized. "In the courtyards below, his brothers play at war and adventure, blood and glory, but he likes to come up here and pretend he can fly. Like an eagle. Or a mage."

"You are speaking like a Syrnte witch," Corey said.

"No one would receive him, except Tzeremond."

"What are you talking about?"

"Him." Eolyn pointed to the boy, but the image faded on the whistling wind. Tears stung her eyes, again. They seemed to come so easy of late. "He was not so different from me, in what he wanted."

Corey took her by the shoulders. "Eolyn, look at me. Have you had visions like this before?"

"No. Yes. A vision?" She shook her head in confusion. "The day my village was attacked, and again, years later, I saw Akmael die, or thought I did, though it didn't happen that way."

Eolyn felt dizzy. She closed her eyes and drew a deep breath, seeking to ground herself. When she opened them, Corey was searching her face with care.

"You may have been born with this ability, though it is unusual for a witch of Moisehén," he said. "Yet there was also your journey to the Underworld..."

Eolyn frowned and looked to where the child Kedehen had stood. Was that all that drove him in the end? A passion for magic? She could imagine the unbearable disappointment of the young prince as one mage after another rejected his petition, not because of the teachings of Aithne and Caradoc, but because of a taboo so ingrained no one had the imagination to see around it. He might have been a different sort of King, had someone other than Tzeremond agreed to teach him. Indeed, he might never have been King at all.

"Only a handful of people have succeeded in doing what you did." Corey's voice called her back from her thoughts. "Perhaps this gift returned with you from the world of the dead."

Eolyn stepped away, wrapped her arms around herself, and shivered. She recalled how she and Akmael had ruptured the vault of the Underworld. Light had flooded the darkness, and the Lost Souls had fled in terror. Where had that power come from? Had she brought it back? Did it lie sleeping inside of her? Inside of Akmael?

"Has the King had similar visions?" she asked.

"I don't know." Corey said. "Perhaps you should ask him yourself."

She flinched at the thought. "I'm weary. I would like to rest."

Corey nodded and escorted her back to her room.

Time passed. The King did not visit, nor did he send for her. His absence unsettled Eolyn, filling her heart with a strange mixture of relief and foreboding. Relief every time the sun set, because she had lived one more day without having to confront him. Foreboding every time the sun rose, for this might be the day that he appeared.

What would she say, when the time came?

Akmael had risked his life and soul to bring her back from the Underworld. He had restored her magic and her spirit. He brought her into the protection of his fortress and assured her all the comforts of his royal household. Yet at the same time, he took away everything that once gave her a sense of home. He permitted the death of her brother and the slaughter of her allies. He had sent her few surviving friends into exile.

Now even Corey was drawn into his service, forcing a wedge between her and the one companion who remained from the time before the rebellion. She found it impossible to imagine this man, Mage and King, was once the boy who brought her such happiness. The laughter they shared in the sun-speckled shade of the forest seemed no more than a distant dream. Everything had changed. Everything had gone wrong.

In the evenings, Corey took her to the gardens, where the sun illuminated lush herbs and fruit laden trees in a green-gold haze. Butterflies wandered from leaf to leaf in search of a place to lay their eggs. Spiders spun their webs in the bushes. Eolyn whispered to the plants, her fingers caressing stems and flowers, her thoughts drifting ever further toward the South Woods.

The yearning for home was growing more intense.

Your magic depends on this forest, Ghemena had once said. *The South Woods will always call you home.*

What would she do if Akmael did not let her go?

"How does one gain an audience with the King?" she asked. "Am I to request it, or do I wait until summoned?"

Corey laughed. "Surely, Maga Eolyn, you must realize that you, of all people, can see the King whenever you please."

"Don't mock me, Corey."

"I am not mocking you. When do you wish to see Akmael?"

"Well." She lifted her chin. "If what you say is true, then now."

She was testing him, of course. Had she known he would acquiesce, she would have said 'tomorrow' or 'next week', but Mage Corey placed her hand upon his arm and led her away from the gardens. They passed through a maze of corridors, up narrow stairwells, and down long hallways.

As they approached the King's apartments, the number of guards they encountered increased, but not once were they detained. Everyone, servants and men-at-arms alike, gave respectful nods as she passed. Their deference disturbed her. "They greet us as if they know who I am. I don't like it."

"You've become far too accustomed to passing through this world unnoticed," Corey replied. "That will have to change now."

They entered the King's antechamber through a pair of heavy doors and proceeded to the receiving room without being announced.

Magical and military artifacts adorned the stone walls, and the windows revealed a wide balcony overlooking the rolling plains below. Akmael stood engaged in conversation with one of his High Mages, a rosy cheeked man with a thick blond beard. They sifted through parchments and other objects on a large polished table.

Akmael wore a simple but finely woven linen shirt, reminiscent of the one he had worn the day they first met in the South Woods. The dark curls of his youth had grown back, and they were bound loosely at the nape of his neck. His broad shoulders were relaxed, his strong hands spread upon the table. His bearing, which gave testimony to his place in the line of Vortingen, filled Eolyn with conflicting emotions of apprehension and pride.

The King looked up. The intensity of his focus made Eolyn catch her breath, though it was clear by his expression that her arrival pleased him.

"Maga Eolyn," he said. "You are well."

"Yes, thank you, Achim...Akmael...my Lord, King." She lowered her eyes, embarrassed by the confusion of names that stumbled from her lips.

Corey and the other mage took their quiet leave.

"Please." The King extended his arm, inviting her to approach. A smile touched his lips.

She remembered how much she enjoyed seeing him smile as a boy, how hard it was to get him to do it at first. Though she longed to close the distance between them, she stopped just beyond his reach. Her hands worked against each other in nervous agitation.

"I wanted to tell you I am deeply grateful for what you did, bringing me back. I understand what it could have cost you, and I am glad no harm came to you in retrieving me. I will..." She drew a breath and steadied her hands. "I will set forth for the South Woods in a few days. I wish to rest there, perhaps the winter through. My magic was drained by the journey to the Underworld, and the battle..." She flushed. By the Gods, why did she have to mention it?

"But you will return?" he asked.

"Yes, of course, I..." She shifted on her feet. This was not the response she had expected, that she was free to go. "Mage Corey told me the prohibition has been lifted. So there is much work to do. There will be students to teach. Many women, I hope. The magic of this land has been so unraveled. It will take a long time to weave it all back together." Her gaze drifted to the table as she spoke. Absently, she picked up an oval object. It fit comfortably in the palm of her hand, and she realized it was a portrait of a young woman. "Who is this?"

Akmael cleared his throat. "The first princess of Roenfyn. One of many candidates I have been discussing with High Mage Tzetobar."

Eolyn set the portrait down carefully. Her fingers were numb.

"The duty of a King," she murmured.

"Alliances must be forged, an heir to the throne secured." He spoke without emotion, as if the matter did not directly concern him.

"So you will marry her?"

"I have not yet decided with whom we will initiate negotiations. Roenfyn has its advantages. It is a neighboring kingdom that offers important territorial gains, and our people share a common history. But there are other possibilities. The Mountain People or the Syrnte, for example, both with magical traditions that could serve us well."

"You just banished them from our territory, and now you speak of alliances?"

"I threw out their hostile armies, but as Mage Tzetobar would be quick to tell you, war must be followed by diplomacy else it will soon engender more war. If the Mountain People and the Syrnte have designs over our territory, it would do well to consider abating their hunger with a royal marriage."

"They did not come to conquer us. They came to assist Ernan and his cause."

Akmael touched her chin and brought her gaze to his. He studied her face for several moments, his expression at once puzzled and amused. "I think what caught my heart on that first day was your capacity to trust so readily, to believe the best of others, even of me. Ghemena worked hard to train you out of it, but she never quite succeeded, did she?"

"My instinct toward trust has little to do with this. I knew them. Khelia. Tahmir. Rishona."

"And I did not." He released her and stepped away. "It is my responsibility, as King, to question their motives in joining this rebellion. You, I am quite certain, were driven by your ideals and by your love for your brother. But they? Why would they send their warriors to die on our battlefields?"

"You think they would so use me?" The insinuation aroused her anger.

"You, and your brother. Yes." He stiffened, and his eyes grew hard. "High Mage Tzetobar will appoint a group of emissaries soon, first to the Paramen Mountains and then to the land of the Syrnte. I could arrange for you to accompany them. Given your ample...*experience* with their people, your assistance could prove useful."

"Akmael, I am not interested in—"

"Perhaps you will find another Syrnte Prince to your liking." Resentment colored his voice. "Would that please you, Eolyn?"

She bristled. "You have no right to question my relationship with him! You knew nothing about him."

"I know a king is always a king in his own land. What you hoped to escape by refusing me, you would have found by accepting him."

"Akmael, I had no more desire to be a Syrnte Princess then I do the Queen of Moisehén! All I wanted…" She faltered. *All I wanted was you.* "I felt so alone. You were gone, and he was there, and I…I needed him. I needed someone to love. That was all."

Her confession did nothing to diminish his look of displeasure. When he drew an impatient breath to respond, Eolyn noticed a glint of silver upon his chest. In an instant, she closed the distance between them, eyes fixed on the parting fold of his shirt. She set her fingers over the finely woven jewel that hung around his neck, mesmerized by the light caught in its many crystals.

"This is what you used to find me!" she realized, astonished. "Where did you get it?"

Akmael went still under her touch. "My mother crafted it and gave it to me as a gift."

"Why have I not seen it before now? Why did you not show it to me?"

"It was my secret, my only remembrance of her. I was accustomed to not sharing it with anyone."

"If only it had been revealed to me sooner." Saddened, Eolyn withdrew, but Akmael stopped her, catching her fingers in his hand. The charge of his touch unsettled her.

"Why?" he asked.

"This is ancient magic of the magas, one of the few spells they held in secret. Its existence was never recorded in the annals. Ghemena told me about it, though she did not have time to teach me how to weave it before she died. The object allows its user to find a friend at great distances, but it will not work unless the intentions of the seeker are true and pure."

"My intentions have always been true," he said, "though it would be an exaggeration to say they were always pure."

"What I don't understand is how it worked. I mean, once you found me in the South Woods, it must have imprinted on my essence in order to allow you to come again, but how did you arrive the first time? Your mother knew nothing of me—had nothing of me—that could have been woven into this web."

Then the truth came to her like summer rain seeping into the soft earth, a slow realization carried on the voice of the dark haired witch who appeared in her dreams so long ago.

You are not the one I sought, little Eolyn, but you are the one who was found.

"Briana meant for you to find Ghemena!" she said. "Your mother must have had something of my tutor. She must have somehow known Ghemena survived. She wanted Ghemena to train you, but this magic could not penetrate the ward of her refuge. It landed you just outside the enchanted forest, and you found me instead."

Eolyn withdrew from Akmael's grasp, her voice reduced to a whisper. "Oh, Akmael, everything you could have learned from her! All the opportunities that were lost because I stood in the way!"

"That's not true." He stepped forward and gathered her face in his hands, igniting a tremor in the deepest part of her spirit.

I had it all wrong. All backwards.

"But you don't understand!" Eolyn said. "My family interfered with your destiny, right from the very beginning. I kept you from Ghemena, though I didn't know what I was doing, and my brother tried to slay you, and my..." Eolyn hesitated, keenly aware of the formidable power that coursed through Akmael's hands, the ease with which he might crush her skull. "The woman who killed your mother..."

Absolute stillness descended upon him, like the silence that precedes a violent storm.

Eolyn closed her eyes, tears brimming on her lashes, certain he was about to strike.

"The woman who killed your mother," she whispered.

"I know who she was, Eolyn," he said. "I know who she was to you."

That was all. Just these words, and then silence.

Eolyn opened her eyes and stared at him, bewildered.

"During the battle of Aerunden," Akmael said, "I recognized her in Ernan's face."

She did not know how to respond. Was this the source of the mindless fury that overtook him during the confrontation with her brother? Was that why he fought Ernan with such indomitable wrath? And if yes, then why...?

"Then why am I still here?" she asked.

Sadness invaded his eyes, and his brow furrowed. For a moment he looked like Achim again, like the boy who spent all afternoon looking in vain for the elusive rainbow snail. A child who could not endure the loss of the one treasure he had never quite found.

"Because I love you, Eolyn," he said. "Because I cannot envision this kingdom without you."

Her spirit unfolded at these words. The room shifted and transformed around them. Rich and varied aromas of the South Woods rose from the stone floor, of bitter earth and crushed pine, of rotting wood and wild roses. She heard wind rushing through trees, birds intent upon their song, crickets chirping in the night, the river roaring in springtime.

She took Akmael's fingers and pressed her lips to them, to the broad palm of his hand, to the tender skin of his wrist. Her kisses coursed over the hard lines of his face before penetrating the sensual depths of his lips. Her desire flared like a rose colored flame, and she melted into him as he wrapped his arms around her.

Just beyond the heat of their embrace, Eolyn heard the closing of heavy doors and the soft hiss of a magic seal.

Was it a trap? She did not care. She wanted only to love him, to love him always.

CHAPTER FORTY-FIVE

Rebirth

EOLYN FELT THE TREMOR of horses' hooves beneath the earth, followed by a steady shiver that passed up through stems of chamomile and sage. Her fingers lingered on the plants to calm them.

Will I ever grow used to it, she wondered. *Or will this sound always bring the same fleeting sense of childhood terror?*

She stood and wiped her hands on her apron, then shielded her eyes from the sun that dipped low over the horizon. The dense garden shimmered in an amber light, and the fresh voice of a sapling fir whispered on the breeze. From the small circle of buildings that comprised her new home, the ground sloped gently down to a small stream, then up again to continue its rolling descent toward the nearby Town of Moehn.

A girl pressed close against Eolyn's skirt and looked up at her. A wisp of ash blond hair fell over her wide hazel eyes. She slipped her small hand into Eolyn's, her grip strong.

"What is it?" she asked.

Eolyn gave the girl's hand an encouraging squeeze. "Look at the far ridge, Ghemena, and tell me what you see."

Riders appeared, flowing over the hill in a short column before descending into a shallow valley.

"Purple banners," the girl said.

"And the sigil?"

"A silver dragon."

"They are the King's men, then."

"They frighten me."

"Yes, well." Eolyn smiled. "They frighten me, too, sometimes. But we are under the King's protection, and these men are sworn to serve him. So we must assume they are friends."

Ghemena compressed her lips into a frown, a telltale indication that she was not convinced. The youngest of three who had come to Eolyn in

276

this first year, Ghemena had seen only five summers. She was just as stubborn as Eolyn's tutor had once been, and just as bright. Like her companions, she was a child of humble origins, whose parents saw the *Aekelahr* more as an opportunity to keep a cumbersome daughter clothed and fed, than as the birthplace of a new era of women's magic.

Eolyn touched the girl's cheek with affection. "I will greet the King's men, Ghemena. Go tell your sisters to lay out bread and drink for our guests."

As the child ran off, Eolyn retrieved her staff. She synchronized her breath with its steady hum and connected her spirit to the solid earth. In truth, she did not like the look of this. With all the people of Moisehén about to converge upon the King's City, Akmael's soldiers had no business in Moehn.

Eolyn strode forward to put as much distance as possible between them and the *Aekelahr*. She met them at a stream, where they reined in their horses. Sir Drostan led the company, with Mage Corey at his side. Among the rest were several members of the King's personal guard.

"What is the meaning of this?" she demanded as Drostan and Corey dismounted.

Corey smiled and spread his arms wide in salutation. She reluctantly granted him an embrace.

Drostan produced a sealed scroll and presented it to her with a bow of respect. "Maga Eolyn, we have orders to escort you on your journey."

Puzzled, Eolyn accepted the document and broke the wax seal. Akmael had written the orders in his own hand. The paper bore traces of his essence, the ink an imprint of his aura. Just touching it ignited her desire. She drew a shaky breath and returned the scroll to Drostan. "Thank you, but it's not necessary. I plan to travel on my own."

Corey chuckled. Drostan shifted on his feet, a furrow marking his brow.

"These are the King's orders, my lady," the knight said, as if that settled everything. As if there were nothing further to discuss.

"I understand, Sir Drostan, and I appreciate this kindness he has extended to me, but this is most unnecessary."

"I'd advise you not to refuse the King's will, Maga Eolyn." Corey watched with an amused expression, though there was an undercurrent of warning in his voice. "I've known Drostan a long time. He will see his liege's will done, even if it means binding you and throwing you on the back of his horse."

Eolyn looked from Corey to Drostan to the men waiting behind them. The truth of Corey's words was apparent in their faces. Resigned, she nodded her consent and invited them to some food and wine.

They gave her the remainder of the day to prepare her things, and departed at dawn. Much to Eolyn's chagrin, Drostan left a handful of men behind under the command of a young knight of Vortingen, a man by the name of Borten, also from Moehn.

"This is a place of learning, not a fortress," she objected.

"They are to look after your students," Drostan said.

"I've hired a matron for that, to stay with them while I'm in the King's City."

"This is the King's command," Drostan replied.

So it was settled once again.

The fields of Moehn were lush that year. The summer had brought steady rains and now shades of russet gold spread through ripening crops. Yet the fertile landscape did little to alleviate Eolyn's discomfort with her forced escort. She had hoped to make this trip in solitude, to chatter with the birds as they gathered in flocks for their journey south, to pray in the Valley of Aerunden where so many had fallen only one short year before.

During their long days of travel, Drostan kept a respectful distance, but Corey's conversation was constant and intrusive. The clatter of metal and the smell of warhorse distracted her to no end. When at last they arrived at the King's City, its turrets adorned with bright banners snapping in the wind, she felt drained and tense and utterly unprepared for the event to come.

Already people had gathered from all parts of the kingdom, crowding the inns, setting up camps outside the high walls, and filling the streets with vibrant activity. Laughter mingled with sharp aromas of ale, wine, and roasted meats.

As they rode toward the central square, news of her arrival rippled ahead of them, bringing men, women, and children out to catch a glimpse of the High Maga. They threw lilies in her path, offered gifts of herbs and flowers, and asked for Eolyn's blessing.

"The Princess will not be pleased when she hears of this," Corey remarked. "Her welcome was not nearly as effusive."

Eolyn shrugged. "There is no room for jealousy in the heart of a maga."

The mage rolled his eyes. "May I remind you Princess Taesara is not a maga. Royal women delight in jealousy. They can't get enough of it."

"This excess of attention is hardly reason for resentment. And it could have been avoided altogether, if the King had not insisted on sending a royal guard."

"I grow weary of your lack of gratitude, Maga Eolyn," Corey replied. "We've been through this before. Tzeremond's companion, Baedon, is still at large, and we cannot underestimate the threat from the Syrnte and the Mountain People."

"They would never—"

"Wouldn't they? Your value to the King is no secret. There is no better way to hold him hostage than to lay threat to your safety. And there are forces that resist change in our own country. Who knows how many have cause to resent you and what you represent. It is not safe for you to travel unprotected. We will not risk losing you again."

"We? Who is 'we'? You? The King? The great Clan of East Selen?" Her retort came sharper than intended, but after so many days on the dusty road, she was tired and irritable.

"You may doubt my affection for you," Corey said tersely, "but you cannot doubt his."

Eolyn said nothing to this rejoinder, reluctant to pursue any conversation that touched upon her relationship with the King. She raised her eyes to the fortress above the city and tried once more to envision herself in his world, weighed down by fine dresses and chains of gold, lost in a labyrinth of intrigue she might never comprehend. Her heart retreated from the thought.

My magic does not belong here.

She thrived on open spaces and forested hills. Confined to the stone fortress of Vortingen, she would grow weak and confused. She would cease to be a maga. She would turn into a woman of ordinary ways, a person Akmael could no longer love.

"Have you met her?" Though she kept her eyes fixed upon the stone towers, she felt the intensity of Corey's gaze, and she could imagine his unspoken rebuke. *All these days we've spent together, and you wait until now to ask.*

"Yes," he said.

"What is she like?"

"Beautiful. Cold. A princess in every sense of the word, prepared to serve her duty and proud of it."

Eolyn nodded and urged her horse forward, though in truth, she wanted to turn back. She did not trust her resolve to hold upon seeing Akmael bound to another. Yet to refuse the wedding invitation would be interpreted as an insult. Not by him, perhaps. Perhaps he would have understood, but everyone else would have noted her absence. She could not risk the disapproval of the noble families of Moisehén.

In the days that followed, Corey's assessment of Princess Taesara proved correct. Though Eolyn did not have a private audience with her, she saw enough of the royal bride at banquets and festivities to gain some sense of the queen to be.

The girl's bearing was regal, her white hand delicate upon Akmael's arm, her smile timid and her gaze sharp. She gave measured attention to each noble who appeared at court, and already knew half the houses and banners of Moisehén. While unfamiliar with the classes of mages, she had an instinct for what questions to ask. She received Eolyn politely, though they interacted only when protocol dictated. And she was beautiful, with no more than sixteen summers, hair the color of ripe wheat, and eyes as blue as a summer sky.

Her aura, however, was dim. It carried little flame or color.

"She'll be a boring take, don't you think? Now that he's tasted the passion of a true maga." Corey's remark, made one evening as they walked toward Eolyn's apartments after yet another tedious banquet, hit her with the sting of cold water.

The stone walls wavered. Eolyn paused in her stride. After a moment, she drew a steady breath and resumed her walk.

"Princess Taesara is everything a true King could want," she said.

That night, frost settled on the city, killing numerous blossoms meant to adorn the ceremony. The unseasonal chill did not dampen the spirits of the people, however. As the sun rose, they gathered to attend the wedding and receive their new Queen.

A host of mages processed first into the central square. Eolyn walked among them in her burgundy robes. Renate took a place beside her, wearing the sapphire gown of a Middle Maga. Opposite them stood noble families of the four provinces.

The King arrived on horseback, surrounded by his personal guard and the members of his Council. When at last everyone was assembled, Akmael stood in the middle of the square to receive his princess, who appeared with her ladies in waiting and men-at-arms, a fur drawn about her shoulders to ward off the chill.

Her sterling gown sparkled in the sun. She held her head high and bore the stately smile of her class. Akmael greeted her with an expressionless face, though his eyes were warm. As High Mage Tzetobar invoked the blessing of Dragon, the King sustained Taesara's hand in his. When the mage finished, Akmael bent to kiss Taesara's lips.

Eolyn closed her eyes against the sting of tears.

This was my choice, she reminded herself. *This is my path.*

She focused on the image of her new *Aekelahr*, a circle of humble buildings nestled in the rolling hills of Moehn. She heard the enthusiastic laughter of her students: Sirena, Melanie, and—as fate would have it—the lively young girl bearing the name of her own tutor, Ghemena.

Already they loved Maga Eolyn, depended on her, and looked to her to help them fulfill their dreams of magic. This year only three had come, but next year there would be more, and the year after that even more.

When Eolyn opened her eyes, the kiss had ended. She felt Renate's hand wrap around hers in warmth, and was grateful for the expression of friendship and support.

High Mage Tzetobar presented the new Queen to her people. They shouted and sang and threw showers of lilies. The surge of joy was unlike anything Eolyn had felt from the citizens of Moisehén, and it filled her heart with gladness. Fear no longer held back their voices. Akmael would build his reign on a very different foundation from that of his father.

The festivities that followed were bright and boisterous, with generous servings of roasted venison, stuffed goose, and wild pig, followed by sweetbreads and dried fruits and honey-drenched cakes. Wine and ale spilled from overflowing cups. Musicians played and sang, acrobats danced on the tables. Laughter rose and fell over a constant din of chatter.

Nobles who had not yet spoken with Eolyn made a point of greeting her now, and Lords Baramon of Selen and Felton of Moehn even invited her to dance. Several former members of the Circle were there to provide entertainment, including Adiana.

Upon recognizing Eolyn, Adiana wrapped her arms around the maga in a tight hug, tears wetting her cheeks as she cried out in delight. Soon Renate joined their happy reunion. They conversed late into the night, sharing news of their lives since the rebellion and recounting fond memories of Corey's Circle.

Only when the King and his bride retired from the feast did Eolyn notice the dull ache behind her eyes. When another cup of wine only intensified the pain, she decided to say good night to her friends.

Dawn was but a few hours away as she returned to her quarters, alone and exhausted.

Eolyn had not spoken with Akmael since her arrival, but she had noticed his hand behind every detail of her stay. She had been assigned a well-furnished apartment on the southern flank of the castle, with a clear view toward the province of Moehn. The servants left no need unattended. Her room was always supplied with fresh fruit and drink.

She poured herself a cup of water now, and dressed it with herbs to subdue her headache. Holding the mug steady between her fingers, she recited the first spell Ghemena had taught her.

Ehekaht, naeom tzefur. Ehukae.

Steam rose off the water. For a moment, Eolyn felt the spirit of her beloved mentor pass through the room.

Laughter and song rose from the streets below. Eolyn drifted to the window to view the city. Inhaling the soothing aroma of her herbal infusion, she watched people dance beneath the distant torches, like bright coals on a dying fire. Last night's frost had dissipated, and the air blew warm against her cheeks.

The essence of the room shifted, and Eolyn felt a presence behind her. She set her tea on the window sill, fingers trembling, and kept her eyes on the rooftops below.

"Why have you come?" she asked.

"To see you once more," Akmael replied. "Why did you not request an audience with me during these days?"

"Because I knew better." She turned to face him, her emotions a churning cauldron of sadness and relief, annoyance and desire. "Your bride is waiting, my Lord King."

"The Queen sleeps under a spell. She will not awaken until I return."

"You cannot stay here."

"I do not intend to."

His words cut deep, and she averted her eyes so he might not notice the pain. He drew close then. Eolyn held still, though she knew she should step away. It was all she wanted in that moment, to feel the intensity of his aura, to remember the intimacy of his touch.

"Don't do this," she whispered, uncertainty breaking through her resolve. "Akmael, please...I can't..."

He studied her in silence, as if registering every detail. Then he lifted his hands to the silver chain around his neck and removed the jewel woven by his mother. He placed it carefully over Eolyn's head, letting the fine medallion come to rest upon her bosom. He withdrew before their lips could touch.

"Mage Corey is very impressed by the work you are doing in Moehn."

It seemed a cold thing to say, so very formal.

"The Gods have sent me worthy students, talented and dedicated to the craft," she replied.

"I am pleased to hear it. The Queen and I will undertake a progress next spring, and we will visit your new *Aekelahr* in Moehn."

"I don't know if that would be a good idea."

"It is necessary. Your endeavor is supported by the Crown."

"Surely you could send a representative, Mage Corey or Thelyn—"

"We cannot avoid seeing each other, Eolyn. You are the only High Maga of Moisehén, and I am the King."

"But we could put it off, until your marriage solidifies and this...this force that draws us to each other fades."

He let out a slow exhale. "How long do you think that will be?"

Eolyn bit her lip, unwilling to give voice to the response.

He rested his hand against her cheek, bringing her gaze back to his.

His fingers traced the line of her neck before descending to the silver web that rested over her heart. "This jewel binds us to each other and to the forest in which we met. I leave it in your power. Use it to find me, should you ever be in need."

Eolyn nodded, her throat tight with pain. The hidden tears of all these days escaped and rolled down her cheeks without restraint.

Then his lips were upon hers, tender and full of desire. She drew him close, unable to resist the flame of his touch.

The embrace proved all too brief. Without warning, Akmael pulled away and stepped past her to the window, where he stood with clenched fists, a brooding look upon his face.

The silence was thick, and Eolyn dared not break it. When at last he spoke, his voice was hoarse. "You said you wanted to restore magic to our people. You said this was the only way."

"It is, Akmael. I can't hope to fulfill my promise to Dragon if I—"

He raised a hand to silence her. In that moment, Eolyn realized Akmael had assumed his father's place, once and for all. Whatever the prince had suffered, wanted, needed or loved was now hidden forever behind the stony mask of Vortingen.

A shimmer passed through him, followed by a flash of white light as he assumed the shape of Owl. In a hush of wings, the Mage King settled on the sill, pausing but a moment before slipping into the night.

Eolyn's heart leapt after him, but she subdued its impulse, halting at the window and watching Akmael's shadow against the starry sky.

"I love you," she whispered as he faded from sight.

Eolyn turned back to her room. It felt barren in the wake of his departure, a vacant space enclosed by stone, a meaningless display of lifeless furniture.

She stood, listening to the silence.

Then she changed out of her dress and into her nightshift, and slipped into her empty bed. She pulled a large pillow into her embrace, inhaling its aroma of stone and earth and timeless magic.

Of him.

Tomorrow, she decided, she would pack early to begin the journey home. She longed to see the girls again, to feel the sun shining on the fields of Moehn and to hear the whisper of the forest. To press her bare feet against the grass and breathe the aroma of warm earth and wildflowers.

Perhaps she would invite Renate or Adiana to travel with her.

She paused at this thought, and her aching heart brightened.

Of course!

Why had she not considered it before? Renate could teach Middle

Magic, and Adiana music, which was Primitive Magic, after all. And who knew music better than Adiana?

Eolyn drew a breath of excitement.

We will weave magic back into this land, united as sisters, like Magas of Old.

Nestling beneath the warmth of her covers, Eolyn closed her eyes. Tomorrow, they would ride south together.

Acknowledgements

The threads of all my stories begin and end with my family, who inspired me long before I understood what inspiration meant. Thank you for your unending support. I couldn't have done this without you.

The forests of the Talamanca Mountain Range in Costa Rica provided fertile ground in which the seeds of *Eolyn* took root and grew. To all the creatures that inhabit those ridges: the great oaks and pumas, the bumble bees and mushrooms, the quetzals, the ferns, the blueberry bushes and mosses. To the duendes who never showed their faces to me, but whose magical presence was always felt, and to all the lush expressions of life in Talamanca: Thank you. I hope I have managed to capture something of your magnificence in these pages.

The greater part of the journey of this second edition was completed when we published the first edition in 2011. All the voices that helped me reach that moment still resonate here. Eric T. Reynolds was the first editor to believe in this novel, and I will forever be indebted to him for giving me an opportunity with Hadley Rille Books. Rafael Aguilar, Suzanne Hunt, Terri-Lynne DeFino, David Hunter, and Carlyle Clark contributed much magic and polish to these pages.

Two writers groups have stuck with me through the years, and continue to help me hone my craft: The Dead Horse Society and The Next Big Writer (tNBW). I'm also fortunate to belong to a wonderful sisterhood of writers, the Dollbabies, who keep me confident and sane.

Most of all, I am grateful to you, the reader, for picking up this book and giving me a chance. Eolyn's story was written for you. May your journey in magic continue well beyond these pages.

About the Author

Karin Rita Gastreich lives in Kansas City, Missouri, where she is part of the biology faculty at Avila University. An ecologist by vocation, she has wandered forests and wildlands all over the planet, but most often in the tropics. Her past times include camping, hiking, music, and flamenco dance. In addition to *The Silver Web* trilogy, Karin has published short stories in *World Jumping, Zahir, Adventures for the Average Woman*, and *69 Flavors of Paranoia*. She is a recipient of the Spring 2011 Andrews Forest Writer's Residency. You can visit Karin at krgastreich.com.

Preview

The Sword of Shadows

Book Two of The Silver Web

Karin Rita Gastreich

Sisters in magic, Eolyn and Adiana seek to revive a millennial tradition once forbidden to women. When war strikes, their fledgling community of magas is destroyed; its members killed, captured or scattered.

In hopes of defending their people, Eolyn tries to escape the occupied province and deliver to King Akmael a weapon that might secure his victory. Trapped by the invading army, Adiana is taken prisoner and placed at the mercy of the ruthless Prince Mechnes.

Even as their world is torn asunder, Eolyn and Adiana cling to a common dream. Courage and perseverance guide them toward a future where the Daughters of Aithne will flourish in a world set free from the violence of men.

"War propels the book forward, and the characters are at their best when the events engulfing them are at their worst." –*Publishers Weekly*

Coming Fall 2016

ORB WEAVER PRESS

Sisters in Magic

"I speak in earnest, Renate." Adiana's words were slurred by drink. "Borten would be an excellent suitor for Eolyn. He's good man and a considerate lover."

Wine escaped Renate's lips in a sputtering laugh. "How would you know Borten's a considerate lover?"

Adiana shrugged. "I can see it in his face."

"See it in his face?" Renate let go a high pitched cackle. "I'll wager you've seen more than his face. You've been restless as a lynx in heat since Eostar."

Adiana gave a mock cry of protest and struck Renate playfully on the shoulder. "How dare you! One does not have to be a maga to see into the hearts of men. I learned a few things working the taverns in Selkynsen, you know. I can read a man as surely as Eolyn reads her books."

"As surely as Eolyn reads her books in bed," Renate replied in crisp tones.

Adiana flopped back on the blanket with an indignant harrumph. They had settled in the courtyard for an evening of wine and companionship, after having tucked the girls into bed. Days had passed since Eolyn departed for the South Woods, and the week would likely see its end before she returned.

"And you accuse me of inventing stories and gossip!" Adiana complained. "Even if I had 'read Borten in bed', what would it matter? The magas always had untamed teachings with respect to that sort of thing. Isn't *aen-lasati* the source of a woman's greatest magic? I swear to the Gods, Renate, sometimes you seem too much of a prude to be a maga."

A prude.

Renate rolled the word over her tongue as she swirled her wine. Yes, that's what she was. Tight inside, dry as autumn leaves underfoot. Forever bound by the failures and disillusions of her past.

"The Magas of the Old Orders were disciplined women," Renate said, "not harlots at a summer festival. To lay claim to their understanding of *aen-lasati* while ignoring all their other teachings does their memory a disservice. It's precisely that sort of myth that led us to the pyres in the first place."

"Oh, Renate." Adiana groaned and reached for the wine skin. "Why must you take everything so seriously? It's finished, remember? The war, the purges, the rebellion, the prohibition. We're free now. The magas have been restored to their rightful place in Moisehén. We've got a proper *Aekelahr*, aspiring young magas, the protection of the Mage King, and a nice little regiment of handsome guards. Even you could have some fun, you know."

The thought of her tired old body wrapped around one of the King's men made Renate giggle until the giddiness shook her ribs and broke upon her lips.

"That's the spirit!" Adiana said. "Here, have some more wine. And tell me, which of the guards do you like the most?"

"Oh, for the love of the Gods, Adiana!" Renate was laughing uncontrollably now, tears streaming down her cheeks. "I am an old woman."

"Age is meaningless for a true maga. That's what Eolyn says." Adiana rested her head on Renate's shoulder.

The older woman returned her warm embrace, inhaling the sweet smells of night mingled with Adiana's vibrant aroma of primrose and summer winds, of the riverside city that had once been her home.

She envied her friend in that moment, not so much for her youth and beauty, but for her continued faith in the possibility that anything could be finished. Someday time and experience would break that faith. Desire and loss, terror and death, treachery and abandonment, all of it stayed with a person until the end of her days, animating the shadows at night, invading dreams, stealing away tranquility in the lonely hours before dawn.

Adiana sighed and lifted her cup to the sky. "I love this moment, when the wine makes the stars shine brighter than ever. Gods bless the vineyards of Selkynsen! Look at the fir, Renate. See how it dances in the torch light?"

"This is but a momentary truce with the Gods," Renate murmured into her cup. "Three years they have left us in peace; it cannot last much longer."

"Hah! There you go again." Adiana took Renate's hand in hers. "What's wrong, Renate? Are you having bad dreams?"

Renate bit her lip and looked away. "Last night I was in the wastes of the dead. The magas came after me with clawed hands and hateful screams."

"Gods, that's awful!" Adiana withdrew from their embrace and studied Renate in the dark. "You burden yourself with far too much guilt, dear friend. It wasn't your fault what happened."

"It was my fault, Adiana." There was no sadness in her voice, no regret, only the cold acknowledgment of truth. "I could blame my youth or my fear and innocence. I could say circumstances went beyond my control, but I would only be hiding inside my own myth. I made my choices. I understood their consequences, and many of my sisters burned because of it."

Adiana sent a slow whistle through her teeth. "You've never said it quite like that before."

Renate shrugged and stared absently into the darkness.

"Does Eolyn know you feel that way?"

"She thinks the Gods have a different way of judging our transgressions, that they interpret our acts across a grander expanse of time and consequence." Renate shivered as Eolyn's words echoed inside her head. "She believes I survived then in order to serve a greater purpose now."

"Well, she's right, isn't she? You're here after all, helping to rebuild the legacy of the magas. I bet all your dead sisters are happy about that."

Renate frowned. How to explain to Adiana that this would not be enough? Dragon was waiting to exact a greater payment, a harsher sacrifice. The old maga had left everything behind and followed Eolyn to Moehn in anticipation of this.

"Do you know what I dream about, Renate?" Adiana's voice became bright, washing the away the shadows of doom, as was her gift. "The Circle. Now those are good dreams, about singing with Rishona, making music with Nathan and Kahlil after the show. I miss those times, all our friends from those far-flung kingdoms, travelling from one end of Moisehén to the other."

Renate gave a short mocking laugh. "Corey had us on a knife's edge with that show of his. Not a day passed when I didn't think the next magistrate would throw us all on the pyre."

"But we laughed about it didn't we? And we created like happy fools. So much defiance in our art! So much beauty. Do you think Corey will ever organize something like that again?"

"I don't know." Renate had cared deeply for Corey. She might have loved him once, had she not been such an old crone and he such a young fool. "He might. But I don't think it would be the same, if he did."

"No, I suppose not. I used to think Corey would be the perfect match for Eolyn."

"Corey and Eolyn?" Renate snorted. "Adiana, you have many gifts, but matchmaking is not one of them."

"What would have been so wrong about that? He's a mage, and she is a maga."

"Corey is like a vine growing in the dark. Eolyn is a flower open to the sun."

"So he turned out to be a treacherous bastard. None of us saw that coming back then."

"I thought you could read a man like a book," Renate retorted.

"I can tell if a man's a considerate lover. It's much harder picking out the treacherous bastards."

"Corey was not so bad." Renate swirled her cup and took another drink. "He only did what he thought he had to do."

"Well, Eolyn will never trust him again, not after the way he betrayed her brother."

The sound of heavy footfalls distracted them from their conversation. One of the men approached, torch in hand.

"Maga Renate," he said, "Mistress Adiana. Sir Malrec requests that you meet him at the north wall at once."

Something in the man's tone extinguished the heat of the wine. Renate's bones creaked as she rose to her feet, and she gripped Adiana's hand for help.

They fastened their cloaks and followed the soldier between the stone buildings and across the gardens. There were no voices to be heard, no soldiers engaged in idle conversation. Crickets and frogs filled the silence with their insistent song. The nervous whinny of horses drifted toward them from the stable. When they approached the half-built wall, their escort brought the torch low. Malrec greeted them in subdued tones and beckoned them to his side.

"There toward the north." He indicated with a nod.

Renate peered over the half-finished wall. In the distance she spotted a luminous mist that wavered, faded then flared again. A memory stirred inside her, nebulous in form, as if she had lived this moment before, though she could not quite capture when.

"What is it?" she asked, not certain she wanted to hear the answer.

"Fire," Malrec replied. "The fields around Moehn are burning. Or worse, the town itself."

Renate gripped Adiana's arm. "We must go to them. We'll need marigold, yellow carowort, and fire-of-aethne, among other herbs and ointments. Adiana, come with me to the herbarium. Malrec, see the horses are readied at once."

"No." The finality of his tone caught Renate off guard.

"No?" she replied. "What do you mean, no?"

"I have readied the horses, but not to take you to Moehn. At least, not until we have some idea of what is happening there."

"Are you mad? We can see what is happening. Those people are suffering! As a maga, I am sworn to help them."

"As a Knight of Vortingen, I am sworn to protect you. You and the Mistress Adiana are not to depart until I give you leave to do so. I have sent a scout to assess the situation. We should have word from him within the hour."

"I will not sit here a prisoner in my own home while people's lives are in danger."

"The town may be under attack."

"Moehn under siege?" Renate threw up her hands in disbelief. "Oh, for Gods' sake. Who would attack Moehn? Some drunken imbecile kicked over a lantern, or a torch fell from its rusted sconce."

"We cannot be certain of that."

A shout from one of the men perched on the wall silenced them. All eyes turned north once again. The night went still. The crickets stopped singing. Renate scanned the darkness, conscious of the unnatural silence. She could hear Malrec's breath, low and steady. A charge filled the air, as if lightning were poised to rip through the starry heavens.

"What is it?" she whispered. "What did they see?"

Malrec hushed her, raising one hand as he searched the obscure terrain.

Once, a lifetime ago, Renate had been a High Maga, and she could change into an owl and see the night world with clarity. But she had long since abandoned those powers, and now the hills so familiar by daylight were amorphous, the distances impossible to judge.

Was that movement she saw along a nearby ridge? A lynx, perhaps, taking advantage of the moonless night to scurry across open fields. But then a flame ignited in its wake, followed by a discontinuous arc of light that spread point by point over the low hill, like a line of small torches. On sudden impulse, the string of flames rose high into the air, slowed against the ebony firmament, then fell toward the *Aekelahr* in a hissing rain of fire.

Malrec took hold of Renate and crushed her against the wall, knocking the wind out of her as the arrows fell behind them, some embedding in the earth, others landing on nearby roofs and igniting the thatch in an instant.

5

"The children!" Adiana cried, and she tore away from the soldier who had shielded her, disappearing into the flickering shadows.

Renate moved to follow, but Malrec caught her by the arm and yanked her back.

"The horses are ready," he said. She had never seen his face so close, so vivid. The rounded cheeks, the rough curls of his beard, the fine spittle that rode on rapid words. "Take them and head south. Do not look back, do not stop, until you reach the forest. Three of the men will accompany you. Go!"

He shoved her away. Renate's feet moved of their own volition, carrying her toward the girls' room even as a second volley of flames descended from the heavens. Behind her raged the shouts of desperate men, followed by the ring of metal upon metal and sudden cries of anguish. Already the assailants were topping the half-finished wall.

Adiana was ushering the girls out of their room. They stumbled, bleary eyed and confused, with summer cloaks thrown over their nightshifts. The soldiers met them with five steeds. One of the men hauled Catarina up to ride with him, Adiana mounted with Tasha, and Ghemena was given to Renate.

As they turned the horses toward the south gate, Renate caught site of Eolyn's study. The roof was ablaze with golden flames, bright as the sun come to earth.

"The annals," she cried in panic and spurred her horse toward the fire.

The animal whinnied and pulled back before they reached the building. Leaving the reins with Ghemena, Renate dropped to the ground. Ignoring the shock of pain in her legs, she raced to the study and burst through the door.

Smoke lodged in her throat and stung her eyes. The room itself was not yet aflame, but the roof roared and burning ash fluttered on the air like black snow.

Renate blinked back tears. Was this what her sisters had seen, as the flames rose up around them? The world aglow with scalding heat, the cold realm of the dead their only promise of escape.

Shaking the image from her mind, she spotted books on the corner shelves. She threw her cloak down in front of them and piled all the volumes she could before tying the corners into a makeshift sack and dragging it back to the entrance. By the time she emerged from the study, every muscle in her body ached.

"For the love of the Gods, old woman!" One of the men shouted. "You kept us waiting for this?"

"The horses will never run with such a load on their backs," another objected.

"We cannot leave this behind! It is all that is left of our heritage." Renate looked from one man to another, and finding no sympathy in their faces, turned to her friend. "Adiana, please! Help me."

After a moment of hesitation, the young woman dismounted and removed her cloak. They divided the tomes between the two of them. Renate heaved her burden into Ghemena's arms and bade the child to hold it tight. Then she swung herself up behind the girl and spurred the horse into a canter.

In moments they were through the south entrance and racing over open fields, hooves pounding against the earth. The horses snorted and drew labored breaths, straining under their loads. Renate leaned forward, molding her body to Ghemena's back, eyes fixed on the black hills ahead.

CPSIA information can be obtained
at www.ICGtesting.com
Printed in the USA
BVHW04s2150170518
516406BV00003B/201/P